'I DON'T WORK FOR SOMEBODY WHO LIES TO ME.

'You can lie to everybody else on this planet, you can lie to God and your mama, but if you lie to me I'm gonna find it out. I'm gonna investigate the hell out of this thing, and I'll know what happened. If I find out you lied to me I'll get you for it. And I don't just mean withdraw from the case. I mean I'll ruin you. Y'understand? Now if that condition's all right with you, you sit there and collect your thoughts for a minute and then start talking. But if it even crosses your mind to lie to me, you get up and walk out now. Now.'

JAY BRANDON

RULES OF EVIDENCE

A SIGNET BOOK

SIGNET

Published by the Penguin Group
Penguin Books Ltd, 27 Wrights Lane, London w8 5tz, England
Penguin Books USA Inc., 375 Hudson Street, New York, New York 10014, USA
Penguin Books Australia Ltd, Ringwood, Victoria, Australia
Penguin Books Canada Ltd, 10 Alcorn Avenue, Toronto, Ontario, Canada m4v 3b2
Penguin Books (NZ) Ltd, 182–190 Wairau Road, Auckland 10, New Zealand

Penguin Books Ltd, Registered Offices: Harmondsworth, Middlesex, England

First published in Great Britain by Michael Joseph 1992
Published in Signet 1993
1 3 5 7 9 10 8 6 4 2

Copyright © Jay Brandon, 1992
All rights reserved

The moral right of the author has been asserted

Typeset by Datix International Limited, Bungay, Suffolk
Set in 10/12 pt Monophoto Plantin
Printed in England by Clays Ltd, St Ives plc

for my old friend Robert Morrow,
who still enjoys practising law

PART 1

CHAPTER 1

In the Monday morning bustle of the courtroom, Raymond Boudro sat at ease. He had already spoken to his client, a truculent young rapist wearing a jailhouse uniform and sitting handcuffed in the jury box, and to the second chair prosecutor, asking for an improvement on the plea bargain offer. Now Raymond was letting them marinate. In half an hour, with the threat of trial more imminent, both the defendant and the prosecutor would probably have grown more reasonable. If not, it was a problem best dealt with later.

Other defense lawyers were still sorting through the State's files looking for their own clients, holding quiet conferences with those clients, or waiting in line to see one of the three prosecutors assigned to the court. In the melee Raymond was probably the only person to see Lawrence Preston come softly through the hallway door and up the aisle. Raymond rose to his feet, quite unconsciously. Mr Preston was in his sixties, should have retired years ago, but probably couldn't afford it – and wouldn't in any event. He looked troubled this morning; not as if he had a hard decision to make – but as if he weren't sure he was in the right place. Raymond held open the gate in the railing, surprising the old lawyer as he reached for it.

'Good morning, Mr Preston.'

'Raymond! What a pleasure.' The old man shook hands with him warmly. Not content with ordinary pleasantries, Mr Preston asked particular questions about Raymond's family, complimented him on his appearance, and would have continued if Raymond hadn't said gently, 'Don't let me keep you from your business, Mr Preston.'

The old man gave him a sunny wink. 'Never let 'em see you hurry,' he advised.

Mr Preston had sounded sharp when he spoke to the younger lawyer, but as he passed on into the busy scene inside the railing of the courtroom he appeared confused again, looking around for a client or a file or a familiar face among the other attorneys. He broke Raymond's heart. When Raymond had been fresh out of law school Lawrence Preston had taken him into his practice. Raymond had been not only grateful but flattered. Even now black lawyers were not common in San Antonio, where the world was divided between Anglos and Mexican-Americans. In those days, fifteen years ago, Mr Preston had been practically unique. He had certainly been the foremost black criminal lawyer in the city.

Raymond had now held that distinction for some years.

Lawrence Preston was a fighter, a 'worthy opponent' of the old school. He fought a lot of battles and sustained a lot of losses. Raymond had learned a lot from him, but had learned more on his own. After five years he had gone into solo practice and flourished. Now his old mentor seemed a historical personage, out of place. Raymond longed to go up and take over for him, but he knew the futility of that attempt.

In a few minutes Judge Fortel had assumed the bench and begun calling the docket. There was a long pause after one defendant's name. Raymond closed his eyes. When he opened them everyone was looking at Mr Preston.

'That would be mine, Your Honor,' the old man was saying, finally. 'And we'll be announcing ready for trial.'

He hadn't even talked to a prosecutor yet, Raymond was certain. The old fighter was charging into battle again, blindly but unflinching.

When Raymond heard his own client's name called he stood and said, 'Will you please mark us conferring, Your Honor?'

Judge Fortel looked at him. Sometimes he called ten names in a row without looking up. Drawing his attention was not desired. But this morning he gave Raymond a small smile and nodded. Raymond withdrew to the railing, where the first chair prosecutor was waiting with the State's file. ''s he gonna take the offer?' the prosecutor asked.

Raymond spread his hands. 'I've gotta talk to the guy some more. And I just don't have the time right now. I gotta be in three other courts. Let me take care of them and I'll be back.'

The prosecutor flapped the file close to Raymond's face. 'This is the third oldest case on the docket. Gotta take care of it today.'

Raymond's face turned immobile as the file flapped close to it. 'I said I'll be back. I'll be back.'

The prosecutor's get-tough expression shriveled for a moment. He stepped back, waving with the file, and said, 'Fine,' in a tone meant to say, 'I don't have time for this shit.'

'Fine,' Raymond said. He stopped at the jury box to speak to his client, then left the courtroom. His nostalgic sadness had turned briefly to anger, equally briefly to satisfaction, then to nothing. He didn't have time. Every judge in the courthouse called the week's docket on Monday morning. Some cases would be disposed of through guilty pleas, many would be put off to another day, some few hapless souls would be put to trial. Raymond had bought time by announcing he was still conferring with the prosecution in hopes of reaching a plea bargain agreement. In the meantime, though, there were other docket calls to answer. If he was lucky enough to dodge trial, Raymond could be through with the courthouse for the whole week by Monday afternoon. But it made for a hectic two or three hours Monday morning.

Out in the hall, lawyers stood in suited clusters or sat on benches talking quietly to clients. In the old red-stone Bexar County Courthouse civil and criminal courts were jumbled together without distinction, so that within ten feet one lawyer would be telling an unhappy woman, 'We'll get custody, there's no problem there, but he says he can only pay four hundred a month,' and another would be telling a glum man in work clothes, 'With good time you can be out in two years.' Lawyers waved and nodded as Raymond threaded his way among them.

At his next stop, the 175th District Court, Alan Porter, the third chair prosecutor and most junior member of the State's team, was leaning against the railing, too calm for a Monday. A prosecutor shouldn't be nonchalant on Monday morning. He should be frantic, wondering which case of the many on the docket would be going to trial. He should also play his cards close, trying to force guilty pleas. But Alan's main concern in life was looking cool. Raymond leaned next to him. 'What's happening?' Raymond said.

'Just waiting for the docket call to be over and I'm outta here. There's a Fam Vio case specially set and it's gonna go. That's the guy in the front row there.'

Family Violence was a section in the District Attorney's office that prosecuted cases of domestic assaults, often murders, baby killings, ugly cases. Raymond saw one of the Fam Vio prosecutors sitting at the State's counsel table, open file in front of her, fingers tented, staring into space with an intent expression. He turned to the front row of the spectator seats where a sweaty, pudgy man in a too-bright suit was sitting next to Don Twyllyn, a defense lawyer, who did not look happy. The two men were not speaking.

'That guy is a wife beater?' Raymond asked.

The prosecutor shook his head. 'Kiddie diddler.'

'Mmm.' Raymond looked again. That made a little more sense. He already had everything he needed from the prosecutor, but now he had to be sociable in exchange. 'Voir dire start this afternoon?' he asked.

Alan Porter shook his head. He didn't smile broadly, but what he was about to say made him happy, the way a punch line pleases its teller. 'Nonjury,' he said.

Raymond straightened from the railing, genuinely incredulous. 'He's trying a sexual assault of a child to Judy?'

The prosecutor nodded. '*Aggravated* sexual assault. Twelve-year-old.'

'Is he crazy? Is there some problem with the case?'

'Nope. It's a slow guilty plea. Pain in the ass for everybody. And the judge'll tack on twenty extra years for puttin' the kid through a trial. Twyllyn's just completely lost control of the guy. I mean, do your job. Get the guy to plead. No skin off my ass, though. Gives me a free couple of days.'

Raymond drifted away, looking suitably impressed by the prosecutor's news. Two or three other defense lawyers had been standing close enough to hear, so they too knew they could make announcements of ready on their cases without risk of being put to trial. The judge would not be pleased if she knew her third chair was giving out such news. Judges liked an active courtroom. 'Get me more trials' was a good judge's constant admonition to prosecutors, and wanting to look like a hardworking judge was only part of the reason. Trials were needed to keep the docket moving. Trials themselves didn't move the docket. You could have cases being tried twenty-four hours a day in the seven felony courts and they wouldn't dispose of a tenth of the burgeoning dockets. Guilty pleas were what fed the maw of the criminal justice machine, disposing of ten defendants in a morning. But you couldn't force guilty pleas except with the constant threat of trial.

So when the judge called the first three cases on the docket and the defense lawyers promptly said, 'Ready,' rather than offering excuses or delays, she knew someone had talked. She directed glares at each of the three prosecutors, especially Alan Porter, who stared back at her innocently. Judge Judy – Judy Byrnes – had only been on the bench three months. She had inherited an out-of-control docket from her predecessor, who had grown tired of his judgely duties and stopped performing them some months in anticipation of his actual retirement date. Judge Judy had pushed the docket hard from day one.

Before her appointment she had been a prosecutor for six years and a defense lawyer for eight. She and Raymond were close to being old friends. They had worked together on two trials. But being an old friend of Judy's was not only indiscernible when she was on the bench, it was a distinct handicap at her docket call.

'Ready,' Raymond said, with the confident expression of a man eager to go to trial. The judge looked at him. Raymond's was the tenth defense announcement of ready. Only two had announced they would be pleading guilty. There was nothing Judy could do about it except harass a lawyer.

'Is your client present, Mr Boudro?'

Raymond hadn't seen this particular client this particular morning. 'He's in the hall, Your Honor.'

Judge Judy said, 'Think he could put in an appearance, just for form's sake?'

Except in the vicinity of the pudgy guy in the front row, his lawyer, and the prosecutor about to try him, a relaxed atmosphere prevailed in the courtroom. The lawyers were watching the exchange between Raymond and the judge with easy interest. They were disappointed when Raymond decided to make the rest of the show private. 'May I approach the bench, Your Honor?'

'Please.'

The third chair prosecutor stepped before the judge too, so the exchange wouldn't be an improper ex parte one. Raymond leaned forward earnestly. 'Judge, Mr Turner is the kind of client who hinders the plea bargaining process by his presence.'

The judge nodded understandingly. 'Looks real guilty, does he?'

'He tends to yell at the prosecutor, Your Honor. And since we're on the subject, may I ask why I get appointed all the black defendants in this and other courts? Am I supposed to have a special rapport with them? Know the secret signs?'

He was just distracting her from his client's absence. There were two or three judges on whom this would have worked. He was not before one of them now.

'Believe it or not, Mr Boudro, you don't get more than your share. There are plenty to go around. And as a matter of fact, some of them ask for you.'

'Really?' For a moment he was flattered. Then he realized she didn't mean they asked for him by name. 'Then may I ask,' he continued, 'why I get appointed to all the stupid, ignorant, *hos*tile defendants?'

9

'I don't give them a personality test before I appoint them a lawyer, Mr Boudro. As a matter of fact I try to get to know them as little as possible. Now, tell your client in the hall if he puts in an appearance actually inside the courtroom before the morning is over I won't yank his bond and put out an arrest warrant for him.'

'Yes, Your Honor.'

'Permission to withdraw granted.'

A moment later Raymond was in the hall, refreshed from the exchange. Some new judges tried to appear not to be taking themselves too seriously; they would cut their friends some slack. Others turned pompous immediately; judgehood confirmed their opinions of themselves. Judy was still doing it right: not full of herself but not taking any shit either. Too bad. The pompous ones could be kissed up and the friendly ones could be walked over. He liked Judy, but she had passed over to the other side now. She had to be handled.

The scene of his next appearance, county court six, in the basement, made him nostalgic again, but pleasantly so this time. Soon after he had started working for Mr Preston he had walked into the office of county court six and met Denise, a clerk in the court. Denise had already been a courthouse insider, and she had shared some of her experience with the young lawyer. The most important thing he had learned from her was that in many ways it was better to have the clerk of the court on your side than to have the judge. Denise didn't take every lawyer by the hand that way. Maybe she had taken pity on Raymond because of his obvious inexperience. No one would have suggested she was particularly helpful to him because of their shared race. Co-workers *did* suggest a mutual attraction that it amused them to hear Denise deny; it amused them even more when the attraction was confirmed.

Raymond's and Denise's courtship had not only had this public quality to it, it had had an air of inevitability they had to work their way around. The cute young clerk, the handsome young lawyer: people winked. Raymond was glad that episode was years behind him. But there were days when he still missed seeing Denise's face when he glanced in the office door of county court six before proceeding into the courtroom.

In this court he actually did some conferring. His client was a DWI, a middle-aged Mexican-American man who'd been stopped on his way home from a wedding and blown a .13 on the intoxilyzer, three points over the legal limit. Triable but not worth the hassle. The prosecutor was a county court veteran, six months in the service of the people. Probation was a given, but the prosecutor and Raymond started out two hundred dollars apart on the fine and could only close the gap to one hundred.

'I can't go lower than four hundred,' the prosecutor said. 'The judge wants us to start getting tougher on DWIs.'

'Man, don't start the get-tough campaign on *my* guy. He's already mortgaged everything he's got to hire me, and you know I ain't gettin' rich on a DWI.' At the last moment he avoided saying 'crummy DWI'. DWIs were a life's work to a misdemeanor prosecutor. Once the prosecutor made felony he could speak condescendingly of DWIs too, but at this stage of the prosecutor's career it wouldn't do to denigrate the seriousness of the offense to him. 'Give him a break.'

'Give *me* a break. It's his only time in court if he's lucky. I've gotta be here every day. If I recommended a lower fine the judge'll be pissed off at me for the rest of the week.'

'No she won't, she likes me,' Raymond argued. 'I'll tell her his sad story and ask her to go even lower. She'll think you're a humanitarian. Three hundred dollars. He can't pay more than that, he'll get revoked.'

'She doesn't like humanitarians, not on DWIs. Let's just try it, see what a jury'll give him.'

'Oh, man, the jury'll fine him a thousand dollars and think they're going easy on him. Be serious. But I might walk him. Look at him: sympathetic old guy, never been arrested before, has one too many at a wedding. You find six people in this town who haven't been drunk at a wedding and you might get a guilty. But in the real world . . .'

'Fine,' said the prosecutor. 'Let's just do it.'

Raymond sighed. He saw Henry Burroughs, another defense lawyer, standing nearby, frankly listening to the exchange. Raymond winked at him. He let silence pass. Neither he nor the prosecutor had walked away. The judge would emerge from her chambers in a minute.

Raymond turned back to the prosecutor. He sounded like a man who'd just had a dash of reality. 'Hey, are we really gonna try this damn thing over a hundred dollars, that the judge'll give him two years to pay off? Come on, I'll *give* you a hundred dollars.' He reached into his pocket.

The prosecutor wasn't going to be outcooled. 'Man, I'll give *you* a hunnerd dollars. It ain't the money, it's numbers. I gotta give 'er the numbers.'

'Then let's monkey with the other numbers,' Raymond said. 'You give me dollars, I'll give you days.'

'Well . . .'

That was how they worked it out. The prosecutor agreed to a three-hundred-dollar fine but raised the underlying sentence, the time the defendant would have to serve if his probation was revoked, from thirty days to forty-five days. This was entirely satisfactory to Raymond. First, he wouldn't be around if the probation ever did get revoked. Second, the underlying was just make-believe anyway. The judge would reform the sentence to something lower if she ever did revoke the guy. But the fine money was real.

Raymond took his file and his deal and sat down to wait his turn at the bench. Henry Burroughs sat beside him. Henry looked slightly out of place in the chaos of county court. There was something scholarly about his appearance. 'Learn anything?' Raymond asked him.

Henry acknowledged the reason for his eavesdropping. 'You get good deals, Raymond. I was hoping I might pick up something of your technique.'

'Wouldn't work for you, Henry. It's a black thing. You wouldn't understand.' Raymond had a T-shirt with those last two sentences emblazoned on the front. He kept promising himself to wear it to court one day.

'Since you brought that out into the open, I'll admit I was thinking that,' Henry said, 'but that's not it.'

'Sure it is. Is it my imagination or did that honky prosecutor start talking a little African toward the end of our discussion?'

Henry smiled but continued to disagree. 'Other defense lawyers get offers as good as yours. Guys the prosecutor has no reason to fear if it came to trial, either. But with me –'

'Yeah. You're a good trial lawyer, you should get better offers than you do. Not that they're hammering you all the time, but you end up going to trial more often than you should, when you could have worked something out.'

'Why is that?'

Raymond felt like a golf pro telling a man in orange pants to keep his head down on his back-swing. 'You really want to know? It's because, Henry, you sound the ringing cry of justice on every case.'

'No I don't.'

'Yes, you do. You think every case is important some way.'

'Every one is, to somebody.'

'See? You start looking at it from "somebody's" point of view, you're gonna be in trial every week. It's not like that, Henry. They're not all important. Fact is, none of 'em's important. It's just a game. You gotta loosen up your attitude. See, you make the prosecutor think it's important too. Then you've made him take an interest in your guy. That's always a mistake. Make it numbers, make it cattle through the chute. You start caring, they start caring, and next thing you know you're saying good-morning to a passel of average citizens eager to ferret out the truth and send your guy away. With me the prosecutor knows I'm on his side. I'm trying to save him trouble. We're pals. With you – '

'I'm supposed to be his opponent,' Henry said. He looked rather solemnly disturbed. 'We're representing different interests. That's how the system works, isn't it?'

'If you press that button all the time, Henry, you're gonna get stepped on a lot. Because all the advantages belong to the State. They can try the cases they like and reduce the ones they don't. And when it comes to punishment the jury's on their side. So you'd do best to lay off the adversarial system crap. Make the prosecutor think it's you and him against the judge and the case.'

Henry chewed his lip. Raymond laughed. 'You're not gonna pick up this technique, are you? I'll see you later, Henry, I've got a plea to take.'

After the plea he was running late to the last two courts on his personal docket, but his secretary had called the courts to make his excuses, so he wasn't in trouble. In Judge Sherman's court he was in no danger of being put to trial anyway. The trial was over, it had been two weeks ago. Today was for sentencing, after the probation department had prepared a pre-sentence investigation report for the judge.

And the first thing the idiot defendant said was, 'I'll take the fifteen.'

He was a black eighth grade dropout who had made it to the age of twenty-one without facing serious prison time. This offense had been aggravated robbery, a holdup at a burger joint during which one of the two robbers, this guy or his partner, got overexcited and pistol-whipped the clerk. The woman clerk. It was an ugly case, the kind in which a jury would think a life sentence was too lenient, but there had been problems from the State's point of view – shaky ID, alibi defense to overcome – so Raymond had managed a pretrial offer of fifteen years, which was the bargain of the month; but the poor stupid defendant had never had anything tougher than a few days in county jail for misdemeanor theft and a five-year probation for stealing a car, and he had balked at pleading guilty for a sentence of fifteen years, four of which he might actually have to serve. So Raymond's hard work to acquire a great offer had gone for nothing and now the trial was over, all the State's problems had been smoothed away by the jury's guilty verdict, and it had changed from a fifteen-year case to, probably, a thirty-year one, and that only because Raymond had had the good sense to go to the judge for punishment rather than the jury. He tried to explain this to the defendant, whose seven tough years of schooling didn't allow him to grasp the logic that meant his fifteen-year offer had gone bye-bye. They were discussing one-week-only sales at Sears when Judge Sherman called them both to the bench. He was frowning.

'Did you really think this PSI report was going to be of some benefit to your client, Mr Boudro?'

'We didn't request the report, Your Honor. I believe Your Honor ordered it on the court's own motion.' Pre-sentence investigation reports contained all kinds of material that wouldn't be admissible at trial: arrest record, hearsay, sometimes written statements from the victim's family. It was risky to ask the judge to order one to use in assessing punishment. Raymond hadn't asked for it in spite of his client's assurance that all his friends and relatives would swear what a swell human being he was.

'We contest much of the material in that report, Your Honor.'

'I'll bet you do. Does he really have four children by four different women?'

The defendant mumbled. 'He denies one of them, Your Honor,' Raymond translated.

'One of the women or one of the children?'

'Your Honor, I think what's important is the heavy weight of responsibility pressing on this young man at such a tender age. Maybe that's what drove him to robbery. And remember, those children will be without a father if Mr Lewis goes to prison.'

The judge made a disgusted sound. He flipped through the last pages of the report, put it down, was obviously still mulling over the appropriate sentence when he had the mean thought of letting the defendant step in it himself. 'Do you have anything to say, Mr Lewis, before I sentence you?'

Mentally, Raymond sighed. He would have intervened, but there wasn't much he could say. His own investigation of his client's life had uncovered no facts in his favor. The kid lived sometimes with his mother, sometimes with one woman or another, occasionally threw down twenty dollars for groceries when he was flush, usually put it up his nose instead. He had no discernible job skills other than a wicked hook shot, but NBA scouts hadn't yet found the playground where he played most afternoons. And he tended to whine when cornered.

'Judge,' Lewis said now, 'I didn't beat up on that woman. I went in there with the gun but it wasn't my idea and I didn't hit nobody and I'm real sorry about the whole thing.'

'That's not what the clerk said at trial,' Judge Sherman remembered accurately.

'Judge, I think that's 'cause Wilson hit her from behind while she was lookin' at me, so I'm the one she remembers.'

Plausible, Raymond thought. Very plausible. The kid had a way with excuses, you couldn't deny him that. Then Raymond looked at the judge's face and remembered what excuses were worth in this court. Responsibility, that was the key. You were supposed to take responsibility.

'Your Honor, as Mr Lewis says, he knows what he did was wrong. I think if he's given another chance –'

'He'll get another chance,' Judge Sherman said, 'but it'll be a while. Mr Lewis, I sentence you to thirty-five years in the Texas Department of Corrections.'

A few minutes later the formalities were over, the defendant was sitting handcuffed in the jury box listening to his mother sob a few feet away while a bailiff filled out a jail slip for him. Raymond was thanking the judge for his time. No matter what they did to you you always thanked them, because you'd always be back.

He took time to talk to Lewis's mother, which made him very late to his last stop, the 186th, the only court on the third floor of the courthouse. It was ten-thirty and Judge Marroquin's docket call had been at nine. Claymore almost climbed atop Raymond as soon as he stepped inside the courtroom. The client pawed Raymond like a big dog out of joy at seeing him.

'Man, they say they put me in jail you don't show up. I keep tellin' 'em you be here, but they startin' to look at me like they like to put my ass in the holdover just for fun.'

'Relax, Claymore, they always say that. You should know that, you're no virgin.'

Raymond was looking past his client at the courtroom. After Judge Sherman's small but brightly lighted courtroom this one appeared dim, because Judge Sherman's was windowless and made bright by artificial lights. This one, the 186th, relied in part for lighting on its rows of windows on two walls, but on cloudy days like this one the windows seemed to emit gloom rather than glow into the courtroom. Raymond wasn't concerned with the visibility. He was concerned with what the appearance of the court told him. It was a bad scene. Empty jury box, sparsely populated courtroom, only one prosecutor left. And the judge on the bench. 'Good morning, Your Honor,' Raymond called.

'Nice of you to join us, Mr Boudro.' Judge Marroquin was a heavy man in his late fifties, ten years a judge, generally pleasant to everyone who came before him, slow to anger but never forgetting anything. He had been a defense lawyer himself for years before becoming a judge and hadn't forgotten what that was like, but those were no longer his problems. Moving the docket came first.

He politely allowed Raymond another minute to talk to the client. Claymore wasn't small, but Raymond was tall enough to see past him. He thought he saw the judge and the woman prosecutor looking at him obliquely, curious at what the two black men standing together near the door of the courtroom were saying to each other. Under that scrutiny Raymond felt a little less like a lawyer. The other lawyers were looking at him as if the conference made him for that moment amalgamated with his client. They must be exchanging secrets and planning strategy.

'You bring the rest of the money?' Raymond asked.

'Yeah, man, yeah. Most of it.' Claymore had calmed down, as if he felt protected now that his lawyer was here, which was a stupid thing to think. The system had only been dozing waiting for the lawyer to arrive, and now that he had the system grumbled into life. It fed on defendants.

'Most?' Raymond said. 'I told you I'm not trying this thing before I get paid.'

Of course, that was not entirely up to him. 'The State of Texas versus Claymore Johnson,' Judge Marroquin said abruptly. 'Announcements?'

'Ready,' the prosecutor said promptly. Her name was Rebecca Schirhart. She was only the third chair, but she'd been a prosecutor for three years and she was good; Raymond had both tried cases and plea-bargained against her. At the judge's announcement she had come to stand by his bench and now stood watching Raymond with an expression he couldn't

19

quite read – expectant, waiting for something to be played out. She and the judge might have been collaborators. The judge was looking at Raymond with the same sort of patient, pleasant expression.

Raymond came forward, past Claymore. The courtroom was cleared out. They were waiting only for him. It looked as if everyone was ready to spring into action as soon as he announced ready for trial. On the other hand, they could already have a case ready to start this afternoon and were just yanking Raymond's chain. He wished he'd been here for the docket call, and to confer with the prosecutor.

'Ready,' he said.

The judge's broad brown face broke into a beneficent smile. 'Good. Everything else fell through this morning. I was afraid we weren't going to have anything to do today.'

Immediately Raymond said, 'Ready on our motion to suppress, I mean, Your Honor.'

The judge's smile faded. 'You filed a motion?' He opened the court's file. 'Oh yes, so you did. All right. Will the motion dispose of the case?'

Raymond made the standard defense lawyer's reply: 'It will if you grant it, Your Honor.' Yes, they all knew that. The motion sought to suppress the cocaine Claymore was charged with possessing. If the judge ruled it had been illegally obtained and so couldn't be introduced into evidence the State wouldn't have a case, they'd have to dismiss. They all knew that. They also knew how often that happened. What the judge meant was, Once I inevitably overrule your motion to suppress, will the defendant take his medicine and plead guilty? But Raymond didn't want the case to end in a guilty plea today, before he'd been paid the remainder of his fee.

'Once Ms Schirhart and I have a chance to confer I'm sure at the next setting . . .'

'All right.' Judge Marroquin understood. 'Let's proceed then. How soon can the witnesses be here, Miss Schirhart?'

'Only one officer, Your Honor, and I believe I saw him in the office this morning, on his way to another court. If he's still in the building I should be able to find him in a few minutes.'

Raymond said a few more calming words to Claymore. He felt a protective pity for this client, who was a relative innocent. But it was lawyers with whom Raymond shared his working days, the nominal other side with whom he maintained his real working relationship.

Becky had gone to use the phone at the clerk's desk. Raymond eased over next to her. 'Why didn't you warn me?' he asked quietly.

'What did you want me to do, wink?' Becky was a tallish young woman with brown hair and pale eyes. Looking at her you could see she had once been a willowy teenager. She was still slender, but not remotely skinny, so she probably thought herself fat. Her skin was too pale, she looked as if she spent too much time in the office. She was a kid, not yet thirty. He couldn't tell if her ambition was to stay in the D.A.'s office until she croaked or just long enough to get experience and go get rich with a big civil law firm. Raymond liked her. She wasn't above an occasional joke in the midst of negotiations. But like and trust were not related.

Most judges would have retired to their chambers while the witnesses were assembled, but Judge Marroquin liked sitting on the bench, overseeing the courtroom, sometimes even talking to spectators. There were a few here even now that all the other defendants had cleared out. A couple of women in the front row of the seats outside the bar, two watchful men in the back. All black. Family or friends, probably, come either to see Claymore off to prison or to watch him slide out one more time.

Raymond looked over the State's file again while he waited, reading the police officer's report for some ammunition to use on cross-examination. I don't feel like trying anything today, he thought. Neither did the judge, probably. Judge Marroquin would be just as happy with a motion to suppress hearing. Use up the morning, get a sense of accomplishment, then go shopping. It was the first week of December. Soon the courthouse would be heavily into its Christmas slack time. Everybody had better things to do than try cases this time of year. Lawyers would rather be out shopping or making some money in their offices so they *could* shop, and prosecutors didn't like to try cases during the holidays. Juries had the occasional misbegotten urge to be forgiving when Christmas was in the air.

The file closed on Raymond's hand. 'The open-file policy is over once we're into trial or a hearing,' the prosecutor said.

'Come on, Becky, let's not be hardasses. What'll you offer me for this guy? 'Course I'd hate to see an innocent man go to prison, but if –'

She laughed. 'He hasn't been innocent since he was five. The offer's on the file jacket, you've seen it.'

'You want to send him off to the joint at Christmas? Leave his presents lying forlorn under the family tree? The judge'd never go for that, Becky. He's a family man.'

They were just killing time waiting for the officer.

He arrived in a surprisingly short time. When Raymond saw him he put the face together with the name on the offense report. Detective Mike Stennett. He must've worked east side narcotics for ten years now. He'd made cases against several clients of Raymond's; they'd gone against each other in court before. This was going to be just a day at the office for Stennett. He'd know just what to say to defeat a motion to suppress and he'd say it with perfect sincerity.

The detective wasn't in uniform. He wore a brown bomber jacket that didn't conceal the fact that he was working on a gut. That was understandable, as he was about Raymond's age, nearly forty. Stennett was of average height or slightly less, with broad shoulders and a solid way of standing as if he'd be impossible to knock over. He wore stubble like a disguise. 'Hope this doesn't take long,' Raymond heard him tell the prosecutor. 'I been up all night.'

'Like to see a copy of your report?' Becky asked him.

The detective sat at the State's table rubbing his eye and glancing disinterestedly at the report he'd written concerning this arrest, but then something on the page caught his interest and he looked up at Claymore for the first time. Then Stennett did something very strange. He winked at Claymore as if they were old pals, meeting in an unexpected place.

Raymond thought he was the only one who saw it. Becky was reviewing her own notes and the judge was talking to his clerk. Raymond couldn't decide what the wink meant so it slipped out of his memory.

'What do I say, man?' Claymore was asking him. 'Give me a clue.'

'Sit,' Raymond said. He took off his overcoat and laid it aside on a chair. For a moment he was the only person in the room standing. Outside the windows that lined the east wall of the room, to the judge's left, the day was overcast, making this room seem isolated. Raymond opened his briefcase and removed a file, placed it on the table and took his own seat in front of his client. There were two counsel tables, but the State's was closer to the witness stand, and for the purposes of this intimate hearing they all got cozy at that table, chairs turned to face the witness stand.

'Are we ready?' the judge asked.

'Yes, Your Honor. The State calls Detective Mike Stennett.'

The cop took the oath and his seat easily, familiar with the routine. As he stated his name, profession, and qualifications, Judge Marroquin turned slightly away from him and his eyes went hooded, as if paying careful attention. In fact he probably could have recited the testimony as well as the detective. Raymond had cross-examined Stennett two or three times before. The judge must have heard him testify ten times as often as that.

Rebecca established the date of the arrest in question, the location, a corner in an east side neighborhood, and Stennett's reason for being there, an anonymous tip that someone was dealing drugs in the vicinity.

'Were you in uniform, Detective?'

'No ma'am, I was dressed about the way I am now.'

'You've just come from an undercover assignment to testify here today?'

'Yes ma'am.'

'On this other day we're talking about, did you approach the corner in a car or on foot?'

'First I drove by in an unmarked car.'

'Did you see anything out of the ordinary?'

'On the corner I'd gotten the tip about, there were

four or five men standing together, in the middle of a weekday afternoon.'

'What did they appear to be doing?'

'I couldn't see their hands, but from the way they were leaning toward each other it seemed one had something the others were inspecting.'

Raymond could have objected to that as speculation, but there was no point, the judge had already heard it. Raymond sat slumped down in his chair, staring at the witness. From the way Stennett had scanned his offense report earlier you would have thought he hardly remembered this occasion, but now he was leaning forward, absorbed in his own narrative, details rolling off his tongue as if he were watching the event happen.

'What did you do?' Becky asked. She had relaxed, realizing she was in the presence of an expert witness.

'I thought I'd seen enough to corroborate the tip I'd received, so I parked the car on another street and walked back.'

'The men were still there?'

'Yes.'

'Do you see any of those men here today?'

The detective identified Claymore, seated at the table behind Raymond. Stennett's eyes lingered on the defense lawyer for a moment as if he could include him in his recollection of the day's events if he wanted to be devilish about it. Raymond stared back at him.

'What was the defendant's position in the group?'

'He was standing mostly with his back to me.'

'Was he the one who seemed to be displaying his wares?'

Just to stretch his legs and register his presence Raymond stood and said, 'Objection, leading. I'm sure the officer can remember his story without help from the prosecutor.'

'Sustained,' said the judge.

'Did anything about the defendant call your attention to him?' Becky asked.

'Yes ma'am. He seemed to be the one the others were looking at. And he was turned a little bit in profile to me and I could see a bulge in his front pants pocket.'

'Did that cause you some concern?'

'Well, it certainly raised the possibility he might be armed. I'm always concerned for my safety when investigating possible criminal violations.'

'So what did you do?'

'As I approached, the men turned toward me. One of them said something and I could see they were about to disband. This one, the defendant, put his hand in his pocket. So I grabbed him, told him to take the hand out real easy, and then I patted down the outside of the pocket myself. There was something hard there. I pulled it out and it was one of those smoky medicine bottles, with something inside wrapped in aluminum foil.'

'What did that mean to you?' the prosecutor asked.

'That's how cocaine is packaged. I've seen it a hundred times.'

'And that's what this proved to be, isn't it, Detective?'

'I'll object to that, Your Honor, unless the witness can demonstrate qualifications as a chemist.' Not to be a jerk, Raymond added, 'We'll stipulate that whatever was inside the foil packet is the subject of this motion to suppress.'

'And the evidence that forms the basis of this prosecution, Your Honor,' Becky added. Raymond gave her a sweet smile.

'Fine,' the judge said. He liked stipulations, they moved things along.

'In that case anything more would be beyond the scope of this hearing, so I'll pass the witness,' Becky said.

Raymond resumed his seat. Judge Marroquin straightened a little and looked at him expectantly, as if in hopes the cross-examination would be more entertaining than the direct had been. Or maybe the judge was only looking forward to wrapping this up and going to lunch. This hearing was little more than a matter of form. With only one witness the judge didn't have much credibility judging to do. Even if Raymond put Claymore on the stand to contradict everything the police officer had said it wouldn't do any good – was the judge going to believe a criminal over a cop? That would set a bad precedent.

And overhanging the whole hearing was the fact of guilt. If the defendant hadn't had an illegal substance in his pocket there'd be nothing now to suppress. Of course, that fact wouldn't weigh in the judge's determination of the legal issue of the search. Not at all.

'Officer, my name is Raymond Boudro. I have a few questions also. If I don't make myself clear please ask me to rephrase.'

Stennett was leaning back in his chair again. 'I know who you are, Counselor. I'm sure you'll be understandable.'

Raymond narrowed his eyes a little. His voice remained affable. 'This tip you received about drug dealing at this location, do you know its source?'

'No. That's what made it anonymous.'

'So you'd never received reliable information from this informant in the past.'

'Beats me.'

'And how recent was the information?'

'I don't know that either. I had just gotten it, but

the tip didn't come directly to me. I'm not sure when the station received it.'

'Maybe the day before?'

'Could have been.'

'Or even days earlier.' The detective shrugged. Raymond went on. 'So for this anonymous, unreliable tip to be worth anything even if it was true the drug dealer in question would have had to set up a stand on the same street corner day after day.' Raymond paused, but he hadn't asked a question and Stennett didn't say anything. 'The tip wasn't worth anything, was it, Officer?'

'It was worth something to me, Counselor. I don't know what it's worth here.'

'Well, you were full of legal opinions in your testimony on direct examination, but if you don't want to offer any now, that's fine. Let me ask you a geographical question instead. This intersection where the tip directed you, what quadrant of the city is that in?'

'That would be the east side.'

'Yes, it would. Is that your normal area of assignment?'

'Yes.'

'For how many years now?'

The detective sighed theatrically. 'Seems like forever sometimes.'

'Would you agree with me that the east side of San Antonio is the area with the greatest concentration of black citizens?'

Stennett appeared to think about it. 'Yeah,' he said.

'And in fact, the five men you saw on this street corner on this day last July were black.'

'Yes, they were.'

'Well, it's a black neighborhood, so that wasn't unusual, was it?'

'No.'

'Then why did you note that in your report, Officer? That the men were black.'

Stennett grew a little exasperated. 'The report's written on a form. You have to identify all the suspects by race, sex, height, all that. Even the witnesses, you have to say what race they are.'

'Yes,' Raymond agreed. 'In the space at the top of the form where you list people you have to fill out all that information. But you also included it in the body of the report, in your written summary of the events leading up to the arrest.' Out of the corner of his eye Raymond saw Rebecca looking at the offense report, frowning a little. 'Do you have a copy of your report in front of you?' he asked Stennett.

'I think I left it on the table over there.'

'Let me show you.' Raymond approached the witness stand with long strides and stood beside the cop, pointing at the page he was holding. Judge Marroquin was looking down on them with some interest. It would have been nice if the witness had flinched from contact with the black defense lawyer, but Stennett only squinted at the report.

'You see?' Raymond pointed. '"Drove to the location, saw five black males on the corner." That is what "B-M-S" stands for, isn't it, Officer? Black males?'

'Yes.'

'Why did you note that? Did you think it added something to your probable cause that the men were black?'

'No.'

'But you already said that when you drove by and saw them your suspicion increased. So seeing five black men together increased your suspicion that a crime was in progress. Would it still have looked suspicious if they'd had a basketball?'

The cop laughed and shook his head. He didn't look concerned, he looked like a man mired in silliness. When the elongated silence inflicted itself on his attention he glanced at the defense lawyer, who was staring at him. 'I'll wait as long as it takes you to think of an answer,' Raymond said charitably.

'I didn't think that was worth answering. It wasn't them being black that made me suspicious. It was five able-bodied young men standing on the street on a workday afternoon with nothing else to do. That made me think maybe they earned their living illegally.'

Raymond looked at him seriously. 'Do you know how many unemployed people there are on the east side of San Antonio, Officer?'

'I know how many drug dealers there are.'

'Perhaps you can regale us with that information if someone asks you a question that requires it. *My* question is whether you know how many unemployed people there are on the east side of town, how many young black men who can't find a job worth having because they don't have the education or qualifications or opportunity to find such a job.'

Stennett held up his hands in a gesture of surrender. 'We're way outside my field of expertise now, Counselor.'

'But you'd agree that the percentage of unemployment is higher on the east side than in San Antonio generally?'

'I don't know.'

'I thought you were rather expert on the east side,' Raymond said. He resumed his seat. For the first time he opened the file beside him. Becky looked at him. The thickness of the file made her suspicious that Raymond hadn't been kidding when he'd announced he was ready to proceed on this motion. The defense lawyer riffled through several pages before he found the one he wanted.

'We've established, Officer, that the east side of town, where you're assigned, is the *area with the largest black population in town, but* in fact it's not exclusively black by any means, is it?'

'No.' The detective sat alertly in his chair.

'No more than fifty percent black, would you estimate?'

'I wouldn't know that,' Stennett said carefully. He had some vague idea where this was leading and he wasn't going to help.

'You see a lot of people over there, don't you, Officer? Would you say more than half of them are black? Or don't you make those distinctions?'

'I'm not a census taker,' the cop said.

Rebecca Schirhart stood up. 'I'll object to any more of these statistical questions, Your Honor. The witness has already said he doesn't know, and I don't see the relevance anyway.'

'Okay,' the judge said noncommittally. That was the kind of ruling you got from Judge Marroquin unless you pressed him. The appellate court couldn't reverse his rulings if he didn't make any. Maybe he was sustaining the prosecutor's objection. It didn't matter. The judge would know the answer to Raymond's question. Even on the 'heavily black' east side, less than half the population was black. The judge knew that. And this was all aimed at the judge. It didn't matter what the evidence showed, all that mattered was how the judge felt about what he'd heard.

'Let's say half then,' Raymond said to Stennett. 'Now, I assume you do have personal knowledge about how many people you've arrested. How many would you say it's been in the last five years?'

Stennett rolled his eyes. 'I have no idea. Hundreds. Maybe thousands.'

'Let's make it easier. How about just in the past year?'

Stennett was silent, calculating. He was intrigued. 'Not that many anymore,' he speculated. 'When I'm undercover I don't arrest every drunk or speeder I see. Maybe one a week, maybe fifty the whole year?'

Raymond nodded. He had a piece of paper in his hand. Pieces of paper lent weight to questioning. 'Very good, Officer. Would you disagree with the figure sixty-two?'

'Sixty-two arrests in the last year? No, I wouldn't disagree with that.' Stennett was no longer casual on the witness stand. He was in a sort of stance, preparing himself.

'And what percentage of those arrestees would you estimate were black?' Raymond asked. He put down his piece of paper, picked up another. He looked over its top at the witness.

Becky was poised to object again, but she saw the relevance of the question; so would the judge. The judge was watching the witness with interest. It was okay, Becky could clean all this up on redirect.

'I guess that would be about fifty percent too,' the detective said.

'Would it surprise you to learn the figure is more like eighty percent?'

'Yes, it would.'

Raymond approached the witness again. 'Do you recognize this as a computer printout of the names of people you've arrested in the past year? And do you see this column that identifies the race of the suspect, as taken from your reports?'

'I object to defense counsel testifying,' Becky said.

The judge didn't even look at her. He was leaning over to look down at the list. Stennett was studying it too.

'I can't vouch for the accuracy of this,' the detective said slowly. 'But I wouldn't be surprised if the percentage is a little higher than the percentage of black population.'

'Because the sight of a black man makes you more suspicious than the sight of someone nonblack? Because you're more likely to investigate a black suspect?'

Stennett appeared to be keeping a rein on his temper. 'If this is true I think it's because statistics will show – '

Becky didn't let him finish. 'Your Honor. This is not only unfounded – the only testimony about the accuracy of these statistics comes from defense counsel himself – it's also irrelevant. The witness has testified to specific facts that gave him reasonable suspicion to conduct a frisk of this particular suspect. What's happened in other cases is irrelevant.'

The judge didn't rule on the objection, but his expression as he looked at Raymond clearly said, 'She's right.' Raymond had taken the point as far as he could anyway. He returned to his seat. 'Let's talk about the specific facts then, Detective Stennett. What was it made you think you had to frisk Claymore Johnson?'

'As I said, fear for my own safety. I was afraid he might be armed.'

'In fact, what you said was there's always the possibility a criminal suspect is armed and you're always concerned for your safety when conducting an investigation. Under that rationale, you'd be justified in searching everyone you see any time. What was it made you fear this particular' – the word was aimed at the prosecutor – 'suspect was armed?'

Stennett looked sure of himself again. 'The bulge in his pocket.'

Raymond stood up. He was wearing his best suit, a midnight-blue pinstripe he had bought after his last major triumph in court. Three years later the suit still fit well, though maybe a little tight in the waist and thighs. Raymond put his hands on his hips, flaring the wings of the jacket back like a gunfighter. 'A bulge about this size?' he said.

Stennett glanced at Raymond's pants. So did Rebecca. So did the judge. 'Could be,' Stennett said. 'I didn't study the size of it.'

Raymond reached into his pocket and pulled out a roll of bills, folded once and held by a money clip. 'Did it occur to you, Detective, that it might be cultural, for a black man to carry a lot of cash on him? Maybe because he doesn't have credit cards, because he can't *get* credit?'

'As a matter of fact, I thought it might *be* cash,' Stennett said. 'That would fit the profile. Guy on the street corner, gathering a crowd, showing something, big wad of cash in his pocket –'

'So you thought it was cash, not a weapon.'

'Possibly.'

'And a black man with a lot of money just has to be a drug dealer, doesn't he, Officer?'

Stennett wanted to say it. You could see the words in his mouth. Becky was tense on the edge of her chair, willing her witness to keep quiet, but the cop wasn't looking at her, he was looking at Raymond, at the taunting look in his eyes. And Stennett said it:

'Not necessarily. He could be a pimp.'

The silence was beautiful. Raymond held it, staying on his feet, not asking another question, the conductor of silence. Judge Marroquin was staring at the witness. It was the kind of joke the judge might have laughed at in another context, even have told himself, but in his courtroom, coming from a white cop, it was appalling. Judge Marroquin had been a well-respected member of the community for many years, but a Mexican-American man in his fifties would remember prejudice, remember the personal effects of it. As a matter of fact, Raymond knew that as a teenager the judge had been arrested and held in jail for a day just because he happened to be the only Mexican in the vicinity of a grocery store robbery in an Anglo neighborhood. The judge always referred to the incident in talks to juries. He didn't laugh about it.

'Or a lawyer,' Stennett said weakly.

'I pass the witness,' Raymond said.

Rebecca started off angrily. 'For the record, Detective, that was a joke you just made.'

'Yeah.'

'A bad joke.'

'Yeah, it was pretty stupid,' he admitted.

'Did the fact that this man was black have anything to do with your searching him?'

'No. None.'

'If he'd been white and you'd had the same information, would you have done the same thing?'

'Yes. Exactly the same.'

'You said you heard one of the men say something as you approached. Did you hear what was said?'

'The only phrase I heard was "the man".'

'What did that mean to you?'

'Cop. They knew I was a cop.'

'They recognized you as a police officer?'

'Oh yes. I'd made a couple of arrests in that set before. If I'd had time I would have gotten a partner for this trip, someone they wouldn't know, but there wasn't time when I got the tip.'

'So when these men, including the defendant, recognized you as a police officer they began moving away from you?'

'Oh definitely. If I'd been a little slower they would've vanished like smoke.'

Black smoke, Raymond thought, but it was too obvious to work into a question.

Becky asked a few more questions. The testimony resumed the tone of a normal hearing. The last question the prosecutor asked was, 'Why did you grab the defendant's hand when he reached into his pocket?'

'Because I was afraid of getting killed,' the witness said with perfect sincerity. Remember that, the prosecutor was telling the judge. Do you want cops to get killed? Want them to hold back because of some ruling of yours?

'I pass the witness,' Becky said.

'No questions,' Raymond said immediately. He'd decided that as soon as Becky began her redirect. He'd already made the best impression he could. There was no point in diluting the effect of that testimony by trying for more and failing.

'Both rest?' the judge said. 'Do you want to argue?' Ominous choice of words. He sounded ready to rule.

Damn straight they wanted to argue. Raymond had made some good points on cross-examination, but nobody ever won a motion to suppress just from crossing the witness. Raymond wanted to drive home what the judge had heard. Becky wanted to remind the judge that this was an ordinary case, the detective had said all the right things even though he'd added some wrong ones.

'This isn't the cutting edge of the law, Judge,' she

began at once. 'This is classic *Terry* versus *Ohio*. The officer had a tip, that gave him reason to investigate, and objective facts he stated here in court gave him reason to frisk the subject. For his own safety. The defendant not only had a bulge in his pocket, he reached for it when he knew a police officer was approaching. We can be glad this was such a veteran officer. A nervous rookie might have blown the suspect away. Personally, a suspect reaching for something in his pocket would scare the hell out of me. That's all this case is about, letting police officers protect themselves.

'And let's not forget one other thing. This wasn't just a hunch. Specific facts, including information from a citizen, led this officer to believe this defendant was carrying illegal drugs, and he was. The officer wasn't just frisking people at random. He had good reason for thinking the defendant was holding illegal drugs and his reasoning was borne out by the facts.'

That was prosecutorial desperation, reminding the judge of the defendant's guilt, justifying the search by what the search had uncovered. But it would probably work. It nearly always did.

'Yes, Your Honor, this time he found something,' Raymond said. 'That's why we're here. But that's not the issue. Allowing police officers to protect themselves is important too, but theirs aren't the only rights at stake. How many times has this witness searched someone without good reason and *not* found something? How many lives has he intruded into without winding up in court? Because the evidence shows this officer thinks every black person he sees is guilty of something.'

'Oh, bull,' Becky said unprofessionally.

'Tell him it's okay, Judge. Tell him he can roust

37

everybody he sees on the east side until he gets lucky and finds something in somebody's pocket. That's what he thinks now. That's what you'll be confirming for him by ruling that this search was legal.' Raymond sounded angry. He couldn't have said himself how much of that tone was real and how much put on.

The detective had left the witness stand but was lingering nearby, at the State's table. Judge Marroquin looked at him as he began ruling. This is the part, Raymond thought, where he tells him, 'Boy, you're walking a thin line,' just before he overrules my motion and lets the evidence in anyway.

'I understand the officer's concern for his own safety,' Judge Marroquin said, staring flatly at Stennett. 'It's a dangerous job he does. But that doesn't lessen other people's rights. If generalized personal fear and a bulge in the pocket was all it took to allow this kind of intrusion, Detective Stennett could search defense counsel. He could search me.

'As for the anonymous tip, that didn't even name this defendant. It named a street corner as suspect. An unidentified voice on the phone can't turn a street corner into a Constitution-free zone, where everyone unwittingly walking through is subject to search.

'Not enough,' the judge concluded. He was still staring at the cop. 'I think something else was at play here. I grant the motion to suppress.'

Everyone sat still, waiting for more, but there was no more. Claymore leaned forward and said into Raymond's ear, 'Grant? What's that mean, grant? Is that –'

Raymond was on his feet. 'Thank you, Your Honor. May we be excused?'

The judge nodded. Raymond glanced at the prosecutor, who looked stunned. He would have bet that as soon as he left she was going to follow the judge into his chambers and ask him to explain his ruling. 'But Judge,' she'd begin.

'Out, out,' Raymond said to his client. He jammed his file into his briefcase, gathered up his overcoat, and hustled Claymore out into the hall. 'Don't give him a chance to change his mind,' he said at the court-room door.

Just before Claymore turned to him in the hall, while no one was watching, Raymond clenched his fist hard. Won! God damn, and won the way hardly anybody ever won one, by ripping the cop a new one on the stand. He wanted to shout in triumph.

'You are free, my man. "Grant" means we won, means the judge agreed with me the search was bad.'

'Mean I walk?' Claymore said, and made a diminished version of the shout of joy Raymond had denied himself. Raymond just stood there looking profes-sional, like he did this every day. A moment later the two black women from the courtroom had joined them. Sure enough, they were Claymore's mother and girl-friend. Mama was crying. 'Oh, Mr Boudro,' she said. 'Oh, you were a terror in there. Thank you, thank you.'

'You're very welcome, ma'am. Claymore –' He had to take the client aside and make the money arrange-ments. The only bad thing about winning the motion was the case was now over and Raymond hadn't been paid.

Someone was squeezing his arm, someone else was thanking him again, when a shadow fell across the small celebration. Something made Raymond turn. The cop was standing there, Mike Stennett, not four feet away. He wore a small ironic smile, aimed at Raymond.

'Congratulations, Counselor,' he said. 'You do good work.

'See you around, Claymore,' he added, and walked away.

Sounds resumed in his wake. One of the women was asking Raymond a question, but the lawyer watched the cop walking away. The smile reminded Raymond of the wink he'd seen Stennett slip Claymore just before the hearing began. It didn't mean casual friendliness. He wondered what the cop was up to. For that matter, why had he given such untypical testimony in the hearing? Raymond would take credit for having goaded Stennett into saying something stupid, but it hadn't been the first time the officer had been cross-examined, nor the fifty-first. Maybe just a bad day, a short temper after a night without sleep. But the detective didn't look irritable as he strolled away down the courthouse hallway.

'What's the matter with that man?' Mama asked. 'Why's he want to harass my boy?' She seemed to think Claymore had just been found innocent. She had a fine judicial capacity: when the cocaine in her son's pocket was ruled inadmissible it vanished from her memory.

'I don't know,' Raymond said. 'But if you're smart you'll stay away from him, Claymore.'

'Man, I run the other way when I see him comin'.'

'You didn't see him coming this time,' Raymond said.

CHAPTER 2

'Saw Mr Preston in court today,' Raymond said that night after supper.

'That old man still going to court?' Denise said, walking back in from the kitchen. Raymond reflected how seldom what Denise said conveyed exactly what she meant. Written coldly, her remark would have looked contemptuous. But her tone made it affectionate, even admiring. Raymond would like to hear her say the same thing of him, in the same way, twenty years from now.

'Still there,' he said. 'Looking a little lost. He needs to stay in his office and get some bright young associate to go to court for him.'

'Why don't you go back to work with him?' Denise asked. She didn't mean that, either. Mr Preston was an institution, but a failing one, while Raymond was prospering on his own.

They sat quietly. Peter had rushed from the table as soon as he was excused. Raymond and Denise were grateful for the minutes alone in the dimness of the dining room. The two of them had once had such a public life. Public meetings in the courthouse, public socializing. Now they were private to the point of isolation, by preference. Most of their evenings were spent like this, alone at home. She saw people at work, he saw people at work, and that was enough people.

Denise had covered her thin arms with a sweater. She was always cold. *She hasn't aged three years in the fourteen or fifteen I've known her*, Raymond thought. He decided to say it.

'You still look like the day I met you.'

She fluttered her eyes, mock flirting. ''Cause you've given me such an easy life,' she said with a laugh.

After the birth of their one child Denise hadn't gone back to work at the courthouse. She was a secretary now at a middle school, so she'd have the same hours as Petey. Raymond was glad she no longer shared the courthouse world with him; he couldn't quite say why. But he was also glad she had the memories to appreciate his stories of his workdays without a lot of background explanation. He looked into his glass, smiling, and Denise indulgently said, 'Tell me again.'

Immediately Raymond said, 'I had him right here,' holding out one cupped hand. 'Couldn't've been better if I'd written his script for him.' For a moment that troubled him again, the way Stennett had said just what Raymond needed him to say.

'Nobody could've done it but you,' Denise said, mocking again, but kindly.

'Damn few would've tried. Or done the work.'

Denise frowned a little. 'Detective Stennett. Isn't he the one arrested Benny that time, in the park?' She still called her brother Benny, though he hadn't called himself that for years.

Raymond laughed. 'Well, you can't hardly hold that against him. Benny does look like the most likely suspect, any given crowd.'

Denise shook her finger at him. 'You better watch what you say 'bout my family. Santa Claus listening to you.' She looked at him as if she'd suddenly reminded herself of something suspicious. 'You sure must not have very busy days lately,' she said.

'What do you mean?' Raymond was genuinely puzzled. What was he being accused of now?

'You must be getting all your shopping done during

the day, 'cause you haven't been out at night at all, and here it's only three weeks 'til Christmas.'

'What makes you think you're getting anything for Christmas?' He smiled.

She gave him that look that hadn't lost its pointedness during twelve years of marriage. 'I don't get something nice for Christmas, you don't get something nice for*ever*.'

'Petey!' Raymond shouted immediately. 'Get your coat, we're going to the mall.'

Denise laughed at his enthusiasm. 'Aw, Dad,' Petey called. They both laughed. Raymond took her hand, and she came around the table to sit on his lap.

'In the meantime,' Raymond said cozily, '*before* Christmas, what've you got to express your admiration for the best lawyer in town?'

Denise murmured it close to his ear: 'I don't know, whyn't you send him around and I'll see how much I like him.'

'Ho ho,' Raymond said.

Two months later Raymond hunched his shoulders, pulling his overcoat tighter. Late February meant spring was near, but winter didn't believe it. Wind whirled down the street, impeded by few trees on this dismal block. The houses wouldn't stop that wind either. Raymond could see a visible chink between the boards beside the front door of this near-shack on the porch of which he was standing. He wanted to be back in his warm car on the way to his warm office. But bills had to be paid or the warmth would stop.

The door opened not much wider than the gap between the boards. A chain held it.

'Mrs Johnson? It's Raymond Boudro, ma'am, Claymore's lawyer. Do you remember me? I'm looking for Claymore.'

The door startled him by swinging closed, but it opened again as quickly, minus the chain. 'Oh, lawyer Boudro,' the old lady said. 'I sure am glad to see you. Step in, step in.'

He didn't like leaving his car unattended. It looked like a white man's car, vulnerable. This neighborhood gave him the creeps. Not because it was so alien but because if he stayed here long it would seem as if he belonged.

He'd come for money. Dunning letters meant nothing to someone like Claymore, who lived so far outside structure he probably seldom saw mail anyway. Raymond hadn't been able to get him on the phone, either. Claymore's old address had turned up vacant, but his mother should know where he'd gone. Claymore still owed Raymond for the case he'd gotten dismissed. Ungrateful son of a bitch wouldn't even think about paying until he got arrested again for something else, then he'd be all penitence and gratitude, expecting the same miracle again. But Raymond didn't want to wait that long.

He stepped inside the house but stayed near the door. 'I was hoping you might be able to tell me where I could find Claymore,' he said. He said it politely as hell, but it made the old lady burst into tears.

'Oh Mr Boudro, I was hoping you could tell me. I haven't seen him. I haven't seen him since before Christmas.'

'Before –? Since the day I met you in court?'

'No, sir. I seen him once since then. One day he came tearin' through here, picking up some of his clothes, borrowin' money, and all he said was he had to get gone. Leave town, he said. He said he call me but he never. Mr Boudro, I just –'

She started crying again. Raymond stood there for

long seconds before he finally put his arm around her and murmured words of encouragement. As he'd feared, she leaned into him, grateful, taking comfort. 'You can find out, can't you?' she said.

Raymond was thinking something terrible, so terrible it was probably true, and undoubtedly could never be proved.

'Where's Claymore Johnson?'

Stennett looked up from his desk. The desk was a mess – papers spilling across each other, two not-empty-enough Styrofoam coffee cups, sprinkling of ashes – and the cop looked like the desk's human counterpart. He was unshaven, his hair was dirty, his clothes wouldn't have looked presentable even if clean. He looked like the end of a three-day drunk, or like a white cop's idea of undercover.

'Okay, I'll bite,' he said, almost yawning. 'Where's Claymore Johnson?'

'I'm asking you,' Raymond said. He would have leaned forward across the desk but he didn't see two safe spots to put his hands down, so he stood straight, glaring. 'He disappeared owing me money and even his mother doesn't know where he is. She's only seen him once since the day your case against him was dismissed, and the day she saw him he was terrified.'

'Someone must've offered him a nine-to-five job,' Stennett said. He was still lounging back in the chair. Raymond suddenly thought he should have done this somewhere else. He was aware of the other cops scattered around the squad room. If they took some interest it wouldn't be favorable to the black defense lawyer. But Raymond had chosen deliberately to come to the police station. He might want to go from this confrontation to Internal Affairs.

Stennett was shaking his head. 'You're a tough audience. I haven't even gotten a smile out of you yet.'

'What did you do to him? You scared him bad. Did you do worse than that? Claymore wouldn't just vanish. He'd let his mother know where he was. Did it hurt you so bad to lose one case?'

'Yeah, right, I'm the Scarlet Avenger; if I can't convict 'em I kill 'em. Grow up, Counselor. You think I kill every suspect whose case gets dismissed? I'd be awful busy, wouldn't I?'

'Not so busy,' Raymond said. 'I've never heard of your arrests not standing up in court before.' Never before, he thought, and the strangeness of the day in the courthouse hall tugged at him again.

Stennett was shaking his head. 'I believe he was scared, but not of me. None of 'em's scared of me. Hell, what's the worst I can do to them, bust 'em? Get 'em put on probation? Or, ooh, horrors, go to *jail* for three or four months? You know what these guys think of prison. It's Holiday Inn for them, just a place to rest up and make some business contacts. Nah. If Claymore's afraid, it's not of me.'

'Who then?' Raymond said.

The cop looked at him, debating internally. Again, as on that day in court, it was clear Stennett had something he was dying to say. Raymond stayed silent and let it come.

'Did you notice our audience in court?' Stennett finally said. 'The two guys in back? You figured they were pals of Claymore's just because they were black too. Kind of a closet racist, aren't you?

'They weren't his pals. They were more like ... business associates. The day after I busted Claymore with that piddling amount of coke, the day after he got out on a P.R. bond, I busted those two guys. With a lot heavier load than Claymore was carrying. Now, I'm not privy to their thinking, but I imagine those guys were curious about the coincidence, Claymore getting popped and a day later me bustin' in on them. So they showed up for his hearing. And when I gave such, let's say, honest testimony that Claymore walked, their suspicions were confirmed. And those guys take a real dim view of snitches.'

'I don't believe you,' Raymond said. 'You testified the way you did just for the benefit of these other drug dealers? You know you ruined your credibility with Judge Marroquin forever.'

'Dream on. Next time I testify to Judge Marroquin I'll have a rock-solid case for him and I'll be respectful and professional as hell and he'll think his little speech did me a world of good and I've straightened out.'

No, this is make-believe, Raymond thought. This is saving face after the fact, after you lost it on the stand, now you've made up some belated justification. But he remembered the wink Stennett had given Claymore, *before* his testimony. Not for Raymond's benefit, not even for Claymore's. For the stone-faced pair at the back of the room.

'You'd throw away a case for that?' Raymond said.

'Throw away a case?' Stennett stood up. For the first time he looked something other than self-satisfied. He was hot. 'That case wasn't worth shit if I'd made it. That little hour's worth of coke in his pocket? That was a probation case anyway. Maybe minimum time to do, and the way they get paroled these days he would've been back here on the same bus that took 'im. What'd I care about that case? I could make ten arrests like that a day, and the factory'd just keep chugging along.

'But I can make 'em distrust each other. That's a lot

better. First they run Claymore off, but they keep 'im in mind. And the next time one of them gets arrested the others start wondering. Maybe they don't like dealing with each other after that. Maybe they do it anyway but at the first suspicious sneeze they start reaching for revolvers. I'll give away every no-account arrest I ever made if I can put a crimp like that in their operation. You ask Claymore which he's more scared of, me and the system or his own pards. If you ever see him again.'

Raymond stared at him. It was always amazing to find someone who took his work seriously. Raymond felt hollow, stripped of triumph, as he realized who had really won their confrontation in court. And realized too how far this cop would go to win.

'You are some piece of work,' he said wonderingly.

And Stennett was his clownish self again. The passionate man sank into a lazy smile. 'Thank you, Counselor. I think you're good at your job, too.'

CHAPTER 3

April night in San Antonio calls people outdoors. The daytime temperature had been in the high eighties, but the heat didn't take forever to dissipate the way it would through the long summer. The air began cooling even before the sun went down. By nine o'clock the breeze made it pleasant to be outside. Mike Stennett had the car windows rolled down. He was leaning back against the door, head out the window, when his radio crackled to life.

'Stennett? You there? Got a call for you.'

'Great, George, now you've blown my cover. I was doing a little undercover vice work. Does this mean the blowjob is off, sweetie? How 'bout if you give back the money and we just do it for love?'

'Knock it off,' the dispatcher said. 'If you don't have anything better to do, and it sounds like you don't, swing by the M.E.'s office. There's a body there you might know.'

'I might? Why?'

'It's an east side druggie with crack in his pocket and looks like a drug deal blew up in his face.'

You never heard anybody say 'nigger' over the police band anymore. You never knew who might be listening, including the chief, who was sensitive. But 'east side' meant the same thing.

'Okay, George. Got a name?'

'I don't. Maybe the M.E. does.'

Stennett had already slipped the car into gear and was letting it roll down the street, next to the left-hand curb, lights still off. 'This isn't another surprise party,

49

is it, George? I get over there and all you guys jump out of the meat locker with presents and girls? You guys are so sweet.'

You couldn't say obscenities over the police band either, so the only response was a loud retiring click. Stennett dropped the radio mike and eased to a stop in front of a two-bedroom house whose tiny front porch was crowded with five or six bodies. He wondered if they could see his face better than he could see theirs. Certainly no one had recognized him, because they remained languid.

'You folks call for a police officer?' he called across the narrow front yard, and enjoyed the ensuing scramble off the porch. One guy vaulted the railing, ran up the side of the house, dived over the backyard fence, and was probably two blocks away when Stennett drove away chuckling. 'Thought so,' he said to himself.

He drove slowly out of the neighborhood, checking locations he knew, taking his time.

The medical examiner's office was a blocky one-story sandstone building that wore its small parking lot like a moat. The M.E. kept begging Commissioners Court for a new building. He had about two thousand square feet where he was and needed ten times that much. The front of the building was dark but somebody opened a side door after Stennett knocked long enough. He didn't have to show a badge. If they didn't recognize him specifically they recognized cop, and they knew they had a stiff the cops were interested in.

He was surprised to see Bob Wyntlowski, Doctor Bob, an assistant medical examiner, when he walked into the examining room. The doctor was yawning over a Styrofoam cup of coffee beside the lone occupied table.

'Kind of late, isn't it, Doc?'

'If one more cop calls me Doc I'm going to weigh his organs for him,' Wyntlowski said without heat. 'Makes me feel like an old half-drunk sawbones in Dodge City. How'd you like it if I called you Cop like it was your name?'

'Geez, sorry. Gah, everybody's so sensitive, it ain't even summer yet.'

'Sorry.' The doctor wiped his hand across his face. 'Long day.'

'That's what I said. What're you doin' here? Thought you saved the autopsies 'til morning.'

'I was down the street at the hospital,' Wyntlowski said. 'Stopped in on my way home and I thought I'd go ahead and do this one. I thought you guys would be interested, since it's a homicide,' he added ironically.

'Is it definitely?'

'Wait'll we put the face back on, you'll see.'

Stennett was avoiding looking at the thing on the table. While they talked one of the doctor's assistants was disassembling the former human laid out – well, you couldn't say face up anymore, but backside down, anyway – on the examining table. There was no way Stennett could ID the guy at this point, because you needed a face for that. They were past the face stage. In order to get to the brain the assistant had made a long cut across the top of the head, ear to ear, then peeled the skin down and forward like latex, exposing the skull, a portion of which he then sawed off in order to remove the brain. In the meantime the face hung down there inside out below the chin. From the inside a face has no individuality.

Stennett could tell from the arms and legs that the corpse was black. The chest cavity was open from breastbone to just above the pubic hair. Most of the organs had already been removed and weighed and were sitting in the sink. The body looked like an anatomical display, no longer human. Sometimes when they were laid out whole on the slab they looked unnaturally stiff, like something assembled by a rubber sculptor who hadn't yet done quite enough study of live models. Other times they were flexible, peaceful, their injuries superficial or invisible, so that a spectator feared the body would sit up and demand an explanation at the first incision. But at the stage this one was in now it was just an empty organ sack, gaping, severed, unnecessarily elaborate. The hands were sad because they were untouched. They could still hold, grip, reach out and clutch. The hands were ready and waiting to do their job if only someone would stick them on a person instead of this grisly thing their trunk had become.

'God, I hate this,' Stennett said.

'What?' Wyntlowski asked. Stennett could never tell if he was joking.

'Wait a minute,' the doctor added to his assistant. 'Let me see that.'

The assistant – did they get hunched like that from bending over a table all day, Stennett wondered, or did the M.E. deliberately hire guys who looked like Igor? – obediently held out a mass of cranberry-jelly-like tissue. The doctor took a scalpel in his rubber-gloved left hand and made a few slices.

'Find something? Is that what killed him?'

'Might have in another twenty years,' Wyntlowski said. 'This is the liver. Heavy drinker. See the dark, stiff areas?'

'So what?' Stennett looked away.

The doctor handed the liver back to the assistant, who rinsed it off and put it in the scale. 'No, here's what killed him,' Wyntlowski said. He moved up to the head. The skull was intact except for the slice that had been removed. There was the skull's face, just like something found in a haunted house except that this one still had eyes in it. Wyntlowski pointed close to them. 'See here?'

'Yeah?' The nose was flat. The small bone that should have indicated it was gone.

'Somebody shoved his nose back into his brain,' the doctor said. 'That's how you usually get killed in a barroom brawl, if you get killed. Get kneed in the face, or punched if it's hard enough, but usually kneed or kicked. And that little sharp bone breaks off and goes right into the brain like a scalpel. Want to see?'

'No thanks, I'll take your word for it. Hey, what're you doing?' He was talking to the assistant now. 'Hey, hold off on that for a minute, will ya? Hey! Hey, come on – oh geez.' Stennett backed away from the indescribable smell that emerged from the intestine the assistant had just opened. Wyntlowski had never put down his Styrofoam coffee cup. He leaned over the open cavity for a better look.

'That's it for me. I'll just wait over here 'til you guys him put back together. Let me know.'

The smell stayed in his nostrils, but it wasn't so bad after he rounded the corner. He took deep breaths and decided he didn't have to look for a trash can. A few minutes later Wyntlowski stuck his head around the corner. 'Ready for you,' he said brightly. As Stennett came back into the autopsy room Wyntlowski said, 'It's a boy.'

They had put the face back on. Presumably the missing slice of skull had been replaced as well, because the corpse didn't look lobotomized. They might have replaced the brain or it might be still lying with the other organs, leaving the slab man brainless. But then, he hadn't been any Rhodes scholar to start with.

The assistant had put the organs back inside the chest cavity, in no particular order, and was sewing up the long incision, using heavy thread, grunting a little as he pulled the flaps of skin together. Stennett concentrated on the face. He had to use his imagination a little about the nose. It was there, it wasn't caved in, but it had no support, just a pedestal of empty flesh.

'See?' the doctor said, pointing out bruises and abrasions on the face and torso. There was a beauty on the cheekbone that probably would have swollen the guy's left eye shut if he'd had time for swelling. 'Your basic beating death,' Wyntlowski said. 'You know him?'

'Yeah, I knew him.'

Wyntlowski waited. Finally, 'By name?' he asked pointedly.

Stennett stirred himself from reflection. 'Old Hoss. What *was* his name? Gordon something. Frazier.'

'Hoss? Sounds like you knew him.'

'Oh, you know. Around. One of the usual suspects. Hell, I probably arrested him before. So, uh, your end of it. Homicide, definitely?'

Wyntlowski shrugged. 'Could have happened in a car wreck. But the way he was found, on the street. Plus the other signs of beating. Yes, homicide.'

'This bone-through-the-brain business. Would that kill him instantly?'

'Like a light switch.'

'It's not something that could gradually work its way back until –'

The doctor shook his head. 'It takes a lot of force. Your nose bone isn't just going to wiggle back into your brain on its own.' He looked at the cop, who

54

seemed to be working on something already. 'Got any suspects in mind?'

Stennett laughed. 'No, but I'm sure we'll have every man on the force on the case by morning. Ol' Hoss. Wonder who he pissed off this time? It would be nice if I could pin it on somebody though, wouldn't it? Kill two birds with one stone. That's always nice.'

'I guess,' Wyntlowski said, in the uninterested tone of a man whose job was always performed in increments of one.

Rebecca had heard the car door but assumed it was at her neighbor's house, so she was startled by the knock on the door. Her first inclination was to stay on the sofa and outwait the person outside. She couldn't think of anyone she wanted to see, and to Becky her living room looked like a mess, because there were two magazines on the coffee table instead of in the rack at the end and it had been two days since she'd vacuumed.

But, 'Oh,' she said when she looked through the peephole and saw Donny Summerford standing there. His head was turned away, looking across Becky's front yard. Donny was company but he was effortless. In fact, in the moment it took her to reach for the doorknob Becky became glad to see him.

'Hello,' she said, mock seductively.

Donny smiled and held up a bottle of red wine in one hand and a cork in the other. 'I was letting it breathe in the car.'

He hadn't overdressed for the occasion. He was wearing a short-sleeved knit shirt, white tennis shorts, and old loafers with no socks. Becky put her hands on her hips and surveyed him. She was wearing shorts herself, but they were old cutoffs. Donny looked tailored even

55

in extreme repose. 'You're such a fucking yuppie,' she said.

He frowned slightly as he stepped in. 'That place has really affected your vocabulary,' he said.

She made a face at his back. 'Civil lawyers don't say *fuck*?'

'Not in every sentence.' But he smiled. She would take high-toned crap from Donny because his reproof didn't seem serious. 'What's the occasion?' she said of the wine.

'Congratulations on your promotion.'

'How did you know?'

'I have my sources.' He tried to look enigmatic without success. Donny's All-American good looks didn't admit of mysteriousness. When she'd first seen him, in a law school class, she'd taken him for a cookie cutter good looker, fonder of himself than of anything else in the world. When she'd gotten to know him better she'd thought his regular features were the disguise he wore to take in dullards while reserving his quirky sense of humor for interesting people like herself. Now on those rare occasions when she saw him in the courthouse the disguise fooled her as well. He looked born for blue suits.

Becky's promotion had been two days ago, plenty of time for news of it to filter to Donny. After only slight nudging a few of the people from the office had taken her to lunch, but that had been the extent of celebration. In fact she had just been sitting here a little depressed over the lack of effect on her life.

'I wanted to take you to dinner,' Donny said, 'but I got hung up at the office. Is it too late for a little . . .?' He displayed the bottle again.

'No, no.' She waved him into the living room.

'Shall I pour into this Dairy Queen cup?'

56

'Not fancy enough for a hotshot civil lawyer, I'm sure. Let me see if the elegant Styrofoam stemware is clean.'

He started to follow her toward the kitchen, but she gestured toward the sofa and hurried away. She'd rather he not see the remains of her takeout dinner. In the kitchen she hurriedly stuffed it into the trash can, washed her hands in the sink, ran a finger across her teeth and rinsed out her mouth as delicately as possible, hoping the running water covered the sound. Wondering if her hair looked as limp as it felt, falling across her forehead, she found the globular red wineglasses, the ones Donny had given her two Christmases ago.

'I hope it's not an expensive bottle,' she said. 'If it's one of your fancy ones it cost more than my raise was.'

'Don't denigrate your promotion. Second chair felony, that's pretty impressive.' He held up his glass; they clinked. 'Congratulations.'

'Thank you.' She was grateful to Donny for making it an occasion at least for a moment, rather than a joke. At the same time she noticed he paused to inhale the fumes from his glass before taking his first sip, and she smiled.

'Actually, it was a little impressive. Mmm, good wine. More impressive than when I made felony. That was during the old administration, of course, and it was just sort of, "We'll see you in the one-seventy-fifth Monday." This time I had an audience with the boss himself.'

'Is that so rare? I thought –'

'Well, you see him, he drops by courts all the time, but it's different when his secretary calls and says, "The District Attorney would like to see you at two if you're not in trial." I thought, Oh shit, this is it, I'm out. After I lost that motion to suppress, you know, he talked to me that time, too.'

'I thought that was all straightened out.'

'Well it was, I thought. When I talked to him he said he just wanted to know if it was something we could make changes to avoid in the future and I said I didn't see how, the cop had just acted like an idiot on the stand, and he said yes, he'd heard the same thing from other people. I figured he must've talked to the judge, in fact I know he did, because then he said Judge Marroquin said I hadn't done anything wrong. But then when I got this second call to go see him I thought, Uh oh, they've been watching me ever since and they've decided it was my fault after all. That's what I thought. This is good.' She held out her glass; Donny refilled it. She realized she was rattling on but didn't care. She hadn't had a chance to talk about this enough and Donny was a good audience. He leaned forward as if interested, and nodded in the right places.

'He didn't tell me right away, first he asked me how everything was going and like that and then asked about my plans.'

At first she'd thought the District Attorney was trying to see if she had somewhere else to go if he fired her or gave her a few weeks to find another job. In retrospect she realized he'd been asking about her commitment to the D.A.'s office. The District Attorney couldn't suffer the illusion that everyone in his employ was a career prosecutor, but it was as if by promoting her he would be admitting her to a higher circle, where just being in it for the experience wasn't good enough.

'And you know what he asked about the most? Another case I lost. It was that theft case, I think I told you about it, where Pat – remember my second chair in the one-seventy-fifth? – said we should just dismiss it and I said no, I'd try it by myself, mainly because the little jerk, the defendant I mean, pissed me off because he was so sure I couldn't prove it. I could have if the judge had let me get in that statement of his. As it was the jury was out all day before they came back not guilty. Anyway, that was the trial the boss asked me about this week. I thought he was summarizing my failures, but he said that was another case he'd checked into and he thought I'd done the right thing by trying it. He said if we just try the ones we know we can win we're letting a lot of people go free who should be in jail. And you know what I just now realized? Pat's gone now and I'm a second chair.'

'Congratulations again,' Donny said. He leaned back on the couch, wineglass resting on his stomach. His flat stomach, Becky thought. It was disgusting the way men could rely for twenty years on the muscles they'd developed in their teens, while if she had one extra French fry or even *thought* about dessert her thighs started looking like curdled milk.

'I'm a little surprised you've stayed there long enough to get this far,' he said.

'I'm a little surprised myself.' When they'd finished law school Donny had gone into one of the two best insurance defense firms in town. Becky had had an offer from a slightly less prestigious firm, one she'd seriously considered, but she'd gone into the D.A.'s office instead because that's where you got the most trial experience the fastest, and trials were the bottom line. If you were afraid of trial the fear might show in the long, long pretrial maneuvering in a civil case. Rebecca *had* been afraid of trials then, fresh from law school, so she'd forced herself into the arena to confront her fear. Fear of trial had stopped being a factor long ago. In the three years since law school Donny had probably gone to trial four times, and two of those had settled before a verdict. Becky's record of jury trials after three years in the D.A.'s office was over a hundred. She wasn't afraid of trial anymore, except that immediate pretrial stage fright she still endured. She was more like addicted to trial. But there was something more than that that kept her a prosecutor, something she wouldn't say to Donny because it would sound like unwonted arrogance.

He began telling her about his own current favorite case, about a triumph he'd had in a deposition. She listened politely, and realized that's the way he had listened to her, too. So she tried to be as good a listener as he'd been. Because she was a lawyer too she asked the right questions, the ones that drew his punch lines, but the story was dry as a textbook to her. What held her interest were the blond hairs curling on his legs. He must still play tennis, she thought; must play with clients because he wouldn't take the time to do it just for the exercise.

She and Donny had dated for three years starting in law school, seriously enough that after the first two weeks they'd each stopped going out with anyone else. They didn't explicitly discuss marriage, but they talked about plans extending so far into their lifetimes they would inevitably include marriage: practicing law together, for example, or where they would take long trips once they were rich.

Becky hated to think she and Donny were so shallow they'd broken apart over work, but that was the case. If she'd gone into that civil law firm she was sure they would be married now, going to the right parties, wondering if they could wait for Becky to make partner before having their one perfect baby. And she would have the casual disdain for criminal law all civil lawyers shared. People didn't go from the top of the class into criminal law. They went into weighty areas like products liability. If she and Donny still had that in common they would undoubtedly have more as well. What he talked about now seemed so trivial to her. All his cases boiled down to money. Enough money could cure any ill in his world. Becky's cases were life and death, horror and hate and lust. Donny, she knew, saw her work as involved with an undersociety best left to their own devices and put out of mind. Donny's world seemed to her filled with greedy graspers; she couldn't understand how it held his interest.

But if she still loved him he would still fascinate her. They'd never had a blowup, they had just – horrible phrase – drifted apart, so subtly they were sometimes, like tonight, still together. From exclusive lovers they'd become what Donny in a light moment had once called friends with sex. He hadn't seen how the phrase had depressed Rebecca, because what it meant, of course, was sex without romance.

But sometimes that beat the alternative.

He had his feet up on the edge of the coffee table, making triangular arches of his legs. Becky faced him, her back against the sofa arm. Barefoot, she stretched her legs toward him. Donny didn't seem to notice. He kept talking. But after a moment he rested his arm lightly on the tops of her ankles. He poured more wine into his glass, stretched to pour the last of it into hers, then looked at the empty bottle as if it were a clock.

'Big glasses,' he said. Becky smiled because it was an old joke between them.

'Donny,' she said, meaning to ask him whom he shared private jokes with now. When he looked at her she asked instead, 'Does anybody still call you Donny?'

He shook his head, smiling as if he'd perpetrated a great hoax. 'Don,' he said deeply.

They sat silently for a minute. His arm was still on her legs but hadn't moved. 'I'm glad you came,' Becky said. 'Your wine's gone straight to my head.'

'Good thing you're already home. Wouldn't do for you to get arrested.'

It hadn't gone to his, she knew. Donny still looked perfectly controlled, though he'd smile at nothing. But he always did.

'Well,' he said. 'I have to be up early tomorrow.'

'Me too.'

'Congratulations again. Next thing you know they'll make you a section chief, then you'll never get out.'

He stood up, putting his empty glass down on the table. Becky just lay back, letting him come, but he walked past her. As he came into her view again, on his way to the door, she hated him, but that passed in a moment. She followed him and he waited. 'Thanks,' she said ambiguously. 'I can always count on you, Donny.'

She leaned into him, he held her, and they kissed, loose and intimate immediately, not a good-night kiss. The tips of their noses brushed. She pushed hair back from her face, flirted with his cheek with her eyelashes. Donny didn't move, just continued to hold her strongly, one arm along the side of her breast. Becky nuzzled his mouth and pressed against him, but she was determined she wouldn't start anything. She had initiated the kiss, but that didn't count, they both knew that was coming. Donny was going to have to start anything more.

But he had more patience than she, or was less affected by the wine. Finally – it must have been two minutes into the kiss – she put her hand inside the waistband of his shorts. It was immediately evident he was interested. Where did he get his restraint, and why did he exercise it? But now that she'd taken the initiative he finally put his hand up inside her blouse.

The undressing part went too fast. There were so few garments between them and nakedness, three apiece. There seemed to be no more than a shimmer of time and she was wrapping her legs around his, pressing her breasts against his hard chest, running her hands over his body that hadn't changed in all the time she'd known him.

'Come,' she said, stepping away and taking his hand. They smiled at the word. Becky flipped down the switch beside the door that turned off the lamp directly behind the sofa. There was another across the room, plenty of light. She didn't take him to the bedroom, just to the sofa. Of the last three times they'd made love two had been here on the sofa. He was edging out of her life. Next it would be the floor in front of the door.

They sat and resumed the kiss until Becky broke away and lifted her head. Donny kissed her breasts, carefully, showing no partiality. She held his back, stroked him, ran her hands up his thighs. She teased him until he grew more aggressive. When he did she turned away and let him come at her from behind, where he could be anybody. But it wasn't someone else she pictured, it was Donny younger, when she had loved him. He had looked different then, though she couldn't say how. She tried to make herself the person she'd been then, the one who had loved him. His hands cupped her breasts, roughly for Donny. She laughed to tell him she approved. Finally she turned around, lying back on the arm cushion, one leg extended along the top of the sofa, and guided him. 'Slowly,' she murmured, but she didn't have to tell him. He was a better lover than he used to be. As at everything, he was damned near perfect. When, some time later, she made the sound that was more in her throat than her mouth, she pulled herself up hard against him, hands clutching his back, her body suspended beneath him. Donny made the same sort of sound, thrust once more, making her shudder, and dropped them both to the sofa. Becky still held him hard, their harsh breaths in rhythm. He kissed her neck. The vision of love faded from her slowly, but it faded. When Donny laughed and said, 'I really do have to get up early in the morning,' she laughed as lightly and said, 'I really do too.' They said a few more words in the tones used for endearments. When she let him out the door she was still naked. She lay back down on the sofa, holding her shirt to her chest. Early in the morning she woke and couldn't think why she wasn't in bed.

CHAPTER 4

Sometimes the papers helped. Usually reporters just cluttered up the scene and tried to ferret out details best left unpublished, but sometimes having a story appear in the newspaper would bring forward a witness who didn't know he was a witness until he read about it. That was what broke the murder of Gordon Frazier.

Until the old man came forward the case was one step away from falling behind somebody's credenza. From day one it was open but virtually ignored. There were some intriguing features about the murder, such as the pistol found at the scene, close to the corpse's hand but without his fingerprints. Intriguing details didn't give the case priority, though. In the five days after Frazier's body was discovered three more people were murdered in San Antonio, each of the victims less worthy of death than Hoss Frazier. There weren't exactly citizens' groups crowding the doors to protest the lack of activity on his case. Not even the usual weeping mother. A sister claimed the body, acting as if she had better things to do with her time. When questioned about suspects she gave her opinion that just about anybody her brother knew was a fifty-fifty bet to beat him to death on any given day. Patrol officers questioned residents surrounding the alley where the body had been found and made the shocking discovery nobody had seen anything.

It didn't seem odd to anyone that Mike Stennett stayed in touch with the case even though he wasn't a homicide detective. After all, he'd had to ID the body, which had been found in his acknowledged east side fiefdom, and the murder seemed drug-related. But he didn't have any insights or turn up any clues. Both the newspapers and the cops had lost interest in the case by the time the old man called the station.

The only story in the paper, headlined BODY IDENTI-FIED, had been of the one-paragraph variety only some-one who pored over the Metro section would read. There never was a follow-up. That's what the old man pointed out when he called five days later.

'Y'all ever arrest anybody for killing that boy on Ghoulson Street?' he asked. The switchboard operator transferred him to Homicide, where he asked the same question of a detective who was eager to get off the phone so he could take a third bite of his barbecue sandwich. 'May I have your name?' the detective asked around his mouthful.

'Haley Burkwright. I live over here on Aransas down the street from it.'

'Uh huh. And can you tell me which case you're talking about?'

'Gordon Frazier, thirty-nine,' the old man said as if quoting from the paper, then deviated from the text. 'The one that got beat to death.'

'Right. No sir, we haven't made an arrest in that case.' The detective didn't ask anything else because the old man sounded like a talker and the detective's sandwich was getting cold.

'Well I saw it.'

'You saw the story in the paper?'

'No son, I saw the murder. Hell, if I had to wait for things to show up in the paper I'd be dead of old age.'

'Then I need to take a statement from you,' the detective said resignedly. 'Can you just hold on while I reach for a form?'

'I got all day, son.'

The detective took a monstrous bite out of his sandwich while fishing the form out of a slot at the back of his desk. Gourmet dining. The wad of meat and bread stuck in his throat and he had to pour cold coffee on top of it until it dissolved. 'Now,' he said. 'Can you spell your name for me?'

Haley Burkwright rattled it off from years of practice, and added his address without being asked.

'And was Mr Frazier a friend of yours?'

The old man made a disgusted sound. 'I don't know that crowd. But I'd seen him around. After I read about it I realized that was him I saw getting the stuffing knocked out of him. More power to whoever was doing it, I thought at the time. But I didn't know he was gonna kill him.'

'Where was this?' the detective asked.

'I stepped out into my backyard. There's a little alley there and then a church parking lot. Missionary Baptist. They were there in the parking lot. I could hear this Frazier fella whining.'

'Did you know the suspect, the one who was hitting him?'

'Seems like I've seen him around too, but I cain't definitely say.'

'Can you describe him?'

'He was a young guy, maybe forty. Average height, little bit heavy around the middle, dark hair. Hard hitter.'

'Black?'

'No. White guy.'

Really, the detective almost said. If the old man was right he'd just eliminated all the suspects and raised the interest level of the case a notch or two.

'Mr Burkwright, I'm going to send a couple of

officers to talk to you further, and if they determine it's warranted' – if they don't think you're just a crazy old fart – 'they'll bring you to the station here to look at some pictures. Would that be all right with you?'

'Sure thing.'

I thought so, the detective thought. By the time he got back to his sandwich it was a fairly disgusting artifact, grease congealed on the beef. He ate it anyway.

Nobody put much stock in the old man even before he made a fool of himself. He took more interest in his surroundings at the police station than he did in the mug books. Kept getting up to wander down the hall to the men's room, then took his time coming back, looking into the other offices. *Groupie*, the detective thought. Old man without much to fill his days just wanted to see the inside of the cop house. The detective indulged him. He wasn't a kid himself: the prospect of a boring retirement didn't seem alien to him. He didn't rein in the old man in his trips around the floor. And he put down his pen when the old man came up to his desk.

'Have you found him, Mr Burkwright?'

Burkwright gave the unexpected answer. 'Yes sir.'

Wouldn't it be something if I solved this case while sitting at my desk, the detective thought, but he didn't believe it. 'Well let's take a look.'

The old man didn't look like a loon. He was alert-faced but not assertive, respectful to the younger man. His hair was gray and thin but he wasn't wearing glasses and he obviously took in everything around him. The detective had to walk faster than was his usual wont to keep up with Burkwright as they walked back to the table where they'd laid out the mug books.

68

And past it.

'Mr Burkwright? Sir? Those are the books there.'

'That's not where I found him.'

He's going to identify one of those wanted circulars in the lobby, the detective thought. Probably the one wanted for robbing a bank in Seattle. He almost bumped into the man's back when Burkwright stopped at another squad room door. 'Look casual,' the old man whispered.

Apparently they didn't do a good job of that, because Mike Stennett, across the room, looked up at the two men staring at him from the doorway. Stennett did look more like a suspect than a cop, the detective realized, with his three days' growth and bloodshot eyes.

'That's him,' the old man said.

'Then he says, "That's him,"' Palomar said, laughing, getting the chuckles in reply. He was about to elaborate on Mike's reaction when his intercom sounded.

Fuentes, the captain, was well known for having no sense of humor on duty. The weird thing about him was if you saw him off duty, at a picnic or something, he'd be drinking beer and telling jokes with the best of them, and guys who'd been to his house said he was a laugh riot there, but nobody had ever seen him crack a smile inside the station. Kept his sense of humor in his locker, some of them said. It was disconcerting when you found yourself standing in front of his desk, which Palomar did three minutes later.

'I hear you turned up a suspect in the Frazier murder,' Fuentes said, making Palomar think the captain was finally breaking his self-imposed on-duty sobriety.

'Oh yeah, you heard about that? Yeah, Stennett didn't find it too amusing, but everybody else –'

Fuentes didn't find it amusing either. 'And exactly what have you done with the information?'

'Sir?' Palomar didn't think Fuentes was referring to the chuckling group around his desk to which he'd passed on the story.

'An eyewitness to a murder identifies a suspect and you did nothing to follow up. Do I have that right?'

'Oh, well, you know, I told the old guy Stennett was a cop, and he kind of backed off.' That was an exaggeration, to say the least. What Burkwright had actually said in response was, 'I kind of thought so.'

'This is a man who reads items in the paper and makes phone calls,' Fuentes said. 'This time he calls us. As time goes by and nothing happens, who do you think he calls next?'

Palomar was no dope; he saw what they were talking about. 'Yes sir, I'll check it out.'

Fuentes spelled it out anyway. 'When we start getting calls from the press we have to have already thoroughly checked this thing out. Know Stennett's whereabouts at the time, how he knew the victim, why we've eliminated him as a suspect. It would be nice, in fact –'

'– if we had another suspect on tap instead. Yes sir.'

'Thank you, Detective. It should be relatively easy to clear Detective Stennett of suspicion. I believe there was a fingerprint on the gun found at the scene?'

Politics, Palomar thought as he left. Politics, press, and paranoia. Did you have to have those three on the brain to make it into the upper ranks of this department, or did they alight on you once you'd made the ascension?

'Mike?'
'Yeah.'

'Jesus, this is shitty, Mike.'

'What is?'

'I'm arresting you.'

'This is exactly why I don't spend more time in this goddamned place,' Stennett said heatedly. 'Between the phones ringing and the civilians walking around and the stupid jokes, it's impossible –'

'It's not a joke, Mike.' Indeed, Detective Palomar looked sober as a black suit. He even had his stomach sucked in, something he didn't usually bother to do around the station house. 'I'm arresting you for the murder of Gordon Frazier. You know, that –'

'Yeah, I know.' Stennett didn't bother to feign surprise. He looked to see if he had a cigarette going, found he did, and inhaled what was left of it. 'This is about the crazy old guy was in here yesterday. Whyn't you put together a lineup and see if he IDs me or the refrigerator?'

'You know I wouldn't do this just on account of that, Mike. Hell, I didn't take the old guy serious for a second. But there's something else. You might as well know now. The gun they found beside the body? It's got your fingerprints on it.'

'Mine?' Stennett stood up, leaned forward on his knuckles. Palomar made a quieting motion at him.

'Don't say anything now, Mike, for Christ's sake. Think about it. Shit, I wouldn't arrest you for it now, you know that, only –' He motioned with his head back over his shoulder. There was nobody there, nobody seen, but Mike knew what he meant.

'You have the right to remain silent,' Palomar said tonelessly.

'Shut the hell up! I know my fucking rights. I taught 'em to you.' Stennett grabbed his jacket as if he'd go storming out. That made Palomar back up a step, but his wasn't the reaction Stennett noticed. For the first time he saw heads at the other desks turned toward him. They'd all been carefully ignoring the scene in the corner until Mike's sudden move. Now they were all looking. There were even two in the doorway. They all know, Stennett thought. Everybody in the damn building probably knows. And nobody'd said a word to him.

'Whyn't you just leave the gun and the badge in the desk drawer,' Palomar said, in the calm, accommodating voice of a cop talking to a jumper. 'That way you'll know where they are.'

It was a little like undressing in public. Most of the heads turned away again as Stennett brought his short-barreled .38 out of its holster at the back of his belt. Fingerprints on the gun, he thought as he dropped this one into his drawer. He lifted the badge in its plastic wallet out of his shirt pocket and dropped that on top. As he did he challenged the few remaining stares. None held up.

'Come on,' Palomar said, embarrassed as hell, and walked out of the room ahead of Mike just to show how much he trusted him.

One of his bosses had called ahead to smooth the way for him at the jail. What he'd said was, 'Treat him like any other prisoner. No favors.'

'We'll get the bond set before they book you,' Palomar said. 'That way you can get out right away. You know a bondsman? Hey, maybe they'll make it P.R.'

But even with bond already set, at the booking desk of the jail Stennett took his first step onto the slide prepared for him by his publicity-conscious superiors. 'We don't got an empty cell right now,' the deputy at the booking desk said. 'Why d'we need one?' replied his supervisor, who had heard the injunction from the upper management of the police department and took it seriously. Treat him like anybody else. 'Pick one,' the supervisor said.

'I'll find that bondsman right away,' Palomar said, but the prisoner was out of his jurisdiction already. He stood there at the booking desk and watched them put Mike into a cell with four other guys. Palomar wondered if he should go over and say something to the others about how hard life could be if one of them got out of line, but decided it was best not to call attention to Mike at all. He hurried out, not looking back.

The cell door closed with an almost gentle click, not the famous clang of movies. Stennett had his back to it, studying the men in the cell with him, hoping not to see a familiar face. He was lucky this time, none of them knew him. Of the four, two were drunk almost to the point of passing out. Only one of the other two met Stennett's eyes, with a sullen smolder, but it was aimed at the world in general, not Stennett in particular. Still, Stennett walked toward him until the guy's eyes wavered. Stennett crossed in front of him, close, watching the hands. Nothing happened. Stennett kicked one of the drunks off the bunk onto the floor and lay back, watching.

Better get used to this, he thought.

CHAPTER 5

It was two minutes until nine. A certain frantic air pervaded the courtroom. The prosecutors were being unusually unresponsive. Raymond hadn't tried to speak to any of them. He just leaned back against the railing, holding his file. Alan, the third chair, passed, stopped, said, 'I gotta tell you, she's hot for a trial.'

'So am I,' Raymond said.

Alan was already walking away, but he looked back to show he appreciated the joke. The look on Raymond's face brought him back. 'You serious?'

'Deadly.'

Alan took the State's file gently from Raymond, who let it go placidly. 'What's wrong with it?' Alan said, leafing through the file. 'Somebody die I don't know about?'

'I just felt like trying something this morning.'

Alan found nothing in the police report to indicate a problem with the case, a simple possession of heroin. He frowned. It was nine o'clock. Any second the door behind the bench would open and the judge would take her place. Something was going to be tried today. Raymond's case was second on the docket. If he announced ready it would probably go. 'I don't see –' the third chair began.

He flipped back to the indictment at the front of the file, which also listed the State's witnesses. 'Oh, shit,' he said, 'Uh, listen, we're going to have to set this one off 'til this thing gets resolved.'

'Dream on,' Raymond said. 'That'll take months. I'm ready for trial today.'

'Listen, man –'

'Tell it to the judge.'

On cue, Judge Byrnes entered and surveyed the room before taking her seat. The two men stood straighter through the bailiff's drone opening court. Alan looked at Raymond a last time and walked to the bench, carrying the offending file.

Less than a minute later Raymond stood and said, 'Ready.'

'Well good,' said the judge. 'State?'

'We have a slight witness problem in this one, Your Honor.'

'Is that an announcement, Mr Porter?'

'I need to talk to the other officers and see –'

'The time for that is *before* docket call, Mr Porter. If you have a written motion for continuance I will be glad to consider it. Do you?'

The first chair prosecutor had come up to see what the problem was. Porter pointed out the witness list to him. The first chair glanced back at Raymond. Then he slapped the file shut and handed it back to the third chair. 'The State will be filing a motion to dismiss in this case, Your Honor.'

Judge Judy appeared slightly mystified. But the copy of the indictment in her file also contained a witness list. She hadn't needed to consult it during the prosecutors' colloquy. 'Fine. Next announcement. Ramon Hernandez?'

At the back of the room a black man in a borrowed suit slumped in his pew and raised his eyes heavenward. Raymond turned and smiled at him. Before he could join his client the first chair prosecutor was in front of him. 'Very cunning, Boudro,' he whispered.

'Hey man, I just wanted to try the thing.'

'I'll bet.' The prosecutor looked again at the damned

indictment, the one listing Mike Stennett as arresting officer, then tossed it toward the counsel table, where it skipped and fluttered to the floor. 'Wonder how many other free rides we'll have to give on account of that asshole?' he said sourly.

That was the capital Raymond made of Stennett's arrest. But not the only capital.

Raymond's first impulse was to jump up and run out and see if it was true. Instead he kept his seat and told the intercom to send him in. And it was true. Mike Stennett walked into the office. Raymond still didn't rise. Stennett looked around the room someone twenty years ago had turned into a large office by knocking out a wall between two bedrooms. The office now comprised most of the back of the old stone house.

The desk would have been too large for a smaller office. It was walnut, with a glass-covered top. If Stennett had taken his best leap and stretched full-length across the desk he might have been able to touch the lawyer's chest with his outstretched hand. Behind Raymond were windows. To his left and right, against the far side walls, were floor-to-ceiling bookshelves. There were a couple of chairs in front of the desk and a large leather couch against the wall behind them. Raymond had taken the desk and the couch in lieu of a fee years ago. They weren't quite to his taste but they were sturdy as old trees. His son used that couch for a trampoline sometimes.

'Usually at this point I say "How may I help you?" In your case I'm really curious about the answer.'

Stennett didn't like standing like a supplicant in front of that ambassadorial desk, so he sat, which wasn't an improvement. 'You may have heard, I need a lawyer.'

'I'd like to take your money, but you know you have a lawyer. A good lawyer.' The Police Association, the cops' union, kept a defense lawyer on retainer to represent its members in criminal cases and disciplinary proceedings before the Civil Service Commission.

'Yeah, I know. A good lawyer very interested in staying in tight with the union. And I don't know what the union's position on me is gonna be. No thanks. I don't plan to have to watch my back all through this thing.'

Raymond was intrigued. Why would Stennett think the cops might not support him? But that's not what he said. What he said was, 'And I was the first lawyer you thought of.'

'I've seen your work, remember? You're good.'

'Very impartial of you. Let's cut the crap, Stennett. You think hiring a black lawyer to defend you'll make some jury think you're not a racist after all?'

'Maybe.' Stennett leaned forward earnestly. 'You want me to deny it? I won't. If that helps, swell. But you think that's my main consideration? You don't see me trying to hire Lawrence Preston, do you? I want you because you're as good as there is in this town. And you know the territory; I won't have to lead you by the hand every step of the way. And if you being black helps me out the least little bit in front of a jury I want that too. Because I'm not taking the fall for this. I didn't do it and I'm not going down for it.'

At least he wasn't going to admit he did it and expect Raymond to defend him anyway. The lawyer studied the cop. Stennett had cleaned up a little, at least he'd shaved this morning, but he'd need more work to be presentable. Sweat veiled his forehead.

''Fraid it'll cost you business?' Stennett asked. 'Or do you have a policy against white clients?'

Raymond's voice stayed cool, as if he were framing a hypothetical problem. 'Tell me why I should try to get you off the hook for murdering a black man.'

Stennett came around the desk. Raymond swiveled to face him but didn't rise, which finally gave the cop the chance to lean down over him. 'I'll tell you why. Because you can win this case. Because this is gonna be a big public trial and the publicity of winning it'll do you as much good as it does me. Because I didn't do it, and you can prove I didn't.'

Raymond was intrigued again by the repeated denial. His face didn't show it. 'There's nothing worse than a confident client,' he said.

'I'm no optimist. I know you can do it because I've seen you do it. Remember Abner Moses?'

'Nah, Stennett, doesn't ring a bell. Abner who?' The sarcastic tone was because Abner Moses had been Raymond's biggest case, a capital murder trial that had generated a lot of publicity at the time. Abner had been a small-time thief elevated to the big time when he was charged with killing a cop during a fight from a bungled burglary. The State had had an eyewitness and Abner had had the kind of record that would make the jury's choice of punishment between life and death easy. Death row was crowded with guys like Abner; everyone had expected him to fulfill his destiny by joining them.

'You weren't a witness in that case.'

'I watched some of it,' Stennett said. 'Of course there were a lot of cops in and out of the audience. Muttering things like he never should've got to the station after the arrest. I think I was the only one who wasn't convinced. I could picture Abner going in an open window, but I couldn't see him pulling the trigger on anybody.'

He hadn't. And the jury had reached the same conclusion. If Raymond closed his eyes he could still call up with textured clarity that moment of the foreman saying, 'Not guilty': Abner looking at Raymond puzzled, his life not having prepared him for those two words; Raymond's palm indented with four tiny slashes where he'd dug his fingernails in so hard he cut himself; the prosecutor, that son of a bitch Frank Mendiola, turning to Raymond with that look of loathing that made the moment even sweeter.

He didn't close his eyes. 'Yeah, luckily the jury saw it that way too,' Raymond said casually.

'And nobody was even bitter about it, 'cause by the end of that trial they knew they'd had the wrong guy. You didn't just poke holes in the State's case, you *proved* he didn't do it.'

Stennett was looking at him appraisingly, wondering if Raymond still had what he'd had then. Raymond wanted to disabuse him of hope. 'That was three years ago,' he said. 'Damn few miracles since then. You can't hope for them. Not too many innocent people get charged with capital murder. Or murder.'

Stennett was untouched. He stared flatly. 'I have to be innocent? I haven't noticed you require that in clients.'

Raymond tried to read him. Was this a murderer two feet in front of him? Stennett looked capable of it. Those hands could do it. Those eyes wouldn't weep over it.

'This case'll do something for you Abner Moses didn't,' Stennett continued. 'Where are you? You should be one of the busiest criminal lawyers in San Antonio. Everybody saw what you can do, and what'd it get you?'

'I do all right.'

'You get your share of pushers and junkies, that's true. But where're the big cases? When some rich boy gets arrested, your phone don't ring.'

'Where do you live, Stennett, comic books? There aren't that many big cases.'

'But there's some, and you don't get any. Why didn't Abner put you over the top? You know why. Because he was a nigger.'

Raymond came out of his chair. Stennett didn't back up, so they ended up standing almost nose to nose, except that Stennett had to look up. He did so calmly, not watching Raymond's hands. 'Thought I'd go ahead and drop the big one so we didn't have to live in suspense,' he said. 'Abner Moses didn't make you a star 'cause he was black and he was a crook. He didn't do that one, but that didn't make him innocent. But you get a cop acquitted, put him back on the force working for truth and justice, that's something people won't forget.'

Raymond pushed him away. Stennett wasn't caught by surprise or off balance, so it took effort, but Raymond managed it. Their eye contact didn't break. Raymond almost wished he'd taken a swing at him instead, when Stennett had dropped the word. But Raymond had been too slow to react, the occasion had passed. It's the things you don't do you come to regret.

'You're not innocent either.'

Stennett looked surprised. 'What do you mean?'

'What happened to Claymore Johnson?'

Stennett made a face as if Raymond had changed the subject to something trivial. 'Claymore? Claymore's in Atlanta.' Raymond, startled, made a mental note to call Claymore's mother. But Stennett was going on. 'Or Kansas City. Vancouver, British Columbia. Wherever he ran into a big city or an ocean in whatever direction he took off in. He's not dead, I'm pretty sure of that. The guys that had it in for Claymore, they're not subtle. They're not ones to do a Jimmy Hoffa with the body. They'd want it layin' in the street. Object lesson, you know?'

Raymond looked unpersuaded. Stennett waved a hand at him. 'I know. You mean me, I didn't do nothin' to Claymore. Except run a scheme on 'im that worked out damn better than I expected. That's the truth.'

He sounded sincere. Raymond pictured him using the same tone of voice in court. He could picture jurors nodding along.

'Sit down,' Raymond said. After a moment's hesitation Stennett returned to the client chair. Raymond took the one next to it, leaning close. 'Now in a minute, I'm going to tell you to tell me what happened. Before I do that you think about it. You know it'll never go beyond me. You know how lawyer-client privilege works. But let me tell you how *I* work. I don't work for somebody who lies to me. You can lie to everybody else on this planet, you can lie to God and your mama, but if you lie to me I'm gonna find it out. I'm gonna investigate the hell out of this thing, and I'll know what happened. If I find out you lied to me I'll get you for it. And I don't just mean withdraw from the case. I mean I'll ruin you. Y'understand? Now if that condition's all right with you, you sit there and collect your thoughts for a minute and then start talking. But if it even crosses your mind to lie to me, you get up and walk out now. Now.'

Stennett looked at him levelly. He nodded. 'That your standard speech?'

'Mouthing off is not one of the choices I gave you. Talk or walk.'

'Jesus, don't go Jesse Jackson on me. All right. So you're taking the case?'

Raymond pointed at the door. 'I've had every kind of low-life scum, degenerate, reprobate, human sewage in this town walk in that door and I haven't turned one away yet. If I've lowered my standards that far I can lower them a little farther.' He held up a finger. 'On my conditions. I mean it. The truth or I ruin you.'

Or maybe both, he thought.

Stennett took his time, pursing his lips. 'All right,' he finally said. 'Now? You're my lawyer, starting now?'

'Starting now. So take your time, think about what you're going to say. I'll know if you're lying. You better believe that.'

Stennett took a long breath and looked away for the first time in minutes, out the windows where the day was turning crystalline, presaging summer.

'I didn't do it,' he began. 'I had no idea who it was gonna be on the slab when I went to the M.E.'s office. I wasn't on duty that night but I was cruisin' anyway . . .'

Raymond's eyes narrowed. It would have been too easy if Stennett had confessed. But Raymond would know the truth before this thing was over.

'Back up,' he said. 'Let's get the details straight. What time was it when you got the call and what street were you on? Picture it. Tell me everything . . .'

'This is one I'm going to try myself,' Tyler Hammond said.

Becky pursed her lips.

'I know that will strike terror in the heart of whatever poor defense lawyer Detective Stennett hires.'

Becky didn't nod along or even smile at the joke, but it was nice to know Tyler didn't think of himself as a formidable prosecutor. In fact, Tyler Hammond was hardly believable as a prosecutor at all. He looked like what he'd been, a professor. He was somewhere in his late forties and could have passed for ten years older. He was thirty pounds overweight; a thick brown beard hid his extra chins but added weight to his face. Even his eyebrows looked heavy, overshadowing brown eyes that looked more often distracted than piercing. He was a man of habits. His empty hand was still cupped around the bowl of the pipe that he'd put back in his desk drawer at the start of this interview.

When Becky had first come to work at the District Attorney's office, Special Crimes had been the worst section in the office. The section was responsible primarily for white-collar crimes, usually complicated thefts that involved paper trail investigations more appropriate to civil than to criminal cases. The section also handled cases that were for any reason odd, and it attracted odd prosecutors, people who hadn't fit in anywhere else but matched up perfectly in Special Crimes, which came to be known unaffectionately as the Geek Patrol. It was their fellow prosecutors who had dubbed them that. Not only was the section's win-loss record far and away the worst in the office, sometimes their cases fell through the cracks and were never heard from again.

The current District Attorney had vowed to turn Special Crimes from a joke into the elite group of prosecutors it should have been, but his choice for chief had not immediately dispelled the geek image. Tyler Hammond was a theoretician, of impressive academic credentials but very limited trial experience. But he had proven a good chief, the guiding mind behind complex litigation. And one of his best traits was that he knew his limitations. In two years as chief he had tried enough cases to feel comfortable in a courtroom, but he had wisely passed off the more difficult trials to the experienced prosecutors he had brought into the section. His insistence on trying this one personally was unusual.

And the fact that he was telling Becky about the case was inexplicable. She was not a member of Tyler's section and had no desire to be. The geek taint still lingered over Special Crimes, as far as Becky was concerned. When Tyler Hammond had asked her to come to his office she'd been afraid he was going to ask her to transfer in. Instead, without preamble, he'd begun explaining the prosecution of Mike Stennett.

'My people work very closely with the police,' Tyler continued. 'More than any other section except Career Criminal. I don't want those working relationships destroyed by this imbroglio.'

'So you're going to try it yourself,' Becky said. 'The chief of the section.'

'Yes. Because I don't share that day-to-day involvement with the police. I can excuse myself from any case I want.'

'But don't you think the chief trying a cop will taint the whole section?' Becky asked. Tyler was not only not a fire-breathing prosecutor, he was the most mild-mannered of bosses. Becky found it easy to question him.

Tyler smiled. 'Do you think anything I do reflects on this office in the minds of police or lawyers? I am the oddity. The last geek. Police may shake their heads in irritation over what I do, but my people can shake their heads right along with them. I am a lonely wandering star whose gravity tugs on no one. And at the worst, if I do feel my efficiency is compromised – or if the District Attorney thinks it is – I can return to the university. I am hardly a career prosecutor.'

Becky nodded noncommittally. A reason for her being here, hearing this, had occurred to her, but she couldn't give it serious consideration. She let Tyler continue, as he was obviously pleased to do. He had not forgotten the pleasure of lecturing.

'By the same token, of course, I need someone from outside my section to sit second with me. The District Attorney wanted that someone to be one of the first chair felony prosecutors, even another section chief, but I resisted that suggestion. Not only would an experienced prosecutor subtly try to wrest control of the case from me, but the same logic prevails. We don't want one of our best people ruined by this case.'

Becky's suspicion deepened. Tyler could no longer maintain eye contact. He cleared his throat. 'I am putting this very badly,' he acknowledged. 'In as ugly a light as possible. The D.A. insisted I do so. He wanted you to understand completely what you'd been getting into.'

She had to resist breaking into a smile. Why did her heart lift like that?

'You see, Detective Stennett of course has friends on the police force. But aside from that –'

'But aside from that,' Becky took over from him, 'the police administration will feel very differently about the case from the way street cops see it.'

'Yes.' Tyler nodded approval at her. 'So no matter what we do we will probably offend some large segment of the police department. So we don't want to look as if we're going after Detective Stennett with our big guns. Only our little guns. You and me.'

'And the District Attorney suggested me?' Becky asked incredulously.

'No. *I* suggested you.'

Becky blinked. She was now engaged in the longest conversation she'd ever had with Tyler Hammond. The second longest had probably been 'Hi, how are you?' She was afraid he had picked her for this strictly because the administration of the D.A.'s office considered her expendable.

He seemed to see what she was thinking. 'I've watched you work,' he said seriously. 'I've reviewed your record – I reviewed *everyone*'s record – and I talked with people who've worked with you. You have quite a nice reputation, Rebecca.'

The compliment was delicious, but she felt compelled to add, 'For someone with so little time in the office. So you decided,' she went on, 'that I was the best inexperienced, low-profile prosecutor on the staff.'

Tyler looked off into the distance. 'There must be a better way to put that,' he mused. After a moment he found the way, and looked back at her. 'I decided that you have the experience I lack to try this important case. You've prosecuted murder cases. This one looks relatively straightforward, I don't foresee any –'

'Spoken like someone who's never felt a case go to pieces under him,' Becky said. 'We have a fingerprint on a gun but the gun isn't the murder weapon. And you never know how good an eyewitness is going to be until he's on the stand. Add that to the natural reluctance of a jury to convict a police officer for killing a criminal, and you have a case, frankly, that a prosecutor would rather see plead than try.'

Tyler looked at her, round-eyed. 'Have you seen my file already?'

Becky shrugged. 'People talk. A high-profile case like this, word gets around the office how good or bad our case is.'

'Is it good enough that you want to try it with me?' Tyler asked, obviously pleased with himself for having found the opening to ask the question to which the whole interview had led.

Becky considered it. It could be a career-threatening case, alienating half the police force. Or the worst possibility, pissing off the cops and then losing the case, too. A not guilty verdict would make it look as if the D.A.'s office had gone after a cop with insufficient evidence. Such a result could put a period to her career in the office. And leaving the office under a cloud like that wouldn't make it easy to get a job with a civil firm, either. The smartest thing for her to do would be to beg off. She could tell Tyler thought so, too – probably half hoped, from the way he was looking at her, that she *would* refuse.

And if she did, she could sit back safely and watch someone else try the case. It *would* be a big case, no matter how the office underplayed it. The prosecutors who tried it would receive a lot of scrutiny, from the press, from their peers, from the boss. And with Tyler on the team, the main burden of trial would fall on the prosecutor who sat second.

Becky felt a sudden lightness, as if she had stepped down to a step that wasn't there. 'Are you kidding?' she said. 'How could I pass up a chance like this?'

'I never understand you real prosecutors,' Tyler said, studying her. 'I put it to you so badly no one in her right mind would agree to this proposition. Why do you?'

Becky smiled. 'A big case, pressure, possibility of disastrous consequences? What's not to understand?'

'The District Attorney said you'd take it.' Tyler shook his head slightly. 'Well. Perhaps it will turn out not to have been so momentous a decision after all.

Odds are there won't even be a trial. Maybe it will end the way they all end, with a plea bargain. I intend to make him a good offer.'

'Not too good,' Becky said.

'He's just usin' you, man. Gettin' the black boy to clean up the white man's mess, like always. Don't you understand that?'

'Nah, Faruq,' Raymond said to his brother-in-law, with heavy emphasis, 'I don't get it. Can you explain it to me?'

Amazingly, Faruq missed the sarcasm and *did* begin explaining. Raymond sipped his iced tea – no beer in Denise's mother's good Baptist home – and watched the children running in the backyard. His mother-in-law was the kindest woman on earth, the sweetest, the most attentive to guests. Raymond always found himself slipping away from her as soon as possible, out onto the back porch like a boy sneaking a smoke. He must not have been the only one the small, fussy house discomfited; all the men eventually gathered on the porch. There were only three of them. Denise's brother, Faruq – née Benny – and her sister's husband, Roy, who never said a word. It was supposed to be a lazy Sunday afternoon, but Faruq had burst immediately into the harangue his mother had shushed him for during lunch.

'You forget I know Stennett,' Faruq was saying. 'You think he's just bad news, but I tell you he's somethin' worse. He's a foot soldier in the genocide war. Maybe even a captain.'

'I know him better than you, Faruq,' Raymond said wearily, again coming down hard on the name. For a long time Raymond had resisted calling his brother-in-law by his adopted Moslem name. Denise still called him Benny, but she had the excuse of shared child-hood. Raymond had eventually come around, after Benny/Faruq had insisted long enough, but to compen-sate Raymond used the new name at every opportunity, with emphasis. 'I know exactly what he is.'

'Then how can you defend him?'

Silence was the best course. Raymond knew it. Re-vealing himself to his militant brother-in-law would just be an exercise in vanity. But Roy was staring at him too – silent, unmilitant Roy, who could have stood for all the masses who'd demand an explanation of him.

'If I'd told him to go away, Faruq,' Raymond said carefully, 'he would've. And I'd be left wondering. And when the case ended I'd still be wondering. Did he do it? Did he get what he deserved for doing it, or did he get away with it? This way I'll know. At least I'll have a better chance of knowing. You find out things having the man for a client that you'll never read in the papers. You know what I'm saying?'

The little speech won him a space of silence, for which he was grateful. He continued to watch the chil-dren, the cousins, at play. Of Faruq's four kids, who'd been at least half raised by their grandmother, Roy's two girls, and Raymond's son, Peter was the second oldest, and the tallest. He looked like a little parent among the rabble of smaller kids.

Usually Petey was in the thick of whatever shrill games they were making up, but occasionally Raymond saw him standing back, watching, as if surprised to find himself here, surrounded by black children. That was a rare experience for Petey.

In fact, it was no longer common for Raymond to find himself in exclusively black company. He was saddened by the realization that he couldn't relax in the little family gathering. He had to tone himself down, become a nostalgic shadow of himself, downplay the fact that he was far and away the most successful member of the family, that his real life was elsewhere.

From the corner of his eye he saw Faruq frankly studying him, sucking the juice from Raymond's explanation for his defense of Mike Stennett and tasting it. Faruq thought him a traitor, Raymond knew, or at least one of the fallen-away. Years ago Raymond had done the right things, attended the correct meetings, made pronouncements, been elected an officer in the Black Bar Association. But where did it get us, Faruq? he asked in imaginary dialogue. Where did it get *me*? What did we change? The changes came before us, man. We inherited them. Pretending we were still struggling was just a way of trying to share in the glory of the old days.

Some of us're still struggling, the imaginary Faruq countered.

It may have been so. But at the same time he'd been posturing with the protesters, Raymond had been finding acceptance in his professional world. He was a good lawyer, that was what counted. That was what won him respect in the courthouse. When he'd discovered that in many ways he'd grown better than old Lawrence Preston, and had slipped away from his tutelage, he'd also left behind most of his pretend-militant associations. Ironically, those associations didn't advance him, they held him back. The lawyers who already accepted him as a professional equal would look askance at his continuing struggle for *supposed* equality.

He could make a better life for himself and his family without all that baggage. After he and Denise had Petey, that became the most important consideration.

So you gave up being black and turned pseudo-white, Faruq would have said.

Well, the hell with Faruq. 'I seem to remember I kept *you* out of Mike Stennett's clutches,' Raymond said suddenly.

'Kept me reporting to a white probation officer for three years,' Faruq sneered. Over the years he had run through the whole spectrum of nicknames – ofay, honky, peckerwood – and now just said 'white', with an emphasis that made the word more bitter than any epithet.

'Well, I could've got you prison time if I'd known you'd rather had that. Lots of good chances for missionary work among your brothers.'

Silent Roy grinned at Raymond, a triumph. And the remark set Faruq off on a tangent, his usual tirade against the criminal justice system. This was less directly an attack on Raymond, who sat back and let it flow over him like the pale spring sunshine. He watched the children play.

'Mama asked too,' Denise said later as they were driving home and Raymond was recounting her brother's attack on him for defending the white cop.

'What?' For some reason Denise's mild remark made him immediately angry. Did he have to explain himself to everybody?

Denise sensed his irritation. 'I don't think she was really asking for herself. Probably just wanted something to tell Benny later, when he'd be goin' on at her and she the only one around to listen to him. She just asked why you took the case. She wasn't upset or anything.'

Mollified, Raymond said, 'And what did you tell her?'

Denise grew uncomfortable, realizing she was on the spot. Had she defended her husband adequately? 'I told her, you know, that he might not even be guilty. And that, well, everybody deserves a defense, no matter how bad they are.'

Raymond was shaking his head. In the rearview mirror he saw Petey half asleep, leaning against the back door, oblivious. 'What have I ever said,' he asked his wife, 'to make you think I believe crap like that?'

Denise didn't respond. She sat looking straight ahead, silent but not withdrawn. Raymond glanced at her, then out of the windshield again, wonderingly. 'You don't know either, do you? You don't know why I'm defending him.'

'I know. But I don't know if you know what you're getting into.'

He was instantly angry, but he kept his voice low. 'I don't believe you, Denise. You think like your idiot brother, you think Stennett's using me, you think I'm too stupid –'

'No.' The syllable was soft but so firm it checked him. Denise turned toward him on the seat and touched the side of his face. He jerked away. 'Not too stupid, honey,' she said. 'Nobody smarter than you, Raymond, I never had any doubts about your brain.'

'Then what?'

'But this man, he's running some kind of game. You don't know what he's thinking. You don't know what he *is*. But whatever he is, his ass is on the line. It's everything for him, and for you it's just a case.'

'No, it's not,' he said, but he said it by rote, and lapsed into silence, still irritated but now more thoughtful than angry. He didn't want to ask Denise what she really meant because he thought he knew. He didn't want to make her say it, have that between them.

Stennett can't outthink you, he thought. But the angry cop had it all over Raymond in intensity. In passion. Mike Stennett, Raymond had learned already, would do whatever he had to do.

He drove down the road, silent, trying to think of a way to change the subject, something else about the day to bring up. He didn't want Denise thinking about the case anymore. And he didn't even ask himself the obvious question.

CHAPTER 6

It was only May, only eleven o'clock in the morning, but the asphalt was warm. Not sizzling the way it would be in July, when the tar would unbind itself and come bubbling up like some ancient ooze, but already the asphalt was warm enough that Raymond could feel it through his shoes. There were stains on the asphalt of the church parking lot, but they looked like oil stains. Whether any of them was blood he couldn't tell. He wondered if the police had taken samples. You'd think they would investigate thoroughly before arresting one of their own, but they never did enough investigating to answer all the lawyers' questions. Probably impossible anyway to lift blood samples from the pavement. That would be a gap in the State's case he could point out to a jury.

He stood in the dappled shade provided by a mesquite tree and looked across the parking lot and the alley behind the church to the backyard where the eyewitness lived. Raymond could see the back door of the man's house. He would have to come back at night to see how good the view was then.

For some reason he had expected to have the answer by now. He had thought unrealistically that Stennett would either confess to him or present an impenetrable defense. Neither had happened. The detective adamantly insisted on his innocence but had essentially no defense. He said he'd been with a snitch about the time of the murder, but wouldn't give Raymond the name. 'He wouldn't testify,' Stennett had said. 'I wouldn't ask him to.'

'He wouldn't come forward to save you from a murder charge?'

'He doesn't owe me that. That's not part of our deal. Our deal is he gives me tips and I give him money. And nobody ever finds out his name from me. That's the other part of the deal.'

Very noble, Raymond thought. *Or a lie.*

'May I help you?'

Raymond was startled, he hadn't heard footsteps, but something about the man's appearance reassured him. The newcomer wore a white short-sleeved shirt, black slacks, lace-up dress shoes run down at the heels. He was a dark black man, the deep, deep brown of his neck and arms making him a shadow inside his white shirt.

'My name is Raymond Boudro. I'm a lawyer.'

'John Entwhistle,' the man said as they shook hands.

'Good morning, Reverend.' Entwhistle's name appeared in much smaller letters on the sign that said Ezekiel Avenue Baptist Church. The minister's hair was receding on both sides from a point above his forehead, leaving an arrow pointing down. A goatee echoed the peak. He could look dramatic in a pulpit, Raymond guessed, but the minister wasn't using his preaching voice. He was quiet, cordial. But he came out to investigate a stranger in his parking lot.

'I'm looking for some sign a man was beaten to death at about this spot.'

Reverend Entwhistle didn't look down, he looked across to the back of the house. Something troubled his eyes briefly. 'Gordon Frazier,' he said.

'You knew him?' Raymond asked. 'But I take it he wasn't a member of your congregation.'

Entwhistle smiled slightly at the idea. 'No. It was out here I would see Gordon. The streets.'

Raymond was looking at the church. He liked the poor look of it, and of its minister. No gold flashed on Entwhistle's person. 'How many times has the church been burglarized?' Raymond asked.

The minister joined him in looking at the small wooden building with the unimpressive cross on the roof. 'Not so often anymore,' he said. He didn't need to add that the burglar bars had been added because of men like Gordon Frazier.

They talked for a few minutes. Reverend Entwhistle knew nothing about the murder except what he'd read in the newspaper. He had a nodding, waving acquaintanceship with Haley Burkwright, the man across the alley, but no more than that. A frown creased the minister's forehead briefly while they spoke, as if he knew something he couldn't call to mind. Raymond couldn't see anything about the physical layout of the church or the parking lot that would be probative one way or the other. He did want to gather opinions from people who'd known the victim. Before he left he asked, 'Think you had a shot at saving Gordon Frazier's soul if he'd lived?'

Reverend Entwhistle's expression acknowledged the unlikelihood, but his voice was optimistic. 'The possibilities are what keep me here. I've seen some remarkable conversions.'

It hadn't occurred to Raymond until he was about to say good-bye, but he asked as an afterthought, 'What about Mike Stennett? Do you know him?'

The minister's face went hard. For the first time he looked militant. Some of the hardness in his glare was directed at Raymond. People tend to identify you with your client, as if you took on his case because you liked him, or thought his cause was just. Raymond had felt that many times. He hadn't expected it in this case. But black people seemed to be finding it easy to put him in Stennett's corner.

'I'm not familiar with the condition of Mr Stennett's soul,' the minister said. 'But I know this.' He pointed at the asphalt where Gordon Frazier had fallen. 'No one should die like that.'

'No,' Raymond agreed. 'Nobody.'

The way Gordon Frazier died was next on his agenda. He took a chance, going to the medical examiner's office without an appointment, but Bob Wyntlowski was the kind of assistant M.E. who was usually at work and would talk to almost anyone. 'We don't get enough visitors who can talk back to us,' he said, shaking hands. He and Raymond knew each other's names, but little more. Cross-examination doesn't grow friendship. But Wyntlowski held no grudges. He brought out the file when Raymond asked for it, and seemed to remember the autopsy. He couldn't possibly remember them all, Raymond thought.

'There wouldn't have been much blood,' Doctor Bob responded to Raymond's summary of his investigation at the parking lot. 'This wasn't a shooting or a stabbing. The injuries, particularly the one that killed him, were mostly internal. Maybe some nosebleed on his shirt. But you're not going to find a lot of blood somewhere that'll tell you where he died.'

Raymond gave him a small, skeptical smile. 'If the cops' reports said there was a pool of blood under him you'd have an explanation for that too, wouldn't you?'

They were sitting on the doctor's office, with its picture window view of the autopsy room, on metal chairs with padded seats and backs. Wyntlowski's arms were resting on the chair arms. He was leaning back, looking tired. 'I could probably think of one.'

'If you needed to,' Raymond said.

Wyntlowski looked like a man so unused to anger he couldn't conjure it up even when he'd been professionally insulted. He gave Raymond a harsh look but his body stayed relaxed in the chair. 'You think I tailor my testimony to fit the State's case?'

'I've seen it, Doctor, I've been in the courtroom.'

'Look, airbrain.' Wyntlowski finally managed to push off the back of the chair. But his voice still wasn't angry. He explained, as to a backward student. 'I take into account information people bring me, of course I do. You can't diagnose in a vacuum. This isn't TV, I can't look at a body and tell you what he was killed with and the store where it was bought. I work with the facts. Police bring me theories, prosecutors do, and I tell them if the body says it could've happened that way. I'll try to apply anything anyone tells me. Defense lawyers almost never do that. You realize that? They treat me like the enemy. I'm not. I'm as impartial as the judge. Tell me what you think are some facts and I'll tell you if they fit.'

Raymond was wondering if the judge remark had been sarcastic. 'Okay, Doctor.'

'Bob.'

'Bob. Here are two facts. Witness says he saw the killing here, but the body was found here, blocks away. Can you tell me if the witness is lying?'

Wyntlowski took the file back from him. He was frowning in a happy way, enjoying the puzzle. 'I might could tell you if the body was moved. Emphasize *body*. If somebody took the guy, unconscious or whatever, from one spot to another just *before* he died I don't know what medical evidence there'd be of that. I don't know why anybody would do that anyway.'

'Unless the beating got interrupted, say by the appearance of a witness, and somebody took the victim somewhere else to finish him off.'

'Right. Or dumps him and a second person comes along and kills him. But if he was dead and *then* moved there might be a sign of it. It's called lividity. When the heart stops beating the blood stops pumping. Only gravity moves it after that. The blood pools in whatever part of the body is lowest. So if the body is dead and it lays in one position long enough for the blood to pool, say in the back and buttocks, the skin will show that effect. Looks like a big bruise. Then if somebody moves the body somewhere else and leaves it laying on its face, I'll see signs of lividity on both the back and front of the body.'

Raymond wondered if lividity might be more easily overlooked on a black corpse, but he didn't sidetrack the doctor. Might save that question for the courtroom. 'Here did you?' he asked instead.

'No.' Wyntlowski had already reviewed his notes. He didn't look down at them again to answer. 'But that doesn't mean it didn't happen. If the body lay on its back and somebody moved it and then laid it back down on its back I couldn't tell you if it was moved. Unless they dragged it through gravel that stuck to the skin or something like that. No, I didn't see that either.'

Raymond nodded. He felt if he concentrated he could feel his own blood moving, slowly, pushed against its own inertia by his terminable heart. Talking to the doctor in this office next to the autopsy room made him aware of the workings of his body, of its destiny. 'So, Doctor – Bob, you haven't helped me out much here. I've seen you do better in court.'

Wyntlowski had used up his small supply of outrage. He couldn't be goaded again. He smiled. 'Actually, this is the State's theory, isn't it? Their witness sees the beating one place but the body ends up somewhere else? I can't help them out. I can't say it happened that way.'

'I'll remember that. What about what killed him? Beating, you said? Beat to death?'

'Not exactly. He got beat up, no doubt about that. But it was one blow that killed him. Or maybe two. One that broke the nose and the other drove the bone into his brain.'

'So you can't say it was intentional?' Raymond asked, uninflected.

Wyntlowski shook his head. 'That's out of my province. Maybe whoever it was would've gone on beating him until he was dead. Maybe it was a surprise to the one doing it. I don't know. It's sure not deliberate like shooting a bullet into his heart. But it was just as effective.'

Now you're rehearsing, Raymond thought. They sat in a moment of silence. 'You'll want to see the pictures,' the doctor said.

Raymond hadn't thought about that, but he guessed he did. Wyntlowski handed the lawyer the file that included a very small stack of photos taken before and during the autopsy. Raymond didn't hear the doctor leave. To his surprise he fell at once into the world inside the folder, as if a hole had opened beneath his chair. For those few minutes of study he couldn't have said where he was, or when.

He skimmed past the short summary of information about the victim, certain that he didn't know Gordon Frazier but could write his life story. Raymond had grown up with a hundred like him. Maybe Gordon Frazier had been a fair student or a fair ball player, an okay kid who didn't make trouble, when he'd hit that year. Eighth grade, maybe ninth, that year when he'd had his first taste of liquor, gagged on it, but come back for more, that year when he'd realized girls could be more than a nuisance and found out there was nobody to say no if you stayed out all night. That year that started out playing catch under the streetlight and ended cruising down the side streets looking for your pusher. And you discovered that everything you wanted took money, but working for it was too slow. But by that time you were far enough into the drug world to become a purveyor as well as a consumer. In not much longer than it takes to lose one's virginity a fifteen-year-old boy could become the king of the world, with money in his pocket, a car, and time for everything but school. A king who'd risen so high so fast, he didn't realize he'd just bumped his head on the ceiling. A hundred bucks a week was a lot of money to a fifteen-year-old, and none of them realized it wouldn't get much better. Your needs soared but your income didn't. A few years later all you worried about was your next fix. Maybe in the few seconds before it took hold you had time to wonder what had become of your glorious teenage kingdom.

Raymond had seen dozens disappear into that one year of discovery and never emerge. He'd begun edging into that year himself when he was fifteen, but for him it had lasted about two days. His father had slapped him down hard, hard enough to carry him through high school graduation, and by that time he had motivation of his own. Ambition had carried him to the point where he could view that lost world dispassionately.

The first picture was a full body shot that just looked like a dead guy. The others were close-ups of portions of the body, primarily the torso. Raymond didn't look at the face for signs of familiarity. He looked at the marks of beating death. 'Beaten to death' was a phrase worn thinner than paper. He could hear it or say it without a thought crossing his mind. The photos of dead Gordon Frazier, though, were not timeworn. They were immediate. Even in death his face didn't look peaceful. It still seemed to flinch from steadily inflicted pain. Raw flesh showed where the skin had been split. Visible scrapes made Raymond want to touch his own face soothingly.

The close-ups of the body showed the pain hadn't been localized. More scrapes, many bruises, some of them maybe older than the fatal beating. Raymond wondered if ribs were cracked. What had the beater wanted? Information? Pain for its own sake? Whoever it was had put this corpse – no, a living, pain-wracked man – through one of the ugliest ways to be murdered. Not a sudden killing with a gun or a knife. The body described the murderer: a man who could smash another man in the face, look at the pain and disfigurement he'd caused, and do it again. And again. And listen to his victim gurgle and wheeze and spit blood. Then step in and kick him in the ribs.

Raymond was picturing Stennett doing it. In imagination Stennett's face was rather dispassionate. He would have incapacitated his victim first with a punch in the stomach or a kick in the balls, then done the rest of the damage methodically, stepping back occasionally like a sculptor to gauge the effect of his latest stroke. The scene was so immediate, more vivid than memory.

Raymond flipped to close-ups of the face. It was amazing how long it took him, but it had been twenty years, and Raymond was studying the marks, not the face as it must have been. It was only when he was turning from one picture to the next that he saw the face whole. In peripheral vision it became unmarked and youthful, the face of a boy.

Raymond stood up, the file sliding off his lap. 'No,' he said, long and so shallow no one else could have heard it. He was staring at the face, the smashed face of a dead man old long before his time. Raymond knew that because his time was Raymond's time.

'When did you change your name, Gordie?' he murmured. It had been Gordie Wilkins when Raymond had known him. They'd known each other all through childhood, but only slightly. The first clear memory Raymond had of Gordie was when Gordie passed a bottle inside a paper sack to him during a parking lot celebration of a freshman football team victory. The burning swig had been followed by a joint that made Raymond cough but otherwise did little but make his ears buzz. The third one had some effect, though, passed back and forth in Gordie's car hours later, as they laughed about what a bunch of jerks the other team had been and how much smarter Raymond and Gordie were than everyone else in the world.

Gordie had been his partner at the start of that famous year. Within a week the joints didn't burn his throat anymore and he was going with Gordie looking to replace the stash that was almost gone. That was the night Raymond had come home to find his father waiting up for him and the year was abruptly over for Raymond. But Gordie hadn't had a father or anyone else to call a halt. And here he was, dead proof that Raymond's father had been right about where that year led.

But for a moment the intervening years, the years that had made Raymond Raymond and Gordie dead, were gone. It would have been so easy. He remembered the laughter in Gordie's car, and knew it would have been easy for that night to slide into a succession of nights that would have kept him Gordie's partner in the life. It was eerie to see your twin, the end of the path you could have taken – had started down in fact – laid out on a slab.

'Want some copies?' the doctor asked.

Raymond's face put a stop to whatever casual inquiry Wyntlowski planned to put next. He stood there respectfully, as if he'd blundered into a funeral. 'What shoes was he wearing?' Raymond asked hoarsely. 'Do you list the clothes?'

Wyntlowski bent to pick the contents of the file off the floor, not saying a word. Raymond helped him. Not tennis shoes, Raymond was thinking, not hightop white sneakers, the last shoes he'd seen Gordie wear. And probably not the pointy black lace-up dress shoes Gordie would have graduated to the next year when he started hanging with the hoods. Mean-looking shoes with taps, so people could hear you coming.

'Let me see,' the doctor said tonelessly. He'd found the clothing list.

'Never mind,' Raymond said. He'd found one of the pictures instead. He held it out, not looking at it.

'You couldn't do something like this without getting marked by it,' he said slowly, picking his way through words, 'could you?'

'You could if you wore gloves.'

Raymond nodded. Still sounding like a man speaking in a foreign tongue, he said, 'My client came and identified the body that night, didn't he? You were here, weren't you?'

'Yes.'

'Do you happen to remember what his hands looked like?'

Wyntlowski's gaze lengthened past Raymond for a minute before he said, 'No. Sorry.'

'Was he hiding them from you?'

The doctor cast again into memory, caught nothing. 'Sorry, beats me. I don't pay much attention to live bodies. If I'd known it was going to be important –'

'No way you could've known.' Raymond stood up. 'Thanks, Bob. Next time we talk we'll probably have an audience and I'll call you Doctor.'

'No problem.'

Raymond walked out gingerly, past two fresh bodies he didn't turn his head to study. He felt his own life very fragile within his thin casing of skin. He walked slowly, like a man awakened to find himself leading an unfamiliar life, unsure of every step he took.

'You gonna put this thing on the front burner? Meanin' we might try it before the end of the century?'

Special Crimes was a satellite section down the hall from the main District Attorney's office. You didn't have to talk your way through a receptionist and a locked door to get into it, you just walked in from the third-floor hallway of the courthouse. As it happened the secretary was away from her desk, so Raymond had just stepped past it and loomed suddenly in the chief's doorway. Tyler Hammond looked up at him mildly, picked up his phone, pressed four digits and said, 'Are you available now? I believe Mr Boudro is here to begin negotiating.'

'It starts with an indictment,' Raymond said. 'Then it's all downhill after that. Ordinary defendant'd already be in the joint over this. We gonna drag everything out because it's a Special Crimes case, or because of who my client is?'

Tyler picked up his pipe, found it dead, stuck it in his mouth anyway. He talked around it. 'You're in a big hurry?'

Raymond didn't answer. He was walking around the small cluttered office, picking up papers, examining an umbrella as if wondering if it was a personal effect or evidence.

'We are being careful,' Tyler continued. 'We're not just looking for a quick conviction, you know, we want the truth. It may be –'

'Save that for the jury.'

Tyler smiled slightly. 'It does need more investigation. Police bring you what they think is a complete case – and in a police officer's opinion, you'd be surprised to hear, it doesn't take much to prove someone guilty – but we need more, because the jury always wants more. They want motive, for example.'

'You have one?'

Becky Schirhart arrived, putting up a hand on each side of the door frame to stop her momentum. She'd hurried down the hall from her office. Her breathing showed it. Raymond looked a question at Tyler, who said, 'Ms Schirhart is going to be my second chair on this case.'

'Really.' Raymond shifted his gaze to Becky. She drew a last deep breath, raising her shoulders, and looked like a deadly serious prosecutor. 'So you had to bring in some trial stud against me for this thing?' Raymond said to the chief. 'Must be serious.'

'Mr Boudro thinks we're being overly ponderous in advancing the case,' Tyler said to Becky.

Becky came all the way into the office, crossed in front of the defense lawyer, and placed herself obliquely between him and Tyler. 'This is the first time you come to talk about the case and what you want is to hurry us up?' She didn't voice the rest of her thought, which was, *Whose side are you on?*

'You're not doing Mike Stennett any favors taking it

106

slow, keeping this thing hanging over his head,' Raymond said. 'Not that you intend doing him any favors. I'm just wondering how different this is going to be, with him as the defendant.'

Becky opened her mouth, but Tyler spoke first. 'It's true I'm not looking forward to prosecuting a cop. We have to do everything by the book or the rest of them will be down on our necks. But it could be worse. I could be prosecuting a popular cop.'

This was Raymond's second hint Stennett might not be beloved by his peers. Again he stored it. 'At least you know how to indict it,' he said. 'You could do that much.'

'We know how,' Becky said. She had already spotted the folder lying on Tyler Hammond's desk. She opened it and handed the draft indictment to Raymond.

'I'm supposed to be the soft touch here,' Tyler said to her mildly. 'You're supposed to keep me from giving in to my reasonable impulses.'

'What difference does it make if he sees it now or a month from now?' Becky said. 'What's he going to do, discover evidence Stennett's innocent? He'd bring it to us if he did, wouldn't he, and we'd all be happy.'

There were two counts to the murder indictment. One alleged the standard assault on a human being with the intent to cause death. The second count was more complicated, alleging Stennett intended to cause serious bodily injury to the victim and killed him in the course of committing another felony, aggravated assault. In other words he didn't necessarily mean for Gordon Frazier to die but he was beating him and he did die. That was murder too.

Becky was watching the defense lawyer as he read. She'd been surprised to hear he would be representing the cop. From Stennett's point of view it made perfect sense. What she couldn't see was Raymond's motive. When Raymond had cross-examined Stennett at their motion to suppress hearing she thought she'd seen real passion in the lawyer, barely concealed loathing for the detective. Now he was representing him. Becky was a prosecutor, she believed defense lawyers were pretty much whores, willing to do anything for money or notoriety, but she hadn't quite believed it of Raymond. At least briefly at the hearing he'd looked like a man with a cause, or one who'd once had a cause and could remember what it had been.

'All right. So take it and read it to a grand jury,' Raymond said of the indictment as he tossed it back onto the desk. 'You can go that far, can't you? You've got fingerprints and an eyewitness. Hell, most of my clients've been *convicted* on less than that. It's sure enough for probable cause.'

'No point tainting him with an indictment if subsequent investigation shows we need to dismiss it,' Tyler Hammond said.

'You think that might happen?'

'No.'

'What else've you got?'

Becky stepped in to do her job. 'You know you're not privy to our investigation. Once he's indicted the file'll be open, not before.'

Raymond looked at her with a level expression that revealed nothing. He does that very well, Becky thought. You don't know if he hates you or if he's about to wink like we're all in this together.

'You could cut it short for us,' Tyler said. Becky shook her head minutely, but he wasn't looking at her. 'If he's going to plead we can get it indicted tomorrow.'

Raymond's expression didn't change except that his eyelids lowered slightly, hooding his eyes. 'I'll certainly convey an offer.'

'It's too early –' Becky began, but Tyler talked over her.

'What's important to me is to know whether he did it. What's important to me is to find out whether there's a cop beating suspects to death and to get him off the force if he is. That's more important than the sentence.' Tyler still looked like a pudgy philosopher sitting at his desk with his pipe in his hand, but his voice didn't fit the image. He was staring hard at Raymond.

'So what's your offer?'

'Voluntary and twenty.'

'No!' Becky said. Both men ignored her.

'Voluntary manslaughter instead of murder and I won't ask for an affirmative finding. I'm cutting right through to my bottom offer.'

'Twenty,' Raymond said. 'You think that's what this case is worth?'

'That's what it's worth to me to find out the truth. If he takes it I'll know.'

'Maybe.'

'Maybe? Have you ever seen an innocent man plead guilty?'

'Oh, who knows,' Raymond said. 'I think I have. Doesn't happen every day, but once, this one guy, aggravated robbery, swore to me so many times he didn't do it I almost believed him. And I thought the ID was questionable; woman who'd only really looked at two black men in her life, the one who robbed her and my guy in the lineup, and maybe they didn't have to look too similar for her to say "That's him." But she wasn't uncertain; she would've nailed him at trial.

And my guy *was* in the vicinity and he had a record and the only alibi he had was his girlfriend. He was perfect casting, you know?'

Becky shifted as if she were going to speak. Raymond didn't look at her. He was talking to Tyler.

'When the prosecutor offered twenty-five I thought my guy was going to cry. 'Cause he couldn't stand the thought of going back to prison for this one but he knew a jury might give him twice that, with his record. And we couldn't go to the judge 'cause it was Fortel and the Fort damn sure would've maxed him.'

Becky nodded to herself. Judge Fortel, called the Fort behind his capacious back, wasn't known as a particularly harsh sentencer but *was* known to have his finger on the pulse of his constituency and he would know when public outrage demanded a high sentence. That part was accurate, Becky grudgingly conceded, silently.

'My defendant just sat there in the jury box like he was never going to move again, with me saying, "I gotta tell her something." And finally I went back to the prosecutor and said, "I guess we've gotta try this thing, 'cause I can't get the poor bastard to say yes or no." And he looked so pathetic sitting there she came down ten years. When I went back and told him he did start crying, 'cause he knew he couldn't turn down fifteen. A few minutes later he's standing up in front of the judge saying "No contest" with his cheeks still wet. That's one I've always wondered about.'

Becky no longer looked about to speak. She had grown a set expression. Her arms were folded. After a silence Tyler Hammond asked, 'What happened to him?'

'Hell, I don't know,' Raymond said offhandedly, 'maybe he's out by now. I didn't become his pen pal.'

Tyler, sidetracked, looked down at his desk for inspiration. Becky said, 'So you're afraid poor innocent Mike Stennett will jump at our offer because it's too good? Which it is. We'll withdraw it if that's what you're afraid of.'

'No, that's not what I'm afraid of.' What Raymond feared was that this wasn't the final plea offer, it was just the opening salvo. Twenty years for murder wasn't a terribly low offer for San Antonio, where juries were notoriously capable of putting themselves in the defendant's shoes. But as an opening offer it *was* too low. Raymond was afraid it was an indication that the prosecutors would take it easy on his client throughout the case, maybe end up dismissing it if they thought they could do it expediently. He was glad to see Becky on the case. Tyler Hammond would dispassionately consider all aspects of the prosecution. Becky could be goaded into seeing it only as a contest. If she was any kind of prosecutor at all she'd still be smarting over her last loss to Raymond. He made sure he was looking down at her as if she were something on the sidewalk he hadn't decided whether to step on or over when he said, 'What do I have to be afraid of?'

Becky returned him a confident smile. 'We'll see,' she said.

There was nothing else to accomplish. A few minutes later Raymond mentioned an appointment and walked out, with another condescending smile. Becky stepped to the doorway to make sure he was gone, then turned on Tyler and said, 'You know what you told him with that ridiculous offer. You told him we're running scared.'

Tyler looked genuinely baffled. 'I told him the truth, that I'm willing to give him a good offer to find out whether Stennett's guilty. I think he –'

'Truth,' Becky snorted, and hurried out. She caught up to Raymond at the head of the stairs. 'Hey,' she called softly.

Becky was not short, but the defense lawyer was almost a head taller. He didn't slump or lean as many tall men do. He made no effort to compromise the disparity in their heights. Her neck would get sore if this were going to be a long conversation, but she had just one thing to say:

'If that poor pathetic agg robber of yours really didn't do that one it just made up for a dozen others he got away with. But I didn't come down ten years on him because I thought he was innocent. I did it because *you* thought he was innocent.'

'Oh, you read my mind, did you? And you thought I could read him better than you could? You thought maybe he told me somethin' brother to brother so's I knew it was gospel?'

Becky hadn't expected anger in return to her anger, at least not this deep-seated hostility. 'I thought you might know something you weren't telling me,' she said quietly.

Raymond didn't want her backing off. He reeled her back in. 'Honey, that is always going to be the case.'

He left her glaring after him.

The twenty years stayed in his mind. Weak opening bid, very weak. Becky had thought so too – unless they'd been good-cop-bad-copping him, telling him what the case was worth while trying to pretend they were really hot to try it. He didn't think Tyler Hammond was capable of that kind of acting, but he didn't know him well enough to say. Tyler was too strange. He didn't play the usual games Raymond knew so well. He might have been telling the truth about his reason for the low offer. One player telling the truth threw off the calculations.

In plea bargaining, real guilt or real innocence isn't a factor. It doesn't matter if you're innocent if the State can prove you guilty. It doesn't matter if you're guilty if the State can't make the case. In an ideal vacuum, the sentence should reflect the type of case and how bad it was. A robber who pistol-whips the clerk should get more years than one who thanks her politely and leaves. But in fact a plea bargain offer is based not entirely on how bad the crime is but on how good the case is. Did you rob a priest who can pick you out of a good lineup, and has, and can climb up on the stand and point the finger and say, 'That's the one'? Or did you rob one to whom all black people look pretty much alike, who's as likely to identify the defense lawyer as the defendant when it comes to court? That's what controls the plea bargain offer. The second guy gets a better offer even if he beat up the priest and torched the church on his way out. It's not the horror factor that controls. It's the certainty factor. That's why the defense lawyer asks for an offer even if he knows his client won't take anything. The offer tells you what the State thinks of its own case.

Raymond was afraid other factors were at play in the Stennett prosecution. What the crime was worth even if it was a lay-down for the prosecution. They – and he – had to estimate what a jury would think of it. A white cop who beat up and killed a black druggie. He knew what other cops would call that: a littering case. Leaving trash on the street. Maybe the prosecutors' own estimation of the crime figured in what they would do with it. Raymond could see it all objectively, work it like an equation. But one calculation he couldn't view objectively. He knew the sum, but he wanted to know what weight to give the two factors. What about Gordon Frazier made his life worth less than another victim's – his crookedness or his blackness? His occupation, or his address?

Now he had reason to see his client again, an offer to convey. And he didn't want to do it over the phone. He wanted to see Stennett's face when he told him.

Stennett's schedule was very flexible. He was on leave with pay, which would become unpaid when an indictment came down. They made an appointment for early afternoon. Stennett arrived for it looking like he'd slept in his clothes, or hadn't slept at all. He carried his own coffee cup into Raymond's office.

'What are you doing?' the lawyer asked. 'You better not be undercover copping anymore. I hope you've got some snappier clothes for trial. You look like you're trying to infiltrate a bowling team.'

'I'm investigating,' Stennett growled.

'Oh good, we got a free investigator on this case. That'll save you some money. If saving money is what counts with you. You know what a free investigator's worth. What've you uncovered about yourself?'

I'll get over this, Raymond was thinking. That he could banter with the cop was proof that the shock of recognition he'd felt when viewing Gordie's autopsy photos was fading. But he'd still gone stiff with tension when Stennett had stepped into the room. Still had the otherworldly sense of confronting his own murderer.

He was obviously hiding it, though. Stennett talked on. 'I've heard Hoss Frazier worked both sides of the street. He was a small-time dealer, but some people say he wasn't above snitching somebody off if he was short of cash.'

'Really. So you think maybe the same dudes that got Claymore Johnson got him too?'

Stennett answered him straight. 'Too much of a coincidence, probably. But it opens up a lot of possibilities, don't it?'

Raymond didn't bother answering. 'So how well did *you* know Frazier? He ever pass you anything?'

Stennett shook his head. 'I never got nothing from him. I'm not sure whose snitch he was, I haven't dug that out yet.'

'Let's talk about your snitch. Suppose I talk to him myself. Maybe he –'

'Fuck that,' Stennett said. 'You don't find him out. Nobody finds him out. Just forget that aspect of it.'

'You're not giving me very much, then. You plan to tell the jury that, assuming I let you testify: that you have a witness who could alibi you but you won't give him up? You think that'll play?'

'You tell me, you're the lawyer. You think that sounds better, or should I just say nobody was with me, I can't prove where I was? Most people can't, you know, any given time.'

'I don't know, we'll have to think about that,' Raymond said as if it were of little consequence. He had just established one thing: Stennett wouldn't blink at committing perjury. Raymond wasn't surprised. He was sure he had seen the detective commit that particular crime.

'Now we have something else to talk about,' he said. 'I've got our first offer from the prosecutors. First and last, they say, but they always say that. Twenty. Reduce the charge and no affirmative finding. You could do a twenty-year sentence in maybe –'

Stennett was good. He didn't even look interested. He was shaking his head before the number was even out of Raymond's mouth. 'They can shove that, and so can you,' the cop said harshly. 'I don't plead for nothin'. You're wasting your time talking about that.'

Raymond kept watching him. The lawyer's hands were folded in his lap. 'I thought for once I had a professional for a client. There's other reasons to keep negotiating than just you might take it. Besides, if I keep pushing they might actually come up with something tempting.'

Stennett was on his feet shaking his head. 'You don't get it. They couldn't come up with something good enough, not if it was reducing it to a misdemeanor. If I get any kind of conviction at all behind this they yank me. I'll be off the force. And I'm not giving that up. I'm a cop. That's what I do, that's what I'm gonna keep doing. There's no compromise, understand?

'And while we're on the subject, let me make things easy for you. All you got to worry about is the first phase of trial. I'm not goin' to prison. There's guys there in TDC who wake up with their underwear sticky 'cause they dreamed I was in the cell with 'em. No thanks, Counselor. If I'm found guilty you just make sure they don't yank my bond. Don't bother preparin' for punishment. I'm outta here. Understand?'

A sarcastic reply would have come easy, but Raymond's mind was on other things as he watched his client. He couldn't have asked for a better evidentiary display. Stennett was pointing at him, index finger extended, but the other fingers folded into a fist, revealing the scarred knuckles, and the scabs on two of them.

CHAPTER 7

If it were a normal case Raymond would be investigating the victim. Every lawyer knows that classic method of defending a murder case: try the victim rather than the accused. This victim was perfect for that type of defense, if Raymond chose to try it that way. As much out of curiosity as to keep up appearances Raymond checked the records. Gordon Frazier's rap sheet – yes, the early offense reports had said 'AKA Gordon Wilkins' – confirmed the life Raymond had imagined for Gordie. Possession, theft, burglary. King declining into jester. Raymond lingered over the few pages of dates and offenses. They told you everything, but they didn't tell you much. The broad outline of a life, but not the details: what Gordie had thought about himself, whether he'd ever tried to change.

After checking the record Raymond dropped into the D.A.'s office for a spot of plea bargaining. He was edgy, he should have gone away. Everyone seemed to be looking at him obliquely. They kept him waiting too long. 'Come on in,' the prosecutor finally said, holding the glass door open.

Raymond didn't make chitchat. 'Said you'd have an offer for me today on Amal Wilson after you had time to look at the file.'

'Oh yeah,' Jack Rieger said, settling behind his desk. Jack was thirty, an old pro. His white shirt was rumpled and his tie pulled loose. He always looked lost; he would sit and blink for a beat or two after a question, but he always had an answer after the blinking. He sorted through the stacks of files on his desk and found the one in question without much trouble. He opened it, saw the offer he'd written inside the jacket, and handed it to Raymond. With an open, accommodating expression, he said, 'Fifty.'

Raymond didn't take the file and he didn't repeat the offer. He just glared, waiting for the prosecutor to correct himself. Raymond used his race in plea bargaining. He knew it. His very presence in the negotiation was enough to trigger any white guilt a prosecutor might still have lurking in him. We all went to college, we know this is society's fault; you're going to take it out on a poor black man who never had a chance? Sometimes Raymond's most effective weapon was this hostile silence, glaring as if he were too dumbstruck to respond. *You've offended me to the depth of my African soul.* But with Jack, who just started looking at other files while the silence lengthened, he had to be explicit.

'Last week you offered me twenty-five on a murder. What makes this one different, that he killed a white guy?'

If Jack had any white liberal guilt it was so vestigial it didn't even make him blink. 'Come on, Ray. You mean Pettigrew? That was just a fight between neighbors that got out of hand. Hell, the complainant was probably cheating at cards. That was closer to voluntary manslaughter than murder. This one's almost capital murder. If I could prove your guy shot the victim because he wanted to steal his wallet it *would* be capital. And look at his record. He's lucky I'm offering fifty.'

Raymond growled a little more, but it wasn't working, so he stalked out. The prosecutor had a good explanation, one he undoubtedly believed himself, but Raymond wondered if that secret component did figure into the offer. Wasn't a dead white man worth maybe five years more, or maybe the black life Pettigrew had taken worth years less?

On his way out of the courthouse he passed the shoeshine stand. The young guy who manned it smiled at him hopefully, which made him quite an optimist, because Raymond had never been a customer of his, not once. Raymond had sat on that particular shoeshine stand only one time, years ago. He'd been a law clerk then, not even a lawyer yet, but he fancied he looked like one in his suit. All he'd needed to complete the image was a fresh shine on his shoes.

Then as now the shoeshine stand had sat just inside the middle doors on the first floor of the courthouse. On a whim Raymond had climbed up. He'd seen lawyers sitting in that seat before, prosperous-looking, benevolent, reading a newspaper or talking to a colleague while the old Mexican shine man worked over their feet. When you sat up there your head was above everyone passing in the halls. Greetings always showered the shoeshine customer. When Raymond took his place he felt on top of the world. He felt silly feeling it, but he felt it just the same.

The shoeshine man was old and fat, and between customers he collapsed on a bench like a balloon going flat. He seemed like a jolly old man. Raymond had heard him keeping up a line of chatter while he worked, and thanking his patrons profusely for dollar tips. Raymond would be embarrassed if the man, so many years his senior, acted deferential to him as well. Raymond would talk to him like an equal, even like a senior worthy of respect.

The man must have been in the bathroom. It was a few seconds before he came lumbering down the hall. A few people had glanced at Raymond curiously, sitting there alone. He was glad to see the shine man coming. Raymond smiled at him. The old man lost a step, and his jolly look. He surveyed Raymond in his chair, looked him in the face, then took his seat on the bench across the way. He picked up a newspaper and hid himself with it.

Raymond cleared his throat. Maybe he's mad because he thinks I'm just sitting here waiting, like it's a public bench. It took him a minute before he got it. Raymond was a child of the sixties, he was used to more subtle racism. But the shine man was old, with attitudes hard as his arteries. When Raymond realized he wasn't coming no matter how long Raymond sat there his skin went cold, then hot. He felt himself glowing like the sun, the most visible person in the city. It was a long, long climb down from the shoeshine stand.

That had happened more than fifteen years ago. Raymond could joke about it now. He never had, but he could. That had been one of his first experiences in the courthouse, but it hadn't been prophetic. When he'd started practicing he'd been treated like a professional by everyone. Courtesy was his typical experience, not that business at the shoeshine stand. Layers of sediment had settled over that ancient hurt.

But he had never climbed back up on that shoeshine stand.

It was time to go east side. Past time. After his one foray to the scene of the crime Raymond had confined his investigation to his professional world. But records couldn't tell him what he needed to find out. And it wasn't Gordon Frazier he was investigating.

The man who owned the grocery store was in his sixties, but he wouldn't let himself be old. He didn't have the time. He wasn't tall, but looked as if he were because he was thin and because he held himself like a soldier. He looked skinny until he lifted a crate and the tendons stood out like piano wire in his forearms. The grocery man had just a dusting of hair across the top of his scalp now, and his skin seemed to have faded. Raymond recalled the man being much blacker when Raymond had been a boy. Now he was oak brown. Raymond was darker, but Raymond got a lot more sun. The grocery man never took a vacation, never got out of his store during the day.

The grocery store had operated in this east location for more than thirty years. It wasn't a modern giant. When Raymond came through the doors in the front corner he could see the owner at the far side of the store, spraying the tomatoes with water. He wondered why the owner didn't turn at the sound of the door chime, but then remembered the big mirror hanging at the ceiling corner and realized he was being watched.

'Hello, Geneva,' Raymond said to the one cashier on duty. Geneva *had* let herself get old – old and fat and so grandmotherly it was surprising how many people had stuck guns in her face. She waved Raymond over and gave him a big hug, but he was clearly on his way across the store, and she let him go.

When Raymond got close the grocery store owner turned and said, 'Must be nice being rich, just running around town on a weekday when poor mortals have to work.' He was smiling.

Raymond gave him a quick hug. They weren't very good at it. They hadn't done a lot of hugging when Raymond was a boy. It was only after he'd gone away to college and his homecomings became occasions that they took it up.

'Hi, Pop,' Raymond said.

'But you don't *look* like you're on your way to the beach,' his father continued.

'Hey, Pop, I'm working. I'm investigating a case.'

'What, a robbery? Digging up something to cross-examine me with? Or Geneva?'

'I got plenty of that already. This is something that doesn't have anything to do with you. I'm just looking for background, thought I'd start here. You know everyone in the neighborhood, don't you? Have you ever heard of Mike Stennett?'

'The police officer?' Mr Boudro went back to spraying his vegetables, turning away. 'You're representing him? Good.'

'Good?' Raymond said. He was usually adept at concealing his feelings when he drew an unexpected response, hiding behind the log and waiting for more, but his father startled reaction from him.

Mr Boudro nodded. 'Because I know you'll do a good job for him.'

'You do know him.'

'Oh, yes. Shops here.'

Raymond looked around the store, finding that image impossible to conjure. Picturing a white man in the store wasn't hard. There was a white woman now, two aisles away looking at cereal boxes. The store's clientele had always been multiethnic. What Raymond couldn't picture was Stennett, the renegade, being a regular customer in any neighborhood. 'Before he got arrested, did you know he was a cop?' Raymond asked.

'Oh, sure.' His father's tone was casual, but his father was a storyteller; he'd adopt a casual tone if he knew it would have a greater effect. Raymond couldn't read him. As if to give him a sporting chance, Mr Boudro turned back to him full face. And sure enough, he started a story.

'About three, no, four years ago I was at the meat counter when he came up to me. I'd seen him in here before, we'd said hello, you know. I guess he knew I owned the place. He knew my name. He said, "Mr Boudro, I'd like you to do me two favors if you would." And I saw he had his wallet in his hand. He set it on the little table behind the scale, so nobody could see it but the two of us, and he stood like he was looking over the meats. I don't guess I said anything, but he went on, "I'd like you to let me out your back door and I'd like you to hang on to this for me." Meaning the wallet. I thought, What the –? But he went on talking real fast, he said, "Something's going on in your alley I'd like to see and maybe get in on, but if they shake me down I don't want 'em to find this." And he flips the wallet open to show me the badge.

'Well, then I knew, of course. I'd seen "Baretta" I knew what was going on. Hell, who needs TV, workin' in this neighborhood, I've seen it all out those picture windows. I just dropped my hand over his wallet and slipped it under my apron and I said kind of loud, "I think we've got what you're looking for in the back here."' Mr Boudro started laughing. 'Like I'm a character in one of those shows, you know? Like I'm in Paris workin' for the Resistance. Idn't that the silliest thing? See the real thing all your life and then when you get in on it for a second you start acting like some bad actor in a show. Anyway, I take him into the back and up to the door and when we get there I see he's been rubbin' his eyes along the way so they're sort of teared up, and about that time I realize he didn't look too good to start with, and now he looks like one of those guys shuffles in here once or twice a day to buy a quart of malt liquor with nickels and pennies. He grins and says, "If they catch me watchin' I'll tell 'em I'm just lookin' for a taste myself."

'I said be careful and let him out the back.'

Raymond was listening to his father's glee over his

role in the little adventure. Raymond knew of the times the grocery store had been robbed, the shopliftings, knew his father had been called to testify in court a few times, but that the old man might have played some role other than victim in a true-life crime story mildly surprised him. 'What happened?' he asked.

'He didn't come back 'til the next day. I was a little worried about him, but there was nothing on the news that night. Next day he came in for his wallet and I asked him if he busted anybody and he said not that time, he wanted to follow it on up. He said he'd let me know. He did, too, about two months later, after I'd read in the paper some hotshot dope dealer got arrested. Officer Stennett came in and said, "That's your collar, Mr Boudro."'

Raymond wondered if his father had made a mistake. He needed to start carrying a photograph of his client, so he could be sure he and witnesses were talking about the right man. This case wasn't Raymond's first knowledge of Stennett. Stennett had figured in several of Raymond's cases, and Raymond had investigated his record thoroughly when he was representing Claymore Johnson. His father's story didn't jibe with the image Raymond had of Mike Stennett.

'That was how long ago, four years? And he still shops here?'

His father nodded. 'I wish more policemen did, but he's the only one, far as I know.'

'Does he ever talk about his work?'

'Oh, nothing important. It's not like we have long deep chats. But he'll say when he's working.'

'You know what he's charged with?' Raymond asked gently.

His father stopped abruptly. 'Mmm huh,' he acknowledged.

'You think he did it?' Silly question. His father'd already said he didn't know Mike Stennett well enough to have a worthwhile opinion. But Raymond was after something else. His father's attitude puzzled him. He approved of the cop.

Mr Boudro answered slowly, as if aware of what Raymond was really asking. 'I think, if he did do it, it wasn't murder.'

'What was it?'

'Maybe, an accident during an investigation.'

'Investigation. I've seen the autopsy pictures, Pop. The man's bruised and scraped from his ribs to the top of his head. And I've had clients tell me they've had exactly that kind of run-in with Mr Stennett, when he wanted to know something they didn't want to tell, or he knew he didn't have enough to arrest 'em and decided to do the next best thing.'

His father looked concerned, but when he spoke it was in an earnest tone Raymond remembered. His father was trying to educate him. 'I don't approve of killing. Nobody. But people like that Frazier are killers too. They're killing this whole neighborhood. Did you keep your eyes open when you drove here? How many closed shops did you see? You know how many businesses here've shut down or moved away 'cause their parking lots turned into dope shops? Or they got broke into so many times they couldn't afford the insurance any more? And I know two myself who got shot trying to do somethin' about it.'

Raymond shook his head. 'That doesn't give cops license –'

'If cops do everything by the book and they do manage to catch somebody, courts let 'em right back out again. The way things are now, cops sometimes have to do something none of us like much. But it's the only thing does any good.'

'These aren't strangers you're talking about, Pop. Some of the people this Stennett's done these things to are people I went to school with. Kids who bought candy in this store. Don't you see that they're –' He tried to think of a flattering way to put this. 'Don't you feel something in common with –'

'Like they're my brothers just because of the color of their skins?' his father said sarcastically. No, Raymond wanted to say, but his father was still talking. 'Look at who I am, Raymond. Would I think that? Put yourself in my place and figure out how I feel. I'm sixty-two years old. Worked ten years for a ten-thousand-dollar down payment to buy this store, just so I wouldn't have to work for somebody else. Worked like a dog ever since, down at the markets at four-thirty in the morning, opening this door before the sun's up, not closing it 'til the sun's down again. And here's that trash on the corner over there every day from noon on – that's when they get up, noon – sitting there staring at me. Wanting what I got but too god-damn lazy to do anything about it but steal or sell dope to other fools like 'em. No, not just what I got. What I got idn't good enough for 'em, just like it wasn't good enough for you.'

The sudden shift made Raymond feel as if he'd been teleported outside the store to mingle with the dopers and thieves across the street. 'Yes it was,' he began automatically.

His father was shaking his head. His expression wasn't angry. He talked fast because of his need to push his words across to Raymond before they lost any of their meaning. 'I would've been ashamed of you if it *had* been good enough. You think I want my son to have no better'n what I had? But you worked for it, Raymond. You did it the right way, the hard way, like me. These trash, all they can think of is scoring a big dope deal. Or breaking into my store or sticking a gun in my face to get what's in the cash register. Now you tell me how I'm supposed to feel about them. Like poor lost lambs? Like they could've been my children? They're nothing of mine. They've turned this neighborhood into a hellhole. Driven businesses away, got children murdered in their beds. If somebody like Mike Stennett has to smudge the lines a little bit to handle them, more power to him. Shoot 'em down, I say. Kill 'em before they breed.'

Raymond had never heard his father go so far, but otherwise the speech was unsurprising. Mr Boudro's personal values were stronger than his sense of group identity. For him the world wasn't white versus black, it was workers against the shiftless. Raymond was sure he'd never hear a white man express the same idea quite so nakedly, but in his father's concluding remark there was a great deal of truth:

'There's lots feel the same way I do.'

'I know. I get juries full of people like you.'

Raymond make the little joke to defuse the tension. He could feel them slipping into the past, into an old argument they hadn't had in years. He'd always known how his father felt about criminals, the way any merchant would feel. When Raymond had begun doing criminal defense they'd been at odds. Raymond hadn't gone into law as much of an idealist, but he had thought he'd be defending principles once in a while. His father saw only the practicalities. He actually asked the standard question: 'How can you defend those people?'

'I don't defend them,' Raymond had said. 'I mean, I don't try to set them free. I'm just there to try to get the judge to be reasonable. Prosecutors try to send every shoplifter to prison for life. That's their job. My job's to say what the case is really worth. And to see that nobody's rights were violated when cops made the case. Somebody has to be there to take the other side; that's how the system works.'

Another way the system worked was prosecutors only heard from cops and victims, and Raymond dealt personally with the accused. It hadn't taken years of poor dumb losers trouping through his office before he formed a view of criminals that differed substantially from his father's. Punishment was almost wasted on the bunch of bed wetters Raymond defended. They thought they were in court not because of anything in particular they'd done, but just because it was their natural lot in life, the way other people think college follows high school. And the idea of anyone being deterred by harsh sentences was laughable. Deterrence required the realization that what had happened to someone else could happen to you. These people weren't capable of that leap of imagination.

His father viewed them as dangerous criminals. They weren't. Some few of them were hardened, in the sense they would literally die before getting a straight job. But most just couldn't compete in the straight world. They didn't have the time sense to hold down a job, or the attention span to keep at one. Hell, they were failures as criminals, or they wouldn't have needed Raymond. How much smarts does it take to walk into a store, point a gun at somebody, take the money, and leave? But there wasn't one out of fifty of them could do it three times in a row without getting caught. And if they did get away with it they netted probably fifty dollars a job. They were pathetic, most of them. Of course, he had come across the occasional sociopath who was in it for the pain, who lived for inflicting humiliation and hurt. They were scary. It was chilly to be in the room with one.

But they couldn't do half the damage a sociopath with a badge could.

'All right, Pop, you're right. We need Robocop out there beating people to death. But you know, the rules he breaks, some of them are designed to make sure cops have the right guy. Like needing probable cause to arrest. That just means you have to be pretty sure you're arresting the right person. Stennett does what he does without being sure enough. Don't you –'

His father interrupted with a question that showed he'd been listening carefully. They were talking about Raymond's client, but Mr Boudro was the one defending him.

'Why'd you take this case, Raymond?'

That was one 'why' Raymond was sure of. He'd resisted his instincts in order to take the case. He remembered the moment Mike Stennett had stepped into his office. It had been one of those rare spooky moments when he didn't like being in the same room with someone. Stennett was the villain in some of the worst stories Raymond had heard from clients over the years, the worst abuses of not only the law but of the human spirit. Of 'curbing' an arrested suspect: stretching a handcuffed man facedown in the street, his lips kissing the curb, so that a stomp on the back of his head would break out all his teeth. He had heard of Stennett sitting in a suspect's living room questioning him while holding the man's young child on his lap, the threat expiicit. Most of these stories hadn't aired in a courtroom because Raymond knew the futility of pitting his criminal clients' stories against a cop's in that setting. But he believed them. Raymond himself had gathered statistical proof the cop was a racist. And now finally Stennett had killed a suspect so blatantly he'd been arrested for it. Killed a black man in the neighborhood where Raymond had grown up, where his parents still lived.

Then Stennett had walked into his office. Raymond had almost thrown him out on the spot. But that response was an old reflex grown slow with disuse. With almost wonderment Raymond had begun listening to Stennett, and as he had he had realized he couldn't throw him out. That would mean watching the case unfold from a distance, wondering, always, what had really happened.

'To find out the truth,' he answered.

He sounded melodramatic saying such a silly thing. He couldn't remember the last time the truth had mattered in a case. You worked with the facts you had, and the client was just the stake in the game. Once events moved from the outside world into the courthouse it didn't really matter if the defendant was guilty or not, or even whether he got convicted or not. What mattered was winning. That was one truth he'd never tried to tell his father or anyone else: the adversarial system made every case into a contest, and Raymond was good at it. Of course, for a defense lawyer winning took very subtle forms. Driving a prosecutor lower on a plea bargain than he'd been willing to go. Better yet, receiving a sentence from a jury lower than the plea bargain offer had been. Or, major triumph, getting the client convicted of only a lesser offense. It was the combat that had drawn Raymond into criminal law. His resolution might have been formed on one of those long-ago Friday nights when he'd realized he could beat them every time on a silly football field without winning anything.

But in this case winning was less important than the truth.

'What are you going to do when you find out the truth?' his father asked quietly.

Trust the old man to ask the tough question, the one at which Raymond had only looked askance so far. But he knew the answer. 'Don't you think people should know if a racist cop is killing black people in your neighborhood, Pop?'

His father looked at him compassionately. He realized his son's risky course. But he wasn't out of tough questions yet. 'If he's such a racist, how come he put his life in my hands? Back when he handed me his badge so the guys in my alley wouldn't know who he was. That would've been worth something to somebody, but he let me know, without hardly knowing anything about me *except* my color.'

Raymond had already been worrying that one over in the back of his mind. 'Well, that's something on his side, Pop. Maybe I'll call you as a witness.'

His father clapped him on the shoulder. The strength in the old hand was his own strength. He felt the kinship to it. 'I've always been proud of you, Raymond. You know that, don't you? I couldn't have hoped for a better son.'

They had been veering emotionally, but now they were back on familiar ground. Mr Boudro gave him another hug, quick as the first one but stronger. 'For once you're on the right side,' he said in a joking tone. 'Don't blow it.'

Raymond put his sunglasses back on before he reached the sidewalk. He gave a long look to the listless lump of black youth on the corner across the street from the grocery store, wondering if any of them were once or future clients.

His father had just laid out a viable defense for him. Mike Stennett wasn't a villain, he was the hero of the east side. A hero to the right thinkers on the east side, that is, and he could count on having some right thinkers on the jury. But Raymond still hadn't reconciled this new view of his client with what he knew of him. He knew too many vicious stories about Stennett, and nearly all the ones he'd heard had been viciousness directed against black suspects, not white ones. Some of the victims had been more bystanders than criminals. What if his father had been on the fringe of the wrong crowd some time when he'd run into the cop, instead of tending his store?

Stennett's respectful treatment of Raymond's father – calling him 'Mister', putting his life in the old man's hands – didn't make sense. Raymond was having such trouble fitting the pieces together that he considered the possibility that Stennett was devious enough to have deliberately muddled his own image – that years ago he had arranged that at least one hardworking old black man would be a character witness for him, when one of the cop's racist brutalities finally caught up with him.

Nearing midnight. Stennett had been on patrol for three or four hours. It was a regular working day for him. He didn't have his badge, but then he seldom carried the badge when he was working anyway. He was armed with something other than his assigned piece, but that wasn't unusual either. It was a quiet night, a Thursday. Tomorrow, payday, would be busier. Mike wasn't looking for trouble, he was looking for witnesses. People who knew Gordon Frazier, who might know people with believable reasons for killing him.

The wind through his open car window was clearing his head. He'd been in five bars, maybe six. It was hard enough to get black people to talk to him; the chance of their opening up to a man standing there without a drink in his hand, who had obviously come in for nothing but information, was nil. Mike had learned that lesson in his early days working under-cover. He'd order a round of drinks then find a way to pour his into a plant, or into somebody else's glass, like he was fucking James Bond. Soon that had come to seem like a waste of whiskey, even though the depart-ment would reimburse him for it. If he ordered a drink he drank it. If he had to order drinks in six different bars while he was on duty, well, a man's gotta do what a man's gotta do.

He missed the badge during the day. He *would* carry it when he wasn't working, when one never knew when a sudden display of authority might be called for. Sight of the badge had a fine effect on clerks and servicemen, but Mike didn't wave it around much. He just liked having it, knowing if some asshole got too far out of line he could make the jerk swallow his tongue by flipping the old wallet open. Once the jerk saw the badge he knew who had to listen to who and who had to shut the fuck up and like it. It didn't matter if the asshole was a brain surgeon or the richest guy in town. 'That's right, I'm a cop, pull over, stand there, what do you think you're doing?' The clown *owed* you an explanation, he knew it, he'd stammer all over himself in his rush to do what you said. Walking around with-out that potential in his back pocket made Mike feel naked. Reduced to a lousy civilian. He didn't plan the demotion to last long.

He had cruised out of his normal area, into a small residential neighborhood. It was still the east side, but this neighborhood could have been anywhere in the city. The yards were mowed, houses neat, trash kept out of sight. Here and there a house had been added onto or a garage made into another room, indicating long-term residents. It was a nice little neighborhood, but not safe. No place was safe. Even here they had to send their kids through the dangerous parts to reach school. And residents could never know when one of their neighboring houses would start looking a little run down, the yard not so scrupulously kept, and cars would start pulling up at all hours of the night, narrow-eyed men and high-strung women easing in and out of the house. Maybe even gunfire punctuating the night. If the neighbors rose up in protest and went to their city councilman or even took matters into their own hands they could maybe drive the infection out, but that would just make things worse for someone else. Community outrage only shifted the bad parts around. Nothing ever cut them out, except, occasionally, someone like Mike Stennett.

He turned the car and drifted back into the business district. The small shops had tight-faced looks, as if their owners had done what they could to protect them but weren't optimistic. It was late for a weeknight. Even the bars were closing. There were no pedestrians. Mike cruised slowly past a parked car and was startled to see someone sitting behind the wheel. The man studied him as Mike got a quick glance and looked away. He didn't change his speed as he drove to the end of the block and turned. He hadn't recognized the man in the car, but he recognized a lookout when he saw one.

He let the car coast to a stop past the mouth of an alley. If he drove down the alley the noise of the engine would be magnified by the buildings enclosing the alley; he might as well have a siren on. He jumped out of the car and ran to the alley, feeling the pistol jiggle under his arm. He took it out and stopped just inside the alley, letting his eyes adjust. The streetlights were long broken out. A hard-edged swatch of moonlight cut across the tops of the buildings at a narrow angle, illuminating the tops of the buildings to his right but leaving the alley and the backs of the shops on the left in darkness. The shops were small, two stories at most, but they loomed in the dark. They were tiny makeshift businesses like upholsterers and small appliance repairs, half of them closed permanently. A few of the buildings had apartments on the second floor but no one lived in them. There were no windows on the ground floors of the backs, only doorways, recessed blacknesses like holes in the paler darkness. Mike walked quickly but softly down the left side, hearing rustlings in the dark louder than his footfalls.

Vibration in his soles matched a sudden rumble in the air, and the alley grew even darker. He looked back and saw a giant truck covering the alley mouth behind him. As abruptly as its appearance, Mike realized the alley was a trap. He stopped dead, trying to blend into the wall. Ahead more doorways loomed, and a dumpster on the right, hiding places enough for a dozen men. Behind him his exit was blocked. The truck had passed but that didn't matter. One man with a gun could cut off his exit just as effectively.

They knew. They knew he had no partner, no backups, he was strictly unofficial, cut off from his lifeline of respectability. Rogue cop, the story would say, and no one would investigate his murder too closely. What had he been doing in that alley with an unregistered gun anyway? This was their chance, all the bastards he had arrested or harassed. They'd heard of him being driven out of the department and had seized their opportunity.

He took a deep breath and cocked the hammer of his revolver. He took two fast steps up to the next doorway and stuck the gun into it like a flail. Empty. He jumped into it and leaned back, protected. Now he too was black as the night. The alley seemed to have grown lighter by comparison. The moon was rising, its light dripping slowly down the wall opposite. Mike breathed more easily. His paranoia subsided. He could see the doorway across from him was empty. He was probably the only person in the alley.

But he knew his rush of warmth was more dangerous than the fear that had produced it. He didn't come strolling out of the shelter of his doorway. He peeked out, looking the length of the wall.

For the most part the shops stood shoulder to shoulder, seamless. But a few stood apart, leaving narrow openings to the street. There was one such rat tunnel between the building in whose doorway he was hiding and the next. He was at about the point where he'd seen the lookout parked on the street. And there was something strange about the doorway of the next building.

He stepped out. Excitement was replacing fear. But his heart hammered again when he had to step past the opening of that narrow tunnel between buildings. It was empty. He had a quick glimpse of a narrow slice of street at the end, fifty feet away. Mike stepped past it and up to the back door of the next shop. It was ajar. With one finger he eased it open farther. Just behind the door a television was stacked atop another.

He should have waited. The thing to do was wait for the burglar to emerge and get the drop on him when his hands were full. But Mike didn't have the patience for that at the best of times, and the adrenal elation of finding the alley wasn't a death trap after all had given him a suicidal eagerness to rush headlong into any opening. He slipped inside and pulled the door closed behind him. He was in a narrow service room crowded with benches and shelves. From the outer room came a rummaging sound, then a whining voice. 'Damn, man, where's the ones that're fixed already?'

He hadn't counted on there being two inside. One lookout, one inside man, that's what he'd figured. He crouched and duckwalked to the interior doorway, trying to locate the second man by sounds.

'Shit, haven't they fixed nothin' here?' the same voice said. 'All right, I'll take the broke ones. They must be worth somethin'.'

He was talking to himself. Nervous burglar keeping his nerve up by talking to himself. Or so out of it he didn't realize he was speaking aloud. Mike might have been wrong, but he decided to risk it. He stepped through the doorway and saw one figure silhouetted against the far wall, which wasn't that far, maybe ten feet. Mike grinned savagely, unaware of what his face was doing.

'What are you doing in my shop?' he bellowed.

The burglar froze. Mike ran the few steps and with that momentum slammed the guy into the shelves he was facing. Something fell with a crash. Mike grabbed the back of the man's collar, twisted it, and dragged him backwards, into the service room. The guy was gagging, his feet slipping out from under him. He would have fallen on his back if not for Mike pulling him along. Mike felt a hand claw at his own hand. Without much effort he banged the guy's head against the door frame as they went through. The burglar made a yawping sound and grabbed his head. Mike let his knee indent the guy's spine as he dragged him back farther. When they reached the back door he slammed the guy's head into that too, and let him fall. Mike was breathing deeply, exultantly. He knew this feeling well. Receding fear of death made one remarkably careless of the rights of others. He kicked the guy just to keep him off balance.

'What's your name?'

Sometimes they'd blurt it out without thinking. This guy took too long, he was thinking, so Mike knelt and let the pistol's point fall into his stomach.

'Stevie Bowen,' the guy slobbered out.

Stevie? What kind of burglar was named Stevie? What was he, a kid? Mike still hadn't gotten a good look at him. He wished he had a flashlight. He wanted to turn on the lights, but then the guy would see his face too.

What to do with him was a problem. He couldn't make an arrest, that would take too much explaining. He would have dearly liked to lay him out, along with his partner, but that was too risky, especially with the trouble he already had.

He picked the guy up again, pushed him through the door into the alley, and slammed the door solidly behind them. He wondered for a second why there was no alarm. Maybe it was out of repair. Maybe a silent alarm *had* gone off. Response time wasn't great in this part of town.

Mike held the guy up against the wall, pushing his face into it. He pulled the head back and banged it for emphasis. The guy was crying. Maybe he *was* a kid, or a junkie in the deep trough between highs.

'I'm so sick of you goddamn thieves,' Mike told him. 'This is the last one for you. You're meat.'

He stuck the barrel into the guy's ear. Too bad he had already cocked it. Cocking it now would be more dramatic, but the effect was good enough. 'No no no,' the guy blubbered, drawing as far away as he could. 'No no no no no, I'm sorry, mister, don't do it, I didn't know it was yours.' Which was believable.

Mike kicked his legs out from under him so he'd feel even more helpless. The guy curled up, waiting to die. He was crying like a baby and emitted the same acrid smell.

'Ah hell,' Mike finally said, like a gruff shopkeeper with a little bit of humanity left in him. 'How old are you?'

'Eighteen.'

Eighteen was old enough. An eighteen-year-old had probably done this a hundred times already. Eighteen was unredeemable. Mike had no illusions that he'd put the fear of God into him permanently. By morning the guy'd be bragging about how he'd gotten away. Mike wished he could arrest him.

'Run,' he said instead. 'Get out of here.'

The guy's legs wouldn't take the invitation. He lurched to his knees but couldn't seem to rise. 'All right then,' Mike said, and fired a shot into the ground beside him, which lent motivation. The kid was twenty feet away in the next second, still barely risen from the ground, but running. Mike fired another shot for good measure. He heard a squeal of tires from the front of the building.

The kid was gone. In the morning Mike would look up 'Stevie Bowen' in the computer and see if he –

No he wouldn't. He didn't have a computer anymore. Mike grimaced. It was fine not having the restraint of partners and backups, not having to worry about fictionalizing a report, but without the real power he was incomplete. His heart was still pounding adrenaline through his system, so hard his hands were shaking. He was still covered with the sweat that had sprung out all over his back when he'd realized he was about to die. The fetid alley air he was sucking into his lungs in great gulps tasted sweeter than mountain water. He wanted a drink worse than another breath.

He would not give this up.

Becky had the witness statements laid out on the desk in front of her like a mosaic, overlapping each other, as if they could form a complete picture. But she could take most of them and drop them into the trash can beside the desk. She had the case laid out to her own satisfaction, but there were gaps she couldn't fill. She kept moving from statement to statement, hoping some hitherto unseen juxtaposition would yield a definitive piece of evidence.

Tyler had tired of the game an hour ago. 'Me too,' Becky'd said when he announced he was going home, but she still sat at Tyler's desk. Everyone else in the section had gone home. At five there'd been a huge exodus from the courthouse that had barely touched her awareness. Now it was after six, the building must have been nearly empty. Down the hall two or three assistant D.A.s were probably still working, or at least putting in the hours, amassing comp time. And there'd be a janitor or two somewhere in the building, maybe lawyers in a court on another floor waiting for a jury. But this end of the third floor was as still as a playground at midnight.

Becky didn't hear the silence. The reports were talking to her. Here was the police dispatcher's. Mike Stennett hadn't been on duty that night, why had the dispatcher called him to go to the medical examiner's office to identify the body? Just put out a call to see if he was there, said the dispatcher. And he had been. Apparently Stennett rarely if ever was actually off duty.

That led to the medical examiner's report, which was as ugly as she could ask for. She picked it up, glanced at some of the lines again. Brutal, methodical beating. For a moment a picture leaped off the page at her, and sounds, grunts of pain. An instant of vividness such as she rarely got from a case anymore. Usually all she would have to do in a case like this was lay out the crime, put the defendant on the spot, and let the jury do the rest. But once in a while you got a jury that asked questions, and she didn't have enough answers this time.

A wisp of smoke made her nose twitch. Tyler's stinky pipe has infected the whole office, she thought.

She went on to the firearm examiner's report. Becky thought she detected a puzzled tone to this one. Yes, this is a gun, the examiner basically concluded of the pistol found lying beside the body. The examiner had no bullet to compare to determine whether the gun had fired it. As far as they could tell the gun hadn't been used at all. There was no serial number on it, no way to trace it to anyone but Mike Stennett, through the fingerprint on it. But why had someone made the gun impossible to trace?

She did have an answer for that one. Stennett himself had done it to make it appear Frazier was armed. He was just the type of cop to carry an untraceable backup gun, for just such emergencies as he'd created in this case. He'd just been careless this time, dropping the gun without making sure he'd wiped all his prints from it.

That was all she had. Go over it as often as she might, there was nothing more. But it was enough. With the eyewitness it would be. Her hand strayed again to his statement.

'I like to work late too, after all the assholes've gone home.'

Becky hated the way her hand shook. She didn't gasp, but the papers in her hand jumped, making her look like a teenage girl. Her expression was all the angrier when she looked up, because whoever it was had scared her so badly for that instant.

Mike Stennett took it easily. People must glare at him every day. He looked as if he fed off anger. Then what he had said registered with Becky. She felt twin cold strands of air raise the skin on her arms. The feeling made her voice louder when she said, 'What the hell are you doing here?'

'Thought we should talk,' Stennett said. He took the cigarette from his mouth, looked around the small office, and came to the desk, where he reached across her to stub it out in the ashtray near Becky's left hand. She didn't give him the satisfaction of drawing back.

'You have an attorney,' she said. 'I can't talk to you about the case.'

'Dudn't that strike you as funny?' Stennett hadn't retreated after stubbing out his cigarette. He sat on the edge of the desk. 'Cop and a prosecutor, and we can't talk except through a defense lawyer?'

'No, in this case that doesn't seem odd to me at all. You being a defendant, you and the defense lawyer are on one side and I'm on the other.'

He made a face as if he'd tasted something both terrible and unexpected. 'It won't be forever,' he said. 'Let's not ruin our whole relationship.'

Stennett was sitting with the eyewitness's statement just under his hand. Becky was resisting an urge to gather up the reports and statements, because that would call his attention to them. She listened and heard the vast silence outside her door. The courthouse was home to her. Even empty, it had never made her nervous before. But it was a hollow old stone tomb. People didn't love the place. They hurried away from it as soon as they could. She felt how unhuman the building was. It was built for work and the work was done for the day and no one should be here. The very air tasted unsafe.

'You have an attorney,' she repeated. 'You take your concerns to him and he'll tell me what he considers –'

'This isn't between him and me,' Stennett said. 'I'm not telling him shit. But you. You should be on my side. We're on the same team.'

'Not this time,' Becky said. She'd started to say, *Not after you killed someone*, but she didn't want to remind him of what he was facing. She had reminded herself, though, of what he was. As he leaned over her, and she smelled the old smoke and body smells trapped in his clothing, she was certain he was a murderer.

He knew just what she was thinking. 'You really think I did this?' he said savagely. 'You think I'm as stupid as those shit-for-brains you prosecute? Listen, 'f I ever took somebody out, you'd never hear about it.'

She stared back at him. 'Really?' she said. 'How often have you done that?'

She wished she hadn't said that. It had jumped out without thought. Stennett drew back, still glaring at her, but he didn't look just angry now, he looked calculating. Becky stood, gathered up the papers, and stuffed them into the file.

'Excuse me. I have someone to meet, down the hall.' A stupid lie. Not only did it not convince him, it probably made him realize how nervous he was making her. Becky stood stiffly, holding the file tight. She was taller than he was, until he slid off the desk. She looked away, picked up her purse, tried to assume a hurried, officious air.

Stennett moved into her path, and closed again. 'What's this about?' he said. His breath was foul in her face. 'This about that case I fucked up for you? I lose you one lousy little possession case and you –'

'If you want to keep that hand you take it off me right now,' Becky said fiercely. She hurried on, hearing a slight tremor in her voice. 'This isn't personal. I was assigned to this case.'

'You didn't maybe ask for it? I'd be a real trophy for you, wouldn't I?'

Becky just glared at him, and tried to edge past him.

'Wait. Hold on.' Stennett raised both hands, palms outward, protesting his innocence. But he was also completely blocking the doorway. 'Just think,' he said. 'Think if I didn't do it. And I swear, I didn't. That means somebody's framed me. Who would that be? Somebody on the other side, somebody you and I're supposed to be putting away. Who's looking into that, who's on my team?'

For just a moment she did consider the possibility of Mike Stennett's innocence. She hoped, for that moment, it was true, that he wasn't a killer.

'We're still investigating,' she said, and pushed past him. He resisted, holding his arm in place across the doorway. Then he let it fall. She walked out into the outer office, hurrying, feeling him close behind her, waiting for the touch of his hand again.

When she reached the outer doorway she looked back. Stennett was still standing in the door of Tyler's office, glancing speculatively inside. 'Detective,' Becky said. When he looked at her she said, 'We're closed for the evening.'

She waited. He crossed the outer office toward her looking a little sheepish, as if she'd caught him at something. Becky stopped being afraid of him.

In fact, as they walked down the empty, echoing corridor toward the stairs, she thought again about what Stennett had suggested, that he might be innocent, that she might find herself working with him again some day. But then she dismissed the idea. She didn't even think of him as a police officer anymore, only as a defendant. Her job was to prove him guilty. If he was innocent, that was his own lawyer's problem.

CHAPTER 8

On the field of boys, two were easy to pick out. If Raymond glanced away, when he looked back his eyes gravitated to Peter. The boy glistened in the June sun. The other boys must be sweating too, but they would never glisten. Peter effortlessly sliced through the other eleven-year-olds. Raymond watched him come across the soccer field, unerringly on an angle that would intersect with the little white boy who'd just taken the pass. Petey slipped past the boy on the other team who tried to block him out and was suddenly at the boy with the ball, who looked up in alarm. Raymond bit his lip. The small crowd moved up closer to the side-line. Petey stuck his foot neatly between the other boy's, hooked the ball out, kicked it past another opposing player, and was galloping toward the goal. Raymond was holding his breath. Like the other parents he followed the action, moving back and forth along the sideline. Unconsciously he too was slipping past people. There was a murmur in the crowd. One, then another shouted, 'Go. Go!' but Raymond was silent.

There was only one other boy between Peter and the goal, and the boy was pasty-faced and lumpy around the middle. Peter was already looking past him to the goalie. Artfully he showed the fat boy the ball then took it away, and he was past. Nothing to it. Raymond narrowed his eyes as if in pain.

And the fat boy reappeared. He was beside Peter, digging for the ball. Quick for a fat white boy. Peter saw him out of the corner of his eye, no problem, he kicked the ball ahead. But the ball wasn't quite where he'd expected, it glanced off his foot and then off his own leg. Trying to recover, Peter stopped too abruptly and lurched forward. The fat boy had the ball in the next instant. He hauled back and kicked it halfway back down the field, to a waiting teammate. Peter stumbled and fell and the action moved away from him.

The crowd drifted back, without Raymond, who found himself standing next to the coach. Their coach wasn't some high-pressure clipboard hurler, he was a middle-aged sporting goods store manager, rather lumpy himself, at ease with the idea that eleven-year-olds weren't pros. He clapped Raymond on the shoulder.

'He'll get the hang of it,' he said. 'Takes a while to teach your feet to do six different things at the same time.'

'Oh yeah, he'll pick it up,' Raymond said. He was breathing again, relieved. 'It's okay, Peter,' he shouted to the field. 'Shake it off.' Peter was already up and running again. He waved and grinned.

Raymond watched him blend back into the crowd, satisfied. He didn't want his son to be a natural athlete. He didn't want Peter to stand out that way. Didn't want to give other parents the chance to say, 'Well, of course *that* one's the star of the team. Look at him.'

In fact parents in this upper-middle-class neighborhood where Raymond lived and Peter went to school weren't like that. They were progressives who'd be embarrassed if their children showed a hint of racism. The children didn't seem to do so. A few minutes later Peter stole the ball again, passed it off to a teammate in position, and when the ball went into the net all the boys jumped on each other indiscriminately, laughing and hugging. No one seemed to shy away from Peter.

Raymond was treated the same way by the other

parents, in a restrained, self-conscious, adult way. They went out of their way to smile at him and elicit his opinion, nodding seriously when he said anything, jumping back into smiles when he looked in their faces. Raymond had the same smile. But he felt the tension. He always would. Peter didn't. Maybe there was none in his relationships with his classmates. His best friend was a red-haired boy with legs the color of teeth. They walked home from school together, they laughed and talked and had secret agreements, but what Raymond liked best about Kevin was that he sometimes argued with Peter, got mad and yelled, but even at the height of his anger he didn't seem to bite back a word that leapt into his mind.

Maybe things would change when Peter got old enough to date their daughters. Having his son go out with a white girl wouldn't be Raymond's first choice either, but there were so few other black kids at the school it seemed inevitable. There was always another step, always another worry.

'Want an ice cream, hero?' Raymond asked when they were in the car.

'I wasn't the hero,' Peter said.

'You made some good plays.'

Peter agreed with that. 'Think any of the other boys want to come?' Raymond asked.

Peter looked around. 'Nah. We all got homework.'

Raymond let the subject drop. His ambivalence sometimes made it hard for him to talk to Peter. He wanted to ask his son how the other boys treated him, if they ever stopped talking when he came up, or slid their eyes away, the kind of thing Raymond would notice. But he didn't want to make Peter defensive. Sometimes the way Peter blended into the white school scared Raymond. The boy wouldn't know what to do if he was dropped into the ghetto. It was other black kids who would think he was weird. Raymond wanted his son to understand what it was to be African-American, but he didn't want to make him self-conscious about it. There were daily stretches when Raymond wasn't self-conscious, but they were always interrupted by realizations that he was the only black person in the room, or that the conversation was being filtered for his benefit.

Raymond wasn't a man of two worlds. He was a man of no worlds. When he returned to his old neighborhood he felt uneasy and conspicuous. But he didn't quite fit into his adult neighborhood and profession either. He never would. Peter would. Did. It was his world, he was born to it. Peter had a heritage Raymond would never have, but unknowingly the boy had had to give up his own culture in exchange. Sometimes Raymond had the wild idea he should move back to the ghetto to raise his son. Let the boy grow up tough, *then* take him out. But that was a crazy idea he and Denise had never even considered. They'd worked to remove their son from that. Raymond thought about Gordie Wilkins, as he'd last seen him. Petey wasn't even exposed to the possibility of that life, the way Raymond had been. Raymond had removed his son one generation from that fate. But Peter could slip back. It only took that one year. And to many people who saw Peter it wasn't apparent how far he was from the ghetto. You could remove him from a dangerous world, but not from his skin, not from people who saw nothing else.

Raymond buzzed his secretary to ask, 'Didn't I have an appointment with somebody?'

'Mr Pruski,' she said promptly. Probably the only

person in the world who called Eddie Pruski Mister. 'Half an hour ago.'

'Have we heard from him? Do we know why he's late?'

'Might have something to do with the police car parked across the street,' Jean said primly.

'What?' This was from Raymond in person, emerging from the inner office. He strode to the window and parted the blinds. A patrol car sat in the sun across the street, yards away from any other car so it was obtrusive to the eye. Two uniformed officers sat in the front seat.

'It's been there about forty minutes,' Jean said. 'Third one today, or the same one keeps coming back.'

Raymond jerked open the door and walked out into the hot sun. His three parking spaces reserved for clients were empty. Raymond stood in the middle of them and stared. No one emerged from the car. When he started across the street the car's motor came alive. The patrol car began moving, slowly, before he could reach it. The driver was young, with blond curly hair. Incognito eyes behind dark shades stared at him. The other patrolman, equally young, was saying something to the driver, gesturing persuasively. The car rolled on, leaving Raymond standing in the street.

What was surprising about the police station was the lack of security. You walked in, you took the elevator, if you knew where you were going you walked to the proper office. If you didn't you stopped somebody in the halls and generally they'd tell you. The D.A.'s office had tighter security. Of course, unlike what you found in other public buildings, most of the people in the station house had guns on their hips. Raymond had the back-of-the-neck feeling that someone was following his progress through the white tile halls that were completely unadorned, giving the same feeling of impermanence as a hospital corridor.

He found Detective Bernardo Martinez at a desk in the Narcotics offices. There were no names on the doors. Martinez wore jeans and a red T-shirt. His hair was a little shaggy and he needed a shave, but if he was successful at undercover he must be able to discard the purposeful air he had, the impression that his time was more valuable than his questioner's. He said 'Uh huh' when Raymond introduced himself.

'I'm representing Mike Stennett. You were his partner, weren't you?'

'That's right.'

'His last partner, as far as I can find out. How long did you work together?'

'Couple of years.'

'Sounds like a long partnership. Did you just get along real well, or did you have an unusual success?'

Martinez laughed shortly. 'Two years isn't long, not around here. Couple of the teams been together ten, twelve years.'

'Oh.' No one had invited Raymond to sit down, so he hadn't. He was happy with his perspective, looking down at the cop. 'So you two broke up early,' Raymond went on, as if talking to himself. Martinez treated the statement as if he were. 'Why?' the lawyer had to add.

'Just worked out that way.'

'Nothing big, no one case that you disagreed over?'

'No,' Martinez agreed, as if the conversation were over.

'Then you just generally didn't work well together,' Raymond said.

Martinez didn't like this corner of the conversation. He chose to ignore it. But it was clear the lawyer was going to go on standing there until there was some response. 'We got along okay,' Martinez tried.

'But?'

'But nothing. Mike and I never had any problems.'

'I see. Then you're still together.' Raymond waited. So did the cop. 'Did your superiors decide to separate you?'

Martinez shook his head briefly. 'Why don't you ask your client if there were any problems?'

'I don't see him here. Why don't you tell me?' Again he waited. 'Look,' Raymond finally said, adopting an entirely different tone. 'He's my client. I'm investigating his case. Whatever you tell me goes no further. In any direction. I'm trying to get a handle on this guy myself. Help me out.'

Martinez didn't drop into any decision-helping nervous habits. He sat still, gazing past Raymond's shoulder. His only movement was to swallow. When Raymond was on the verge of giving up or asking a different question, the detective suddenly began speaking. It almost sounded like a prepared speech.

'We have an unusual degree of autonomy in this section. They give us money for buys, we write reports once in a while, but other than that we're gone. You develop your own contacts, you follow them up, you take the case from beginning to end. They can't supervise us too close, because out there you're all alone.'

'Except for your partner.'

'Except for your partner,' Martinez agreed. Now his eyes had fastened on Raymond's. 'And if your partner starts throwing you crazy it's pretty fucking scary. Because you're supposed to be the only straight ones out there.'

'Crazy like what?'

'Like you don't blow your cover just to throw the

152

fear of God into some punk. You're shuffling around out there like Joe Pathetic Junkie, and if you suddenly *descend* on some guy like the wrath of heaven it might make him start wondering where you're coming from.'

Raymond and Martinez were studying each other. Raymond thought the detective was watching him to see if what he was saying surprised Raymond. 'What would he do to put the fear of God into somebody?' Raymond asked.

Martinez shook his head as if he wouldn't answer, but he was still watching the lawyer. Finally he said, 'These aren't subtle guys we're dealing with. You don't scare them with cutting remarks.'

'He'd get physical sometimes?'

'Let's drop it. Mike's a good cop. I still think that. Let it go at that.'

'Would you testify to that?'

This question removed any confidentiality from the tone of the conversation. Martinez started making getting-ready-to-leave moves. He stood and turned away. Raymond walked around the desk so that when Martinez turned back they were face-to-face. 'Would you? I might need character witnesses.'

'Don't put me on the stand. You don't want that.'

'Why not?'

Martinez shook his head. 'I wouldn't take him down, but I wouldn't do him any good, either.'

'Why? What could the other side bring up?'

Martinez turned away. He opened a locker and took out a light windbreaker. After it was on he checked his pockets, seemed satisfied, and gave Raymond a 'You still here?' look.

'Okay.' Raymond gave up. 'But let me ask you something else. How long've you been in Narcotics?'

'Fourteen years.' Martinez looked as if he was in his

mid-forties, so that was most of his career in the police department.

'How?' Raymond was genuinely puzzled. He'd wondered this about Stennett. How could someone make a career out of undercover? 'Once you've made a few arrests, don't they start catching on?'

Martinez grinned. 'I've sent some of these guys away three, four times. I get 'em popped, they go away, first week back they sell to me again.'

'And then they get arrested and they don't make the connection?'

Martinez shook his head. ''Course, you never make the arrest yourself. You just make the buy, go away, write the warrant, and somebody else serves it, some sheriff's deputy. The suspect don't know who made the case on him. And he's made enough sales by that time that he can't track it down.'

'What about court? Once you testify, doesn't word get around to other people?'

'Yeah, if it comes to that you got a problem. You'd be pretty stupid to try to make a case on that same guy again. But it doesn't come to that very often. If it's a good case it gets plea-bargained. I haven't been to court in two years.'

It was true the detective didn't look familiar, and Raymond specialized in drug cases.

'Now, you don't wanna get notorious. But if you just take it easy, keep your head down, you can do it forever.'

Raymond thought about that, and it returned him to the subject at hand. 'If somebody in the life found out what you were, that might be reason to kill him, wouldn't it?'

Martinez became remote again. 'Not for me,' he said. 'Just be reason to stay away from him.'

'What about my client?' No answer. 'Do you think he did it?' Raymond asked explicitly. Still no answer, but this time Raymond moved to the doorway and stayed there. 'Listen,' he said. 'I want to know. This isn't about the case. I want to know. Do you think he killed this guy?'

The detective rolled his eyes as if the question were too stupid to answer, but Raymond didn't move. 'Look at me. You think I have reason for wanting to know if this guy I'm defending is a racist murderer?' They stared at each other, black and brown. The white cop in question seemed to be a sinister presence just outside the door. 'Did he do it?' Raymond asked quietly.

Martinez appeared to think it over as if it were the first time he had. After several seconds he said, almost as if reluctant to reach his conclusion, 'I don't think so.'

'You think he could?'

That one didn't require any thought. 'Could?' Martinez said. 'Oh yeah. Yeah.'

'"Could" doesn't count for much, does it? Lots of us *could* kill somebody. But it doesn't count unless you really do it.'

That's an interesting remark, Raymond's face said clearly as he asked his wife, 'Who have you thought about killing, Denise?'

'Mostly you, honey.' She said it affectionately, but it reminded him of troubled times he hadn't thought about in a long time.

The problem in the early years of their marriage had been that Raymond knew what a great catch he was. An educated black man who made a good living: those were in very short supply. That he was attractive on top of it was something other women noticed.

Raymond noticed their notice. That awareness sometimes made him late getting home. Denise would make mildly threatening remarks, but Raymond didn't think she was in a position to say anything ultimate. After their son was born, a year into their marriage, Raymond settled down but not completely. There was still the occasional evening out.

Until one late night he eased the front door open to find there was no need for stealth. Lights burned in the empty rooms. There was no note, just a missing suitcase and depleted clothing drawers. Petey's favorite stuffed animal, a floppy dog, was missing along with his pajamas and several changes of clothes. Raymond sat on the couch for a long, long time, the liquor draining out of his system leaving him headachey and tired, afraid to call Denise's mother or friends, picturing the diverging futures. He raged and kicked the furniture, he said who needed her anyway, but he kept ending up despondent on the couch. He thought about being a bachelor again, about losing his son, losing Denise, starting over. He thought about spending a life with the woman he'd just spent the evening with, and shuddered.

There wasn't much point in being a great catch if you didn't want to be caught by anyone but the one you already had. When Denise called the next day she said, 'I gave you one night to decide what you want.' 'Please come home,' he'd said before she stopped speaking. She'd been back home that night, and for the last ten years so had Raymond, every night. They didn't have much of a social life. Denise was his best friend.

'There was another patrol car pulling away when I got back to the office,' he told her. 'Jean said it went by every few minutes.'

'What are they trying to do, scare you?'

'I don't know. Scare me into doing what? I asked Martinez; I told him what was happening and I said, "Why are some patrol officers running off my business?"'

'What did he say?' Denise lounged at ease on the couch, glass of wine in hand. Peter was in his room doing homework. One of them would go check it in a few minutes.

'I said, maybe they don't like me representing Mike Stennett? Like he's done something to make them mad? Martinez just laughed and said, "Think who you're talking about. Think he's ever done anything to offend anybody? But so they'd want to ruin his lawyer's business? Shit, they know *some*body's gonna represent him."'

'Well, but . . .' Denise said.

'But they don't want me in particular representing him? I thought about that, but why? And Martinez said something else interesting. He said Stennett knows a lot of the younger officers. He doesn't have a regular partner anymore, so once in a while he gets some young patrol officer to work undercover with him on some particular case. When he needs a backup or something.'

Denise nodded. He didn't have to spin out the rest of his speculations for her. But she wasn't concerned about the case as a case. She was concerned about him. She knew Raymond was desperate to find out the truth. He knew she must have wondered already what she finally asked him that night: 'Ray. What if you find out he really did it?'

'I don't know. I can't let him go on being a cop.'

'Seems like the cops and the prosecutors're already done investigating. What if you find out something more, something they don't know, but that would clinch the case for them?'

He shrugged, looking at her. 'What should I do?'

'There's rules –' she began softly. He cut her off with a laugh. Those law school hypothetical questions about ethics didn't count when it was life or death. He didn't have to tell her that.

Denise set down her glass. On her way past him she laid a hand on his shoulder. Raymond stared at the vacant TV screen while she was gone. It might have been ten minutes or half an hour. When she returned from Peter's room she had a more intense expression. Raymond stood, pulled from his daze, trying to think of what he'd neglected. Denise stopped him.

'You think he's a racist, and a murderer,' she said.

'I don't know.'

He started to step past her, but she hadn't finished her thought. She put a hand on his chest. 'What if he did do it, and you're the only one who finds out? And he knows you know.'

It wasn't a question that called for an answer. He just looked back at her until she dropped her hand, and he went in to see his son.

The indictment, worded just as he'd seen it in Tyler Hammond's office, came down in early July. Judge Judy Byrnes was presiding that month, so it landed in her court. Raymond made his first court appearance on the case. Someone had thoughtfully set it on a Thursday, so it wasn't the bedlam a Monday docket would have been. It was a first setting, it should have been an occasion just to look over the State's file and maybe set another date for pretrial motions, but the judge treated it a little differently. She called Raymond and Becky up before the bench. She had a jury waiting in the hall to resume a trial, the regular prosecutors in the court and the defense lawyer and defendant were quiet at their respective tables. The courtroom was uncrowded. The judge had a discreet voice. It was clear to the two before her but didn't carry.

'Let's give my docket a break and not drag this through a lot of settings,' she said to Raymond. 'I'm sure your client doesn't want to keep trudging in here and rubbing shoulders with the other defendants.' Nice subtle tone on 'other'. To Raymond she said, 'When will you be ready to try this thing?'

He took a thoughtful pause. 'October,' he said.

'October,' Judy said. Becky looked at him strangely too. That afternoon in July the temperature would flirt with a hundred degrees. October sounded like a fairy tale land, infinitely remote. 'I was thinking more like early September,' the judge said.

Raymond spread his hands. 'I could say that'd be fine, then come in in September and give you a sad tale and get it put off. See what happens?' he said to Becky. 'Judge asks you to be honest with her and you do and she fusses at you. Then she'll complain that nobody ever tells her the truth.' He turned back to the judge. He almost called her Judy, but he'd never called her anything but Judge in her own court and he didn't now. 'I'm trying to be honest with you, Judge. I've got a lot of investigating still to do on this case. I'll be ready in October.'

The judge tapped a pencil. 'You'll be calling witnesses?'

'Quite definitely.' Becky was still giving him a puzzled look. He was doing everything he could to encourage her uncertainty.

'All right, October,' Judge Byrnes said. She consulted her calendar. 'The thirteenth. That'll be a Monday, it won't be unlucky for anyone. We'll make that a special setting, I'll clear the whole week for you.

Unless you think there's a chance this might end in a plea after all?'

Raymond looked at Becky. 'No,' they both said, almost in unison.

'You need to work on your rhythm if you're going to be a duet,' the judge said. Writing on her calendar, she waved them away without looking up.

Raymond hadn't removed anything from his briefcase for the short session. Becky had. He waited while she gathered up her papers, and they walked out together. Without knowing either of them, another lawyer could have told at a glance what they were. The defense lawyer carried a briefcase, because he's far from home and all alone. The prosecutor carried only a file folder, because her office was just one flight up.

'I'd like to get a copy of the indictment and your witness list,' Raymond said. Becky nodded as if he needed no excuse to follow her.

'October, huh?' she said as they passed the Special Crimes office. 'I hope I can count on that.'

'Already tired of Special Crimes?'

'I didn't say that.' But she gave him a look.

They were buzzed through the door into the main D.A.'s office without a word. Down the hall Becky said, 'I'm just ready to try the thing and get it done with. Other cops treat you funny when they know you're preparing a case against one of them. Did you know that?'

Her office was a cramped cubicle, made more crowded but less drab by her framed posters. Becky did all her work here now, inside the beige maze, not down the hall in the unprotected Special Crimes offices. She thought about telling Raymond about the visit from his client. She wondered if he already knew. He hadn't approved the idea, she was sure. A good lawyer like Raymond would never do that, send his client to negotiate with the prosecution. He'd probably be furious if he heard about it.

Sometimes as a prosecutor you start thinking the defense lawyer truly represents his client, believes in him, will get around you any way he can because the client comes first. Becky had thought that about Raymond a time or two, though usually he was as ready as she to joke about the losers he represented. With this case it sometimes seemed the lawyer was antagonistic to his defendant's interests. She had to be on her guard, though, remember that that could be only a ploy. No matter what else it was it was still a case. Lawyers always want to win.

'You mean you're already ready to try it?' Raymond asked.

Becky calculated whether to tell him anything. It took the free and easy tone out of her voice. Finally she said, 'You showed me how to try this case. Remember our motion to suppress? You had Stennett convicted way back then.'

See that you remember, he thought, without lifting his eyes from the witness list she'd handed him. Beside more than half the names was the notation 'SAPD' and a four-digit badge number. 'Lot of cops here,' Raymond said. 'You really got this many cops lined up to testify against a cop?'

'You know how it is. Chains of custody, scene investigations. None of 'em really has anything to say against Stennett.'

'Couple of these guys develop bad memories, it could really wreck your case,' Raymond mused. 'Somebody can't testify he took the gun to the fingerprint examiner, your chain loses a link, you can't get the gun or the fingerprint into evidence.'

'That won't happen.'

Raymond shrugged, still looking at the list of ten or so witnesses. There were no names on it he didn't know. 'So this is it?' he asked the prosecutor. 'You don't have any surprises?' It was a serious question. This was a discovery session.

'What surprises do we need? We've got an eyewitness and a fingerprint.'

'And that's all?'

She smiled, but she didn't look as confident as she thought. 'What about you? Who are these fabled witnesses of yours?'

It wasn't an improper question, but she wasn't entitled to have it answered. The defense has certain rights to discover at least the broad outlines of the State's case prior to trial. The State has no such reciprocal right. But prosecutors usually got some idea, through sessions such as this, lawyers trying to maneuver each other. If a defense lawyer had a viable defense he'd usually give the prosecutor at least a peek at it, in hopes of getting a better plea bargain offer, or a dismissal. Or just to show what a swell investigation he was doing.

Raymond gave her nothing. 'They ain't character witnesses,' he said. 'And so far I got nobody to testify what a swell probationer he'd make.'

He stood up. 'This isn't gonna be a coast for you. First of all, you can absolutely forget about a plea to anything. I give you my guarantee of that. And you better be damn sure of your witnesses, 'cause I'm gonna be damn sure of mine.'

Baffled by his change of tone, Becky fell back on what prosecutors always think but seldom say, what they come out with only when surprised by a defense lawyer committed to defense. 'You know he did it,' she said.

'I *don't* know it. I don't see enough here to convince me. Let me know when you get more. I'll be checking back.'

He left her looking irritated and uncertain, like a woman about to pick up a phone and call an investigator. Exactly as he wanted her.

Finally he had another appointment with his client. As Raymond continued to investigate, Stennett had become a monstrous though contradictory figure in his thoughts. It was always a surprise to see him reduced to flesh. He expected the cop to slink into the office like a creature out of place in daylight. He expected what he was to show in his face. It didn't. Stennett looked smaller than he remembered, and weary, like a man with commonplace but besetting problems; too many bills, or a bickering marriage. Raymond didn't even realize he felt a flicker of sympathy, but he did feel the urge to step on it, hard.

'I've been asking about you. Why is it you don't have any fans in the police department?'

'You're not looking hard enough.' Stennett pulled one cigarette out of his pocket and put it in his mouth, but didn't produce a lighter.

'I looked in your own division. Are you the only one in Narcotics who doesn't have a partner?'

Stennett grinned. 'I got more partners than I know what to do with. Who needs a partner anyway?'

'Your last one seems to have some problems with your style.'

Stennett's grin turned into a chuckle. 'Ah, you been talking to 'Nardo. Lemme tell you 'bout that. Ain't nothin' wrong with 'Nardo, he's as good a cop as they got.' He paused as if that sentiment needed revising, but disdained clarification and went on. 'But 'Nardo doesn't want to be a street cop the rest of his days.' He paused again, trying to assemble his thoughts. Almost as if he's about to tell secrets, Raymond thought. Or maybe just thinking of the best way to tell them. Is he about to tell me something I can use in other cases? Raymond wondered, then wondered if that's what Stennett was wondering. Beneath the microscopic layer of mutual interest imposed by this singular case, they were still opponents.

'Look,' Stennett said. 'Beyond detective any promotions are political. You gotta kiss the right ass, you gotta . . . make the right impression. Soon as I made detective I knew I wasn't going any further, and that was fine by me, because detective was all I ever wanted to be. But 'Nardo's got ambitions. And it didn't take him long to realize associating with me wasn't gonna do him any good. That's the whole story of that. He'll be a lieutenant pretty soon, and maybe one day he'll be the first Mexican chief this department's had. And I wish him well. But we were never destined to be lifelong partners.'

'Plausible,' Raymond said, as if weighing the story for courtroom use, but Stennett heard the rebuke in it, too.

'I can't help it if there's a good explanation for everything.'

'But you didn't pick up another partner. What's wrong with everybody else?'

'It's just dumb. Isn't it?' Stennett had toyed with the cigarette until he'd broken it and it was useless for smoking, but he kept moving it from his fingers to his mouth. 'When I'm undercover I'm supposed to be some shiftless junkie. How many of them got the same running buddy for ten years? Stupid.'

'But sometimes you need a partner.'

'Yeah. And when I do I pick up somebody for the one job. Some patrolman, you know, or young detective. Somebody who still gets a kick out of it. They like it, it's good for their promotion chances, and I get a new face. And when the case is over they go their way and I go mine.'

Raymond let silence answer, the answer being he was no longer interested. It had nothing to do with the case. Stennett looked even wearier when he stopped talking.

'Found out anything useful?'

Stennett shook his head. Raymond had made his own discreet inquiries among his clients and other sources and hadn't turned up any hint of a conspiracy to frame Stennett. Not that anyone would necessarily tell Raymond the truth about it. But he didn't believe any of the habitual criminals he knew or knew of had the initiative or the organizational skills to arrange something this well. Plus –

'Let's talk about this,' he said to his client. 'Time to start roughing out a defense. The State's case is going to be pretty straightforward, if they don't come up with something new. They have somebody who saw you beating up the victim –' Again that scene as Raymond had imagined it flared briefly in his mind. 'And they have your fingerprint on a gun next to him. Now what do we have to counter that? You weren't there, you say. So where did the State's evidence come from?'

'Somebody's setting me up.'

'Yeah. Who?'

Stennett shrugged again. Sullenness was hardening his face, driving the weariness out. If the prosecution managed to put this face before the jury they'd convict in about five minutes.

'Let's forget about who and say how,' Raymond

said. 'We've been figuring it was somebody you busted, or were about to bust. Somebody wanting revenge or you off the case. Some bad guy. How does some bad guy arrange this?'

The quickness of Stennett's response showed he'd been wondering the same thing. 'Getting the old man to make the charge is easy. Who knows what they got on him? Maybe just fear. Tell him do this or we blow you away. Torch your house some night with you in it. I've been lookin' into that –'

'I'll talk to him. See if I can get a feel for that. But that leaves the gun. How do these cunning criminals get your fingerprint on a gun? Walk up to you and say, "Here, Officer, would you mind handling this gun for us? Thank you very much."'

'Maybe it's one I took away from somebody and then gave back.'

'You in the habit of doing that? Givin' guns back to people you just arrested, or almost just arrested?'

'If I was undercover at the time and didn't want to blow it off. Maybe I traded somebody a gun for dope, so I'd look like a burglar. Or they realized later I was a cop, or even knew at the time, and once they had the gun they realized they had my prints on it. So they –'

'So they kill somebody just to set you up. But instead of killing him with the pistol that's conveniently got your prints on it they beat him to death. Then they find a convenient witness and blackmail him and hope the whole thing holds together long enough to get you convicted.'

Stennett stood up and threw the cigarette in the direction of the trash can behind Raymond's desk. 'I didn't say it was a *good* plan. Maybe it was more spur of the moment. They had something against Frazier anyway, and once they killed him they realized –'

Raymond gave a sardonic look past Stennett's shoulder, as if there were a rational observer listening to this.

'This is all great stuff, Mike, this has the sound of a really winning defense, but do you think we could come up with maybe one witness who could tell this to the jury? I'd like to just tell it to them myself, but those tightass prosecutors'd probably object.'

'*I* could tell it. I could take the stand –'

'I can think of an objection to that that'd be sustained too. Let's look at it a different way. Who would be more likely to have access to a gun with your print on it?'

Stennett frowned. Raymond watched him closely. If his confusion was an act, it was a good one. 'I haven't had any guns stolen . . .' Stennett mumbled.

Raymond wanted him to think of it on his own, so he didn't give a hint. Stennett muttered something about his locker. Then he got it, or he decided it was time to look like he got it. His eyes went distant, then narrowed.

'Cops,' he said.

An hour later they had a list of fellow officers who might have a grudge against Mike. The list threatened to engulf the entire force. 'But nobody'd have it in for me this bad,' Stennett said for about the eighth time. He was pacing. His face was hard again, his eyes darting, his hands clenching. Raymond had the satisfaction of having turned him against all his brothers in blue. 'If some fucking administrator wanted me out so bad he could taste it, but didn't have anything the Civil Service Commission would uphold – I'm not saying they'd kill somebody, but they might let me take the fall for somebody already dead.'

'Not an administrator,' Raymond said. 'Don't you know your whole administration is scared to death of this case? It's called civil liability. When you get tried a lot of dirt could get dragged into the open. Like your overforceful handling of certain suspects. Gordon Frazier's family could sue the city. That could bring on other suits, too. If they could prove your administrators knew what you were doing but hadn't reined you in, the city could be liable for millions.'

'Well, that's just one of those things,' Stennett began hesitantly. 'I can't see them shootin' themselves in remorse over costin' the taxpayers big bucks.'

'No, but city employees who cost the city millions tend not to get promoted any higher. Once in a while they even get fired or demoted. This case of yours puts the whole administration of the police department in jeopardy. None of them would bring that kind of grief down on themselves just to get rid of a jerk like you. No, it had to be more personal.'

If that's what it was, Raymond thought. But the whole idea sounded ludicrous to him. Stennett's guilt was the only simple, straightforward explanation for Gordon Frazier's murder. The more they explored other theories the more certain that guilt seemed. If Raymond couldn't find the evidence that would definitely prove Stennett guilty, he could at least close out other options.

'Let's think about the gun,' he said. 'You've seen it?' Stennett nodded, which meant somebody had gotten it out of the policy property room to give him a look at it. Or he'd already seen it. 'Did it look familiar to you?' Raymond asked.

'Sure. I've handled ones like it. You know how many guns I've held in the last twenty years?'

'Nothing special about that one?'

Stennett shook his head. Raymond was studying him for a pattern. Lots of liars were like that. Did he speak when he was telling the truth but only nod or shake his head when he was lying? With a really veteran liar, though, the lie tripped out more convincingly than any true statement.

Stennett had grown increasingly restless. Raymond had planted a new idea in his head. Either it was an idea – a class of suspects – he was anxious to investigate, or a whole new realm of lying possibilities for which to manufacture support.

'I gotta go,' he said abruptly.

Raymond followed him to the outer door. Stennett never looked back. Raymond watched him go. 'Now here's something new and curious,' he said to himself.

A patrol car – exactly like the ones they'd seen so often in the past few days – was cruising slowly by. It was following Stennett's dilapidated heap.

Was it Stennett the cops were keeping an eye on, rather than his lawyer? That tended to make Raymond's silly theory that a cop or cops had set him up more plausible. Raymond frowned. But why follow him so conspicuously, in a marked car?

'We're gonna get to the bottom of this,' he said to Jean. 'If they come back, buzz me.'

She did, an hour later. 'Patrol car,' she said shortly. Jean was too ladylike to say 'Cops.'

Raymond peered through the blinds. 'What the hell?' The car was parked in its usual prominent spot, but it was empty. 'Now this is just about –' He walked hurriedly to the door and yanked it open.

Mirrored insectile eyes confronted him. Raymond was already rushing out before he realized they were there. He stopped short less than a foot away. The uniform cap, pulled down low, poked toward his nose.

Between the hat and the shades the face was almost concealed. Only the white chin showed.

Behind the cop stood another one, also in shades. They were in their short-sleeved uniforms, with uniform sweat crescents under the arms. Their guns dragged down their belts. Their hands hung on their belts near the guns.

'Like to talk to you,' the one in front said.

CHAPTER 9

Raymond stepped back. 'There's the lady you make an appointment with.' Jean looked startled.

The lead cop hastily doffed his hat and sunglasses. He was the dark one. A mustache made him look like a kid on Halloween rather than older. The sunglasses had concealed a wide, flat nose. Maybe *flattened* was the word. It was the only thing that kept him from looking sixteen. 'Hello, ma'am,' he said to Jean. 'But we only have a few minutes,' he said to Raymond. 'We're on our lunch break.'

Raymond looked him over, as well as the one in back, who'd also removed his mirrored lenses and hat. He was the one with blond curls.

'All right, come in, since it's just a minute.' Behind their backs he looked at Jean, pointed at the cops, outside toward their car, and finally to her phone. She nodded imperceptibly.

He escorted the cops into his office, closed the door, and crossed to the window. He folded his arms and leaned back against the glass. The patrolmen hesitated. The blond one looked at his partner as if they'd made a mistake. The dark one shuffled his feet a little, then lunged across the room.

'Steve Montoya,' he said, hand extended.

Raymond said his own name and shook, trying to make it look as if his hand had leaped out to do just that.

'This is my partner, Darryl Kreutzer.' Pronounced 'Kroyt-zer'. The blond one, who'd dropped into a chair, gave a little wave. They were embarrassed,

Raymond realized. To put them at ease he said, 'You the only two been hanging around running off my clients, or are there more of you?'

The cops looked at each other, then Montoya hastily said, 'Oh, hey, we didn't mean to do that. Why didn't we think of that, Darryl?' Kreutzer just rolled his eyes.

'You probably thought most of my clients're CEOs of major corporations coming to ask my advice on how to fuck Japan.'

Montoya looked confused, decided he should laugh, laughed, frowned, looked at his partner again. 'You want to talk?' he asked.

'No,' Kreutzer said. It wasn't his idea to be there.

'Okay, here.' Montoya spread his hands. 'We just wanted to see what you, I mean, your office – No, not see. We wanted to meet you and offer –'

'Mention Mike,' Kreutzer said. Montoya gave him a look, shrugged, and said, 'Yeah, that's it. We just wanted to tell you we back up Mike a hundred percent.'

Raymond sighed. He crossed to the door, stuck his head out and told Jean, 'Call off the SWAT team. They're here to be my pals.' Back inside he said, 'So it's taken you two weeks to work up your nerve to come inside?'

Montoya looked startled. 'No, no, it was just, you know, a silent show of support.'

Raymond mouthed the last phrase, looked heavenward, sat. So did Montoya. Raymond wished he still smoked. Lighting a cigarette and blowing the smoke toward them would look so cool at this point. 'And there were others?' he asked, gesturing outside.

'Yeah. Lots of us.'

'So you know something that's going to help me?'

'No, not really,' Montoya said. 'Just that Mike's a real good guy and we know he didn't do this.'

'You've worked with him?'

'Sure.' Montoya dropped into a heavy Mexican accent, said, 'Hey, man, how much for a dime bag, man? I need it real bad,' and grinned. 'Only couple times.'

'No kidding. Ever see him push somebody around?'

'No,' Kreutzer said quickly. Raymond looked at him curiously, forcing the kid to continue, but Kreutzer'd said his whole piece. Beside him Montoya was staunchly shaking his head.

'And you guys never pushed anybody around either, right?'

Kreutzer looked disgusted. Montoya said, 'Hey, we don't know anything about the case, really. We just wanted to do whatever we could to help. You know.'

Raymond looked them over. So Stennett did have his supporters in the police department. Were all of them of the younger generation?

'Really,' Kreutzer said suddenly. 'If we can do anything, tell us. We'd like to do something, we just don't know what.' He sounded younger when he talked longer.

'Here's what you can do. Find out where that gun came from, the one that has Stennett's fingerprint on it.' He didn't want them blundering around in the eyewitness's life, but they probably couldn't do any damage asking around among other cops about the gun. 'If we could trace that maybe we'd have something.'

'Okay.' They stood up hastily, looking happy to have an assignment. It was Kreutzer who spoke. 'That'll be great. If we find anything we'll let you know.'

'Be discreet,' Raymond said, just to be humorous.

'Right, right. Oh and hey,' Montoya continued, 'sorry about running off your clients.'

173

'Yeah, we didn't realize,' Kreutzer said. 'Next time we'll be cool.'

They went out, jostling each other in the doorway.

'Can't wait to see that,' Raymond said.

'See this scar right here?' The black man indicated a tiny triangular depression on his cheekbone. 'Almost put my eye out. 'Nother half inch I be blind.'

Raymond inspected it like a medical student, like he'd never seen a scar before. 'What was that, a ring?'

'Yeah, ring. Big old heavy lump of gold, you know, with ragged edges?'

Raymond nodded and sat back on the couch. The stuffing shifted under his weight and the cushion he was sitting on sank a little too deep. The supporting springs had separated, or a slat had broken. He sat up again, delicately, trying to balance his weight on his thighs, which were pressing down on the wood frame.

He had gotten as far as the living room of the shotgun shack, and hadn't been offered a tour of the other three rooms. Someone was rustling around in the back. In the living room Raymond had the couch and the man he was interviewing had the rocking chair, the only other piece of furniture. There was little else to see. The only decorations were photographs of people, mostly children, some of them just Polaroid pictures thumbtacked to the walls.

'What did he want?'

'Didn't want nothin' far's I could tell. Wanted to beat the shit out of somebody and I was available.'

'Maybe he was dissatisfied with the quality of something you sold him?'

The man didn't respond. He was probably about Raymond's age but looked like he could have been in his fifties. He'd said his name was Ali. He wasn't a client. One of Raymond's clients had given Raymond Ali's name and said he had a story. But it was a short story. Raymond had heard it twice already, he'd killed five minutes, he was ready to leave. It was Saturday morning. He'd had trouble deciding whether to wear a suit and look like a lawyer. Instead he'd decided to go casual, look like a brother. He was wearing old corduroys and his 'It's a black thing, you wouldn't understand' T-shirt, which had been a mistake. In this setting it made him feel like Gene Wilder trying to be black. The man he was interviewing wore torn jeans, no shoes, and a hacked-off sweatshirt that said 'Newport refreshes'. Effortless authenticity.

'He didn't tell you anything? Ask for names, nothing?'

Ali looked up and stroked his chin, as if it were the first time he'd ever considered anyone's motive for beating him up. After a second he started shaking his head and didn't stop.

'All right. Just so we're sure, was this him?' Raymond handed him the photo. It was a poor reproduction of a bad likeness from Stennett's personnel file, but it was the only picture Raymond had been able to find. Both the newspaper libraries had turned up several articles but no photos. He'd known better than to ask Stennett for a picture of himself.

'Probably him. Got a better picture? Yeah, I think that's him. Mean bastard, shoulders about like this? Why you asking? Who is he? You gonna sue him?'

Raymond decided to protect Stennett's cover for the time being. 'He's a client of mine.'

Ali's face lit up. 'He got busted. Good. I hope it sticks. What'd he do, kill somebody?'

Raymond suddenly caught a whiff of something cooking in the back of the house. It wasn't food.

He asked Ali if he'd heard of the same thing happening to other people. Sure, all the time. By the same guy? Who knew? They didn't have pictures to compare. Just scars. He gave Raymond a couple of names and the interview drifted to a close. At the door Raymond suddenly turned. The question came out more harshly than he'd intended. 'You got children here while you're cooking that shit?'

Ali scowled. Darn, the meeting was ending on a note of rancor. 'What're you, my probation officer?'

'No, but I might have a talk with him.'

It was a rejoinder, that was all, a snappy comeback, but the man looked startled, and it was a poor idea to startle a paranoid meth dealer. Raymond stepped out and when the door didn't close behind him he had to make himself saunter down the front yard. He looked back with a menacing expression. Ali was gone from the doorway, so Raymond didn't have to look intimidating, he could do what he wanted, which was run. The sound of his engine starting without a problem was delightful music. Two blocks away he started laughing at himself, but his eyes were angry. That's what made him such an effective investigator, he thought, his uncanny ability to blend smoothly into every stratum of society.

But he was the Shadow compared to Darryl Kreutzer. The next time the cop appeared he had adopted a civilian outfit that worked about as well as an I Am Undercover sign. His T-shirt said 'North Texas State University', but it might as well have said 'White Boy Cop in Disguise'. 'You worked undercover with Mike Stennett?' Raymond said. 'Was he trying to get you killed?'

'Well, I only made a buy once. I was supposed to be

some college boy from the suburbs home on spring break.'

'Which is what you were, right?' Raymond wondered briefly at the source of his desire lately to annoy everyone he talked to.

But Kreutzer took it amiably. 'Not the suburbs. I'm from Kerrville.' He named a town a ninety-minute drive northwest of San Antonio, center of a farming and ranching community founded by German immigrants in the early 1800s, which accounted for Kreutzer's name and looks. Kerrville was also a quaint tourist town where big-city shoppers went looking for bargain antiques only to discover the shopkeepers knew very well the value of a quilt.

'What brought you to San Antonio?' Raymond asked. And why do I care? he added to himself. But there was something about Kreutzer that intrigued him. Big, eager, open-faced kid who seemed the antithesis of Mike Stennett. Raymond wondered how short a time Darryl had been a cop.

'Came to the academy. I've always wanted to be a police officer. And Kerrville, well, I'll probably go back there some day, but I wanted to get experience on a big-city force. I guess you can see it all here. See lots you'd never see in Kerrville, anyway.'

Like Negroes, Raymond thought. No, be fair. They'd probably had black people pass through Kerr County. Or at least seen the Platters on 'Ed Sullivan'.

Kreutzer looked a little uncomfortable at being back in Raymond's office alone. He'd get up, pace to the window, glance out. Raymond had to keep swiveling to keep up with him.

'That's why Mike was such a buddy. He kind of showed me the ropes, you know? Things you can't learn in the academy, or on patrol. I don't know why, he just picked me up for that one assignment, but then he kind of kept in touch. Used me and Steve as backups a couple of times. Just –'

'You know some of his other partners haven't been too thrilled with him,' Raymond couldn't resist saying. He wasn't in the mood to hear any more about heroic Mike Stennett. 'And seeing his current difficulties, he's not the best role model you could –'

Kreutzer turned from the window and looked at him, so penetratingly it stopped the lawyer's tongue. Under that stare Raymond felt suddenly like a traitor.

'He didn't do this,' Kreutzer said. His tone was so certain it was a rebuke to Mike Stennett's lawyer, who should believe in him.

'Right. That's why I'm defending him.' It was a subtle relief to see that Kreutzer thought Stennett innocent, that he didn't 'back Mike up a hundred percent' while believing he *had* beaten a suspect to death. 'So what can we do to help him? You find out anything about that gun?'

Kreutzer shook his head. 'I looked at it. The serial number's been filed off, so it's impossible to trace it. Somebody'd just have to remember the gun, but how could anybody? It's not an unusual gun. Only –'

'Only the person who dropped it there would know where it came from.'

'I guess so,' Kreutzer said reluctantly, still looking for possibilities.

'Okay. Well, I didn't think that'd pan out.' That was all Raymond had to say, and he didn't think Kreutzer had anything to add, but the young cop wasn't ready to leave. He did his pacing routine again. Raymond was about to start ushering him out when the kid suddenly said, 'I heard the old man's story, you know. The guy who said he saw Mike do it, what's his name?'

'Haley Burkwright?'

'Yeah. They sent Steve'n me to bring him to the station. He wanted to tell us all about it. That old guy, he doesn't know what he's talking about. I think he's just looking for attention. He probably knew who Mike was from the start. Somebody could –'

'You don't go anywhere near him,' Raymond said. 'That's just what we need, other cops harassing the State's star witness.'

'No. I won't.'

'I'm going to talk to him. His story's the key, all right.'

'But he's wrong, he's all mixed up.'

'Yeah.' The kid's faith in Stennett was touching. Also irritating. 'If your pal Mike didn't have a history of this kind of thing maybe nobody would've taken this one seriously. You know about his ... methods, don't you?'

Kreutzer just stared at him. Had trouble lying out loud. But Kreutzer obviously wasn't ready to let his character witnessing end in silence.

'I know this,' he said. 'You say Mike gets picked on because he has a rep. But let me tell you, sometimes a cop needs a rep like that. I had a suspect once, who gave me a tip about a much bigger deal going down. Trying to talk his way out of trouble, you know. I didn't know whether it was even worth following up on. I gave the guy a look, you know, like "You better not be lying to me," but who am I? Me giving a look doesn't count for anything with guys like that. But Mike happened to be handy at the time. I asked him if he thought the guy's story was worth checking out and he said, "Let me talk to him." He went into the room with the guy and when he came out he just said, "Yeah, it's a good tip." Just like that. Nothing to it.'

'And what did your suspect look like afterward?' Raymond asked.

'He looked fine. I'm not talking about roughing people up. I mean they don't lie to Mike. They know better than that.'

'And how do you think he earned this degree of professional respect?' Raymond asked, wondering if the kid would recognize irony.

Kreutzer looked a little uneasy. 'Well, you've got to back it up sometimes, that's true. But you have to, it's one of the tools you need if you're going to be an effective cop.'

'Other cops don't seem to think so. I haven't had a lot of veterans shouldering their way in here offering to be character witnesses. You think about that.' Kreutzer wanted to continue the discussion, but Raymond cut him off and sent him back out on the trail of hot leads. After he ushered the kid out Raymond felt vaguely disgusted, mostly with himself. First he came off like a cop to some poor hapless meth dealer, then to a real cop he's suddenly an ethics instructor. Who died and left you in charge of the world?

'Think any of the partners in your firm'll see you here?' Becky asked, joking.

'I hardly think so,' Donny said. 'And if I saw a client here we'd pretend we hadn't seen each other.'

It sounded like his blue suit talking. It was the prim voice Donny used to use when he was adopting a persona. Becky wondered if now the persona had adopted him. 'Let's get a drink.'

The bar wasn't the kind of vile place that would have justified Donny's reaction. In fact, it was just the kind of place where they used to spend hours when they were dating. Formica-topped tables without cloths, jammed too close together, a wooden floor with about six square feet cleared for dancing, and a three-piece band that had its amps turned up as if it were playing Yankee Stadium. There was even a certain amount of cigarette haze in the air, a nostalgic touch.

Donny steered them to a table in as quiet a corner as there was, where eventually the desultory waitress found them. Some time after they ordered she returned with four drinks. 'Happy hour,' she said.

'I thought they'd made this illegal,' Donny said of the two-for-one drinks, after the waitress had gone away.

'We're beyond the reach of the law here,' Becky said.

The place was filling up. The customers made Becky feel old. She drank her first drink quickly. Mercifully, it began at once to make her head feel lighter. She started the second. Donny had finally decided he could compete with the band. In a loud voice she could barely hear he was telling her about the case that had brought him to the courthouse today, where Becky had run into him as they were each trudging away at the end of the long day. They'd decided to make it a little longer, the kind of spur-of-the-moment decision neither of them made anymore.

At first all she saw were the legs. They were quite long, or her chair was quite low. She couldn't be sure there was a torso at the top of the legs, and she didn't bother to look up to make sure. They'd move out of her line of vision in a moment. When the legs stayed in place for several seconds she saw Donny looking up, then look at her, expectantly.

'I believe you're over the age limit for this place,' the legs said. 'I know I am.'

Becky looked up at Raymond Boudro. 'Oh,' she said. 'Don't tell me I've tracked you to your lair.'

'Yes I will, thank you,' Raymond said. He looked around, delicately lifted a purse and a jacket off a chair at an adjacent table, excused himself, and pulled the chair up to the hubcap-sized table Becky and Donny shared. He set down his drink. Both the men looked at her, and Becky made the introductions. They professed themselves pleased to meet. 'Lawyer?' Raymond asked Donny in a friendly way.

'Civil,' Becky said, and Raymond turned back to her.

'I always go straight home after work,' he said.

'Me too,' Becky agreed.

'What I really hate is hanging around with lawyers at the end of the day.'

'God, yes. Ten hours is enough.'

'And the absolute worst is sitting in some bar talking about your cases. Like you can't turn it off, like you don't have any other life.'

'That is pathetic, isn't it?'

'Have you thought about the gun?'

'Of course I've thought about the gun,' Becky said. 'It's my main piece of evidence. Except, of course, for the best eyewitness you've ever seen.'

'I'll get us another round,' Donny said politely. 'What are you having, Mr Boudro?'

'You can't trace it to him, can you?' Raymond said.

Becky grew more animated. 'I'd say a fingerprint traces it to him pretty damn well.'

'Something amber,' Donny concluded, studying the dregs in Raymond's glass, and went off in the direction of the bar.

'But you don't know where it came from,' Raymond insisted. 'If you could show him in possession of the gun some time *before* the murder, it'd make your case stronger.'

'And you know how I can do that?' Becky asked, expecting evasion.

Raymond rubbed his hands together. He looked resigned. 'No,' he said.

They sat in what passed for silence. The band was doing a Hank Williams number, though the lead singer obviously fancied himself Mick Jagger instead. 'Did I really pick a bar where you hang out?' Becky asked.

Raymond shook his head. 'I followed you here.'

'You're not just a lawyer, you're a sleuth.' Raymond heard what Becky meant to say, but in fact what she'd said was 'sweuth'.

'How many of these have you had?' he asked, picking up her second drink, which was nearly gone.

'About four too few,' she said. Raymond nodded in sympathy.

Becky watched him. She thought she understood his troubled look. She leaned close. 'This is flat off the record,' she said. 'And the answer won't change anything I do. But tell me. Did Stennett do it?'

'I wish I knew,' Raymond said. 'If I did I'd tell you.' He held her gaze. 'And if you find out for sure, will you tell me?'

She grew cagier. 'Give away my case, you mean.'

'No, that's not what I mean.'

They continued to watch each other. I'll have to ask around if he's done this before, Becky thought. Catch his opponent after hours, sidle up as if making friends. He's very likable when he wants to be, it occurred to her, a thought that should have made her wary, but didn't.

'Your client came to see me,' she said. 'He told me he and I are on the same team, so I shouldn't be out to get him the way I am. I sort of got the impression *you weren't* on the team.'

Raymond didn't respond directly. 'You have to find some way to counter me,' he said. 'When the case comes to trial. My – presence.'

'Nobody'll fall for that,' Becky said confidently. 'Jury'll see right through that.'

He leaned in closer. 'I don't mean my being black. I mean my cunning ways and sly moves in trial. Ask Frank Mendiola about Abner Moses, ask what I did to him on that one.'

This time Becky didn't let herself be goaded. She thought the defense lawyer was actually trying to tell her something – or had been trying, and then had backed off.

'You showed me yourself what Mike Stennett is,' she said. 'You had the statistical proof. I may not be able to get any of that in at trial, but you know and I know he's as dirty as they come.'

Prove it, Raymond wanted to tell her. But he didn't say it, only partly because he didn't want to give himself away. He didn't know what he did want. He didn't want the drink the pretty boy in the blue suit was bringing toward him. 'Gotta go,' he said suddenly to Becky. 'Tell your boyfriend thanks anyway.'

He's not – Becky started to say, but didn't. Watching Raymond leave, gracefully sliding between tables, she felt obscurely flattered. Donny had to put his hand atop hers to return her attention to him. Then Becky looked at the hands and thought, *Amazing. Look, almost holding my hand in a public place*. But her mind stayed on the departed Raymond.

'So that's him,' Donny said. 'Your opponent, the fabled trial lawyer. Is he really that good, or do they just say that because – '

'I think he's really that good.'

'What did he want?' Donny actually sounded interested. He pulled her hand closer.

'I'm not sure. Talk about the case. You know, this is a big case. Be a big win for him if he wins.'

'And a big loss for you,' Donny said.

'But it's almost as if he has something else in mind. As if he really wants . . .'

'Just trying to rattle you?' Donny suggested.

'Maybe.' Becky tried to stop thinking about it. It was after hours. She looked at Donny. His attention was flattering. *You see?* she wanted to tell him. *My world is more interesting than yours.* 'I'm glad I've got as solid a case as I do,' she said instead.

'Otherwise he'd be making you nervous,' Donny said ironically.

'Mmmm,' Becky acknowledged. She was looking at the door again, frowning.

'Over there's where the two orphans lived. Boy was three, girl five. It was bedtime, eight-thirty, nine. Mom'd just put 'em to bed, went to get glasses of water. Shot came through the kitchen window. Right through her throat. Knocked her down, smashed her voice box, but it didn't kill her right away. She was just bleeding to death. Went stumbling back into the kids' room. Some shock to them. Mom goes to get water, comes back gurgling blood all down her front. She was trying to tell 'em something but she couldn't talk. Couldn't hardly breathe. Maybe trying to get 'em to call an ambulance because she couldn't do it herself. Maybe just trying to tell 'em she loved 'em. Finally sat down on the floor between the two beds and died. Neighbor found the two kids the next morning, in bed together, Mom dead next to 'em.'

Raymond didn't say anything. 'There's the window,' Mike Stennett continued. 'Look, second floor. They didn't shoot her on purpose. They couldn't even see her. They were shooting at somebody else. Maybe just shooting. Drive-by. No telling if they meant to get somebody else or if they just didn't give a shit. You remember that case?'

'Vaguely,' Raymond said. Stennett nodded. The silence lasted until Raymond had enough mastery of his voice to ask, 'What happened to the kids?'

'They've got a grandmother. She's sixty-three years old. Not a lot of energy. Maybe she'll live long enough to get 'em through school, maybe they'll end up in state custody.'

'Just absolutely random,' Raymond said. 'Little girl –' Stennett was looking away, out his car window. He stopped and cleared his throat. 'Girl still wakes up crying at night. She blames herself, you see. She thinks she could've saved her mama's life if she'd done something.'

Raymond thought about Peter, about how his life would be wrenched out of shape if he were orphaned by utterly inexplicable violence. He'd have money, he'd get by, but who could explain to him why he didn't have a father anymore? He wanted to tell Stennett to step on it and speed the hell out of this east side battle zone.

Instead he said, 'They ever catch anybody?'

'No, *they* never caught anybody,' Stennett said sarcastically. '*I* had my suspicions, but not enough to make a case.'

'Did you act on your suspicions?' Raymond asked only because he wanted to hear that Stennett had, that some bastard had paid for creating two horrified orphans who would never outgrow their memories. For a moment Raymond was his own father, wanting instant pacification of his outrage.

'Yeah, right, the bodies're in the river. Cement

shoes. Over there, see that burned-out store? Junkies got careless with matches. They weren't even breakin' in, just huddling in the doorway, but the door was wood and they had a little fire going 'cause it was cold . . . Insurance probably pay for it, if the store owner'd had insurance. You know what it costs to insure one of these places in this neighborhood?'

'Yes, I do.'

Stennett looked at him for the first time in a while. 'Oh that's right, your dad's store.'

'That's right, this is my neighborhood. I don't need the tour.'

Stennett laughed. 'This was your neighborhood twenty years ago, Counselor. When's the last time you spent the night here?'

'Look, Stennett, cruising the streets and tossing back a couple in some after after-hours joint doesn't make it your neighborhood, either. You don't have any stake in what goes on here.'

Stennett didn't take up the challenge. He just drove.

'I've heard stories about you,' Raymond began. 'Been talking to different people about you. And I've heard about others who disappeared shortly after a visit from you.'

Again Stennett didn't respond. He glanced at Raymond, listening, waiting for the point of the story.

'I bet if I collected your reports I wouldn't find any of these stories. As I recall, none of 'em involved arresting anybody. Just putting the fear of God into 'em.' He used Detective Martinez's phrase. 'Or actually the fear of Mike Stennett.'

The car rolled to a stop. Raymond looked up quickly, unaware of where they were. What Denise had said hurried through his mind: What if he finds out you're the only one who knows?

But they were just parked on the sunny September street. Stennett was looking past him, making Raymond turn and look too.

'What happened here?'

'Nothing,' Stennett said. 'It's my house.'

They were in one of those pleasant little residential neighborhoods that abided in such peril on the east side. Raymond had grown up a few blocks away. The house they were looking at was as well kept as most of the others on the block: bushes trimmed, curtains drawn across the front window. There were also curtains darkening the windows of the garage door, giving the house a slightly wary look.

'What do you mean, your house?' Raymond asked brightly.

'The house where I live. The house where I grew up.'

Raymond stared as the car started rolling again. 'You grew up here?'

'And still live here. The population's not even fifty percent black, remember? My wife – ex-wife – she hated it, kept telling me we had to move. And after Tracy got old enough for school we did. Lived in the same district you do. Tracy and your boy probably go to school together.'

Raymond had never told Stennett where he lived, and didn't like hearing the cop recount details of his life. Stennett was leaning back, relaxed in his seat, steering with his wrist flopped over the wheel.

'But I kept the house. After Penny 'n me split up I kicked the tenants out and moved back in.' The houses slipped by. Raymond waited for the narrative to resume. A boy who should have been in school pedaled across the street in front of them. Stennett turned, picking up speed the length of a block, turned again.

Soon they were in a worse neighborhood, near the public housing courts. Stennett became more watchful, as if he were spotting landmarks. Raymond slouched in his seat, wondering which of their reputations would suffer more if they were seen together by someone who knew who they were.

The area was obviously a mine field of memories for Mike Stennett. When he started talking again it might have been triggered by the sight of the run-down housing unit beside them or by the man who turned his face and hurried away between two buildings. 'Man, I hated patrolling this area,' Stennett said. 'When I was a uniform? First of all you feel like you got a big red bulls-eye painted on your forehead. And the hostility just gets to you. The ones that don't hate you are afraid of you. Even the ones who like seeing you around 're too scared to be friendly.

'You go on a call, domestic violence, you show up in your blue suit that makes you look like the man from Mars, and by the time you get there she's sorry she called the cops, she says nothing's happened. There's a baby crying, another kid looking scared, and maybe food stain on the wall and a broken plate in the trash. Guy looks like he's gonna jump on you if you look at him crooked. And you look around and you just know you're at the scene of a future crime. You don't know how bad it'll be, but odds are some day soon there'll be detectives here taking samples and paramedics carrying out a body.'

'Did you worry about it when you went home at night?'

'You don't have to *worry* about it. It's a certainty. It happens every night, somewhere. Man, I was glad to get out of that uniform.'

'How did that help?' Raymond asked. He was

touring not just the east side but Stennett's mind. He let him talk about whatever he wanted.

'I felt like part of it again, I didn't feel like some goddamn soldier in an occupation force. Folks could talk to me even if they knew who I was, 'cause I wasn't in that damned uniform.'

And it gave you the opportunity to work off some of those frustrations, Raymond thought. Stennett wasn't dumb, he knew just what his lawyer was thinking.

'It would've driven me crazy,' he said. 'Knowing something like what happened to that lady with the two orphan kids and knowing who did it and not being able to do anything about it but go around in a uniform and ask their relatives dumbass questions. "Do you remember where Dennis was that night, ma'am? Home, you say? Let me make a note of that." Sometimes, you know, you know something. You don't know it good enough for a warrant or a court, but you *know*. Any things like that you know?'

'So you'd do something about it?' Raymond asked. It was his earlier question, now with some hope of an answer.

'I never killed anybody. But sometimes if you squeeze a little you'll get a name. Or something. You know what it's like to know somebody's hurting somebody else, over and over, every day, hurting the whole community, and know you'll never get a witness to it? Sometimes you can have a little talk with somebody like that and he'll remember he's got relatives he always liked in Cincinnati. Some of those ones you said "disappeared" after I saw 'em? You go back and ask if anybody missed 'em afterwards. Ask if anybody was real torn up to see 'em go.' He looked at Raymond for just a second. 'Ask your father if he'd approve.'

'And that's what happened to Gordon Frazier?' Raymond asked it quickly, while Stennett remained on his talking jag. He'd already justified his pattern, he could admit to one example.

'No.'

'I'm not saying it was on purpose, but if he fought back, you had to defend yourself and he fell on something . . .?'

'No,' Stennett said adamantly. 'I barely knew Frazier, I had nothing against him. He wasn't somebody I heard of very much. From what I know he wasn't important enough to anybody to kill him.'

He was important to me, Raymond thought, but the thought had no edge. It was hollow, even in his own mind.

They glided down the street, not talking much, each of them holding back, knowing what they knew but not knowing enough. Touring the rot of their old neighborhood. The quiet blocks stood like memory, whole and untouched in places, blasted or faded away in others. The silence was almost companionable.

'Who wants to know?' the woman said, folding her arms and making no move to let him in.

'Lady, I already do know,' Raymond said wearily. 'It's taken me weeks to find you, through a lot of people who don't give a damn, and I was hoping maybe you do.'

Nothing in the woman's posture or expression responded. Her name was Kathy Pease. Raymond knew she was about thirty-five, though in appearance she could have been as much as ten years older. He could see she'd been pretty, though; still was, behind the frown. When Raymond was young there'd seemed something untouchable about girls like this. He was still surprised occasionally to find prettiness was no protection from life.

Kathy Pease had the distinction of being Gordon Frazier's last girlfriend. Without knowing she existed Raymond had tracked her through the leavings of Gordie's life: dead mother, father a lifelong unknown, Gordie's only acknowledged sibling a sister who didn't seem to care that her brother was dead. He'd found guys Frazier had hung with for twenty years who didn't even seem to realize Gordie was no longer among them. Finally from a parole officer he'd gotten Kathy Pease's phone number and her address, the one Frazier had given as his own; not the address on his driver's license, the one listed on the police report of his death.

Kathy Pease had had time to memorize the business card Raymond had handed her. It didn't lighten her attitude. 'I'm representing a police officer named Stennett,' he began.

'Yippee for you. I got nothing to do with cops.' *Or their black lawyers*, one could complete the sentence from her face.

'I want to ask about Gordie.'

'Ask what? About what a bum he was, how he was a junkie, how he stole from his own mama 'til she died, what a worthless life he had, how it don't really matter to anybody that he's dead?' She glared at him, defiantly, making his case for him but hating him for it. She knew what the lawyer for a murder defendant would want to know about the victim.

'Is that why you let him live with you?' Raymond asked quietly.

He made no move to push his way into the apartment. He just stood there with his hands folded in front of him, a stone block of patience, as if he'd keep standing there if she closed the door in his face and still be standing there an hour or a day later when she opened it again. Kathy Pease turned abruptly away and crossed the room, leaving Raymond to close the door after he came in.

He took in the room in a glance. It looked as if it had started life as storage space, then been halfheartedly turned into living quarters. A large front room was living room, dining room, and an open kitchen in the corner. Wooden floor, wallpapered walls peeling at all the edges. The main impression of the apartment was odor. It was over a restaurant, and smelled as if someone were cooking garbage. It must have been unbearable later in the summer day, and Raymond saw no sign of air-conditioning. There was a fan going, sitting alone on the floor, turning to sweep the room. When its breath hit his face for a moment he realized it was no favor to the inhabitants to have the air in this place stirred up.

He followed Kathy Pease to the living area. She dropped to the couch beside a still-smoking cigarette. Raymond sat gingerly on the edge of a metal folding chair.

'Have you ever heard of Mike Stennett?' he asked.

She gave him a sarcastic look. 'No.'

'Gordon never mentioned him, having a run-in with him?'

'No' again.

'How long did you know Gordon?' Raymond had to keep himself from saying Gordie.

She shook her head like that one was too tough for her. Instead she said, 'He lived here the last six months or so.'

'Do you know' – Raymond was trying to put this delicately, to remain on the fringe of her tolerance – 'who he associated with, what he was doing?'

Kathy Pease started crying. Not bawling, nothing

showy about it. She pressed her lips together while tears welled out of her eyes and ran down her cheeks. Through them she kept glaring at Raymond, hating him for seeing her care. She didn't speak until she thought she had her voice under firm control, but it still skittered on her.

'If you found me you must've talked to lots of other people,' she began, 'and I know just what they told you. They told you Gordie was forty years old –'

'Thirty-nine,' Raymond said, but she didn't hear.

'– and never done a day's work. That he wouldn't know how to work if he wanted to, that he wasn't good for nothing but hustling anybody that gave a shit about him for two minutes, that he didn't care about nothing but putting something in his arm or up his nose.

'Let me tell you, though.' Her voice was rising. Raymond didn't think she knew it, or that she was leaning forward pointing at him. 'Before I let Gordie move in here I saw he hadn't been high for two months. I told him, "I'll let you stay here, but if you ever once come around me carrying something I won't just kick you out, I'll put a gun in your ear and pull the trigger." I wouldn't have that –'

She cut off that thought, but started another. She was still glaring at Raymond as if he were arguing with her. 'And he did it, mister. Let me tell you the most amazing thing you've heard this year. You smell that restaurant down there? Well, Gordie was working there. That's right, a job. Gordie Frazier had a job. The worst kind of job, too, washing dishes and sweeping up and cleaning tables. But he stuck with it. He'd been there three months. They were talking about making him a waiter, and you would've thought it was president of IBM they were going to make him, from the way Gordie talked about it. He got a *Social Security*

Card. Thirty-nine years old, first one in his life. And I mean a real one, I don't mean he bought one off some guy. He was coming back, Mr Lawyer. Gordie Frazier was on the way back. You tell that to some damn jury.'

She made Raymond so sad he wanted to run out. Gordie sweeping floors and busing tables, the kind of job you had when you were a teenager. But Gordie'd been king of the world when he was a teenager. He'd had to start over twenty years later, start trying to have a life. Raymond had clients like Gordie, he knew the impossible triumph of holding a real job for even a month.

Kathy Pease said it, she didn't just let it hang unspoken between them. 'And you gonna get off the man that killed him,' she said.

Raymond just shook his head. 'Gordie hadn't been in any trouble at all lately?' he asked.

Unexpectedly, she laughed. 'You know what he said? He said he couldn't go back if he wanted. Told me one day he was hanging on some corner – he swore he was just talking to the dudes, and I believed him, or his ass would've been in the street. Well, I half believed him. I knew Gordie backslid once in a while, but as long as he didn't bring it around me and kept trying I'd let it pass. Anyway, this time was probably good for him, 'cause he said he was there on the corner when some cop car pulled up and some honky cop threw down on all of 'em. Gordie laughed about it. Said, "Picture that, somebody sellin' dope right next to me, and we all so dumb we don't even see a squad car parked around the corner."'

'Squad car?' Raymond asked, startled. The story was secondhand, and obviously wrong. Mike Stennett certainly wouldn't have been in any squad car.

But she nodded. 'Scared the pee out of Gordie, too,

I tell you. He couldn't get arrested. He was on parole. He knew if he went back to the joint I wouldn't be here waiting for him when he got out.'

'What happened?'

'Said he talked his way out of it. Ran, more likely, I figure. Gordie could talk, nobody knows that better than me, but can't nobody talk the man out of it when he's making busts.'

'When did this happen?' Raymond asked. He was surprised. He'd just come for background information, really just to satisfy his own curiosity about Gordie. He hadn't expected to uncover evidence.

'Few days before he was killed,' Kathy said.

'And you don't know who it was almost arrested him?'

She shrugged. 'Gordie didn't say names.'

The end of the story imposed silence on them. Kathy Pease was winding down into depression. She fought it off with anger. 'You really working for the son of a bitch that did Gordie?'

'I just want to find out what happened,' Raymond said.

She looked at him, still sullen, debating. She had something else. Raymond thought it better to wait than to ask for it. Kathy looked no less angry when she suddenly stood up and said, 'Come here.'

Raymond followed her, surprised, growing wary, as she strode out of the room, down a short hall at the back, and into a tiny bedroom. Raymond was even more startled to see there was a child there. He hadn't heard her make a sound all the time he'd been in the apartment. The little girl was probably four years old, he didn't think as old as five. She just wore panties and a shirt. There were toys scattered around the room, books, even a television, but the child wasn't playing with anything. She sat on a cushion against one wall, rocking herself. When the adults entered she turned away, hiding her face.

The tears were welling from Kathy Pease's eyes again. 'Debby? Honey? Don't you want to come out front with me? We got company. Honey?'

The little girl didn't make a sound or a move. Raymond felt a tingle of the skin along his spine. The little girl looked like some creature he'd almost stepped on in the forest. She kept her face covered, desperate for solitude.

'You want something to drink, honey?' Kathy Pease was saying. She had knelt, to put herself on the child's level, but it didn't help. Debby pushed herself along the baseboard, away.

Raymond felt intrusive. He was backing out of the room. Kathy Pease looked back over her shoulder at him. 'No. Look. Look at her. This is what your client did.'

Raymond stared at the child, horrified. He had never heard of Stennett abusing children. Whatever else he'd heard, not that. Kathy joined him in the doorway. The child peeked at them then hurriedly turned away again.

'I kicked her father out when she was two years old,' Kathy said stonily, reciting a case history, 'when I caught him touching her. I don't know how long it'd gone on. But she was always scared of men after that. Hung on my leg if there was one even in the building with her.

'When Gordie and I started up I had to meet him other places while my mother stayed with Debby. But Gordie kept wanting to see her, wanting to come home with me. I finally let him, thinking I'd prove to him it wouldn't work.

'You wouldn't've believed him.' She spoke as if aware that Raymond had known Gordon Frazier. 'Gordie Frazier, worthless junkie. You'd've thought he was a child psychologist. He didn't go near her at first, didn't try to get close to her. But he kept coming 'round, and he'd bring things. Not big things, you know. But a book or something. And he'd sit over in the far corner reading it to himself, out loud. Laughing over the pictures. When he seen Debby was creeping closer he'd turn the book so she could see it. At first she'd run back to me, or out of the room. I thought Gordie'd give up. Who'd think *he'd* have patience? I didn't have it, not enough. But Gordie kept on. If it wasn't a book it was a toy that moved or something.

'It was like charming a squirrel. She finally got to where she'd run up and snatch it out of his hand if he held it out far enough. But then she had to bring it back for him to read the book or start the toy.

'This went on for three months. Months! And one day I come home and Gordie's here alone with her, which almost made me scream, but she's just sitting on his lap, happy as a clam, reading about Grover or some damn character.'

She stopped speaking for a moment. Raymond was watching the child under discussion. It was impossible to tell if Debby knew she was being talked about. She just kept scooting along the floor until she was in a corner.

'That's when I let Gordie move in,' Kathy Pease said when she'd recovered herself. 'How could I help it? He said that's how he got to me, and it damn sure was. She loved him better than she did me. And Gordie, it was like the first time in his life he realized he could do something worthwhile. Like nobody'd ever needed him like that child did.

'And now look at her. How'm I supposed to tell her it's okay, to let anybody else close to her ever again? Tell me what to –'

Kathy's resolve gave out, she sobbed and ran out of the room. Raymond lingered only for a moment, wanting to hold the girl, comfort her, but realizing he'd only do more harm by drawing close to her. He didn't have Gordon Frazier's patience, or time to devote to the task.

He returned to the living room feeling hopelessly out of place and inadequate. Kathy Pease had resumed her original posture, standing straight, arms folded, but now the stance was obviously defensive rather than hostile. She looked as if she were trying to hold her insides in.

Raymond had the background he'd come for, but he wasn't the one who could use it. 'Has anyone from the District Attorney's office called you?' he asked.

Kathy Pease shook her head.

'Have you tried to call them?' he asked. She just gave him a look. 'You should,' he said. She rolled her eyes.

A minute or two later he was in the hall outside the closed apartment door, wondering who he could call, what he should do next. He leaned his forehead against the wall and closed his eyes.

'God damn you,' he said aloud.

CHAPTER 10

It was Jean who took the call. Raymond wished the caller had known his direct line. 'What did he say?' he asked again.

'He asked to talk to you,' Jean said patiently. She was holding the pad on which she'd alertly made notes.

'By name?'

She shook her head. 'He asked to talk to the lawyer. When I asked if I could say who was calling he didn't answer, as if he hadn't expected that. I thought he had hung up. Then he said, "Tell Stennett to remember when he arrested Patrick Casey".' She was reading from her notes. 'I asked him to repeat the name and he did. Patrick Casey. And he mentioned arrest again. Then he asked, "Got it?" and when I said yes he hung up.'

'Definitely a man's voice?'

'Oh yes. Very deep. He was making it deeper, but it wasn't a woman.'

'No idea who?' Raymond asked helplessly. 'Was it a black voice?'

Jean looked at him reprovingly. 'You can't always tell, you know.'

Raymond tried to think of a better question.

'I'm sorry,' Jean said. 'He was speaking very softly and distorting his voice. I don't know if I've ever heard him before.'

'Not your fault,' Raymond said. 'But try to hold it in mind. What I want to know is, could it have been Stennett himself?'

She thought about it and shrugged. 'I haven't heard him enough.'

Stennett appeared late that afternoon in response to the call from Jean. He dropped a form on Raymond's desk. 'I arrested somebody named Patrick Casey, all right. A year ago. Stupid case. He was waving a gun around in a coffee shop. Not a robbery, just a crazoid. I should've let the uniforms make the bust, but I thought I had a better chance of takin' him down without anybody getting hurt.'

'Serpico in action again,' Raymond said. 'What did you do, talk him into repenting?'

'More like knocked him down and sat on him. I think he got a class C misdemeanor out of it.'

'And the gun?'

Stennett nodded, pointed to a line on the arrest report. 'Thirty-eight automatic. Right brand and make. It didn't have a serial number.'

'Just like the one lying beside Gordon Frazier.'

'Yeah.'

'What did you do with it?'

'I confiscated it, of course,' Stennett said. 'And then I turned it in to be destroyed.'

'But it didn't get destroyed.'

Stennett shrugged.

'Are you sure you didn't keep it for a throw-down?' Raymond asked. He didn't expect much of an answer. He just wanted to keep Stennett talking. Jean was sitting beside him making notes of the conversation, something she hadn't done before, but Stennett had barely glanced at her.

'If I had I wouldn't've mentioned the gun in my report, now would I have?' Stennett said logically. 'This only happened a year ago; believe me, I already had my share of back up pieces.'

'Who handles it after you turn it in?'

'All kinds of people,' Stennett said. 'It stays in the property room until the court case is disposed of. Then the assistant D.A. gets an order from the judge to have it destroyed, unless some D.A.'s investigator wants it instead. The order goes back to some evidence tech to do the destroying. Guns fall through the cracks every step of the way. Cop could get it, prosecutor. I've even heard of a judge ending up with one. Or the defense lawyer collects it for part of his fee.'

That narrowed the suspects down to the list they already had: everyone in North America. Raymond asked, 'And who do you think made the call putting us on to it?'

'Could've been just about anybody, couldn't it? Maybe Montoya or Kreutzer found out but didn't want to finger the one they found out from. Or they asked around and stirred up somebody's memory –'

'And he wanted to do you a favor.'

'By letting you know I had access to a gun like the one with my fingerprint on it that ended up next to the dead victim? That hurts more than it helps, doesn't it?'

'Everybody already knew you had access to it from the fingerprint. This opens up the possibilities to include a lot more suspects. The guy who called wouldn't've called your defense lawyer if he meant to hurt you. He would've called the D.A.'

True, Stennett acknowledged with a shrug. 'Could've been just about anybody, couldn't it?'

Raymond looked at Jean, who had dropped her pose of note taking and was just sitting there listening to Stennett's voice. When she saw Raymond looking at her she gave the same sort of shrug, in miniature.

Who knows? her eyes said.

★

The first cool front of the season usually hits San Antonio the very end of September. Not one of the blue northers that will come later, sweeping the sky clean and turning skin icy between one minute and the next; this is just a cool front, finally blowing away the summer that's oppressed everyone for five months. The temperature drops below seventy for the first time since April. Usually a blustering wind will accompany the front. The world is still green. The first leaves don't fall from the trees; they're ripped.

Lifelong residents exaggerate the effect of this first coolness at the same time they welcome it. 'You picked a hell of a night to play James Bond,' Denise said, turning up his collar for him.

'Cadillac might've heard something,' Raymond said. 'He's the one guy I trust who might be able to find out.'

'What with being a criminal and all,' Denise said.

The front was a few days early this year. Raymond had dressed comfortably this time, not thinking much about what he put on: jeans, tennis shoes, sweatshirt, comfortable old jacket. He kept an eye on the rearview mirror as he drove, even turned out of his way once, pulled into a driveway, and went back the way he'd come. Denise would have laughed, and he did feel silly, but he owed his old friend some care.

He circled the big parking lot when he got there. Two or three other cars were scattered around. They could have been sitting there broken down for two weeks. He didn't see any people. Even dogs had slunk under houses to escape the wind.

Raymond parked in the shadows cast by the stands that reared above him. He left his collar turned up, as much to cover his face as to protect it. He felt singularly alone. It was a Tuesday night. In three days those stands would be packed with fans, but tonight the wind whistled through the iron framework. Ten people could have been hiding in that darkness, behind girders, but Raymond felt the tingling distinction of being the only visible person in a silent arena. He passed the ticket booths, stepped over the chain that guarded the entrance, and entered the deeper darkness under the stands, where the concession booths stood shrouded.

Cadillac did him a favor, he stepped out of hiding while Raymond was still fifteen feet away, didn't try to be funny, just waved and let Raymond approach. They clasped hands at shoulder height like arm wrestlers. Raymond wondered if African-American men still did that or if Cadillac just staged it for him to let him think he was still in. He also gave the obligatory greeting. 'How ya doin', man?'

'Good,' Raymond said, 'good. You?'

'Cain't beat it.' Cadillac Pierce – Raymond couldn't even remember his real first name, this many years later – was three or four inches shorter than Raymond, still wiry, full of nervous energy. His head kept bobbing, his hands went in and out of his pockets. He smoked, of course.

'Didn't see you at the reunion last year,' Raymond said, breaking the ice. It had been more like three years since he'd seen Cadillac, though he'd heard of him occasionally.

The shorter man smiled ironically. 'Don't seem like twenty years to me, man. I must spend half my life hangin' around this place or the old corners or the school. I didn't need no event to memorialize it for me. 'Course I would've gone too if I was a big-time stud lawyer.'

Cadillac had been one of Raymond's first court triumphs. Pierce had come to him already on probation and with a new case hanging over him, when Raymond was a new young lawyer and Cadillac was already old in the life. His previous lawyer had retired, so Cadillac had given Raymond a shot on the strength of their shared past as high school football teammates. It was the first case Raymond won, on a motion to suppress; Cadillac had thought he was a wizard ever since. He'd picked up two more cases, both drug related, in the years since then, but had had the good sense to pick them up within a few months of each other so they could be plea-bargained together and he'd only gone away for a year or two. If prison hadn't rehabilitated him it had wised him up. He hadn't been caught at anything since, as far as Raymond had heard.

'So you picked this place for our own little reunion,' Raymond said. 'I'm touched. I didn't know you were nostalgic.'

Cadillac gave the same slightly pained smile. 'Had a meeting with somebody else here while ago. Thought I'd just consolidate.'

Raymond felt briefly chilled by realization that touched him more coldly than the wind had. Cadillac must have been meeting some kid football player. Still making a living from his contacts with the sport that had brought the two of them together. Raymond liked Cadillac. He'd always enjoyed running into him again and talking as if they were both outlaws putting over another scheme. He knew he lived vicariously, through his old wide receiver, the life he could have had. But Raymond had grown up. More important, he had a son approaching his teen years. He realized how scared he'd be to learn that Peter had met someone like Cadillac, a grown man hanging around schoolyards and football stadiums making new young friends.

He became a little more business like. Cadillac had heard, of course, that he was representing Mike Stennett. He asked how it was going, in a neutral tone that made Raymond defensive. 'It's goin' too swell,' he said angrily. 'I ain't puttin' no racist cop back on the streets to kill more people. Not if he's guilty. But I still don't know. You know how it is, man, nobody knows nothin'. That's when I thought of you.'

Cadillac could ask around. He could get answers more freely than Raymond. Stennett had denied even knowing Gordon Frazier, beyond his bare identity. Raymond wanted to know if that was true. Anyone ever seen them together, did any of Frazier's friends know of some more intimate link between the victim and the cop?

Raymond didn't have to spell it out. Cadillac was nodding in a sentence or two. Smoke trailed away horizontally from the cigarette in the corner of his mouth, the smoke first a thick cloud then more and more ghostlike into the recesses of the stadium.

'And somebody who knows tells me and I tell you and then what happens?' Cadillac asked. 'You make him plead guilty? Or just get off his case?'

'No. I'm on his case to the end. I just want to know what the end should be. What a jury says doesn't mean shit to me, not on this one. I have to know. When I do – I'll work that out, don't worry.'

'Not my worry. What d' I care?'

Raymond looked as closely at his old teammate as he could in the dim light. Cadillac's eyes looked a little glazed, but that could have been from weariness. Smoke made the sides of his head look gray. In the shadows he could have been the wizened old man he would become, if he lived that long.

What a life, hanging around school kids, dealing

with murderers and thieves on one end and hustling like a salesman on the other. Cadillac's squinting eyes had given up any hope of the big score years ago, and there was no pension he was working toward. If he got out now, found a real world job, he could still put in twenty or twenty-five years at it. They were still young. Raymond was afraid of sounding like some dorky social worker, but he asked it anyway:

'Don't you ever get tired of this life, man?'

Cadillac looked surprised. For a moment he was surprised into honesty. He looked away as he said, 'Some mornings I wake up and I think, "It'd be better t' be blown away today than t' do this shit again." Man, I am tired to *death*.' Then the mask was back on. He looked at Raymond with a bright, false grin, the painted alertness of a ventriloquist's dummy. 'Think I go be a stockbroker instead. Yeah, that's it. I think I go apply t' Merrill Lynch tomorrow.'

Raymond tried to look equally disillusioned, like they were both in the same fix. But his question had ruined the casual, intimate tone of the interview. Cadillac grew brusque. Busy man. Raymond managed to say he'd pay for information without sounding insulting. 'I do what I can for you, man,' Cadillac said. He looked at his watch, a bulky item on his thin wrist. 'Gotta be somewhere.'

'Right.' Raymond watched him walking away, briskly, glancing from side to side as if an importuning crowd would have delayed him with more requests. Raymond followed more slowly, rolling his shoulders to unbunch them. If this didn't work he had nothing left but trial and its unreliable result. The State had a good case. At the beginning of his involvement Raymond would have said it would be better, if his doubts went unresolved, for Stennett to be convicted. Now he had doubts on top of doubts. If Stennett wasn't guilty he was some kind of skulking hero, like Raymond's father thought, maybe stepping over the line but doing it because he had to, doing more good for the east side than all the rest of the police force, approved of by the best people in the community. But if he was guilty he was a murderer. Society might tolerate that but Raymond couldn't. He had to know the truth. This was the first time he was unwilling just to take his shot in court and let what happened happen.

Cadillac was long out of sight. Raymond began following him out. The wind had died down for the moment, leaving a booming silence under the stands. Silent echoes waited to fill the hollowness at the first sound. He could hear his quiet steps coming back to him from the darkness. He stopped, and the steps continued for a moment. Raymond hurried forward and the sounds grew hurried too. There was a sound that might have been a rat gnawing or a twig hitting a wooden bench, but it wasn't. It was an artificial sound, a human sound, maybe a plastic button snagging momentarily on a girder, with a tiny click.

Still walking, Raymond glanced to his right then abruptly ran to his left. He was at full speed in a couple of steps, back under the stands. Sounds grew to full volume in his ears: the scrape of his soles on the gritty asphalt, breath coming harshly, the ragged scrambling sounds of men in full flight. Raymond got a glimpse, dodged a beam, caught up, and slammed full force into his pursuer, mashing him back against a girder.

'You son of a bitch,' he said.

Stennett held up a hand to block the punch that seemed to be coming. Raymond released him instead, pushing back away from him. 'What're you doing following me?' he said.

That was obvious. Stennett knew Raymond was investigating, using his contacts to try to get a lead in the case. Stennett wanted to know who those contacts were. He was still a cop, still chasing suspects, and not above using his own lawyer to ferret them out.

Stennett almost confirmed it. 'Who was that you were talkin' to?' he asked. 'Some dealer?'

'None o' your fuckin' business,' Raymond said. He was disgusted with the whole case. What did he do now? Beat up his client? Withdraw?

'Who you selling me out to?' Stennett asked.

Raymond's brief sense of resignation evaporated. 'Selling? What d' you think you're worth to anybody? Who the hell could I sell you to?'

Stennett was glaring at him as if he were the aggrieved party. 'Lot of people like to see me get convicted. You know some of 'em.'

Raymond almost laughed. 'There you go again,' he said. 'The big conspiracy. Here's the shocking news, Stennett. You overestimate your importance in everyone's lives.'

Raymond turned away. Stennett took his sleeve and tugged it just enough to change his direction. They walked side by side, not out from under the stands but back among the concession booths. Raymond didn't have the interest to ask where they were going. They turned into one of the tunnels rising into the stadium itself. At the end of it they were blocked by a chain link fence with a gate and a padlock. Raymond looked out at the empty football field lit by starlight. Stennett took a thick ring bristling with keys from his pocket and unlocked the padlock. Raymond looked at him in surprise.

'We burglarizing the place?'

Stennett showed him the key ring. 'I'm the security guard.'

'What?'

'I gotta eat, don't I?' Stennett was inside the gate, looking back at him. Raymond followed him. Stennett was heading toward some steps leading down to the field.

The empty stands rose all around them, lifting Raymond's gaze. There was not a soul in the seats. It was eerie to be a solitary human in a place built to hold tens of thousands. The place was designed for crushed, roaring crowds, not for emptiness. Even empty, the stadium retained its grandeur, its public character. The silence seemed to expect something of Raymond. This was a showcase for spectacle. Moonlight populated the stands with the ghosts of the millions who'd sat here over the last fifty years. They sat silent, waiting.

Stennett seemed unaffected by the size and silence of the stadium. He walked down the concrete steps as if they were the driveway of his home. Raymond followed him, down the steps and out onto the field. Here the sideline benches held other ghosts. Stennett looked at him quizzically when Raymond laughed.

'This is funny, you bringing me here,' Raymond explained. 'I used to play here.'

'Tell me about it,' Stennett said. 'We could've been city champs your senior year, you weren't such a fuckup.'

Raymond stared. 'That's rich. What do you mean "we", paleface?'

'I mean we. My school.'

'You went to Sam Houston.' Raymond should have realized they were former classmates when Stennett had shown him his house, but somehow he hadn't grasped that. He had assumed Stennett had gone to private school, like so many of the white kids in the neighborhood. Raymond didn't remember him.

'Two years behind you,' Stennett said. He pointed up into the stands behind Raymond. 'I was sitting right there for the big game.'

'How come you weren't down here?' Raymond had stepped out onto the field. The grass was slightly damp. He pivoted in his tennis shoes, turning back to Stennett as if he'd just taken the snap from center and was handing off. Silly how long these memories of reflexes still lived in a body that hadn't needed them for half its lifetime.

'You wouldn't believe this, but I was a scrawny little thing in high school,' Stennett said. 'On the day in question I probably weighed a hundred and twenty-three pounds. And I was slow. I didn't quite see where I'd fit in on a team full of black weight lifters who were all taller than my father.'

Raymond barely listened. He was looking downfield. He hadn't stood on this field in twenty years. He wasn't one to come back for homecoming games and wave to the crowd and watch kids who had taken his place compete for the same honors. Raymond had put all this behind him the second his senior season ended. How pitiful to keep reliving it as if life had peaked at seventeen. But standing here now he couldn't help feeling it again, the triumph of just walking onto the field. Every eye had been on him and he'd known it. He had been the biggest thing you could be in a Texas high school. He'd been the quarterback.

'I couldn't talk for three days after that game,' Stennett said. 'And my knees were sore from jumping up and down on that damn concrete. We took more punishment in the stands than you guys did on the field.'

Neither of them had to say which game Stennett was talking about. There had only been one big game. Raymond's senior year his high school had won district, then bi-district. In the second round of the play-offs they'd faced Robert E. Lee, a north side power-house. Everyone was certain the winner would go on to the state finals.

'We scored on every possession,' Raymond said. He felt silly saying it, but not as silly as he'd felt a minute ago. He was slipping back.

'And so did they,' he heard Stennett say faintly. 'Real defensive struggle.'

But all Lee's scores had been touchdowns and two of Sam Houston's had been field goals, so Raymond's team had trailed by one when Raymond went out for the last time with a minute twenty-eight left. He'd fumbled the first snap and stood there frozen, thinking it was all over. But his fullback had recovered. On the next play Raymond had hit Cadillac on a quick slant that was good for fifteen to their own forty-three but had used up their last time-out. They stalled out there for three plays, a run and two incomplete passes. On fourth and eight Raymond had dropped back, unable to hear anything, vision obscured by reaching hands, and gotten one tiny glimpse of his star receiver, Jerry Sloan, apparently alone at the left sideline. Raymond had leaped, the only jump pass of his career, and thrown a clothesline at Jerry, who grabbed it for his sixtieth reception of the season, saw a tackler coming, sidestepped him because he had a clear line up the sideline, and then gotten blindsided and went down still in bounds with eighteen seconds left. Raymond had hustled them up without a huddle and thrown an incomplete pass to stop the clock. And there they were, far outside their kicker's range, almost fifty yards away from scoring and with time left for one play.

'Ah, shit, who cares?' Raymond said, eyes roving down the empty field.

'About fifty-three thousand people up there cared,' Stennett said. 'Did you notice how quiet it got there at the end?'

No, he hadn't noticed. They didn't matter, those people in the stands. They didn't exist. The world was composed of only this green rectangle and twenty-two boys, ten of them on your side and eleven of them hating your guts, and glory and horror encasing the field like a tight, opaque dome, out of which the air was quickly leaking.

But as soon as he'd stepped back from center it had all come alive. Raymond had rolled right, spreading the defense and his own team. It was amazing how much room there was, how little of the field the twenty-two players took up. He could see for miles. And in that second a six-foot-four tackle who should have already been playing in college had reared up in front of him. Raymond had ducked and scrambled, eluding him for the moment. But when he looked back downfield it had all unraveled, there was no order at all, his players were lost in tangles of Lee players and others were converging on Raymond.

And Jerry Sloan was alone in the end zone, jumping up and down.

Jerry had pointed to the opposite corner and run toward it, the defender belatedly finding him but far too many steps behind to catch Jerry. Raymond had cocked his arm, reared back – and stopped.

'Why didn't you throw it?' Stennett asked. 'He was wide open. It was six easy.'

'You didn't know Jerry,' Raymond said, twenty years after the fact. 'He had great instinct, the best. If you hit him on a buttonhook, just as he turned in, the ball'd stick to his hands before he even knew it was there. But when he went long and was all clear, like on that play, when he had time to think about it, he was a lot bigger risk. He'd try to catch it while it was ten yards in the air, he'd jump too soon, he'd trip. That's just what he'd done on the series before.'

'Well, maybe,' Stennett said skeptically. 'But it sure looked . . .'

Raymond had tucked the ball and taken off. He dodged the initial crush of tacklers and the field looked clear. He angled for the sideline, because he had five seconds left. He was already at the thirty, in sight of the goal line, maybe in field goal range, when the first tackler caught him. Standing on the field twenty years later Raymond could feel that last run. The tackler was down around his ankles. Raymond stepped over him, pulled one leg free, then the other. But the pack had caught up by then. He was only five yards from the sideline, he could reach it in the few seconds left. Hands clutched at him. He saw one pale face inside a helmet, teeth gritted like the world would end if he lost his grip. Raymond stiff-armed him. He had a death grip on the ball. It was death that was in the air, for all of them. He struggled as if life lay just beyond that sideline. The tacklers moaned and cried as if they'd turn into dust if he crossed it. Three of them had his legs. Raymond remembered the last massive effort to rip free, and he had, but he was going down. He saw his hand outstretched, holding the ball, seeing it hit the turf a foot inbounds.

'You could run, but you were a hell of a passer,' Stennett said. 'You should've thrown. At the end you didn't do what you did best because you didn't trust anyone else.'

Raymond turned his back on the field. 'Easy to say from the stands,' he said. 'You know what Jerry Sloan said to me afterward? He thanked me. He said, 'Thank God it didn't come down to me at the end.'

It took only a moment of quiet for the past to recede from them so they felt silly talking about it. Bringing them forward, Stennett asked indifferently, 'That game kept you from playing college ball?'

'I played, enough to keep my scholarship. But I wasn't big enough to turn pro, so what was the point?' In fact, he'd made up his mind before that last high school game. That game had been for all the glory, but glory wasn't worth anything. He could've crushed Lee that night, and the white boys would have picked themselves up and gone back to their nice white suburb and taken their college entrance exams and started the careers that would keep them rich. And black boys like Raymond would whoop their triumph and drink and dance their victory party and go cheerfully on their way to becoming janitors and gas station attendants, working for the white boys.

That's what had sent Raymond to law school. He arrived there four years later feeling he'd found his true vocation, only to discover the school filled with those same white boys and girls who ended up in law school only because Daddy still had some money left when they'd finished college. But the field was level from then on. Raymond had as good a shot at winning as anyone, and when he did it mattered.

Stennett was still mulling over being helpless in the stands. Probably remembering half the stadium erupting as time ran out, while the other half fell into sullen dejection. In a strange way his thoughts mirrored Raymond's.

'White people suck,' Stennett said.

Raymond was startled into laughter. 'I hate to be the one to break this to you . . .'

'Yeah, I know. But being white and poor is like being rich and black. Don't do you no good to belong to the club if nobody'll dance with you.'

Raymond couldn't let him get by with that. 'Poor white boy still has an advantage.'

'That's true,' Stennett said musingly. 'I might could make some money, but you'll always be a nigger.'

Raymond lashed out. His fist was in the air before he had time to think whether this was the proper response. His racial reflexes had sharpened in the past few weeks. It was a short punch and not very accurate, catching Stennett in the temple. Good way to break a knuckle. Raymond shook his hand to free it of the pain, but at the same time readied the left.

One of the many insulting things about being called a nigger is that it reduces a person to that one aspect. You are no longer complex, you are no longer unique, you're just one indistinguishable head of cattle. Using it between members of the same race may be a matter of camaraderie, emphasizing that in spite of their differences they have that one essential in common. In the mouth of someone like Stennett, though, it meant the opposite: no matter what we have in common, we will never be anything but adversaries.

Maybe Stennett hadn't meant it that way. He looked stunned by the punch. He still hadn't raised his hands. Still, Raymond was prepared to hit him again, and probably would have, if not for the tuft of grass a few feet away. The tuft of grass chose that moment to leap into the air. It seemed a long moment later before they heard the crack of the shot.

Raymond stood there, still puzzled over what had animated the grass. Stennett yelped something, pushed Raymond hard, turning him, then ran in the opposite direction. Raymond was running as well, propelled at first by Stennett's push, then by his own legs. He heard another shot, couldn't tell where it had gone or originated, but imagined he heard the bullet whiz by

216

him. He was facing the field, empty as a target range. He swerved, looking for a way back into the stands, and saw instead a blocking sled on the sidelines. He leaped into the middle of it, banging his ribs and one shin, and scrambled underneath, where the pads and metal offered the illusion of protection. A marksman could still kill him.

Raymond looked up, into the stands on the opposite side of the field, and saw nothing. He looked closer above him and saw no movement there, either. Finally he looked back the way he had come. Stennett had picked up one of the sideline benches and was carrying it like a shield, struggling back toward the stands. He was also trying to fumble his gun out from under his shirt in the back, but that was one action too many. He stumbled and fell, the bench falling on top of him and then off.

Raymond was pinned down. There was no way he could lift the sled the way Stennett had lifted the bench. He crawled to the edge of his cover and prepared to dart out, but the sound of another shot stopped him. 'Stennett!' he shouted.

Stennett was up. He gained the entrance they'd come in. Protected there, he fired his pistol wildly in different directions. No shot responded. Stennett frantically waved Raymond toward him. Oh, right. But staying under the sled was no better. Raymond got his feet under him and leaped out. He ran straight toward the head-high wall that surrounded the stands, not on the longer angle toward the entrance. From the corner of his eye he saw Stennett leap out of hiding, both hands holding the pistol, aiming back up above them. Of course, if the sniper were in the stands opposite, both Stennett and Raymond were completely uncovered then.

Raymond gained the wall and ran along it, toward the entryway. The sound of his own breathing was too loud for him to tell if there was another shot. He didn't slow down enough to take evasive action, just ran. He passed Stennett and dived into the open doorway. His momentum slid him along the concrete floor, down the tunnel to where the chain link fence stopped him. He pulled open the gate and hurled himself through it, sliding again. More ragged breathing gave him an instant's warning before Stennett fell on top of him. They landed in a heap back under the dark stands.

Stennett struggled up and squatted in a listening pose. Raymond just lay there until his breathing slowed and he could listen too, to the acres of quiet under the stands. He stared at the back of Stennett's head.

'Does *every*body hate you?' he asked.

Stennett turned. 'Me? He was shooting at you.'

'No.' Raymond thought about it. He *had* imagined the bullets had followed him when he and Stennett had run in opposite directions. But there remained an important distinction between them. 'Nobody's ever fired a gun at me before. It happens to you every week.'

Stennett appeared to think about that. Then he pivoted, making Raymond cringe, pointing the gun past the lawyer's head. They both waited. 'Let's get the hell out of here,' Raymond suggested.

'Yeah. *You* wanta walk across that parking lot? Go ahead, I'll cover you.'

So they sat in their bunker with concrete walls on two sides, and Stennett glided back up the ramp to relock the gate. Raymond was glad to see him return. They huddled silently. As minutes passed they grew calmer but not enough to emerge from hiding. They were obviously thinking similar thoughts. 'First the anonymous call, now this,' Stennett said eventually.

'That's right,' Raymond said immediately. 'Somebody's trying to help us and somebody's trying to kill us. Who would those people be?'

'Well, it would be the real murderer who's trying to kill us. And the one trying to help us is, uh . . .'

'Yeah, "uh",' Raymond said. He still considered Stennett a good candidate as the anonymous caller himself. And after he thought a little more about it, 'And come to think of it, why would the "real murderer" be trying to kill us anyway? You're already taking the fall for him. It's perfect. Why's he want to mess with things?'

Stennett sounded like a man struggling to shore up a losing theory. 'We must be onto something he's afraid of,' he said.

'Oh yeah? I'm not on to anything. I don't know shit. Do you?'

Stennett sat in the dimness and chewed on his lip. Raymond watched him.

Talking to the eyewitness probably wouldn't help much, it never did, but it was the last thing he had to do. So on the sunny last day of September Raymond appeared on the doorstep of the tiny asbestos-shingled house. It looked as if it could contain no more than four rooms. That would remain a matter for speculation, because he got no farther than the front porch.

Raymond was dressed like a lawyer, three pieces to his suit, even carrying a briefcase. Maybe that wasn't the way to win anyone's confidence, but he wanted to be official. Haley Burkwright actually seemed glad to see him. He came out onto the porch, nodded, talked, took Raymond around to the back so he could see the view the old man had had of the church parking lot.

But he didn't say anything. Someone had talked to him, probably Becky Schirhart. Burkwright didn't commit himself to any statements of fact. Raymond had a feeling he could have stood there all day, listening to the old man talk happily about the decline of the neighborhood, without hearing anything useful.

The view to the parking lot was unobstructed. Raymond looked forty or fifty yards to the spot where he'd stood looking for bloodstains. After he left the old man Raymond returned to the church. He had a feeling John Entwhistle's early warning system would detect him momentarily anyway, but this time he knocked on the door. The minister, too, looked glad to be interrupted. He gestured Raymond inside, putting his arm around his visitor's shoulders briefly as if putting a penitent at ease. The floor of the lobby was linoleum that was cracked in spots but shone. When Raymond said he'd just met Haley Burkwright, Reverend Entwhistle gave a judicious smile.

'You said you'd talked to him a few times. You wouldn't have any indications about his eyesight, would you?'

''Fraid I can't help you there. He recognizes me from his backyard, I know that. And his hearing is excellent.'

Raymond's look asked for explanation and the minister obliged. 'A couple of times he's mentioned the singing on Sunday night. Not complaining, just commenting. He's mentioned the names of specific hymns he'd heard, and he was right.'

Raymond whistled appreciatively and Entwhistle nodded. The minister was wearing a white shirt identical to the one Raymond had seen him wearing the last time. When he folded the arms that erupted from the shirt's white sleeves Entwhistle looked rather like a wall. Those arms had had some unministerly former life.

Raymond asked more about Haley Burkwright. Entwhistle seemed willing to help, but just didn't know his neighbor well enough to offer anything useful. As the interview wound down, though, he began to look troubled again. Something nagged at his memory. Raymond let silence worry it further.

'There's something about him, isn't there?' he finally asked. 'Or is it about Gordon Frazier? Or Mike Stennett?'

'Let's go upstairs,' Entwhistle said, and led the way up to his study.

Twenty minutes later Raymond sat alone in his car, briefcase flung on the seat beside him. He pulled open his tie and collar but made no move to start the engine. 'Well, shit,' he said disgustedly. He had just broken the back of the prosecution's case.

PART 2

CHAPTER 11

Raymond had had a terrible night. He always did the night before a trial, but this was worse. He lay on his back for hours, eyes sometimes closed, the darkness behind his eyelids the same as the darkness of the room. If he slept he dreamed he was awake, waiting, so his mind had no rest at all. But he rose very early, full of energy, twitching with it. It was energy carried strictly by his nerves; it might die away in an hour, leaving his body heavy with the unslept night.

When he was dressed it was still much too early for Peter to be up. Raymond sat by his son's bed in the dark for some time, watching him sleep. He put his hand on the boy's narrow chest and watched it rise and fall, felt Peter's heart pulsing, open then closed. At the door Denise held him without speaking. He kissed her temples beside her eyes. There were wrinkles there, but tiny ones. Her skin was still almost as smooth as melting ice cream. In the dimness she looked twenty.

'Thanks, Winston,' Raymond said to the janitor who let him into the courtroom. Winston was young, black, almost always happy-looking. He was smiling even at this hour of the morning. This wasn't the first time he'd unlocked a courtroom door for Raymond. They were the only two people in the building. Winston leaned in to flip on the lights, then withdrew.

The 175th District Court was in an unusually designed courtroom on the second floor of the courthouse. From the hallway Raymond entered a tiny anteroom from which one could peer through a second set of glass doors into the back of the courtroom. A convex mirror mounted high on the back wall gave a view of the front of the room, including the judge's bench. Raymond passed through those doors and made a sharp turn to the right to walk to the front, through the gate in the bar. He laid his briefcase on the defense table.

Again he felt the isolation of being alone in a place designed for very public use. Unpopulated, the courtroom was stripped of its function. It looked like a historical exhibit, meticulously reconstructed but never used. There was a pristine air foreign to a court, which operates on conflict and noise. The emptiness of the room seemed to mock whatever would fill it as empty as well, ritual without application. The silence that filled the massive building was more profound than any sound that could break it. Only Raymond would know that silence. The others would arrive to an already bustling building. By that time Raymond would have made the room his own. He had his own pretrial ritual, unprescribed by any code of procedure. First he went and sat in the jury box. In the 175th the jury box was to the lawyers' right, directly facing the witness stand, an arrangement that focused attention on the judge and the witness and put the lawyers and the defendant almost offstage. Raymond sat in each of the juror chairs, checking the angles of vision. He said a sentence aloud to hear the sound of his voice in the empty room. It sounded squeaky and insincere.

From the jury box he moved behind the bench and sat in the judge's chair. It was padded, high-backed, on both a swivel and rollers. A chair it would be easy to nap in. He began to feel tired.

A voice startled him out of his reverie. 'You get promoted?'

Mike Stennett lounged against a pew in the back of the courtroom. Raymond wondered how long he'd been there. Stennett was wearing gray slacks and a plaid jacket, not quite clownish-looking. He looked like a man who didn't get dressed up very often, and that wasn't bad. 'I thought we were supposed to meet in the coffee shop,' he said.

'We are, in half an hour.' Raymond came down from the bench. He took off his suit coat and arranged it on the back of the chair at the counsel table.

'What're you doing here?' Stennett persisted. 'Anybody else around?'

'I like to get the feel of the room beforehand,' Raymond said, coming through the gate.

'Oh yeah? You about to get undressed? Want me to leave?' Stennett grinned. His grin disappeared when Raymond said, 'Yes.

'I want you to leave,' Raymond amplified.

Stennett suddenly looked as if he realized he was intruding, and like a man who didn't often have such a realization. 'Oh. Okay, sure. Uh, anything I need to know first?'

'I'll tell you downstairs. In the meantime practice saying "Not guilty" and sounding sincere.' Ignoring his client, Raymond sat on the back row of the courtroom. He pictured the backs of the lawyers' heads, the judge high above everyone, the jurors almost hidden in their corner.

'Hey?'

He turned to look. He'd thought Stennett had already gone, but he was standing in the doorway. Raymond raised his eyebrows. 'You know why I hired you?' Stennett asked, looking straight at him.

'Yeah, I know.'

'No you don't. I hired you because I've been

watching you for twenty years, and the one thing I know about you is you hate to lose.' They looked at each other. Raymond didn't respond. 'You won't lose this one,' Stennett concluded. The door swung shut where he'd stood, leaving Raymond alone in the courtroom.

In three weeks Judy Byrnes was facing her first election. Appointed to the bench, she had to run for it in the next election, which had happened to be only a few months away when she took office. Traditionally in Texas the Democratic primary was the election: whoever won that primary might as well have been sworn in the next week. But in the last couple of elections a scattering of Republicans had been elected, particularly in judicial races where they ran as reform candidates, so Judge Byrnes, appointed by the Republican governor, had a fighting chance. Her opponent was a longtime defense lawyer who made party contacts, appeared at as many public functions as were held, and relied on his bland, familiar-sounding name.

Judicial candidates don't usually have the money for radio or TV campaigns. This trial, over which reporters would swarm, would be Judge Byrnes's most public exposure in the weeks before the election. That fact didn't show in her expression as she took her seat and called the short docket preceding *The State of Texas v. Michael Stennett*, but she could not have missed the reporters lining the front row of the spectator benches.

Tyler Hammond looked relaxed and easy sitting next to the empty jury box. The table in front of him was covered with the foot-tall stack of papers he'd removed from his expanding file. Becky had brought her Penal Code and Code of Criminal Procedure and a legal pad. Tyler had come over and shaken hands with Raymond and looked momentarily nonplussed as he decided only to nod at Mike Stennett sitting beside him. Becky had looked levelly at Raymond and given him an ever so tiny nod of recognition.

Tyler sat whispering to Becky as the prospective jurors began filing into the courtroom, taking their places in the spectator seats. The lawyers' chairs had been moved to the opposite sides of their tables so they faced the prospective jurors seated out in the audience. The judge sat behind the lawyers. *So we all present a united front against them*, Raymond thought. The lawyers would only let twelve of those prospective jurors inside the bar.

Tyler kept whispering to Becky, not looking at them. Becky stood and tugged Tyler to his feet as well. Raymond was already standing. Tyler began smoothing his clothes. His right hand kept returning to his beard, grooming it incessantly. He managed only occasional looks at the thirty-six potential jurors. Becky and Raymond looked over the crowd, smiling, making eye contact with everyone. The prospective jurors sometimes smiled back, more often dropped their eyes or glanced around the courtroom.

After the judge's remarks were over Becky addressed the panel. She smiled, she moved around, she introduced herself and Tyler Hammond. She didn't carry notes, Raymond noticed. All she picked up was a copy of the indictment.

'At the beginning of trial I'll read you this indictment,' she said. The jurors' eyes fixed on the document. 'It names this man' – she stood behind Mike Stennett's chair – 'and says certain acts he did, resulting in a man's death. The indictment wasn't issued by the D.A.'s office, it was issued by a grand jury, citizens like yourselves who decided the case should be brought to trial. But it isn't evidence. It's just a guideline. The judge told you the heavy burden of proof the State has – beyond a reasonable doubt – but that burden only applies to the facts stated in the indictment. Other issues may come up at trial, but we are only required to prove what's stated here.' She held the document up. A few people nodded. The prosecutor had a piece of paper on her side. The prosecution had already proven its case to one panel of average citizens, Becky was telling the prospective jurors, without putting it in so many words, because that would have been objectionable.

'The *allegations* in the indictment,' Raymond corrected her when it was his turn. 'Not facts. They're not facts until you decide they are.'

During individual voir dire Tyler asked a few perfunctory questions of the potential jurors he questioned, always ending with, 'Can you be a fair and impartial juror in this case?' None of the interviewed admitted to harboring unfair intentions.

He looked down at his notes while he spoke. Becky watched the jurors closely. Jury selection is the single most important phase of trial, and it is mystical. There were many theories of selection and Becky had tried several, but didn't subscribe to any. No lawyer knows what magical question to ask a potential juror that will make him reveal himself as a guilty or not guilty voter. Most would-be jurors give the answers they think are being sought rather than examining their feelings. She knew lawyers who tried to be sly, others like Tyler who asked questions just to take up time. Becky believed in watching. She liked jurors who looked interested, whose eyes moved around the courtroom, who frowned or nodded at answers their fellows gave.

The question Becky asked a few of the potential jurors was, 'Do you think police officers should be held to a higher standard of behavior than other citizens?' 'Yes,' was the invariable response. After Becky nodded the first time that answer was given the subsequent responders knew that was the right answer, and gave it unhesitatingly.

'You work for City Public Service?' Raymond asked one bespectacled man who'd brought two pens and a pencil in a shirt pocket protector. 'The electric company. How long?'

'Twenty-two years.' The man sounded a little wary. He liked getting a question that had a numerical answer.

'All your working life? Never owned your own business?'

The man shook his head with a slight smile.

Raymond was standing, with a hand in his pocket. He struck a conversational tone. 'You said police officers should be held to a higher standard of behavior when they're on the job,' he said, expanding the juror's answer. 'Why is that?'

'Well, they have a position of public trust.'

'Sure. And they carry guns and they have some authority we don't want them to abuse.' The juror nodded along. 'They also have some unusual pressures when they're working,' Raymond continued. 'Has anyone ever fired a shot at you while you were working, Mr Rector?'

The man smiled again. 'No.'

'Stabbed you, or swung a club at you or anything like that?'

The other potential jurors showed by their expressions that they got the point, but Mr Rector didn't just want to be the straight man any longer. 'Once when I was shutting off somebody's meter they sicced their dog on me,' he said.

'Really. What did you do?'

'I got my behind over the fence in a big hurry,' the juror said, drawing the laughs he wanted, including from Raymond. When Raymond finished laughing he said, 'What if there hadn't been a fence to protect you? Do you think you would have been justified in hitting the dog?'

'You bet. I was just there doing my job.'

'If you'd had a gun, and that dog had come at you and wouldn't quit, growling and foaming at the mouth, and with its two-inch teeth bared and lunging for your throat, and you couldn't have gotten away, would it have been all right for you to shoot the dog?'

Mr Rector gave the answer about two seconds' thought, he didn't want to sound like a hothead, but there was only one answer. 'Yes. If there was no other way.'

After the questioning the jury panel was removed and the parties separated to make their strikes. Each side was allowed ten, ten people they could remove from the jury without giving any reason. This was the real voodoo, Becky thought. From a handful of biographical facts and answers to mostly irrelevant questions we're supposed to decide who we can't live with having on the jury.

'I think we should strike Rector,' she said to Tyler.

'Why? Solid citizen, same job for twenty years, he works for the government just like we do . . .'

'He said it would be okay to shoot the dog,' Becky said. She expected the look Tyler gave her; she weathered it without changing expression. 'Dogs are warm and lovable and friendly, Tyler. Everybody likes dogs. We, on the other hand, have Gordon Frazier on our team. Nobody liked Frazier. Nobody on the jury's going to. Mike Stennett was just doing his job when a big, mean dog came at him and he had to defend himself.'

'You think that's going to be their defense?' Tyler asked, looking across the courtroom to where Raymond was conferring with his client.

'Maybe. Why else would he have asked that question?'

'Since you bring that up,' Tyler mused, 'I was wondering why he asked people if they owned their own businesses. Should we strike those people who said yes? Or no? Stennett doesn't own his own business. Is he saying Gordon Frazier did?'

Becky shrugged. She pointed at another name on the juror list. 'What about her?'

The juror information forms didn't include a line for race, not anymore, but the prosecutors had made notes of the few blacks on the panel. Becky didn't have to say it aloud. This should be easy. The victim was black, the defendant white. Normally the defense lawyer would strike blacks from the panel without a moment's thought. But would this one?

'Leave her alone,' Tyler said. 'Let Mr Boudro take her off if he wants. We want her.'

In this way they arrived at a jury of twelve people, each side trying to prevent the other from having the jurors it supposedly wanted. The twelve jurors – ten white, two black, seven women and five men – were sworn, seated in the box, and retired into anonymity.

After lunch the courtroom began to fill with people who hadn't wanted to sit through jury selection but somehow knew that testimony was about to begin. While the parties waited for the judge to appear Tyler Hammond's composure revealed itself as the thin pretense it was. 'No,' he whispered urgently, shaking his head at Becky. He wouldn't look at the spectators, the jurors, or anyone else.

'Take the first witness, Tyler, it'll settle you down.'

'No, no, you take the first one, give me a chance to ease into it.'

Becky spoke calmly, even though the door behind the bench had just opened and the judge emerged into the courtroom. Becky and Tyler rose with everyone else. 'If you sit there for half an hour while we do the first witness it'll just get worse, Tyler, it will seem like that much more pressure. Just do the first one. It's Officer Gilmore. He doesn't even know anything, there's no way to mess it up.'

Tyler shook his head again. Becky said, 'I'm sitting down and I'm not getting up again until the second witness.'

She did. Judge Byrnes said, 'Call your first witness,' not looking up until the silence imposed itself on her attention. 'State?' she directed at the State's table. Becky sat there. Tyler hastily stood and mumbled, 'Officer Gilmore.' The bailiff had to ask him to repeat it.

Most of the State's witnesses were cops or other professionals accustomed to testifying, but Becky had given them her standard pretrial speech, and the judge had instructed them as well, that once trial began the witnesses were to remain outside the courtroom, unable to hear other witnesses' testimony. In consequence, given the layout of this peculiar courtroom, each witness had a long entrance to make. Officer Gilmore came in through the hall door and up the aisle. He creaked and clanked a little from his belt and cuffs and gun. Gilmore was young, a patrol officer, and walked the way young cops walk, rolling his hips a little, feeling the weight of the gun.

'Give him an encouraging smile,' Raymond whispered to his client, who obliged with a ghastly parody of friendliness. Gilmore almost flinched away from him.

Gilmore had discovered the body of the victim. That was all he had to say, and Tyler made it very boring, his voice a low drone, his head usually down as he read from his notes. Raymond thought about making an objection, just to see if the prosecutor would shake into little pieces when he had to stand to respond, but refrained. It would have been mean.

But Tyler began to breathe easier as his examination drew to a close. Nothing to it. He sat back looking a little self-satisfied. He had run out of questions before eliciting the one piece of information that had to be obtained from this witness. Becky leaned over and reminded him.

'Oh,' Tyler said aloud, the loudest thing he'd said so far. 'Did you find anything near the body, Officer?'

'A gun,' Officer Gilmore obliged. Tyler leaned over to fumble in the cardboard box at his feet. Becky handed him the gun.

'I hand you what's been marked State's Exhibit number one,' Tyler said, doing so. He had managed not to trip over the leg of the counsel table as he crossed to the front of the courtroom. Once the officer took the gun from him Tyler put both hands in his pockets and hunched his shoulders as if he'd come a great journey in the cold and didn't look forward to the return trip. He sneaked a peek at the spectator seats, which were filled with people who seemed to be leaning toward him. 'Can you identify that?'

'This is the gun I found next to the body,' said the patrol officer, turning the item in question over in his hands. It was a heavy, long-barrelled revolver with fake pearl handles, rather Old West-looking. Tyler offered it into evidence. At that point Raymond could object, say he had no objection, or question the witness about the piece of evidence. He chose the latter.

'Is there a serial number on that gun, Officer?'

'No sir, it's been scratched off.'

'Had you ever seen it before the night you found it beside Gordon Frazier's body?'

'Not that I know of,' said the policeman.

'You mean you might have but there's nothing special about the gun that would have allowed you to identify it?'

'No sir, nothing special.'

'Then how can you identify it now?'

'I scratched my initials on the handle before I put it in the property room that night.' Officer Gilmore smiled as if he'd invented this trick himself. Raymond nodded and said he had no objection. Tyler was finally allowed to return to his seat and pass the witness, so Raymond's questioning of the officer continued. It was short.

'What was the name of that street where you found the body, Officer Gilmore?'

'It was in an alley between Ghoulson and Jenkins.'

Becky displayed no reaction. She knew the flaws in her case. The jurors didn't know what they'd just heard. Raymond would tell them later. He repeated it for emphasis.

'Ghoulson and Jenkins, thank you. Did you know this man you found in that alley, Officer?'

'The body? No, sir.'

'What about this man sitting next to me? Do you know him?'

'Yes, sir.'

'Will you please identify him for the jury?'

The officer shifted in his chair, wondering how much to say. 'His name is Mike Stennett. He's a narcotics detective.'

'A police officer.'

'Yes, sir.'

'Have you ever worked with him, Officer Gilmore?'

'No, sir.'

'But you know his reputation within the police department.' Raymond didn't phrase that one as a question. His tone gently implied that only an ignoramus wouldn't know another officer's reputation.

'He's supposed to be a good detective.'

'By good you mean thorough, careful? I guess if an undercover narcotics officer isn't careful he doesn't last very long.'

That wasn't a question either, but the witness agreed with it. The jurors appeared a little more attentive than they had during Tyler Hammond's questioning. Becky was whispering something to her co-counsel. A couple of jurors turned in their chairs to look at Mike Stennett. He sat there stoically, as if he were the guest of honor at an awards ceremony, about to give a speech of acceptance.

Raymond asked deliberately, 'Would Mike Stennett's reputation lead you to believe he's the kind of man who would kill someone and then carelessly leave a gun with his fingerprint on it right next to the victim's body?'

At Becky's urging, Tyler was on his feet before this question was finished. 'Objection, Your Honor. That calls for hearsay. And, uh, speculation.'

'Sustained,' said Judge Byrnes, giving Raymond a look as if he'd gotten away with something in spite of her ruling.

A string of other police witnesses followed. The prosecution was being careful, thorough, and trying to make it look as if they had a massive, airtight case. The jurors might have noticed that several of these witnesses had nothing to say that implicated the defendant, but they would not wonder why some witness mentioned in the case was not called. Tyler had recommended eliminating half these witnesses, but Becky was experienced enough to know that jurors who wondered why someone hadn't been called might start inventing things that missing witness might have testified.

Also, she knew the State's case wouldn't be finished that first day, and she wanted to save her big guns until the next day, so the effect of their testimony wouldn't dissipate overnight.

But she needed a witness today to put some life in the case, to add some revulsion. 'Dr Robert Wyntlowski.'

There was a short recess while the pathologist came over from the medical examiner's office. 'It's going pretty well, isn't it?' Stennett said, sipping from a Styrofoam cup of coffee. He kept his back to the reporters on the front row.

'It hasn't started yet,' Raymond said.

'They haven't hurt us any.'

They haven't tried yet. They're saving it for tomorrow.'

'You think you should've brought up about my print being on the gun?'

Raymond looked at him a little disgustedly. 'You think they won't? Might as well have the jury thinking about a reason for it before it even comes in.'

'That was a good point you made about me not bein' stupid enough to drop it there.'

'I can think of an explanation for that,' Raymond said. 'I'm sure they can too.' And he went to talk to the prosecutors.

Becky and Tyler broke off their conversation and looked up at the defense lawyer. Becky made her mouth small and crossed her arms. 'Better watch yourself on this next one, Rebecca,' Raymond said. 'I already talked to Doctor Bob, he's given me some fuel.'

'Oh, right.' As if the M.E. had ever helped a defense lawyer.

Raymond read her meaning. 'This isn't an ordinary case, Miss Becky.'

'That's why they have me trying it,' she said. He gave her a little smile, then looked serious again. When he spoke he sounded like a collaborator.

'I haven't heard anything about motive. Have you ever figured out a motive?'

Becky shrugged. This was obvious. 'It was an interrogation that got out of hand.'

'What was he interrogating him about? I haven't found anybody to say they even knew each other.'

'It doesn't matter. You obviously weren't listening to my voir dire,' Becky said. Tyler was just looking back and forth between the two of them. 'We don't have to prove motive.'

'Yeah. Tell *them* that in your final argument.' Raymond gestured at the jury box. 'Just let 'em be curious about the reason. Then listen to what *I* have to say.'

He turned on his heel. Behind him Becky was glaring. Tyler looked worried. 'He's right,' he said. 'But we can't even get in what we know.'

Becky looked at him fondly. 'Tyler, you're good, but there's some things you need to learn.'

'Like what?'

'Like how the rules of evidence can help you by keeping out some answers.'

'You can see the distinction between these bruises in the left side of the rib area and this one, for example, on the right cheekbone.'

'May I publish these to the jury, Your Honor?' At the judge's nod Becky passed the two photographs the medical examiner had been comparing to the first juror. One was a close-up of Gordon Frazier's face, the other a longer view of the torso. Becky handed them to the first juror and walked back to the witness stand. She didn't look at the jury. It was Tyler's job to do that. He saw the first juror, a Mexican-American woman in her forties, glance at the first photo, flinch, and hastily pass it on. The second juror, also a woman, studied the picture a little more closely. Her expression was very sober as she handed on the photo and accepted the second one.

Raymond sat very still, watching the jurors. He had let the autopsy photos in without objection, hadn't even looked at them when Becky offered them in evidence.

Becky waited for the photos to be well on their way through the jury before resuming her questioning. 'What is that distinction between the types of bruises?'

'Size, mainly. The smaller ones are from glancing blows, the larger ones are vivid, penetrating bruises.'

'What inflicted those bruises, in your opinion?'

'I'd say a fist. Possibly an implement, but there's one particularly well-defined bruise on the abdomen just below the rib cage where you can actually see the deeper indentations of four knuckles.'

'How much force would be required to make these marks, Dr Wyntlowski?'

'In terms of pounds per square inch I can't say, but considerable.'

'Not just a hearty slap on the back.'

'No.'

'Someone was trying to hurt him,' Becky added, and paused, expecting objection. So did the judge. She looked at Raymond, who was watching the witness attentively. 'Yes,' the doctor answered.

'Did you find any other marks on the body, Doctor?'

'I found needle marks inside both elbows. They were not fresh.'

'Did you find any narcotics in the victim's system?'

'No.'

Becky had returned to her seat. She appeared to glance at a paper on the table beside her but in reality was looking at the jury. They were all watching the witness. Still, Becky raised her voice.

'Were you able to determine what killed Gordon Frazier, Doctor?'

'Yes. It was a blow or combination of blows in this area.' With a pointer he indicated the nose on a generic outline of a face he'd brought, as personable as a crash test dummy. Becky wanted the real thing. She returned to the witness stand and found another photograph of dead, mutilated Gordon Frazier. 'Could you show us on this, please?'

'Certainly. Right here. The bridge of his nose was broken and the nose bone was shoved up into the brain.' Doctor Bob had an admirable habit of dropping medical jargon at effective moments. Most of the jurors reacted in some way, if only wrinkling their faces. Two of them touched their own noses.

'Now, one blow could do that in the same motion, but it would take a great deal of force. More likely it's two blows to the same spot, one quickly following the other.'

'So it wouldn't require as much force?'

'No, but still a great deal. It's not something that would happen accidentally.'

That was another spot for an objection, but none

came, though Raymond was paying close attention. So was Mike Stennett, as if he'd never heard a beating death reduced to clinical terms before.

Becky had the other photographs introduced and circulated them through the jury box. The jurors seemed to study these longer. 'Pass the witness.'

'Did you see any sign the body had been moved after Gordon Frazier died?' Raymond asked.

'No.' Wyntlowski described lividity, the blood pooling in the lowest part of the body. Even when it remained contained, blood left a trail.

'Is there any way the victim could have been beaten in one location and died as a direct result of that beating at another location several blocks away?'

'It's possible,' the doctor said. Raymond's eyes snapped up and locked on him. Three feet away, Becky showed no sign of triumph, but inside she was delighted with herself.

'His nose could have been broken at the first location,' the doctor was continuing, as if unaware of Raymond's stare. 'He could have walked – staggered, crawled, whatever – some distance and then perhaps fallen forward, passing out from his other injuries, and *that* impact could have driven the bone upwards. That's possible.'

'But this isn't the type of injury that would gradually cause death?' Raymond asked, having recovered himself.

'Not like internal bleeding, no. When it happened it would be abrupt.'

'You said it couldn't have been accidental,' Raymond said, 'but could it have been unintentional? Could someone have killed Gordon Frazier without meaning to kill him?'

'Sure. Someone just trying to hurt him punches him too hard in the wrong place. Oh yes.'

But that would still be murder, Becky thought, in the terms of the second count of the indictment. Trying to hurt someone so badly you kill him instead would be murder of the same degree as setting out to kill him and accomplishing it. That's not going to do him any good. She made a note to herself to mention this in final argument. But Raymond was continuing, his voice rising.

'In the heat of the moment, one vicious punch, maybe even in response to something the victim did, and boom! Gordon Frazier is dead – abruptly, you said – shocking the killer, leaving him with an unexpected result, a dead body on the street in front of him,' Raymond said, as if seeing it. Becky was looking at him, as were others. The doctor didn't answer, unsure that he was being addressed. 'I suppose,' he finally said.

Raymond passed the witness in a distracted tone. Becky asked one question. 'What race was the victim?'

'He was black.'

Raymond had no more questions.

Becky found herself with about forty-five minutes of the court's working day left on her hands, and she didn't want to put on either of her two most important witnesses yet. She had one left in reserve, one whose testimony she expected to be very brief. 'Detective Bernardo Martinez,' she said. She enjoyed the expression on Mike Stennett's face as she said it.

Martinez was wearing a navy blue suit. His hair was cut, his nails clean. He looked like a mid-level executive of a large company or a successful small businessman. Becky quickly established his occupation and his connection to the defendant.

'Frankly, you don't look as if you could pass for a junkie, Detective.'

'It's Sergeant, actually. I've been promoted recently, and my duties no longer include street investigations.'

Stennett smiled and shook his head slightly, admiringly. Martinez looked at him, didn't smile or nod, and looked back at his questioner.

'You worked with Mike Stennett for two years,' Becky said.

'Yes.'

'Did you ever know him to beat a suspect?'

There were pulses of silence. Becky felt a moment of panic and wanted to withdraw the question. Judge Byrnes looked sharply at Raymond.

'I don't know what you mean by "beat",' Bernardo Martinez said hesitantly. 'Sure, I've seen him slap somebody around a little. It was in character –'

Raymond had risen slowly to his feet. It wasn't automatic at all. 'Objection,' he said. 'This raises an irrelevant extraneous offense, or offenses, with no reason for admission.'

Finally, Becky thought. 'Sustained,' the judge said.

They nudge. Good trial lawyers know where the boundaries are, and try to nudge them outward. A good question can be more effective than an answer, especially if the other side objects. You ask the question to draw the objection, to let the jury know the other side doesn't want them to hear that answer. That's what Becky was doing. She knew she couldn't get into other illegal conduct of the defendant's. Too much of that and she'd risk having the conviction reversed on appeal. But when she asked the question, relying on Raymond to object, she told the jury just as effectively that it was true, Mike Stennett made a habit of beating up suspects. This way was even better than getting the specific testimony in. Unsupplied with details, the jurors could invent them for themselves. She kept at it.

'In the time you worked together, did he treat black suspects differently from white suspects?'

This time Raymond didn't take the bait. He sat there with his legs stretched out in front of him looking indifferent to both the question and the answer, as if he already knew. Becky looked at him and saw he wasn't going to rise.

'In my opinion he treated black suspects more harshly,' Martinez said. 'He was more likely to get physical with a black suspect. One time he –' Martinez had started reluctantly but was warming to his subject.

'Thank you, Sergeant,' Becky said hastily, and passed the witness. She'd gotten in just enough, she thought, to be effective. But she stared at the defense lawyer, irritated that he hadn't played his part. Raymond still sat there lethargically.

'Ever know him to kill anybody?' he asked loudly.

Martinez shook his head.

'Think he killed Gordon Frazier?'

The stir rippled through everyone in the courtroom, but for different reasons. Becky and the judge both looked alarmed. This was an objectionable question – at least, it would have been if a prosecutor had asked it. When the defense lawyer asked it, there was no one to object. *Becky* wasn't going to object, and have the jury think she didn't like the answer. But this departure from the orthodox made her chew her lip.

Reporters happily made notes, waiting for the answer to the kind of direct question they never heard asked in trials. Jurors looked interested; it was a question they would have asked if they could.

Bernardo Martinez glanced at the prosecutor, then grew a thin shell that could have meant he was retreating or that he was steeling himself to say the truth. 'I don't now why he would have,' he said.

Raymond persisted. He looked more alert now. 'But if he had a good reason you think he might.'

Martinez looked at his former partner. 'If Mike thought he needed killing real bad, he'd do it.'

'Coolly. Deliberately.'

'I don't think he'd lie awake over it.'

Stennett was giving Martinez a long, level look. Stennett didn't look insulted.

'Thank you, Sergeant.'

Becky felt lucky to escape. She asked no more questions, and Judge Byrnes recessed for the day. She instructed the jurors not to discuss the case overnight and dismissed them. Before leaving the bench she looked at the lawyers as if she might call them into her chambers, but turned away without saying it.

Raymond and Stennett said nothing to each other. Like most cops, Stennett thought he knew trial procedure pretty well, but in fact he was under the impression trials followed more sensible rules than they in fact did. He didn't realize what an aberration had just taken place in his. Raymond walked away, leaving his briefcase on the table. Stennett sat. His old partner was still sitting too, on the witness stand, maybe hoping Stennett would go away before he had to walk past him. But Stennett waited. There appeared no other way out except past him, and Martinez wouldn't have taken another way if one had been available. He crossed slowly to within a few feet of Stennett, nodded to him, and walked past.

'Congratulations,' Stennett said. 'Finally made your way out of the ranks. You'll look good behind a desk, 'Nardo. Up there where arrests don't matter, all anybody talks about is image.'

Martinez stopped, he knew there had to be at least a small scene, but he didn't turn back. 'I'm sorry for your trouble, Mike. I hope you come out of it okay.'

''Nardo?'

'Yeah.'

'You're one of them now, you're an administrator, maybe you can tell me how they think. Maybe you've thought like them all along. How come nobody's ever even pretended to back me up on this deal? How come I've been left swinging in the wind from day one? They think I've done so little I'm not even worth one sentence of support in the papers?'

He was trying to sound offhand, but he didn't, he sounded hurt. A speech like this from Mike Stennett was the equivalent of sobbing and screams from someone else. Bernardo decided to tell him the truth.

'You embarrass them, Mike. You're a dinosaur. We're trying to create a modern police department here and you're something out of the forties. Hell, you're like something out of Chicago in the twenties. Couple that with this idea of yours that you're the honky auxiliary of the east side and I don't know *what* you are. I think you're schizo.'

This blast left Stennett grinning. It removed all trace of self-pity from his voice. '"Honky auxiliary", what the hell's that mean?'

'I think you wish you *were* black. Or you think you are, but nobody can recognize it and you resent it. Your lawyer should've asked me that. I think you come down harder on blacks because they're your brothers and they've disappointed you.'

'You've been taking courses again, haven't you, 'Nardo?'

'What're you trying to do, set up an ineffective assistance claim?' Becky was asking Raymond. 'Have you decided not to apply the rules of evidence to this trial?'

'There are no rules.'

They had a few moments of privacy. Reporters knew

they could catch the trial participants in the hall when they emerged, and all the media representatives had retreated to that hall, where a citizens' committee was staging some sort of demonstration that displayed no spontaneity. The group's placards stressed 'law and order', which had aroused the reporters' curiosity. How did a law and order group stand on a policeman charged with murder?

'What do you mean, there aren't any rules?' Becky said. She had seen Raymond serious while questioning witnesses, putting on passion for a speech to a judge or jury, but he always came down off it as soon as he was offstage. He wasn't a crusader, he could joke about his own posturing. Now he looked like he'd lost his objectivity. His answer confirmed that suspicion.

'Only games have rules,' he said seriously.

'He's on a mission from God,' Becky said to Tyler.

'I am on a truth-seeking mission. Don't you see? I don't care. The old rules don't apply. Do what you want, who's stopping you? Let it all in, let God sort it out. I don't mean the judge, I mean those twelve average citizens, let them decide it the way we decide things in real life. Let them know everything you got. I am.'

He had not made a disciple. Becky looked at him, thinking all around what he was saying. 'Whose side are you on?' was the way she finally summarized what she was wondering.

Raymond leaned toward her earnestly. 'Becky, are you so steeped in this shit you can't remember there's a real world beyond all this? There aren't sides. The truth is too elusive anyway for us to fight to try to keep it out. Do what you can. I won't stop you.'

He hadn't made a dent in her suspicion. He left her wondering what he really meant and how she could make use of it. 'Thank you for your encouragement,' she said primly, gathering up her materials. She looked like a schoolgirl going to her next class. Tyler Hammond looked like her rumpled professor. 'Interesting idea,' he said to Raymond. 'Becky –'

'We need to talk about tomorrow,' Raymond said to his client as they walked toward the door. 'They've run through almost their whole witness list, they'll wrap up tomorrow morning probably. I have a couple of witnesses and then we'll do the smart thing and rest or we'll put you on.'

'Oh, I'm gonna testify, don't worry about that. I know what the jury thinks if the defendant sits there and exercises his right not to incriminate himself.'

'Sometimes letting them speculate about it is better than climbing up on the stand and shooting yourself in the foot right in front of them.'

Stennett made a face as if the suggestion of that possibility offended his nostrils. 'What're you scared of? I've never testified yet that the jury didn't believe me.'

'They didn't believe you, jerk. They just listened to you and nodded and winked and thought, It's okay. We know you're lying. We know the search was illegal. We know you beat him up a little afterwards. But we're gonna pop him anyway, cause he's a goddamned burglar. You think you got that going for you this time, too? You think they'll listen to you and nod and look solemn and think, It's okay. We know you killed him, but he was just a nigger drug dealer? Is that what you think?'

They were the last people out of the courtroom. As they pushed open the hallway door a flash went off and they heard the whir of a TV camera. Raymond sighed at the thought of being interviewed. Mike Stennett's reaction was more primitive, and instantaneous. He flung up an arm and ducked his face into his shoulder. While Raymond turned, thinking his client was still behind him, Stennett had spun and darted back into the courtroom. Instinctively, Raymond followed. Stennett's reaction was so violent that for a moment Raymond thought they were being shot at again. He turned the lock on the hall door and slowly followed his client back into the courtroom. Stennett was already back inside the bar, heading for the court offices. His shoulders were hunched. He whirled, saw who was following him, and called, 'There another way out through the offices?'

'Their door goes into the hall, too,' Raymond said quietly. Stennett stopped, caught in indecision. His eyes lit on the windows on the far wall. 'Fire escape,' he said, snapping his fingers.

Raymond rolled his eyes. 'Don't do that. You make yourself look guilty. Like one of those forties mobsters with his hat over –'

'I'm a cop!' Stennett spun to shout at him. 'I'm not having my face all over the evening news. I work undercover, don't you get that? And I will again. When this is over I'm going right back.'

He turned away again without seeing the effect this speech had on his lawyer. Raymond looked as if he knew the secret way out and was debating whether to reveal it. His eyes seemed to deepen, turn multilayered, as he watched Stennett reach the wall and sidle along it, fingers skittering on the glass of the windows, searching desperately for the way back into his life.

When he called Jean for his messages she said he had a visitor. 'Tell him some other time,' Raymond said wearily. 'I'm going home. I've gotta –'

'You'd better come by,' Jean said. 'He's a police officer. He says he has to see you tonight.'

It was too damned hot for the middle of October. The temperature had hit ninety late that afternoon. The air was dead still now, impenetrable. That stillness probably presaged the first good cold front of the season, but in the meantime Raymond felt the weight of the whole deadened atmosphere as he got out of his car in front of his office.

'Go home,' he said to Jean as soon as he walked in. 'Take care of your children.'

She already had her purse in her hand. She inclined her head toward the open door of his office and was gone. Raymond carried his suit jacket into the office and dropped it on the couch. Darryl Kreutzer, dressed like a college boy on his way to play in a basketball game, stopped in mid-pace. 'How'd it go today?' he asked, as if he'd dropped by for conversation.

'Oh, great. They haven't hurt us yet,' Raymond quoted his client.

'Well, good. Oh, hey. How come I never saw anything in the papers about that sniper shooting at you guys in the stadium? Don't you think that'd be useful, make it look like somebody else did it and's tryin' to stop you guys from finding out?'

'If that's Stennett's theory let *him* hold a press conference and announce it,' Raymond said wearily. 'So why're you here, Officer Kreutzer? You've solved the crime?'

Kreutzer's expression became serious instead of merely interested. 'I know Mike didn't do it,' he said.

'To tell you the truth, Darryl, at this point your opinion of his character isn't worth much. Now if you had the real murderer in hand –'

'I'm not talking about character, I mean I *know* he didn't do it. I was with him.'

Raymond's responses slowed. He leaned on a corner

of the desk and watched the young cop, who ran his fingers through his hair nervously but looked back at him unfalteringly. 'You saw him with Frazier?' Raymond said.

Kreutzer shook his head. 'He was never there. We were miles away at the time Frazier was killed. We were staking out another location, waiting for some dope deal Mike had heard was gonna go down. Nobody ever showed, but I was with him the whole time.'

Raymond spoke gently. 'Darryl, this could ruin your whole career. It's not worth it. Stop for a minute just thinking he's your friend and you want to help him. Think about what he did. He's not the wonderful cop you think. There are better men on the force who won't even work with him, because they have the discipline to follow the rules, while Mike Stennett's just some roving –'

Kreutzer interrupted. 'It's the truth. I was with him.'

'I don't think this'll fly, Darryl. First of all, you were probably on duty that night. It'd be very easy for the prosecutors to check.'

'I *was* on duty. But, uh – this is the part I wouldn't want to come out, so maybe we could fix it up somehow – Steve has a girlfriend. I dropped him off at her place and I cruised over to meet Mike by myself.'

'You're out riding in a patrol car, subject to being sent on a call at any time, and you drop off your partner at some private residence where he'll be out of touch? Did you do that often?'

Kreutzer looked embarrassed but rather proud of himself at the same time. 'Wednesday night, you know. Not a lot of calls. It was almost time for our supper break anyway. I just gave him an extra half hour or so. It wasn't that risky.'

'All right, so then you hurry over to meet Mike, right at the time of the murder – which was when?'

''Bout seven thirty, eight o'clock.'

'Eight, okay. Where'd you meet?'

'At these public housing apartments over here right on the edge of downtown. Victoria Courts? There was an empty unit that Mike had the key to somehow and we waited in there, because somebody was supposed to show up next door.'

'Who?'

'Well, he never did.'

'But what was the name of the guy you were expecting?'

'Uh, Hector. Hector Garcia.'

'And he never showed. So you and Stennett sat there in the dark for how long?'

'Hour, little more. I had to get back.'

'What'd you talk about?'

Kreutzer looked surprised. 'This was six months ago.'

'But you haven't had that many conversations with Mike Stennett, have you? Surely something stands out in your memory.'

'Well, the guy. We talked about the guy we were waiting for. He was some big dealer and he was coming to make a sale.'

'What were you going to do if he showed?'

'That's why I was there, so I could arrest him and Mike could stay out of it.'

'Did you have a warrant?'

'Uh, no. We were hoping to see enough ourselves to justify –'

'How long did you say you've been a cop, two years?' Raymond asked suddenly. Again, Kreutzer looked surprised at the shift.

'Two and a half.'

'Ever testified before?'

'Sure, lots of times.'

'Then why aren't you a better liar?'

'It's true!' Kreutzer raised his voice but stopped looking at Raymond. He licked his lips.

'It's a crock. You got the time wrong, your story doesn't make any sense, and I'll bet you haven't bothered to set it up, either. Let me call Stennett and see if he's ever heard of any Hector Garcia, the big dealer who makes personal deliveries to Victoria Courts.'

Kreutzer didn't say anything. Raymond had to actually reach for the phone to start him talking again.

'All right, all right. So I got some details wrong. You *tell* me what to say. We'll get it straight with Mike.'

Raymond shook his head. 'I can't use you.'

'Why *not*? Don't you have some sort of ethical obligation to use a witness if you know he's willing to testify?'

'Not if I don't believe you.' Raymond was still watching Kreutzer with some compassion for his distress.

'Oh, great, Mike's got himself the one moral lawyer in town,' Kreutzer said, sarcasm sounding unconvincing in his mouth, like a punch line he mangled in the retelling.

'Becky Schirhart'd take your head off and hand it to you, 'f I's dumb enough to put you on the stand. You'd never even feel it was missing.'

'But, look. You got any other defense?'

Raymond shrugged. 'I've got something. I don't know what it's worth.'

Kreutzer blew loudly and shook his hands, like an athlete shaking off a small hurt, readying himself for the next play. 'Okay. Okay then. What can I do to help?'

'Nothing. What you could do is talk to somebody like Sergeant Martinez. Ask him if the department thinks Mike Stennett is the best role model for your career. He's not the hero –'

'Martinez,' Kreutzer said. 'That bureaucrat. You don't know what it means to have somebody like Mike on the force. You join up, you have some ideals, you really want to accomplish something. I know it's corny, but there's a few of us who really think we could do something about crime. Help people. Then you get in and find out it's all just bushwah – community relations and paperwork and not stepping on the wrong toes because somebody might be connected. But then there's a few, a very few, like Mike, who can still make a difference. And look what they do to him.'

Bitterness returned to Kreutzer's face, aging it. Thinking of the conspiracy against his friend cast suspicion on everyone. He pointed, sternly. 'You better win this. If Mike goes down and I get the idea you laid down and let 'em do it to him –'

He didn't put the rest into words. It was in his face. He gave Raymond another view of it for a long moment, then stalked out. Raymond heard the outer door slam. He looked after the kid compassionately. Deny Mike Stennett what noble qualities you would, he was capable of inspiring loyalty. It was one of the most dangerous things about him.

CHAPTER 12

'How old was that fingerprint, Officer?'

'No telling.'

'What?' Raymond looked surprised. 'You can't tell how long that fingerprint had been on that gun when you examined it?'

'No.'

'Can you give me some idea? Two weeks, a year?'

'Yes, either of those.' Detective Eseverino Barrientos shrugged his heavy shoulders. He had already explained to the jury that in his opinion the fingerprint found on the gun lying beside the murder victim was Mike Stennett's fingerprint. He didn't grow flustered under Raymond's cross-examination. Barrientos was a happy case of a man who had found his niche in life. He was tall and broad-shouldered. Raymond, who still had the habit of placing men by appearance at the position they should have played on a football team, would have started him at tight end. The detective's fingers were broad and blunt, unshaped for the seemingly delicate work he did. But he had been a fingerprint examiner for fifteen years, chief of the section for five. In spite of his size he no longer looked like a police officer. He looked like a lab technician. When he put on his half-glasses, as he did for reading his report, he looked like an experimental chemist.

'The oils from the finger are there,' he explained. 'They stay there until something removes them, like water, or rubbing.'

'So if we put that gun with that fingerprint on it in a time capsule it would still be there in a hundred years?'

'Well, I doubt that. There would be some very gradual evaporation, unless the time capsule was airtight.'

'Ten years?'

'Very likely it would still be there.'

Raymond leaned forward, being experimental himself. 'Then can't you tell from how faded the print is about how old it is?'

Barrientos smiled. 'We're not that precise.'

Raymond sat back appearing to absorb the information, letting the jury do so.

'Let me ask you something else, Detective, just for my own information.' This sounded like the beginning of an irrelevant line of questioning. Tyler Hammond, whose witness this was, became more attentive. 'In your opinion you can tell from all these swirls and spirals and loops and ridges and curlicues that this is my client's fingerprint on this gun. How come you couldn't tell that before my client was identified as a suspect? Didn't you already have his prints on file?'

Tyler started to rise. Becky stopped him. 'It's irrelevant,' Tyler whispered. 'Sure it is,' Becky whispered back. 'But it doesn't make any difference and we don't want the jury to think we're hiding something. Sevey'll handle it.'

Detective Barrientos was quite prepared to handle the question. He smiled at the opportunity. It wasn't often enough someone asked him to explain the fine points of his occupation. 'We have more than four hundred thousand fingerprints on file,' he said. 'On cards, not microfilm. We have country and city employees, convicted felons, anyone who's ever been arrested in San Antonio.

'Four hundred thousand prints is a lot to look through,' he went on happily. 'I could do it in about a

year, maybe, if I didn't do anything else. Now, fingerprints can be broken down into categories. Thirty categories. Everybody's prints fall into one of thirty different categories. If we could place the unknown print,
like the one we found on the gun, into one of those
categories, then we'd narrow the possibles down to a
thousand or two – assuming it matched one of the
prints we have on file. You could compare a thousand
or two by hand, that wouldn't be so hard. *But* – to
determine the category you need ten prints. The prints
from all ten fingers.' He displayed his own fingertips.
'Here we only had one. So we couldn't categorize it.
So we're back to four hundred thousand plus possibles.
It's not possible.'

'Couldn't a computer do it?'

'Yes.' Barrientos nodded for emphasis. 'Relatively
new computer, very expensive. The FBI has one in
Washington. Houston has one. The computer costs
about six million dollars. We don't have one.'

Raymond shrugged. That really had been something he pursued just for his own curiosity. Why
hadn't the police pinned Stennett as a suspect sooner?
He had one more real question of the fingerprint examiner.

'Detective, where did you find that print on that
gun?'

Barrientos consulted his notes. 'On the bottom of
the grip. The underneath part.'

'You have the gun in front of you there? Would you
please show us how a man would have to hold it in
order to leave that print in that location?'

Barrientos picked up the gun and placed his thumb
on the telltale spot, the bottommost part of the gun.
Then he awkwardly wrapped his fingers around the
handle. This left him holding the gun upside down, its

barrel pointing forward and toward the ground, or toward his own foot if he let it dangle too carelessly. It was no way to hold a gun.

'Could you fire the gun holding it like that?' Raymond asked.

It made a small funny show, the large detective trying to reach the trigger with his index finger, then his little finger. 'I don't think so,' he said, giving up. 'I wouldn't want to try.'

'That's where you'd leave a print if you were just carrying the gun very casually, isn't it?'

'I suppose.'

Upon having the witness passed to him, Tyler asked, 'Officer, did you find any other fingerprints on that gun, either identified or unknown?'

'No.'

Tyler steeled himself to ask the objectionable question. Becky had written it out for him. 'Officer, what happened was, someone wiped that gun clean of fingerprints but missed that one spot. Wouldn't you say that's what happened?'

Raymond objected to that as calling for speculation, but the answer wasn't the point. The question had been. Tyler felt rather pleased with himself. He had learned a trick.

'Officer Steve Montoya,' Becky said.

Mike Stennett looked mildly surprised. He didn't know any connection the patrolman had to the case. Raymond didn't look up from his note making when the name was called. He'd seen it on the State's witness list, he'd questioned Montoya himself. All he could testify was that he'd brought Haley Burkwright to the police station. He was just there because Becky was being a tightass, bringing in every witness no matter how insignificant. For a moment Raymond considered the idea of amusing himself by questioning the relevance of every question asked of this witness.

Montoya edged into the courtroom from the back. If Raymond had looked at him he might have wondered why Montoya looked so tired and wary. The defense lawyer had no way of knowing about the two hours Montoya had spent in the District Attorney's office the evening before, being questioned not only by the trial prosecutors but by two of his own superiors. Montoya glanced at Stennett but didn't return his smile.

Raymond didn't raise an objection, in fact he didn't lift his eyes as the patrolman testified about being sent to fetch the old man to police headquarters. This testimony was less than scintillating for the jury, who didn't know who Haley Burkwright was. Becky didn't try to elicit hearsay testimony as to why Montoya had been sent for the witness. She just established the facts in three questions and answers. Raymond was thinking he wouldn't do any cross-examination at all, when Becky changed course.

'Officer, do you know this defendant?'

'Yes.' Montoya was quiet. At a sharp look from the prosecutor he cleared his throat.

'He's a fellow police officer, isn't he?'

'Yes.' Montoya spoke up this time.

'Have you ever worked with him?'

'Not regularly, but two or three times.'

'I want to ask you about an occasion about a year ago when Detective Stennett had you and your partner meet him at a bar on the near east side. You remember the night I mean?'

Montoya remembered. He'd confessed it last night. Becky had gotten lucky. Montoya had been the last police witness left on her witness list. If he hadn't known anything she could use she would have had to call a witness off the list, and in order to do that she would have had to show good cause. She couldn't have used her real good cause, which was that the defense lawyer had just told her he'd let her get away with it. Luckily, it had soon become clear Montoya did know something. She'd had to call in a couple of his bosses to threaten him into revealing it. Now he sat on the stand looking tight as stretched cable, but ready to do as he'd been told. Mike Stennett was frowning.

'Were you and your partner in uniform?'

'Yes.'

'What were you there to do?'

'Mike said he wanted to talk to some drug dealer, and he wanted –'

'A black drug dealer?'

'Yes.'

'When he described this suspect to you, did he use the word *black*?'

'No,' Montoya muttered.

'What did he say?'

This was a hard thing, to talk like this in front of a crowded room. But he wasn't saying it, he was quoting. Montoya answered hurriedly. 'He said "nigger".' And he spoke up so he wouldn't have to repeat it.

Before the answer the judge's head swiveled sharply from the witness to the defense lawyer. Her eyes remained on Raymond, who was watching the patrolman, frowning.

Becky noticed the judge's stare and was glad it wasn't directed at her. Feeling a little self-conscious, she shifted the burden to her witness. 'What were you and your partner there to do?'

'I think Mike wanted to sort of good-cop-bad-cop the guy. He was going to get tough with him, you know, and then Darryl and I'd step in and stop him and tell the guy, you know, "You're lucky he didn't kill you. He's killed other people." Like that.'

'You were supposed to say this about a fellow police officer?'

'Well, he was pretending to be another drug dealer who was moving into the territory. He wanted to scare the guy off.'

'Is that a standard sort of police operation?'

Montoya shrugged. 'I don't work narcotics, I don't know.'

'Did it happen the way it was planned?' Becky asked.

'No.'

'Why not?'

'Darryl and I came through the bar. Mike and the suspect were in the alley out back. We were supposed to let it go on for a minute and then bust in. There was a little window in the alley door we could watch through. But once they started gettin' into it Mike waved us off. So we just stood there and watched.'

'He was conducting a little course for you, wasn't he?' Montoya didn't have an answer to that and Becky didn't want one. 'What do you mean by "getting into it"?' she asked immediately.

The voice that answered was crisp, authoritative, and unexpected. 'Wait,' Judge Byrnes snapped. For the first time she took her eyes off Raymond, to ask the witness, 'What was this suspect's name?'

'I don't know, ma'am.'

'Was it Gordon Frazier?'

'No. No, ma'am.'

'We'll have a fifteen-minute recess, I believe. I'll see the attorneys in my chambers.' She didn't look at anyone on her way out. No one had time to react. The judge was out of the room before anyone could rise. They found her pacing in her chambers, still in her robe. Raymond came forthrightly into the room, looking impatient and slightly puzzled. Becky and Tyler Hammond looked more sheepish. They edged into the room.

'Close the door, will you, please, Tyler? Thank you.' The judge turned immediately on Becky. 'What is this we're hearing out here? Something about the defendant getting rough with another suspect on another occasion? What does that have to do with this case?'

'It's to establish a pattern, Your Honor.'

'Why do you need to establish a pattern? It appears you have a very solid case. No one's questioned any element of it as yet. No one's claimed accident or anything else that would open the door to this.'

Becky said stiffly, as if from a script of which she had a low opinion, 'I believe accident has been hinted at through cross-examination.'

'*Hinted* at? Has your legal training really been so inadequate that you think a *hint* raised through a *question* would allow you to introduce an extraneous offense like this? Professor Hammond?'

Judge Byrnes's authority did not derive from her age – she was younger than Tyler – or from her robe, but from their knowledge of what a competent attorney she was. She was sharp and precise and had a sudden laugh – she was a pleasure to have a drink with. If the other lawyers in the room hadn't liked her and thought highly of her, the current tone of her voice wouldn't have had such a shriveling effect.

Tyler said uncomfortably, 'I believe under the circumstances –'

'You think rules change with circumstances?' Judy said. 'Is that what you taught your students?'

'Of course they do,' Tyler said quickly, but Judy ignored him. She was looking at Raymond. Seeing himself off the hook, Tyler subsided.

The judge looked at her old friend the defense lawyer for several seconds. Raymond was the tallest, most conspicuous person in the room, but he had a way of sinking into himself as if he had gone away, leaving only this shell behind. To him the judge spoke formally.

'Evidence is getting before the jury in this case, notably about the defendant's racial attitude, that is both inadmissible and harmful to the defendant. I would exclude this evidence if an objection were offered. Raymond, I am forming the impression you are not representing your client to the best of your ability. If that impression persists at the end of the trial I will feel obligated to report it to someone in a position to suspend your license to practice law. Do you understand?'

'Yes.' The word seemed to crystallize out of the air.

Judy's face softened. She looked troubled rather than angry. 'I know you know better. That's all. We'll resume in five minutes.'

She turned away and sat behind her desk. When she looked up the prosecutors were gone. Raymond was closing the door behind them. His mask of imperviousness had shattered.

'It is *my* right to invoke the rules of evidence or not,' he said, his tone low but rising. '*My* discretion, not yours. I may be laying traps for those people. I might just be fucking up. But this is *my* case to try, not yours. You don't tell me how to try it and you damn sure don't threaten me in front of prosecutors. When it's over you do whatever you think you have to. Do *you* understand?'

For a moment he had actually frightened her. By the end of his speech she was staring at him curiously. Raymond didn't wait for an answer. When he turned and walked out, leaving the door open, letting air and light back into the office, the judge realized how small and close the room had seemed for a moment.

Steve Montoya had turned into Haley Burkwright when the judge returned to the courtroom. She looked a little surprised by the transformation. The witness smiled at her. Tyler hastily rose to say, 'Neither side had any more questions of Officer Montoya. The State calls Haley Burkwright.

'Please tell the jury your name,' Tyler added, resuming his seat.

'Haley Burkwright.' Without being asked, Burkwright spelled it and added his age, sixty-three. He sat easily in the witness chair, happily, as if it were where he'd wanted to be all his life.

'Occupation?'

'I'm retired from the Missouri Pacific Railroad. I was a brakeman.' He scanned the jury for signs they were familiar with the profession. Mostly they smiled back at him.

'Where do you live, Mr Burkwright?'

'Three-oh-one Aransas Street. Like Port Aransas down at the coast? It's a few blocks from East Houston Street.'

Keep a rein on him, Becky had said to Tyler. *The old man loves to talk. Don't let him open himself up to any side issues. He's our whole case. We want to expose him to Boudro as little as possible.*

'Were you at home there the night of April sixteenth of this year?' Tyler asked.

'Yes, sir.' Burkwright nodded, confirming his

testimony, and gave the jury another little peek, enjoying the anticipation.

'That was a week night.'

'Well, weekend, week nights pretty much all the same to me now, but yes sir, I think it was a Wednesday night.'

Tyler nodded. 'Did you ever step outside that night?'

'About ten o'clock, I went out onto the back porch. Thought I'd heard something.'

'What can you see from your back porch, Mr Burkwright?'

The witness leaned forward, ready. 'I seen two men. One of 'em was on the ground already –'

'No, no, Mr Burkwright. I mean generally. What building or scene can you see from your back porch?'

'Oh. The church across the alley, that's my view. The back and the side and the parking lot of the Baptist Church.'

'That's the Ezekiel Avenue Baptist Church?'

'Yes.'

That's one question Tyler saved me having to ask on cross, Raymond thought. He wondered what significance the church had for the prosecutor. Probably none. Probably just being overthorough again. Raymond sat watching the witness, watching him enjoy himself on the witness stand. He felt sorry for the old man.

'Do you have a good view of the church parking lot, Mr Burkwright?'

'Oh, yeah. No trees in the way or nothing. The streetlight's on the other side of the church and half the time it's busted out, but they always leave some lights on inside the church and they kind of spotlight the parking lot.'

Tyler nodded again. 'What did you see that night, April sixteenth?'

'Two men, like I started to say. In the parking lot, back up in the corner furthest from the street, which means closest to my house. One of 'em, that would be the black one, was down on the ground, on his back, reaching out toward the other one like "Don't hit me again." And the other one, this gentleman here, was standing over him with his fist doubled up.'

Tyler felt very little control over the examination. Information was coming in willy-nilly rather than in the dramatic way he wished to present it. He had to leap into the witness's pauses for breath.

'When you said "this gentleman here", whom did you mean, sir?'

'Him.' Burkwright pointed.

'I'm sorry, so we can be sure, would you mind standing up, please?' Tyler's inexperience worked to his advantage. Raymond would have objected to such a display if requested by a prosecutor who knew better. But it would have been surly to refuse Tyler Hammond's mild, polite, flustered request. Stennett rose to his feet. Raymond would have told him to keep his hands unclenched, but whispering instructions to him in front of the jury would have been as bad as leaving him uninstructed, so he said nothing, and Stennett kept his hands loosely clasped in front of him, rather like one fist atop another. The shoulders of his jacket looked a little strained.

'That's him,' Haley Burkwright said.

Stennett sat down, feeling he'd just tried on the public stocks for sizing.

'And what was the defendant doing the night you saw him in the church parking lot?'

'Well, he reached down and pulled the other one to

his feet and hit him in the stomach. Oh, and I mean hard. Just doubled the boy over. Made me wince.'

The very distinct bruise on the abdomen, Raymond thought.

'Did the black man fight back?' Tyler asked. In the configuration of the courtroom his voice seemed to come detached and disembodied, while the jurors kept their eyes on the witness.

'No, sir. Never got a chance, that I seen. He'd try to crawl away, that was about it.'

'Did you ever hear them say anything?'

'This one, the one doing the beating, he said something like it wasn't a game, that this was pretty much it for the other one. Something like that.'

Tyler carried one of the autopsy photos of Gordon Frazier, one of the close-ups of the face, to the witness stand. 'Was this the man you saw being beaten?'

'Yes, sir. I'd seen him around the neighborhood before, but I didn't know his name. And it's kinda hard to tell this is him, isn't it?'

Tyler let silence comment on that while he resumed his seat. 'What about the other one, the white man, did you know him before that night?'

'I thought I'd seen him around too, but I wasn't so sure. That's why I went up to get a better look.'

Raymond, surprised, looked at Tyler and saw he was *not* surprised. 'How did you do that?' Tyler asked.

'Just walked down to the corner of my backyard. I got a pretty good-sized yard, and it slopes down toward the church, so when I come down to the corner there I's just across the alley from 'em. Maybe twenty feet. And they didn't see me at first, being busy, so I just stood there and watched. I wanted to see how serious it was before I decided whether to do anything about it.'

'How serious was it?'

Haley Burkwright looked thoughtful, as if it hadn't occurred to him before that he'd be telling this part of the story. 'I hadn't seen a fight like that in a long time,' he said slowly. 'One where somebody really means to hurt somebody else? I'd forgotten what it *sounds* like. It didn't look all that terrible. If I'd been watchin' it from inside my house, through a window, I wouldn't've thought much of it. But when you get right up close like that and hear it –' He shook his head. 'The sound the bones in the fist make when they hit the bones in the face, the crunching sound, like a boot walking on gravel. And you hear the grunt, the straining, you know, of somebody really tryin' to put something behind his punch. And the other guy goes sort of *whomph!* like he's gonna throw up.' The old man stopped, looking faraway. They could see he was hearing it now, trying to get it right. 'Then his breathing comes loud, you can hear it, but there's – a hole in it, too, like something's caught in his throat and he can't get it out and he can't breathe around it.' Burkwright hunched his shoulders inward. He was sobered, no longer joyous at telling his story. 'When I heard it, that's when I decided I'd better say something.'

'Did you?' Tyler asked quietly. The old man had fallen into a reverie he didn't like to disturb.

Burkwright looked up. 'Oh, yes. I didn't have to say much, just "Hey", you know, something like that. Just let 'em know somebody was watchin'. I thought that'd break it up. The other one, the black one, he was down on his face, I thought he might've been out already. But this one heard me, he spun around and looked at me, just stared for a minute, and he still had his fist bunched up. I thought if I stepped back he'd come after me, too. But we just looked at each other. Closer than I am to him now.'

269

'Then you're positive of your identification?' Tyler asked.

'Oh, yes, sir. Even without him taking his shirt off.'

'What?'

Raymond glanced at Tyler and saw he *was* surprised this time. Raymond probably understood faster than the prosecutor. He leaned over and spoke to his client.

Haley Burkwright said matter-of-factly, 'It'd been a hot day, and he was wearing one of those shirts, what do they call 'em? Made like undershirts, you know, with no sleeves and the shoulders cut out. And before he turned around I saw he had a mark right here.' He reached across his chest to pat the back of his right shoulder. 'Looked like, like an old burn or something. That what it was, a burn scar?' He asked that directly of Mike Stennett.

Everyone was looking at Stennett: the judge, everyone. Except Raymond, who was staring straight ahead. And Becky, who was looking at Raymond.

'Ask for a display,' she whispered to Tyler. A risky request. If the old man was wrong they would severely undercut his credibility. Maybe behind Raymond's closed expression the defense lawyer was hoping they would do just that. He had already received an answer from his defendant; he knew. But the prosecutors had to make the request. If they left the question open the jury would wonder why they hadn't asked. If there was no scar Raymond would certainly bring that out during his own case, so they couldn't avoid the bad news, if it was bad news. Better to find it out now, so they could explain away the old man's mistake. Damn him, why hadn't he mentioned this before?

Haley Burkwright seemed to have no idea of the furor he had caused. He sat in the witness chair at ease again, leaning back, looking at the jurors as if he might strike up a conversation with them.

Tyler rose. 'Your Honor, we ask that the defendant display his shoulder to the jury.'

Raymond also stood. 'Approach the bench, Your Honor?'

Thank you, God, Becky thought. It was true, there was a scar. The defense lawyer didn't want the jury to hear his objection, didn't want them to know he was trying to keep it from them. But we asked, Becky thought. *They'll know we wanted to show it to them, even if the judge doesn't let us.*

The three lawyers gathered in front of the judge. 'Your Honor, I have to object to this,' Raymond said quietly.

'Why?' Judge Byrnes was a model of impartiality. One way to read her expression was, *Just because I told you to start objecting doesn't mean I'm going to sustain them when you do.*

'Your Honor, asking my client to strip and display himself like an exhibit to this jury would be barbaric. It would be extremely prejudicial. The State doesn't need it. They already have a positive identification.'

'Which will be severely undermined if we're not allowed to prove the truth of this claim by our identification witness, Your Honor,' Tyler said. Becky was proud of him. Speaking only to other lawyers, he could be smooth as glass.

'I agree,' said the judge. 'The hole that would leave in the State's case outweighs the embarrassment to your client. However, I will clear the courtroom first.'

'Oh hell, let 'em all see. The jury's the only ones that count. If you're letting it in let's be public about it. I don't care about his sensibilities.' Raymond stalked away and resumed his seat without a word to his client, who looked at him questioningly.

'Mr Stennett, I'm granting the State's request,' the

judge explained helpfully. 'Please stand and display your shoulder to the jurors.'

Some people could have done it icily, as if personally uninvolved. Mike Stennett was not one of those. He leaned toward his lawyer, received a shrug in response to his whispered question, and slowly stood. He made an awkward moment as awkward as possible, and as long. Standing beside his chair, he removed his jacket and his tie and laid them across the table. Acutely conscious of the roomful of people at his back, he went and stood directly in front of the jury box, which afforded him some protection from the spectators as he unbuttoned his shirt. His face had turned red and it kept darkening until there seemed no more shades of red to which it could deepen. He unbuttoned only his top four buttons, found that wasn't enough, and unbuttoned all the rest, pulling the shirt out of his pants and dropping it down below his shoulders like a shawl. He turned and stood in front of the jurors like a statue. Their heads moved to get better views. So did Haley Burkwright's.

'Yeah, burn scar,' he said. 'Or is it a bullet wound?' he asked Stennett as if he expected an answer, and shrugged when he received none.

Stennett stood for five seconds, then pulled up his shirt, kept his back to the jury while he tucked it in, so they couldn't see the look he was giving the witness, then hastily buttoned up while returning to his seat. He shrugged into his jacket and sat with his necktie in his lap, not looking at anyone. His head looked as if it would explode from the pressure of blood.

That was the moment to pass the witness, the moment of highest tension. Let the defense lawyer cross-examine the witness while the sight of that affirming scar remained vivid in the jurors' minds. But Tyler didn't seize the moment. He hated to let go of his most important witness before wringing him dry of information.

'What happened after you spoke?' he asked.

'Well, while the defendant here and I were staring at each other, the black boy came to his senses and took off. I saw him raise up and shake his head and then he just took off like a sprinter. This one turned around and yelled at him and took off after him.'

'Did the victim appear seriously injured?'

'He was down on the ground facing away from me and he run off without looking back, so I didn't get a look at his face. From what I heard and seen he must've been hurt some, and he wasn't running all that great. But . . .' He shrugged.

'And the defendant, you say he ran after him?'

'Yes sir. He was going faster, looked like he'd catch him, but they turned the corner around the church and that's the last I saw of 'em. But when I saw in the paper that Frazier was dead, beat to death, that's when I put two and two together and called the police.'

Tyler nodded. He was formulating another question when Becky leaned over and whispered to him. He said something back, she became more emphatic, and Tyler stood up to say, 'I pass the witness, Your Honor.'

No voice replaced his. The silence lengthened until the prosecutors left off their whispered colloquy to turn to their left. The judge was also looking in that direction, as was Mike Stennett. Raymond sat, still slumped as he'd been since dropping into his chair after his objection to the display was overruled. He sat staring at Haley Burkwright, who was one of the few people in the room not looking at the defense lawyer.

You are mine, old man, Raymond thought. *From*

where I sit I can stretch out my hand, tap you on the forehead, and you will crumble like a column of ash. It was sad to see the old man sitting there unaware of the nearness of destruction.

Raymond sat up. 'No questions,' he said, and began scribbling notes on the legal pad in front of him. Stennett grabbed his arm. Raymond shook him off.

Judge Byrnes watched the defendant frantically whispering to his lawyer, watched Raymond ignore him. She felt the trial slipping away from her. She had seen many incompetent lawyers but she had never before seen one deliberately betray a client. She wanted to call a halt to everything. But she didn't. It wasn't the anger of Raymond's response to her last reprimand that kept her from calling another conference in her chambers. It was the correctness of it. She couldn't try the case herself and she couldn't make him try it.

'Call your next witness,' she said to the prosecutors.

That was not what Tyler had expected her to say. He required another hurried exchange with Becky. Afterwards, 'The State rests,' he said.

Becky was thinking that this was where a case usually ended. Sometimes the defense called a witness or two, to contradict some part of her case, but at least half the time they called none. One of the many good reasons for a defense lawyer not to let his defendant testify was that he usually came off looking like a liar. In this case Raymond knew the kind of ammunition she had if he put Stennett on the stand. And a defendant often had no one else *to* call. So the State's case was often as not the only case. After the scant opposition Raymond had put up so far, Judge Byrnes obviously didn't expect a defense in this trial. 'Are you ready to begin?' she asked the defense lawyer as a matter of form, the signal for him to rest as well.

'Yes, Your Honor,' Raymond said snappily.

The judge should have done a better job of keeping surprise out of her voice when she said, 'You have witnesses to present?'

'Yes, Your Honor. I can have the first one here in twenty minutes.'

The judge looked at her watch, looked at the jurors shifting restlessly. 'We'll begin after lunch. You'll be kept together for lunch,' she said to the jury. 'Don't discuss what you've heard today, even with each other. One o'clock,' she said to everyone else.

'What the hell was that?' Stennett raged. 'That old man's gone, you know, you've lost your chance to destroy his testimony. And they can throw everybody else's testimony in the shitter as long as they've got him.'

'He was compelling, wasn't he?' Raymond said quietly.

Stennett stopped pacing and glared at him. There was an uneasiness beneath the glare. He had realized that morning how badly he might have miscalculated in his choice of lawyer. 'But he was wrong,' he said forcefully.

'How'd he know about the burn, Mike? *I* didn't know about the scar on your shoulder. The prosecutors didn't know about it. You spent a lot of time at the beach with the old man?'

'How the hell do I know? He said he's seen me around. Or maybe somebody told him. It's no big family secret. My partners've seen it. I don't try to hide it.' He was looking away as he spun these possibilities. When Raymond didn't reply the silence grew cumbersome.

Raymond was looking at his client. Something was

wrong. The evidence of what he knew and what he could see were irreconcilable. Raymond had shared what he had learned from Reverend Entwhistle with Stennett; the State's case was a bust. But Raymond had seldom seen a stronger case and he had never seen anyone act more guilty than Stennett looked now.

Stennett was finally looking at him again. 'Are you gonna give me a defense? Or do I go to the judge and tell her I want a new lawyer? I think she'd give me one.'

'I'll give you a defense.'

But Stennett didn't like the tone of that reply. He leaned across the table. 'You know I didn't do it.'

Raymond stirred. 'I know you didn't do it the way and the place they think you did it. I know you *would* do it, if you thought it needed doing and you could get away with it.'

'I think I'd better see the judge,' Stennett said. But he didn't turn away. Raymond continued as if they'd only been discussing the defense.

'Time to stop being coy about this alibi witness, Mike. You testify you were with him but don't let the jury see him, it looks like the world's most obvious lie. We have to put him on. I don't care if he lies on the stand. They'll expect him to lie. But they have to see he exists.'

'And how long do you think he'd live after he walks out of this courtroom, after I testify he's been my informant on twenty cases? That he's put that many people in the joint?'

Raymond shrugged. He was going to press this to the wall, at least for his own benefit, make Stennett produce or admit he'd been lying. 'If we burn him, we burn him. That's the business he's in. Tough.'

Stennett rocked back, studying his lawyer. His expression changed from adamant to crafty. 'All right. You give him a call. He'll be glad to hear from you.'

'No, you call him, he's your snitch. Arrange a meeting. I'll be –'

'You call him,' Stennett repeated, interrupting. 'He's your friend. Cadillac Pierce. Tell him you want a favor.'

'Bullshit.'

'Bullshit yourself. Why d'you think we were at the stadium that night? I didn't follow you there. I work there, remember? I'm the man with the keys. Cadillac was meeting me there. Not for the first time. He's a little worried about this trial. I told him don't sweat it. But you tell him we've decided to burn him instead. He won't mind it coming from you.'

If it was a lie it was a good one. Raymond remembered the silly evasive measures he'd taken while driving to the stadium. He didn't think Stennett could have followed him there. It made everything make sense. And Cadillac had been in the life long enough to be playing both sides. He *had* stayed arrest-free for a remarkably long time. The story solved something else, too.

'You think Cadillac tried to kill you that night? Maybe you didn't convince him he could trust you?'

'I don't *think* so,' Stennett said carefully. 'I don't see Cadillac pulling the trigger like that. But he's sure a good candidate, isn't he? And he did miss. Maybe he tried and couldn't do it. I don't know.'

Stennett had lost his evasiveness. He looked sincere now. But a good liar could lose himself in a good lie. It didn't matter, though. If Stennett's alibi witness wasn't Cadillac it was someone like him. Someone whose life was at stake, who would lie, wriggle, maybe kill to avoid the trial. They'd never find him.

Even if he existed.

Raymond's expression cleared. 'Then it's all up to you, baby. Sound real convincing.'

Stennett looked surprised. 'You don't think it'd be better if I just say I was alone?'

'No. You tell the absolute truth.'

'Let's get in there.'

Judge Byrnes was a portrait of the impartial majesty of the law. Raymond might have been someone she had never seen before. 'Is the defense still ready?'

'Yes, Your Honor.'

'Call your first witness.'

'The defense calls Harold Boudro.'

CHAPTER 13

It had been a long time since Raymond had seen his father testify. Years ago he'd gone out of curiosity and to offer support, but he'd soon seen his father didn't need the support. He was solid on the stand, even the first time. It was just part of the job if you ran a public business in a high-crime neighborhood, and Mr Boudro did it as well as he did every other part of his job. He had always testified as a State's witness. He'd been coached by prosecutors who'd done their job well. Raymond hadn't had to spend much time prepping him for this, his first appearance for the defense.

'Please state your name and occupation.'

'Harold Boudro. I'm an independent grocer.'

I'll testify to that, Raymond thought.

'Where is your store located, sir?'

'Boudro's Market, on Perkins Street.'

'Is that on the east side of San Antonio?'

'Yes, it is.'

Mr Boudro sat in the witness stand composedly but not as if he took his appearance there lightly. He had gotten dressed up to the extent that he had removed his apron and put on a jacket. The white shirt and tie were his daily uniform. He looked at the jurors when he answered the questions.

'Mr Boudro, it's obvious to the jury, but just so the record will reflect it, what is your race?'

'I'm a black American.' Raymond's father was aware that the preferred political term was now African-American, but he had never cared to be politically correct. From 'negro' to 'black' was the last vocabulary adjustment he would make in his lifetime.

'Do you know this man to my left?'

'Yes I do. He's a regular customer of my store. He's also a police officer.'

'You know him personally, then?'

'Yes.'

'I'd like you to tell the jury about the occasion when you first learned that Mr Stennett is a police officer.'

'May we approach the bench?' That was Becky, on her feet. Raymond rose too, but as Becky started around her table toward the judge Raymond remained in place.

'I don't think that's necessary, Your Honor,' he said. 'The State is obviously going to object to the relevance of this testimony. It goes to the defendant's racial attitude, a subject the prosecution was allowed to explore thoroughly during its case. This is rebuttal.'

Becky gave Raymond a withering look. She would obviously have liked the jurors left out of this discussion, but as the judge didn't say anything Becky stayed where she was to respond. 'The State's evidence was specifically related to the defendant's performance of his duties as a police officer, which made it relevant to the murder.'

'This testimony will be, too,' Raymond said laconically.

Judge Byrnes was looking at him speculatively, wondering if this had been his plan all along or if he was just scrambling to save face – and his license – after her threat in chambers. This was turning into a novel trial. Judges hate novel trials.

'If that was an objection I'll overrule it,' said the judge. 'You may continue, Mr Boudro.' She nodded to indicate she was speaking to the witness.

Mr Boudro told the jurors of the time when Mike Stennett had placed his wallet and his life in the store owner's black hands. He told the story simply, looking at the jurors, letting the implications raise themselves.

'Has he ever treated you less than courteously?' Raymond asked at the conclusion of the tale.

'No. He is always perfectly polite.'

'What does he call you?'

'He calls me Mr Boudro.'

'And he remains a regular customer of your store?'

'Yes.'

'Thank you.' As Raymond passed the witness he also passed a note to the prosecution table. The note said, 'Rip him to pieces.' Tyler handed the note to Becky, who was already asking her first question as she read it.

'You never encountered the defendant in a dark alley, did you, Mr Boudro?'

'No.'

'You were never questioned by him as a suspect in a crime?'

'No, I wasn't.'

'Were you in the parking lot of the Ezekiel Avenue Baptist Church the night of April sixteenth?'

'No, ma'am, I was nowhere near.'

'So you don't know what Mike Stennett did to Gordon Frazier that night?'

'No I don't. Or if he did anything.'

Becky glanced again at Raymond's note, and at the defense lawyer himself. 'Mr Boudro,' she said to his father, 'just so the jury can place your testimony in perspective, would you explain why you and the defendant's attorney have the same last name?'

'I'm his father,' the grocer said, looking at his son with measured pride.

'Thank –'

'But if you think I'd lie for him because of that, you don't know me.'

Becky had forgotten, as lawyers often forget, that witnesses have lives outside the trial. Witnesses took their place in the stand as on a stage. She had a use for them or had to damage them; during a trial she put out of her mind that witnesses had lives, and characters, apart from their roles in the drama. But Harold Boudro's quiet statement forced Becky to look at him as a real person for the first time, not just as a defense ploy. 'I *don't* know you, Mr Boudro,' she said, 'and I didn't mean to impugn your honesty. I apologize.'

Raymond wanted to lean across the narrow space between the tables and say, 'He does that so well, doesn't he? Makes you feel this big,' but there was no opportunity. Spending all his energy keeping his face straight, he excused the witness.

In his father's place Raymond called two more east side merchants familiar with Stennett. They had dealt with him for years and never received the impression he looked down on them because of their race. They hadn't had occasion, like Harold Boudro, to learn of Stennett's undercover work, but after being informed about it prior to trial they were lavish in his praise. Their business and their children were in danger because of the lack of men like Mike Stennett. The defendant in his public seat began to look embarrassed but pleased. But this was no testimonial dinner.

'*Why* do we need more like him?' Becky asked the second of the witnesses, a garage owner who'd been robbed and assaulted by what he called 'dopeheads'.

'Because he does what he had to do to clean out that element,' Isaiah Prescott answered.

'Whatever he has to do?'

'Yes, ma'am.'

'And understandably, you approve of that.'

'I don't think he should kill anybody –'

'Not deliberately, but if it happens, it happens, right, Mr Prescott?'

'Well –' The mechanic shrugged his heavy shoulders.

'Did you know Gordon Frazier, Mr Prescott?'

'No.'

'He never robbed you, did he?'

'No.'

'He was just maybe suspected of something, possessing drugs, maybe.' She was far outside anything to which this witness could testify, but Raymond let her continue. 'A lot of cars pass through your garage, don't they, Mr Prescott?'

'In a good month,' the witness joked.

'Some of them can't be fixed, so you strip the usable parts out of them and sell the parts and sell what's left for junk, does that happen?'

'Yes, some.'

'That would be a good front for a stolen car operation, wouldn't it? I'm not saying it happens' – she cut off his belligerent response – 'I'm saying someone could get the idea. Get suspicious. It could be you Mike Stennett wants to question some dark night in a parking lot, couldn't it, Mr Prescott?'

There was no good answer. Raymond saved the witness, finally, with an objection, but the point had been made. *And that's how you play the game when there are no rules*, Raymond thought. He was proud of Becky.

'Reverend John Entwhistle,' he said to the judge and the bailiff and the courtroom. The prosecutors mouthed 'Who?' at each other and turned to watch the minister make his way up the aisle. Raymond leaned over and said, 'This is the big bomb. I tried to warn you.'

'I'm the minister of the Ezekiel Avenue Baptist Church,' Entwhistle said moments later. The prosecutors sat stiffly, not even making notes yet.

'Reverend, we've been hearing about an event that supposedly took place in the parking lot of your church Wednesday night, April sixteenth of this year.' A good objection to that question occurred to Becky: informing a witness of an earlier witness's testimony, but it wasn't important, it would come in another way. Becky just sat there tight-lipped. Raymond continued, 'Can you tell us what was taking place at the church that night?'

'We had a revival meeting.'

Becky gripped Tyler's arm.

'What time did it begin?' Raymond was asking the questions gently, as if broaching a painful subject.

'We were to start at eight o'clock, but we were a little late. As usual.' The witness smiled.

'And how late did the meeting run, Reverend?'

'Our evangelist' – the minister shook his head, admiringly, a little embarrassed – 'was filled with the spirit. And his altar call drew a great response. Many souls came forward to pray and weep and be saved. Afterwards no one wanted to go home. They lingered on and on. I was the last to leave, and it must have been after eleven o'clock.'

Raymond nodded, made a note. 'Was the meeting well attended, Reverend Entwhistle?'

The minister nodded and smiled again. 'It was one of our most successful ever. Our attendance was more than two hundred people.'

'Did they come in cars?'

'Yes sir. The parking lot was full. Cars blocked other

cars in, and people had to park on the street for blocks around.'

'Did people remain inside the church during the whole meeting?'

'People came and went. Not all our congregation has renounced every vice, I'm sorry to say. At any given time there might have been two or three men outside smoking. And of course there were a few crying babies who needed to be taken outside for air, or feeding.' *There always are*, said his indulgent expression.

'Did anyone report to you a disturbance in the parking lot?' Raymond's voice had grown softer and softer.

'No, sir.'

'Pass the witness.'

It was moments before Tyler realized this was his witness to cross-examine. He looked at Becky, but she had nothing to say to him. 'Are you certain about those times, Reverend?' Tyler finally asked.

'Well, roughly. I know I was at the church by seven-thirty to make sure everything was in order, and it was late when I left.'

'And the date? April sixteenth?'

'Oh, yes. It was on my calendar. And I brought a program.' From his inside pocket the minister produced a many-folded sheet of paper. As he unfolded it gentle Jesus appeared on the cover, carrying a lamb under his arm. 'Would you like to see?'

'That won't be necessary. Thank you, Reverend.' Tyler looked again at Becky. She had been thinking frantically for minutes, but no question had come to her. Were they talking about the wrong place? But it was the church their own witness had named. And Haley Burkwright couldn't have been confused about the location, it was his home. As for the time, the medical examiner's report had established that the body was already in the morgue by eleven o'clock. Time, date, place. Wait, wait. She scribbled a note. Tyler read it off.

'Do you remember what time it got dark that night, Reverend Entwhistle?'

The minister looked surprised. 'Early April, not on daylight savings time yet . . . I'd guess –' The word *guess* was a signal for an objection, but Raymond sat quiet. He was curious about the answer. He was curious about the question. 'I'd guess by six-thirty it was dark.'

'Thank you,' Tyler said, then repeated aloud what Becky whispered to him. 'That's all.'

That was all for Raymond too. He shook hands with the minister as he passed on his way out. *Here he's charged with killing a black man, and I'm calling all the black witnesses to defend him*, it occurred to Raymond. But he was about to break the pattern.

'We wish to recall Haley Burkwright, Your Honor.'

Ripple through the courtroom. After the testimony they'd just heard, it seemed cruel to bring the old man back.

'Is he here?' the judge asked the prosecutors.

'No, Your Honor, we thought he'd been excused. I assume he's at home . . .'

'This will take a while, won't it?' Judge Judy asked Raymond, who shrugged as if to say, How long would *you* spend on him? 'Let's do it in the morning,' the judge concluded.

The next morning, looking at the witness, it was obvious to Raymond, and didn't surprise him to see, that Haley Burkwright knew what was up. When Burkwright took the stand that morning he was no longer happy to be there. He looked grim, chastened, almost belligerent, as if someone had already accused him of lying. Raymond had expected as much, but it was improper. The witness should have been left completely uninformed of what had happened in court besides his own testimony. Raymond leaned across the narrow space between the tables and said softly, 'Correct me if I'm wrong, but it looks as if someone has violated the rule.'

'There are no rules,' Becky said, looking straight ahead.

When he began his examination, Raymond took it very gently.

'Mr Burkwright, you testifed during your first appearance about a beating you said you saw take place on the church parking lot behind your house . . .'

'I could've been wrong about the time,' Haley said immediately. 'Like I said, time's not that important to me. I don't watch TV –'

Raymond held up a hand. 'That's not my question, Mr Burkwright. I want to ask you about your familiarity with the defendant.' He waved the hand at Stennett. 'You know him, don't you? You knew him before you saw him in any muscle shirt in any parking lot, didn't you?'

'I *said* I thought I'd seen him before. I guess somewhere around the neighborhood . . .'

He stopped because Raymond was shaking his head. 'Not around the neighborhood, Mr Burkwright. Not in the streets. You saw him dressed pretty much the way he is today, in another courtroom. When he testified against your grandson.'

A gentle stir ran through the crowd in the courtroom. Gentle because they continued to watch the old man for reaction. He showed none at first. Just sat there, bowed slightly, waiting for a question. He shifted his attention from the lawyer to the defendant, as if the question might come from him instead.

Raymond glanced at the prosecution table. They too were watching their witness intently. They looked stoic. They did not look surprised.

'That *was* your grandson, wasn't it, Mr Burkwright, Edward Navarro, who was arrested for possession of more than five pounds of marijuana? Who Mike Stennett arrested?'

'Was that him?' Burkwright said quietly. 'I didn't remember the officer's name. I came to the trial but I couldn't stand to watch all of it. I kept going out into the hall.'

'Maybe you ran into Detective Stennett there,' Raymond suggested.

'Maybe so. I knew he looked familiar. But if you're saying I held a grudge because of that you're dead wrong. Getting arrested for that pot was the best thing that ever happened to that boy. He was nineteen years old, he'd dropped out of school, he wouldn't work, he thought he could get by messing with dope and his ignorant friends. I was *glad* when he got busted. I told his mother, "This'll be good for Eddie. He'll learn a lesson." And he did. He served his probation, he's got a job now –'

'Was it good for him to get beaten up in jail while he was waiting for trial? Was it the best thing that ever happened to him when someone tried to sexually assault him in his cell? That's not what he said in the civil suit he filed against the county, was it, Mr Burkwright?'

The witness's voice dropped to a mumble again. 'I don't know anything about that. I don't know if that was true or not. I know he dropped that suit.'

'Well, to be accurate, he settled it. At any rate, it

didn't leave you any great love for the man who put Eddie in that cell, did it, Mr Burkwright? When you went through the police station looking for a suspect to name, that was the familiar face you were looking for, wasn't it?'

The old man was looking down at the floor, shaking his head. 'I had nothing against him,' he said again.

When Raymond passed the witness he was surprised to see Tyler prepare himself to cross-examine. They must have decided Tyler could more gently draw out the old man, who sat on the stand looking broken. But when Tyler spoke it was in a voice Raymond had never heard before.

'So you lied?' he said loudly. 'To get even you went to the cops and lied about this man, then you came to the District Attorney's office and lied to me and lied to Ms Schirhart, and then you got up in front of this jury –'

Haley Burkwright's head had snapped up. His face was growing red, but it took him that long to interrupt, as if he couldn't believe what he was hearing. 'No!' he finally shouted. 'No. I never –' His eyes blazed. He pointed a bony finger. 'I would *never* come in here and take an oath to tell the truth and then lie to these people.' He looked at the jurors as if they were old friends whose confidence in him was in jeopardy. 'And I would *never* say I saw a man do what I saw this man do if I hadn't seen it with my own eyes. I saw him in that parking lot, hitting a man like he meant to kill him. And when he heard me and turned around, and he gave me that *look* that just took me back, that made me realize my own life was on the line. You don't forget the face that gives you a look like that. Look at him. Look at him right now. No, sir. I don't remember him from that damned trial. I remember him from that parking lot, when I saw him beating a man to death.'

The jurors were looking at Stennett, at the appraising look he was giving Haley Burkwright. How should you look at the witness who makes an accusation like that? Give him a big smile? A look of pity? Stennett was obviously thinking hard about the question, but all he could come up with was that thoughtful stare.

Tyler's angry voice having accomplished its purpose, it was discarded. Raymond was looking at him, amazed, admiring. The rumpled professor had reappeared, replacing the hardassed prosecutor Raymond had never suspected existed.

'But are you sure of the time, Haley?' Tyler was the only person in the room old enough to sound justified in calling the old man by his first name.

'No. *You* told me the time.' Oops. There was a bit of prosecutorial misconduct they hoped wouldn't get mentioned again. 'I just remember it was that night some time. After dark. Could've been seven o'clock. I didn't remember it was the same night as their big revival meeting, but that don't mean nothin'. I told you nights're all the same to me. I know what I saw. Just because I don't remember exactly when I saw it doesn't mean it didn't happen. It happened. You know it happened.'

The last remark was directed to Mike Stennett. It was a good stopping point, and this time Tyler took it. So did the judge, calling a short recess. The lawyers and the spectators stood and stretched, and the jurors filed out of the box, but Haley Burkwright just sat, watching them trickle past him, the witness looking as if he were the one on trial.

'Did you know Gordon Frazier?'

'Sure,' Stennett said. 'I'd seen him around, in bars, and in places where drug deals were going down. I'd be undercover and he'd be doing business. But I never saw him selling, only buying, so I never had him popped. Other people did, but I didn't. I was kind of waiting for him to move up in the world, but he never did.'

'Did he know you?' No one was studying Raymond as he put the questions. All eyes were on Stennett. Raymond was doing an impression of himself, duplicating the performance he would give in any other trial. But if anyone had looked at him they would have seen that the performance didn't extend to his face. He was studying his client in exactly the same way the jurors were.

'He knew my face, and he probably knew my name, but he wouldn't've known they went together. He would've known there was a narcotics cop named Mike Stennett. Your name gets known, I mean it's a matter of public record. Your name appears on the affidavits for their arrest warrants, and once in a while you have to testify and your name gets out that way. But as long as they don't know the name goes with the face you're okay. He may've even used my name in vain once or twice.'

'What do you mean by that?'

'I heard from another cop once that he was about to bust Frazier for something but Frazier took him aside and said he was working for me. Used my name. But it was just a name he'd heard. Because I'd see him sometimes and he didn't even know me.'

The answer, imparting news he hadn't heard before, stirred something in Raymond's memory, but he didn't have time to consider it, and he certainly wasn't going to ask questions in front of the jury to which he didn't know the answers. 'But he could have been a useful source of information anyway, couldn't he?' he asked instead.

'He could have if he'd wanted, but I had others. I had nothing to do with Gordon Frazier.'

'You just knew him well enough to identify him at the morgue that night.'

'That's right.'

Raymond would have phrased it differently for an ordinary client, but Stennett was a professional, a professional witness. So Raymond put the important question in terms with which everyone in the room could nod along. 'All right, Detective, you've been here, you've heard it. What we're talking about is a Wednesday night, April sixteenth. In the parking lot of Ezekiel Avenue Baptist Church. Were you there?'

'No.'

'Where were you, from, say, dark on?'

'Between about six and about eight I was with somebody, an informant of mine. We met on the other side of town, out Bandera, 'cause of course he didn't want to be seen with me. And we had a couple of beers and talked.'

'In a bar?'

Stennett gave him a stupid-question look. 'That would've been too chancy. We just got a six-pack and drove around a little.'

'Was he providing you with information?'

'He gave me a couple of things but I never got the chance to follow up on 'em. Mostly he just wanted to talk. Snitches're people too, you know. Sometimes they just want a beer and a chat.'

If this was Stennett's attempt to look like a warm, personable guy, it didn't come off with Raymond, but Raymond wasn't on the jury, not officially.

'What's this informant's name?' he asked.

'I can't tell you that,' Stennett said. He looked a little smug. This was the stance he'd been waiting to take. But he was surprised to see his lawyer rise to his feet.

'Your Honor, will you please instruct the witness that he can be held in contempt if he doesn't answer the question?'

Judge Byrnes looked hard at Raymond, but no one was watching her. Mike Stennett's reaction was much stronger. *You son of a bitch*, his expression said more clearly than words.

'Detective, you've been sworn as a witness,' the judge said tonelessly. 'You have no privilege not to answer the question. If you refuse I can hold you in contempt, which would mean placing you in jail until you agree to answer.'

'Then you'll just have to put me in jail,' Stennett said hotly, 'because I'm not giving the name. I already told *him*, this guy's made cases for me. He's put people away. If I say his name he'd be dead. He'd be dead. I don't have to get him in here, all it takes is me saying the name. And the one thing I promised him a long time ago is that nobody'd ever find out his name from me. I didn't think it'd be a judge doing the asking, but it doesn't matter.' He was glaring at his lawyer.

Now that time you sounded sincere, Raymond thought, and resumed his seat. 'I'll withdraw the question,' he said. 'So that's from six to eight,' he continued mildly. 'Where were you after eight?' Not that it mattered. From eight on nothing had happened in that church parking lot except people parking their cars and going in to be saved.

Stennett took a moment to recover. He had just flung himself against a stone wall to discover it was only a paper drawing of a wall. He had the surprised look of a man rising from the ground. 'Uh – About eight I dropped off – my informant – back at his car and I went cruising around a little by myself. Nothing much was going on. I had a party staked out when I got a call from the dispatcher asking me to go by the M.E.'s to see if I could ID a body.'

Raymond was looking upward, beyond the walls of the courtroom. He felt a little like an orchestra conductor. *Isn't this nice? What shall I ask you next? Shall I make you deny what everyone knows is your method of operation? Force you to explain yourself? The prosecutors aren't going to object if I ask you something that makes you look bad. Shall I take you by the hand and lead you over a precipice? Or into a blank wall?*

For some reason he thought of his father. The jury was full of his father. They didn't care about rules of procedure. They wanted to know what had happened. Abruptly, he decided if Stennett was going to be betrayed, it would be by himself.

'Detective,' he said, 'we've heard allegations from some of the State's witnesses that you may mistreat suspects. Is that true?'

'I've never killed anyone.' Stennett glowered, looking capable of it. 'I've never even come close. But I've had to protect myself once in a while.' He shook his head, lifted his hands helplessly. 'To come in here and try to explain what it's like out there, it's a losing proposition.'

'It's a jungle,' Raymond suggested.

'No. A jungle you know what to expect. You don't have to worry when you're surrounded by gazelles or monkeys. Even an elephant won't hurt you if you leave it alone. But out there – You can't turn your back on anybody. People do things out of character. You can trust somebody twenty times and the next time he'll get you killed. Even your partner . . .' He backed off that subject. Stennett was looking down, twisting his hands, looking more victim than accused. 'Nobody's harmless. Even a docile old duffer like that Burkwright'll come out of nowhere and lie you into something like this.'

'Was he lying?'

Stennett stopped shaking his head. 'I think he just made a mistake. Maybe way in the back of his mind he was mad at me over that business about his grandkid, but I think he just remembered me from that and when he tried to get himself some attention –'

'I object to this speculation,' Becky said. She was mad at herself for letting Stennett ramble on so long before remembering there was something she could do about it. She had fallen into the rhythm of Raymond's trial, she had forgotten there were rules she could use. When Raymond passed the witness the whole world seemed open to her. Mike Stennett's entire life was hers to dissect. She sat for a moment besotted with possibility.

'So you only used force to defend yourself?'

'Well, what do you mean by force?' Stennett asked. Being coy with her was a mistake, Raymond thought. But forthright denial would have been, too, because she had the ammunition to make him out a liar.

'What was the term your lawyer used? "Mistreating suspects"?'

'No, I never did that.'

Becky didn't have to look at the documents, but she picked them up so Stennett would know she had them. 'Isn't it true you received an official reprimand three years ago for using excessive force during an arrest?'

'That's funny, isn't it, who gets to decide what's excessive? Not the officer whose life –'

'Yes or no.'

'Yes.'

'And six years ago you were suspended for ten days for slapping a handcuffed suspect?'

'That was very stupid of me,' Stennett said. He sounded sincere. 'Letting somebody get to me like that just by mouthing off. That doesn't happen anymore.'

'But you were suspended? You don't deny the reason?'

'No.'

They had established their positions quickly. Becky hadn't tried to edge up on him, or make any pretense at being his friend. She looked at the cop like a clogging clump of hair her drain had belched out. He sat up, watching her levelly, waiting. She rose, holding his stare like a dog on a leash, and walked to the evidence on the ledge in front of the judge's bench.

'Do you recognize this gun?'

He hesitated. *Damn you*, Raymond thought. *Say it or don't but don't sit there looking like you're trying to decide the best thing to say.*

'No,' Stennett said. 'I know where it was found, supposedly.'

'But it's not familiar to you?'

'I've seen guns like it. I've handled a lot of guns in my time. Some like that one.'

'In fact you've handled this one. Or do you have some other explanation for your fingerprint being on it?'

'I guess I must've.'

'But this gun hasn't been in a time capsule. It wasn't kept in an airtight canister. It was lying on the street next to a dead body. And you can't explain why it had your fingerprint on it?'

Stennett hesitated again. He looked at his lawyer.

Jerk. 'It's the same make and model as a gun I took off a suspect a while back and turned in to be destroyed. Could be that's how my print got on it.'

'But that one was destroyed,' Becky said.

'Well, it was supposed to be.'

'You mean sometimes what's officially supposed to happen to a gun doesn't? Somebody hangs on to it? Do you have any guns you acquired that way, Detective?'

'Not that one. I turned that one in.'

That was a pretty good answer, from Becky's point of view. She hesitated herself, deciding whether to pin him down. Yes, she decided. Let the jury see him lie again. 'But that wasn't my question, Detective. I asked if you have any unofficial guns like that. What do they call them? Backups?'

It would have been nice if she could have baited him into using the term 'throw-down', but he wasn't that easy. The effortless way he came out with the obvious lie was almost as good, though. 'No. I don't have any like that.'

Becky nodded. Slowly she replaced the gun on the shelf, slowly resumed her seat, until the jurors were watching her. She looked thoughtful, as if there were so many ways to pick him apart. When Becky settled on one the jurors returned their attention to the defendant. It wasn't like a tennis match. The ball stayed in Stennett's court.

'You and Detective Martinez, who testified yesterday, were partners for a while, weren't you?'

'*Sergeant* Martinez. Yes. Two years.'

'That's not very long for a team in Narcotics, is it?'

'Well, I never stayed too long with any partner.' Stennett shrugged.

'That doesn't sound like a recommendation to me.'

This was strange, cross-examination unpunctuated by objection. Becky naturally paused, waiting for it. The silence made her seem to stumble. 'But let's just talk about you and Sergeant Martinez. Didn't you get along?'

'Yeah, we got along fine, we did some good work together.'

'Then why didn't you stay together?'

Stennett sighed and looked distant, as if this were irrelevant. It was, strictly speaking. But again, it was a question that interested the spectators. Stennett had his ready explanation.

'Bernardo's ambitious. You can see that, he's already passed me up on the promotion ladder. It didn't take him long to see that being hooked up with me was holding him back.'

'Why, are you such a lousy cop?'

'I don't think so. I do the job –'

'Don't be so modest, Detective, you're damned good, aren't you? Nobody has a better arrest record than you, do they? Nobody's ever had.'

'Yeah, I think my arrest record compares to anybody's.'

'Then why wouldn't Bernardo Martinez, who's so ambitious, want to hitch his little red wagon to your star? Maybe if he'd stuck with you he would've made sergeant even faster.'

Stennett was talking to an innocent. 'Arrests don't count. Being good at the job don't count. It's politics, and I never played the game.'

'Well, it was *some*thing else, anyway. Did you see him start to testify about the way you make arrests? Did you see the distaste? That's what drove him away from you, wasn't it, Detective Stennett? He didn't like your methods.'

'He never said anything to me,' Stennett said, didn't like that answer, and started over. 'I never did anything out there 'Nardo wouldn't't've done himself.' No, that wasn't quite it either. 'I never done anything to be ashamed of,' he concluded. He remembered to look at the jury.

'Maybe that's a reflection of your capacity for shame,' Becky said.

'Counsel,' the judge said sharply, not waiting for an objection that wouldn't come.

'I'm sorry, Your Honor, I withdraw that. Detective, you heard Mr Burkwright testify. Do you honestly believe he would have gotten up there and lied about you, a police officer, risked a perjury charge, just because you arrested his grandson years ago?'

'I think he made a mistake,' Stennett said, no anger in his voice. He sounded almost compassionate.

'A mistake? A misidentification? Do you think his testimony left open that possibility? Could you demonstrate for us the look you gave him that night, that burned itself into his memory so he said he could never forget?'

He was expressionless with the effort not to do it, not to glare at her. 'I was never there.'

'You weren't in the parking lot, you didn't even see Gordon Frazier that night?'

'Only in the morgue.'

'Only in the morgue. Did you have any reaction when you saw him lying there? Did you wish you could bring him back? Did you think, I didn't mean to kill him? Just rough him up a little?'

'I never touched him,' Stennett said, strongly but not shrill. 'Never. Not that night, not any time. I never laid a hand on Gordon Frazier.' It was the most honest he'd sounded. But it was the line he'd had the most time to practice.

'Would you admit it if you had?' Becky asked. There was no good way to answer the question. He couldn't say no, and if he said yes he'd sound unbelievable. Becky let him chew it over for long seconds before saying, summoning all the contempt she could, 'I pass the witness.'

Raymond tried to think what he'd do for a normal client. Conventional wisdom said you didn't let the State get in the last word, but Raymond often disdained the conventional wisdom. He could rehash the evidence, let it dribble away boringly, quashing the drama of Becky's questioning. But Stennett had already made his best showing in his last, strongest denial. Raymond decided to let that stand or fall on its own. 'No more questions,' he said, and added, 'The defense rests.'

He didn't take the prosecutors as much by surprise, they had lost much of their capacity for surprise, but they still had to confer for a moment before Tyler stood to say, 'We close.'

'Close,' Raymond said as well. No one could have accounted for the sudden bitterness in his expression. No rebuttal witnesses for the State? He stewed through the judge's explanation to the jurors that final arguments would come after lunch. As soon as they began filing out and the spectators rose, and noise reclaimed the room, he turned to the prosecutors and said harshly, 'Couldn't you come up with one damned witness to say something good about Gordon Frazier? Couldn't you even have come up with a good picture of him, something besides mug shots and autopsy photos? His high school graduation picture –'

'He didn't graduate,' Tyler said gently.

'– or a wedding picture, or just some smiling Polaroid from a good day in his life? Couldn't you show he had a life? Couldn't you find anybody who knew him to say one kind word about him?'

He bit off what else he had to say, leaving a loud pulsing silence that ended when Becky said quietly, 'Maybe you could suggest someone, Raymond.'

He turned away with a silent snarl. But he wasn't angry at any deficiency in the prosecution. He could have prosecuted the case himself, and it wouldn't have mattered, he'd still be angry at this stage. Because they hadn't convinced him and he hadn't convinced himself. One way or the other, he still didn't know. It had turned out to be only what it always was, a show for the jury. Now they'd convict or acquit, he couldn't guess which, but he still wouldn't know. He saw his client walking toward him and wanted to choke the truth out of him.

They seemed to be arguing each other's cases. When Raymond began arguing, after Tyler's tidy summary of the evidence, the jurors suffered a temporary disorientation and the judge a deepening suspicion, because the defense lawyer seemed to be arguing the State's case.

'You will be tempted,' he said, 'when this turns out to be a difficult case to decide, when you've argued and found yourselves in disagreement, when you weigh a very solid eyewitness identification against an equally solid denial, and you match the discrepancies in the State's case against the defendant's lack of proof of his alibi defense – you will be tempted to say, "Well, it's not a very important case. It wasn't much of a life that was lost here."

'I tell you, if you start thinking that way you'll be putting every man, woman, and child in this city at risk. Do you want to say if your life isn't entirely respectable it's free for the taking? No. We're not in the business of judging lives here. We don't decide degrees of guilt based on the worthiness of the victim. Gordon Frazier had a life that was worth as much as yours, or mine, or his.' Pointing at Stennett, who was trying to keep his expression neutral, but his eyes were wide. 'Taking it from him was murder.'

Raymond stood over his client, not looking at him. He stood lost in thought, as if deliberating with the jurors. 'Then you might think,' he continued, '"Well, it wasn't murder. Beating, maybe, but he didn't mean to kill him. He just got unlucky." Look at these photos if you think that. You think this was just one poorly placed blow, delivered a little too enthusiastically? Look at these injuries. Look at the number of them. Then remember the indictment. Read the instructions the judge has given you. If you start beating someone, and beat him so badly he dies, it doesn't matter if you didn't mean for him to die. It's murder. Unjustified, first-degree murder. No matter what. No matter how good a reason he had.'

Again pointing at Stennett. But after he had drawn the jury's attention to him, Raymond walked away, toward them, on their side. He appeared struck by a new thought again.

'And while we're thinking about how good his reason was, what *was* his reason? Have we heard one? I was listening for one and I didn't hear one. Did you? From what we've heard here, Mike Stennett and Gordon Frazier had only the most casual, nodding acquaintanceship. Why would this detective suddenly be somewhere beating him to death? Was he arresting him? Interrogating him? Why? Frazier was no drug lord. He had no high-level contacts. He was somebody scrambling for his next dollar, his next meal. What could he give this police officer? There's no sense to it. It doesn't hold together.

'But all right. Let's play let's pretend. Let's say this defendant did have some very good reason for wanting Gordon Frazier dead. Let's give that one to the State. Because his own partner said he thought Mike Stennett would kill somebody if he thought they needed killing. So let's say he did, and then let's look at how he went about it. He could have lured Gordon Frazier to some spot so private they wouldn't be seen by a cat. He could have taken him out with one shot and been gone, and no one would ever have suspected. Instead he picked a church parking lot with houses all around. A church, incidentally, that was crowded with people that night.' He looked at Becky with gentle sympathy. 'She's going to get up here in a minute and tell you her eyewitness made a little mistake. It wasn't at ten o'clock the way he testified, it must have been earlier, about seven, *before* the crowd arrived for the revival meeting. It couldn't have happened when Haley Burkwright said it did, and it didn't happen later, because Gordon Frazier was in the morgue by the time that revival meeting was over. So it must have been earlier than he said.

'But that means this ruthless, cold-blooded killer picked a very public spot for his murder, and he picked seven o'clock in the evening for the time. Just half an hour after sundown, if that. A time when everybody in this city was still awake. When children were still playing outside. When a scream from his victim might bring a dozen neighbors running.

'And by the way, we've been calling Haley Burkwright an eyewitness, but he wasn't, was he? He didn't say he saw a murder, and he didn't. Gordon Frazier's body was found five blocks away, in an alley. When

Haley Burkwright saw him last, Frazier was alive and mobile. So Detective Stennett must have chased him down to finish his foul deed. Boy, he must've been mad, huh? He's just been seen beating his victim by an eyewitness who got a good look at his face, but that didn't deter him. He had to chase Frazier two, three blocks, but that didn't give him time to cool off. No, he wanted him so bad he chased him down, and killed him, and then he fumbled out a gun with his finger-print on it and dropped it and ran.

'Does that sound like what you know about Mike Stennett? This thorough, careful, highly experienced police detective? What else did his partner say about him? If Mike wanted to kill somebody he'd do it – coolly, deliberately. With cold calculation. Not this half-assed botch the State has described to you.'

He held up a hand. 'And *now* we can talk about Gordon Frazier's worth. Now it becomes relevant. Not what we think about him. But what he was worth to Mike Stennett. Because he took a hell of a risk to take Gordon Frazier out. He put himself here, in your hands, a cop risking prison. You think Gordon Frazier was worth that to this man?' He turned and looked at Stennett. They looked at each other. The big room was silent, as if they were alone in it.

'But what about Haley Burkwright?' Raymond asked quietly, turning back to the jury. 'You mean he lied? Well, he had reason to lie.' He picked his way slowly, looking down. 'We know *his* motive. Whether he *did* lie, that's one of those hard questions you have to answer. Let's give the old man the benefit of the doubt and say he made a mistake. We know he made at least one. We know he didn't get it right. But he probably did see something, some time, in that parking lot behind his house. Maybe it had something to do with this case, maybe not. Some stranger did give him that hate-filled look he remembers. But when he read that somebody had been killed nearby, and he went to the police station to try to help, he saw Mike Stennett. And he knew he knew that face. We know where he knew it from. The court where he'd seen the detective testifying against Haley's grandson.'

Raymond's voice had grown soft as the whisper of conscience. 'He just made a mistake. Don't you compound the mistake.'

Hard to read their expressions. Raymond didn't try, he turned his back on them and walked to his seat. And Stennett was watching his lawyer, not the jury.

As Raymond had started out arguing the State's case, Becky appeared to feel obliged to return the favor. She made a defense argument.

'During jury selection I asked you if police officers should be held to a higher standard of conduct than other people, and most of you said yes. Now I have to tell you you were wrong. You can't hold him to a higher standard just because of his occupation. His superiors in the police department can. They can reprimand him, or suspend him, as they've done in the past, or even fire him. You can't. We are not here to enforce the rules and regulations of the police department. There's no occasion here for us to tell him, "We don't like the way you do your job." Or even, "We think you're despicable."

'Let's remember what his job is. He's an undercover narcotics detective. He makes his way incognito among some of the vilest people in this city, the most violent, the least conscience-bound. He lives with stresses you and I can't imagine. I wouldn't last a week at his job. We can't ask that he do this dangerous, terrible job and at the same time adhere to a higher code of conduct none of the rest of us is bound by.

'*But* – we *can* insist that he be bound by the *same* laws. We must. We can't say, "We're going to make an example of you because you're a cop, and you can't step out of line." But neither can we say, "You've got a tough job to do so we're going to let you get away with murder."'

She stood in front of them looking from face to face, asking for a commitment. They gave her nothing. Becky became more conversational. 'He's got a hard job, but he makes it harder, doesn't he? On himself and on everybody else. It's not part of his job to be beating a suspect. If the danger to Mike Stennett increased because of that, that's danger he brought on himself. He can't escape his responsibility under the law because of it. He can't tell you, "Well, he lunged at me, I had to protect myself." The answer to that is, "You shouldn't have been beating him in the first place." And beating is what it was. It wasn't a struggle the defendant got caught up in. You heard our witness. The victim never even fought back. He never got a chance. The only thing he did was try to get away.

'But Mike Stennett wouldn't let him get away. He followed, to a less public spot, an alley, where there were no witnesses to interrupt him, and he finished what he'd started. Defense counsel has suggested he wouldn't have done that once he'd been seen beating Gordon Frazier. But Detective Stennett didn't have to worry about any eyewitness. What were the odds he'd ever be identified? His picture wasn't in any mug book. And he was in a position to keep track of the investigation – as he did – and deflect any suspicion from himself. It was just a fluke that Haley Burkwright had some vague inkling that the man he'd seen was a police officer, and was able to identify him at the police station. Something Mike Stennett hadn't anticipated.

'Not that he was thinking clearly enough to worry about consequences anyway. Look at these pictures. Look at this systematic beating death. Is this the work of a man making reasonable decisions? No, this is a furious man. It's ironic that the defense has tried to paint the defendant as a cold-blooded killer because that makes him less likely to have committed this enraged murder. The truth is he was furious at Gordon Frazier and he made some mistakes as a result.

'*Why* was he furious? That's a clever question by defense counsel, because he thinks it will distract you and he knows we can't answer it. Only two people could tell you what prompted this brutal encounter. One of them can't tell you now and one of them won't. Luckily, it doesn't matter. That's a question we don't have to answer. Look in the charge. Motive isn't one of those elements the State is required to prove. Don't be distracted by that. We just have to prove what he *did*, not why. And we have.

'What about the gun? Defense counsel would have you believe his client was too smart to have left a gun with his telltale fingerprint on it at the scene of the crime. But he didn't think it had his print on it. That gun had been wiped clean, except in one out-of-the-way spot Stennett neglected to wipe. He didn't know the gun would be traced to him.

'So maybe he dropped it on purpose. Why does a police officer carry an untraceable gun like that, one not registered to him? So he can do what Mike Stennett did here. Make a murder look like self-defense. Drop the gun by the murder victim's hand so it looks like he was armed and dangerous when he was killed. Again, that's something we can't know and don't have to prove. If you're worried about the gun, just remember this: we know it came from Mike Stennett and we know it ended up beside the dead body. How else did it get there if he didn't leave it?'

Becky was wrapping up and it scared her. She was the last to argue and she felt the weight of the whole case. Had she answered all Raymond's arguments? Did the jurors have questions she hadn't anticipated? At the end she tried to make it both strong and simple.

'We can't explain everything. Did anyone expect we could? Did anyone think we'd have the whole thing on videotape? Murder is an ugly, furtive business. We're lucky we got any witness to it. He didn't count on that. He didn't count on Haley Burkwright.

'Mr Burkwright got the time wrong.' She pointed at Raymond. 'He told you I was going to tell you my witness made a mistake, well, obviously he did. A very understandable mistake. Look at Haley Burkwright, at the way he lives. He's retired, he lives alone. What's three hours to a man like that? Who sleeps when he wants and eats when he wants and probably goes out on his back porch a dozen times a day? What's a couple of hours' difference to a man like that? You and I probably can't put a precise time to everything we see, and we're bound by clocks, by our working lives. Haley Burkwright isn't.

'But do you doubt what he told you? The essential truth of it? He saw a man beating another man and he went closer to get a better look. So he was this close to the killer when the killer turned and saw *him*, and gave Haley that look that froze him where he stood, because it looked like the killer was going to come after *him*. Do you think he could forget that face? He knows. He may be off on the time, but he knows that face. He'll never forget it.

'But the defendant says he wasn't there, and he was pretty adamant himself.' She backed up and pointed at

Stennett, who was watching her, trying to keep his face neutral, but even a neutral expression on his face looked pretty grim. 'Now you get into comparisons, and motives, and that's when things get murky,' Becky said, as if troubled herself. 'Mike Stennett certainly has good reason to lie. He *has* to lie. But maybe Haley Burkwright has reason, too. Do you really think he'd lie away another man's career, and risk prison himself for perjury, just because of a marijuana case against his grandson? Not as good a reason, is it? But once you start comparing, doubt can creep in.' She still looked doubtful. Then the confusion on her face cleared wonderfully, as she hoped theirs would.

'But we're lucky again. We don't have to decide it just by comparing their certainty. We have something else. You saw it. We made him show it to you.' She was pointing at Stennett again. 'It wasn't just the defendant's face Haley Burkwright identified. It was the burn on his shoulder.

'And he didn't see that in any courtroom. Mike Stennett didn't go on the stand shirtless when he testified against Haley Burkwright's grandson. There's only one place Mr Burkwright could have seen that scar. On a church parking lot, where he saw this man beating another man to death.'

She stood there for long seconds, holding their attention on Mike Stennett, until she dropped her eyes and resumed her seat. Even Judge Byrnes seemed lost in thought for a few moments longer, before remembering her own responsibilities. In a few words she gave the case to the jury. At the counsel tables, only Mike Stennett watched them file out. The lawyers sat with heads slightly bowed, rehearsing what they'd just done, hating the fact that it was over.

★

As Raymond had predicted, the jury had trouble. After they'd been out for two hours everyone settled into waiting. The jurors must have taken a vote by then. When they didn't appear it meant they were stalled. They were talking. There was no easy way out for them. At his client's insistence, Raymond hadn't asked that the jury be allowed to convict of the lesser offense of aggravated assault, a possibility that had been raised by the evidence. For Stennett, one conviction was as bad as another; he didn't want the jury to be allowed to compromise and think they were doing him a favor. It was going to be murder or nothing.

Making it hard on the jury made it hard on everyone. No one stayed in the courtroom, but the participants kept dropping by, finding reasons to return, and when they did they'd talk quietly to the bailiff, or to a newspaper reporter who might be lingering, and they'd look at the closed door of the jury room, wanting to creep closer and listen – no, wanting to go boldly inside and argue some more, ask, 'What's your problem?' and answer the questions that followed.

For the prosecutors it was a little easier. They went to their offices one floor above. Raymond could have returned to his own office, but it was too far away. He called it, called Denise at work, called his father to say the case was over except for the verdict. He found an errand to run downtown, went by the coffee shop, always checking back at the courtroom, letting them know where he could be found. Glancing at the jury room, wondering what the hell they were doing in there. Had they killed each other? Or slipped quietly out a window and gone home? No, the bailiff muttered. They were in there. He'd heard raised voices.

Raymond went by Becky's office for a conversation composed mostly of silences. He congratulated her on her adaptability. 'I think it was an honest trial. We gave them everything they'd want to know,' he said. 'Not like most trials where you spend half your time playing hide-the-ball-from-the-jury.'

'So it should be easy for them to decide, right?' Becky said ironically. She watched Raymond smile unhappily. She asked, 'Have *you* decided?'

There was no place else to go. And so, gradually and by default, Raymond found himself in the company of his client. Stennett had gone from the courthouse to the police station, two blocks away, found no one there he could stand for long, and returned to pace more or less the same confines as Raymond, though he didn't have the lawyer's access to the inner offices. Raymond came across him in the courtroom. They walked without a word of arrangement to an empty conference room. It was a Thursday afternoon, quiet. Once they began talking the silence seemed to grow even deeper outside the room, as if the courthouse were being quietly disassembled and all the employees were tiptoeing away to their homes. 'They didn't prove dick,' Stennett said abruptly. 'Did they? I didn't hear 'em prove anything.'

'That's why the jury came back so fast with a not guilty,' Raymond said.

'Well, the old man –' Stennett began, and seemed to finish the thought without speaking it, then give it a different ending aloud. 'They feel sorry for him, they don't wanta make him look too bad.'

Raymond was silent and still. Stennett paced.

'I don't think it'd hold up even if they did convict, do you? I mean, you proved it didn't happen. It couldn't have. You did a great job, Raymond.'

Raymond didn't accept the compliment or shrug it off. He didn't acknowledge it at all. It hadn't happened. 'Don't pin any hopes on appeal,' he said. 'The jury decides the facts. If they say something happened it doesn't matter if I had ten angels swearing it didn't.'

'But there's no way they could think the Reverend would lie for me. They can't believe that parking lot was empty like the old man said.'

'No,' Raymond said quietly. He looked up at Stennett. 'But he was awfully convincing, wasn't he? And how'd he know about the mark on your back?'

Stennett didn't answer. Raymond stood. 'It's true, isn't it? He saw what he says he saw.' The silence convinced him, but he wanted it said. 'I know some bad things about you already, Stennett. This one must really be terrible if you don't want me to know it. The trial's over. Tell me.'

At first he thought the cop wasn't going to speak. Stennett was obviously thinking furiously, trying to devise an explanation. Raymond watched, waiting for the lie. He saw thought slow, grind to a halt, watched Stennett's face grow smooth. 'He saw something,' Stennett said grudgingly. 'He saw me.'

That was all he was going to say. But he didn't have to say more. 'Oh, my God,' Raymond said, 'I get it. Who did you beat up in that parking lot, and when?' Stennett didn't answer, but it didn't matter. It was all spinning out right in front of Raymond.

'It couldn't've happened the same time as the revival meeting, not there, and it didn't. Burkwright didn't just get the time wrong, he got the whole damn day wrong. Isn't that right? He saw you putting it to somebody real good, but it wasn't Wednesday, was it? He just thought that after he read about Gordie in the paper.'

'Gordie?' Stennett said.

'But you did beat him up – what? the night before?

two nights before? – in that parking lot. The old man saw you, and nobody thinks he was lying about that.'

'No,' Stennett said sullenly. 'I said I never touched Frazier and I didn't. I didn't have any reason –'

'Then who did you have reason to beat up? Burkwright got that wrong, too, huh? He just thought it was Frazier 'cause that's who he read about in the paper. But he never got a good look at the guy on the ground, he just got a good look at you. He just saw it was' – Raymond almost laughed, but not a laugh of amusement – 'a black man.'

Stennett looked off into space. He looked like the most put-upon man on the planet. No one understood. 'It was no big thing.' He finally sighed. 'The old fool made it sound like a matter of life and death. It was just – you know, it was just a little object lesson. And it wasn't Frazier, it had nothing to do with Frazier. *I* had nothing to do with Frazier.'

'You're making this up as you go along,' Raymond said. 'Why didn't you tell me this before? Don't you know how it would have helped?'

'Yeah, right. So my defense woulda been, "No, I didn't kill him, it was some *other* asshole I was beatin' up in that parking lot." But that together with what the old fool thought he saw and it would've been an easy conviction, a lay-down. I know how juries think. Even if they'd believed me, they would've convicted me for the *other* thing. No. You can't have half a defense. You gotta deny everything.

'Besides, I haven't seen the guy since. And even if I could find him, what d'ya think the chances are he'd come into court and save my ass by backing me up?'

'About the same as the chance I'd buy this,' Raymond said. 'No, you did it. Isn't it funny, you should've got away with it, 'cause nobody saw you do

313

Gordie in that alley. But they got you anyway 'cause the old man'd seen you before and got mixed up. Ain't that the most hilarious thing?'

'No.' Stennett was shaking his head furiously. 'No. I didn't kill anybody.'

'But you did,' Raymond insisted. 'You were there in the alley, too. You left your gun.'

'No!'

Raymond leaned toward him. 'Convince me. Prove it to me. I'm the jury. I'm the judge. Make me positive you didn't do it. Make me certain.'

Stennett looked at him suspiciously. 'Why? What'll you do about it?'

Raymond grew calm. He picked up his briefcase. 'All right, don't. I've got enough.'

'For what? Where're you going?' Stennett looked concerned. As if Raymond would walk out and leave him locked in the tiny room forever.

Raymond didn't answer. He started for the door.

'What for? What for?' Stennett shouted again, and started around the table. Raymond didn't look back. But the door opened before he could reach it. A bailiff stuck his head in.

'We've got a verdict,' he said.

CHAPTER 14

There was time. Even when a courtroom stirs to life again, the pace is hardly hectic. The players had to be assembled from all over the building. Even the judge was out of her office and had to be tracked down. The bailiff went to look for her. The door of the conference room closed behind him.

'Well,' Raymond said to his client. 'I think it'll be guilty. Way they looked at you, way they looked at Haley Burkwright. That's all it is, you know, a swearing match between you and him. Plus he's got the gun on his side. I think you better take a deep breath.'

'And what're you gonna do about it?' Stennett said tightly.

'I'm gonna be satisfied.' Raymond opened the door.

'So you're gonna give whoever really did it a free one?' Stennett asked quietly.

It stopped the defense lawyer. It made him close the door and turn back. 'Are you?' he said.

Stennett spoke quickly. He felt the weight of that jury, he heard the sounds of the courtroom filling up. 'If they come back not guilty,' he said, 'like I know they will, I can take it from there. Don't worry about a thing. Job well done. I just may need a little help if they've gone crazy and come back guilty.'

'No shit. You'll need a *lot* of help. Here's how we do it.'

Raymond spoke only a few sentences, but as the lawyer talked, his client wondered when he had had time to come up with these ideas. Stennett began to scowl but when Raymond stopped talking and waited for an answer, the detective finally said, 'All right, all right. If it's necessary. But it won't be.'

When Raymond emerged from the conference room, he took up his station at the door of the courtroom, waiting for Tyler. Others filtered past him slowly. At the same time the official word was going out to the participants, unofficial word spread even more quickly. Reporters trickled into the court, a witness or two, a scattering of cops. Haley Burkwright gave Raymond a glare that the defense lawyer didn't bother to try to deflect with a kind word. He'd never make a friend there.

Raymond caught Tyler in the doorway, Becky behind him. They both looked worried, Raymond was glad to see.

'Come with me,' he said, taking them back out into the hall.

'Why? What's happened?' Tyler tried to peer over Raymond's shoulder.

'Nothing in there. Come on.'

There were reporters in the hall, spectators, any number of people. Raymond led the way across the hall. He glanced down a short side corridor to the men's room, glanced back at Becky, kept going. He ducked through the swinging doors into a stairwell, and down a short flight to a landing where they were alone. The worried looks on his audience's faces had deepened. Raymond started without preamble.

'You going to be satisfied with this verdict? Whatever it is?'

'If it's guilty,' Becky said.

'Really? You that sure he did it?'

She hesitated. 'Yes.'

'Well I'm not. Not sure enough. Tyler? You said you wanted to know for sure. You said that was the most important thing. Was that just bullshit?' He turned back to Becky. 'And what if the verdict's not guilty? You gonna live with that? Will that convince you? Whatever the jury thinks, that's what you think too?'

Becky said, 'What is this, plea bargaining? Are you making an offer?'

'No. I'm asking for help.'

Tyler looked much less decisive than his partner. 'How? It's too late for anything.'

'No it's not. I think I can prove it, one way or another. I just need some support from you.'

'*After* the verdict.' Tyler was puzzling over that one. It was a strange idea to him. The verdict was supposed to be the end.

'Well?' Raymond was looking at Becky. 'You so sure of what it's going to be? Will you be happy with a win? You decide, Becky. What are we about here? The truth? Or just a verdict?'

Becky stepped close to him. A lawyer came clattering down the stairs behind her. They waited for him to pass, silent, looking only at each other. 'Just tell me one thing,' Becky said when they were alone again.

'Is *he* in on this? Your client?' She sounded as if his name were too vile to repeat.

'He thinks he is,' Raymond said.

Stennett was the first one to take his place in the courtroom. He was alone for a long time. The trial grew up again around him, like ice crystals forming. Raymond took his seat without speaking to his client, closely followed by the prosecutors, who leaned their heads together to talk. Judge Byrnes entered from the door behind her chair, still adjusting her robe, and nodded to the bailiff, who disappeared down the short hallway to the jury room.

The jurors didn't fidget. They'd had time to grow bored. They had nothing to anticipate. 'Have you reached a verdict?' the judge asked.

No one instructs jurors in the protocol of the courtroom. They devise their own. The foreman, a white man in his fifties, a man who owned a small print shop, Raymond remembered, decided it was appropriate to rise. 'Yes, we have, Your Honor.'

Some judges read the verdict themselves. Some let the foreman do it. Judy was new enough on the bench to bother to explain as the bailiff took the paper from the foreman and carried it to her. 'After I check the verdict for proper form you will read it aloud, please.'

The judge unfolded the half sheet, read it expressionlessly, and didn't look up at anyone. Raymond watched her to see what she thought of the verdict, but there was no clue. He heard the foreman clear his throat.

'We the jury find the defendant, Michael Stennett, guilty of murder as charged in the indictment.'

The foreman said the whole sentence, conscientiously, but no one was listening after the operative word was spoken. Stennett leaned forward, unbelieving. His hands were clenched on the chair's arms as if he were restraining himself from leaping up. But he didn't restrain his expression. 'You sorry –' he muttered. The jurors were lucky he was unarmed.

Raymond slumping in his chair, blew out a long breath, and watched Stennett from the corner of his eye.

Judge Byrnes, forewarned, was completely composed. 'It's late,' she said to the jury. 'We'll begin the punishment phase at nine o'clock tomorrow morning. You're released, but remember my instructions not to discuss the case with anyone. The trial isn't over yet.'

The bailiff led the jury back out of the room, their

tiny little part done with. There was another bailiff, bent over a desk doing paperwork. Raymond saw Stennett look at that one, then back over his shoulder.

Judge Byrnes began unzipping her robe. Informally she repeated to the lawyers, 'Nine o'clock,' and started to rise. Raymond beat her to it.

'Your Honor, I have reason to believe the defendant will not appear for the punishment phase if he remains free on bond.' To Judge Byrnes's flat stare he added, 'As an officer of the court I feel it's my duty to advise the court of that.'

'You bastard!' Stennett shouted. Raymond put a hand on his shoulder to hold him in his seat. Stennett knocked it away. The remaining bailiff came to his feet.

'Very well, I revoke the bond. Take him into custody.' From the direction of her look one would have thought the judge was ordering the lawyer to jail, rather than his client.

'No! Judge!' Stennett shouted, in the voice he used to freeze suspects. The judge had already turned away. She didn't look back. The bailiff was at Stennett's side. He reached for his gun as Stennett drew back his fist. The other bailiff appeared in the hall doorway and stood flat-footed, looking baffled. Stennett turned and punched Raymond in the jaw, taking him completely by surprise, dropping him. The bailiff pulled Stennett back to keep him from kicking the lawyer.

'You son of a bitch!' Stennett screamed. 'I asked you for help!' Raymond shook his head groggily. The other bailiff finally arrived. One holding each arm, they dragged the defendant away. Stennett didn't go quietly. He dug in his heels and jerked one arm free. The larger bailiff drew his revolver and leaned in to say something to him. 'I *will* shoot you,' was what he murmured. Stennett looked sullen but stopped struggling.

Through slightly blurry vision Raymond saw that two of the cops in the audience, Darryl Kreutzer and Bernardo Martinez, were on their feet. Martinez might have been armed under his jacket. Kreutzer, in uniform, obviously was. Both started forward.

Stennett shook off the restraining hands, gave his lawyer one more look that made everyone in the room think he was going to go after him, and turned and stalked away. The bailiffs followed closely, holstering their guns.

Tyler helped Raymond to his feet. 'Can you talk?'

'Four score and seven years ago,' Raymond said distinctly.

'It's not broken, then.' Tyler kept his grip on his arm. Raymond looked as if he had been jarred loose from the whole scene. He was not quite among the living. But Becky was standing in front of him and he looked at her, quite comprehendingly, not at all vague. She looked as if she was concerned about something other than his health.

'You did the right thing,' Tyler said solemnly. 'You have a higher responsibility than the one to your client.'

Raymond made a derisive sound that didn't require a functioning jaw, picked up his briefcase, and left.

He kept his hands from shaking, but the effort made them stiff. The jailer had to do the delicate work for him of unfastening his watch strap. Losing the watch made him feel more naked than it should have. Stennett kept rubbing his wrist. His empty pockets made him feel stupid, as if he'd left his house without filling them. But this was home now. Keys would have been as useless as money.

The bailiffs had passed him on to other sheriff's deputies, but these were jail guards who gave no sign they had any dealings in the outside world. No one said anything to him, no word of encouragement. He was just another prisoner. The last jailer led him down a concrete path made narrow by the cells that pressed in on both sides. Each cell looked darker and more crowded than the one before it, and smelled worse. They went far down the row before they stopped. This time the cell door did clang when it closed behind Stennett, loud enough to lift some of the heads in the cell. The jailer gave the door a good shake to make sure, and left. His footsteps sounded as light and free as a tap dancer's.

Stennett glared around the cell, but he could feel his true expression beneath the fierce one. His lip wanted to tremble. In fancy he could see a gleam or two of recognition in the eyes turned toward him. Someone sat up on one of the bunks. *Come on*, he wanted to scream. He wanted them to come at him *now*, get it over with, smash a few faces before he went down, be buried under a mass of cursing, gouging bodies, rather than find a seat and wait, nerves itching for the feel of fingers reaching in the dark. Eyes wide open or barely hooded until dawn. It was going to be a terrible night, but not the worst. Those would come after he got to prison. There were no hard-timers here. Most of these weren't even convicted yet. They might be in for too many tickets, or drunk driving. It was after he got to prison that the true horrible nights and days would begin. Once word spread who he was. How many nights could he endure without sleep? How many homemade shivs could he take out of how many hands, how many gang attacks could he survive? How many whispers through the dark?

★

'You mean they tell you everything here? 'Cause they don't tell me nothing. I just do what I'm told.'

'Just curious. I figured they might not leave him here, I just wondered what excuse they'd use.'

'Want to ask him about other cases, they said. I don't know. Maybe he can still make some kind of deal.'

The jailer shrugged and took the paper, picked up a phone and said a few words. The uniformed police officer didn't even look around. It wasn't his first time to pick up or drop off a prisoner from the jail; he'd already seen everything he wanted to see there.

Stennett came out looking irritable, like they'd awakened him from a restful sleep. 'What now?' he growled. 'I was just gettin' settled in.'

The uniform looked unconcerned. 'Detectives wanta talk to you.' He took one of the prisoner's arms, Stennett shook off his hand, and the uniform didn't make an issue of it. He put his hands in his pockets and let Stennett follow him out.

The night was cool. The air felt so fresh it burned his lungs. 'This?' Stennett said as the young uniformed officer circled a brown Chevrolet Caprice and opened the driver's door.

'Get in,' he said. Stennett did. He slumped against the door panel. The uniformed officer's pistol in its holster was only two or three feet from his hand. A little leather thong held it in place. The uniform's hands were high on the steering wheel. Then one of them dropped, covering the gun.

'Who wants to see me?' Stennett asked. He didn't care enough to ask again when there was no answer.

The police station was less than a mile from the jail. The way the uniformed officer drove, though, it would take them forever to get there. He took a wrong turn and compounded it by turning again. Stennett frowned at him. The car slowed even further.

'What are you doing, Darryl?'

Kreutzer pulled to a stop at the curb, in a neighborhood that looked as if it had been built as a movie set thirty years earlier and then abandoned.

'Bus station's about two blocks that way,' he said. 'There's a cab stand there, too.' He snapped open his shirt pocket. 'Here's three hundred dollars. That's all the cash I could get. If you call me I'll send you some more after payday. I'll drive you to the airport if you want, but I don't know, I thought you'd feel too helpless up in a plane. I'll have to report you escaped in a couple of hours or so. If I don't they'll probably call from the jail, anyway.'

Stennett just sat. He looked pained.

'You got a raw deal, man,' Kreutzer said more passionately. 'Even if you did kill him, it's a littering case. A cop shouldn't go to prison over scum like that. Go on. Hurry up. I'd appreciate it if you'd give me a little tap first to make it look good, but I can manage without it if you don't feel like it.'

'Then what?' Stennett said quietly. 'That's it, that's my career? What d' I do now, roam around the country looking for a fucking one-armed man? Move to Colorado and be a ski instructor? You know where I've lived besides San Antonio? Nowhere.'

'I'm sorry, Mike. I thought this is what you'd planned if you lost the trial. I don't know what else I can do.'

When Stennett spoke again he sounded less hostile but more determined. 'Yeah. It was what I planned. But now I've got something left to do before I split. Shove over, will you?'

Kreutzer hesitated. 'Where are you going?'

'Don't worry, I'll leave the car where they'll find it fast.'

Kreutzer hesitated longer. He should have been in charge here, but somehow Mike still outranked him. 'I'll go with you.'

They drove uncrowded streets. Stennett gave directions in a low voice. Darryl avoided the expressways. For several blocks silence was as heavy as the night, darkening the interior of the car. The dashboard lights fell short of Kreutzer's face, making it appear disembodied hands were driving.

Mike was obviously lost in many thoughts. When he finally stirred he said, 'This could cost you your job.'

'I figure a suspension. That's the worst they ever do to somebody for losing a prisoner. Even if they think I did it on purpose, some of them might not think that was so terrible. And if they fire me I might still catch on somewhere else. I'll risk it.'

Stennett didn't say thanks. 'Stop up there,' he said when he saw a pay phone on a stand at the edge of a parking lot. Darryl sat in the car looking around as he waited. Two blocks ahead a police car was parked at a donut shop. 'Hurry up,' he muttered, and as soon as his passenger returned he turned down a side street. 'Where to?'

'He's in his office,' Stennett said. 'Getting ready for the punishment phase.'

Kreutzer's nervousness changed source and deepened. 'Mike, I –'

'I told you just to let me have the car. You don't have to be part of this. It's mine.' He sounded hurried, anxious to be on his way, but he was watching the young cop, not making a move to take the wheel himself.

Kreutzer steadied himself by pushing back farther

into the seat, arms rigid and locked on the steering wheel. 'No,' he said. 'I'll come.'

Stennett shrugged. 'Suit yourself,' he said.

Raymond sat alone in his office. He felt as if he were alone on the planet. Jean had gone home hours ago; the door to her outer office stood open. Dark and quiet out there. Darker in the street outside. If headlights passed they didn't reach Raymond.

Who would approve of what he had done? Not the judge, probably no other lawyers. Not his father. He could picture his father's scowl if he'd been in the room to see Stennett led away to jail. The abstract black community? Maybe. If only he knew some of them. His clients would approve. Yes, that was one crowd that would back him up a hundred percent. Having that invisible crew on his team did not reassure him.

He didn't even know if he approved of himself. He only knew he hadn't had any choice. He couldn't stand back this time the way he always had. On this one he had to be more than a lawyer. He was a party. He was a victim.

When they parked across the street and looked at the building head-on it looked dark and empty, but they'd already seen the light at the back as they were driving up the street. Kreutzer turned the key the wrong way, grinding the engine, then hurriedly shut it off. Stennett didn't even jump at the unexpected noise. He looked dead still, wound down almost to nothingness. Even his eyes looked uninhabited. It was startling to hear him speak. 'You got another piece besides that one you're wearing? Goddamn it, I know you do. Give it.'

Kreutzer pursed his lips, then bent, rummaged

under his seat, and pulled out an automatic. Stennett took out the magazine, inspected it, popped it back in. He stuck the gun in his waistband and was out of the car without another word. Kreutzer had to run to catch up.

The front door of the office was unlocked. They eased inside, comfortable in the dimness, and up to the open door through which light spilled. Kreutzer would have paused to peer in, but Stennett stepped boldly through and the younger man followed. He saw the lawyer at the desk jerk his head up, looking badly startled at the appearance of the two white cops.

But then Raymond's expression changed, became knowing. It was Darryl he looked at, ignoring Stennett, as he said, 'I thought so.'

Stennett drifted off to the side, out of Raymond's line of vision. Kreutzer stayed where he was, puzzled. Suddenly he wanted to back away, but he wanted worse to understand what the lawyer meant.

'Just doing Mike a favor?' Raymond asked. 'It's an awful risk for somebody you hardly know. Do you go to church, Darryl? Where'd you get that conscience?'

Darryl just stood there, watchful, saying nothing. It was Stennett who spoke, sounding dreamy, abstract, as if reminiscing.

'It must've been scary going to interview the old man, when they sent you and Montoya to pick him up. Hearing him say he'd seen the killing. Standing back letting your partner talk to him so the old man doesn't get a good look at you. Pulling your hat a little lower. Realizing you'd blown it, startin' to sweat. Glancing at your partner and wonderin' if you'll have to do him and the old man both, or if you can trust him to help you out. You must've gone shaky with relief when you finally realized the old man didn't recognize you. He was talking about somebody else. Me.'

Raymond said, 'That's why Haley Burkwright got the day wrong. He didn't tell you the day, you told *him*, because you knew the day Gordon Frazier was murdered. That's how Burkwright got mixed up, talking to you, when what he'd really seen had happened a day earlier, when the church parking lot was empty. The night of the revival, the night of the murder, Gordon Frazier was being killed half a mile away. By you, Darryl. In that alley. Why were you beating him?'

Kreutzer was shaking his head. 'No,' was all he said.

'I should have suspected you,' Raymond went on, 'because you came in here and told me you could've done it. Your story about being with Mike was garbage, but part of it was true, the part about how you dropped off your partner sometimes and rode alone. That meant you could have been alone at the time of the murder, free to have done it yourself. I can check with Montoya and find out. I think he'll admit the truth when he realizes it clears *him* of suspicion of murder.'

'It doesn't matter,' Darryl said. His fidgeting had gone away. He chose his words carefully. 'Being alone doesn't make me a murderer. Mike. You going to let him do this to me?'

'And you told me something else,' Raymond said. He came around the desk like a professor making a point. 'You told me about the sniper shooting at Mike and me in the stadium. Like you said, it wasn't in the paper. There wasn't even a police report on it. We didn't bother, because half the people we suspected were cops anyway. I figured Stennett had told you about it. But he didn't.'

Raymond and Stennett glanced at each other. If they'd worked together from the beginning, if they'd trusted each other enough to share all their information *before* the jury verdict was imminent, they might have figured it out sooner. But Raymond didn't know if that would have changed anything.

'But that's neither here nor there,' Raymond said. 'You weren't trying to kill us, you were just trying to do what you told me, point suspicion away from Mike. You did it because you felt so bad about accidentally making him the prime suspect in the murder you committed by dropping that gun to make it look as if Frazier had been armed.'

'I gave it to you, Darryl,' Stennett said. 'That gun I'd taken off that crazoid, that ended up next to Frazier's body. I didn't turn it in to be destroyed, I gave it to you to turn in. You should've told me you were gonna hang on to it, I wouldn't've put it in my report. After I looked at that arrest report and saw your name I remembered. After we got that anonymous call. Thanks for trying to help out again, Darryl. That was risky too, but I guess you thought you owed me.'

'And you were the one who had the grudge against Gordon Frazier,' Raymond said. He had drawn even closer to Kreutzer. 'You were the one who pulled up to a corner one day in a squad car, who caught Frazier with the others and was going to arrest him until he told you he was snitching for Stennett. Only he wasn't. And when Mike told you he wasn't, you got pissed off. And you knew what your pal Mike would do in a case like that, didn't you? Fact, he'd probably told you what he'd just done to somebody else. Part of your training.' Stennett gave Raymond a sharp glance, but Raymond wasn't looking at him. 'You knew what Mike'd do about somebody who lied to him. He'd make sure it never happened again. Have a talk with the guy in an alley. Point out his mistake. Rough him up a little. When Frazier fought back it surprised you, didn't it, Darryl? And you overreacted and what? kneed him in the face when he lunged at you? Or picked up a rock? Scared the shit out of you when you realized you'd killed him, didn't it, Darryl? You panicked. You got your throw-down gun, you thought you'd try to make it look like self-defense, but then you remembered you had no business being there anyway, you should've been patrolling with your partner. So you just ran.

'Mike and I were thinking somebody'd deliberately set him up, but we couldn't make that work, it didn't make sense, no cop hated him that much, and it had to be a cop. We didn't realize it was an accident, a stupid accident, that you had that throw-down he'd handled and you were too sloppy to wipe it completely clean. If you'd just been more thorough, the way he would've been, you wouldn't've put your hero in that spot.'

If that didn't do it, Raymond thought, they'd have to beat a confession out of him. It was certainly the most telling thing he'd said to the young cop. Kreutzer looked stricken as he turned to Stennett.

'Mike, I never meant – You know that wasn't on purpose.'

Yes, Raymond thought, but Stennett, like an amateur, interrupted the confession. He looked as if he were confessing himself.

'I thought I could do it, Darryl. Take the heat, be a stand-up guy, all that crap. But I never thought they'd convict me. And once they did I thought *you'd* stand up for me.'

'I did, Mike, I got you out. I couldn't –'

'To be on the run for the rest of my life? To never be a cop again?' Stennett's voice was raised for the first time. He looked like his old self, reassuming his identity. That jail sweat had finally dried.

'You still can, Mike,' Kreutzer said quietly. Raymond froze. He understood faster than Stennett did. Kreutzer's hand was on his gun. He had slipped the leather thong off the hammer. He was speaking to the other cop, but he indicated Raymond. 'He's the only one who knows. He hasn't told anybody but you. We can work this out, you and me. We can come up with evidence that'll clear you, without implicating me, either. I'll alibi you, I'll come up with somebody who got the gun from me. We can do it, Mike, as long as we take him out.'

Raymond knew the futility of appealing to Kreutzer. The young cop was speaking of the black lawyer as if he weren't in the room, as if he were incapable of objection. Raymond looked instead at his client. Stennett was looking back at him appraisingly, sizing up the possibilities. Raymond realized he couldn't guess what Stennett would have done if all those possibilities had been open to him.

Darryl Kreutzer jumped as if someone had poked him from behind. Nothing had touched him, it was just a sound that had scared him, the sound of Bernardo Martinez stepping into the room from the outer office. 'Take it easy,' the sergeant said.

Ten yards to his right, two uniformed officers pushed open the bathroom door and came into the office, hands on hips. From the wild look Kreutzer gave them Raymond couldn't tell if he knew them. The outer office was no longer quiet. There were the sounds of at least two more people coming toward them.

Kreutzer opened his mouth, but couldn't speak. There were too many people, too many to involve in a scheme, too many to deal with. But none of them had drawn a weapon. Kreutzer was the only one with his hand on his gun. He jerked it out by instinct. He leaped aside, grabbed Raymond around the throat from behind, and put the gun's point against the lawyer's temple.

There were exclamations and curses, and people ducked, involuntarily, as if shots had already been fired. One of the uniformed cops dodged back into the bathroom, the other hit the floor. Stennett and Martinez dropped into crouches, sliding away from each other. One could see how they'd been as partners. Kreutzer didn't move. He was already protected by the lawyer's body. He waited for everyone to freeze, as they did after their first startled reactions.

'Just let me out of here,' he said quite calmly. 'Or I will blow his head right off, and take out as many of you as I can.'

'Just hold it,' Martinez said, putting out a hand, drawing attention to himself. 'Give yourself a minute to think, Darryl, this isn't –'

'I know the drill, Sergeant, I know how you talk somebody out of this, stall 'til you get help. But I'm not waiting and I'm not negotiating. Just get the hell out of my way.' He started forward, pushing Raymond.

Raymond knew he was dead. He'd known it from the moment he felt the cold barrel of the gun touch his forehead. Darryl Kreutzer would kill him in the next moment or kill him when they got to the front door or kill him after they'd driven a block away. To Kreutzer Raymond was barely alive anyway, a cipher, a different species. And who were his saviors? These cops arrayed in front of Raymond, looking past him, or at him as if he were the black outline on the targets they fired at for practice.

Knowing he was dead already made it easy. He just

went limp. When Kreutzer tried to push him forward Raymond dropped straight down, slithering out of his grip, reaching upward for the gun but missing, grabbing at Kreutzer's forearm. As he fell he saw Kreutzer looking down at him, hating him, hating Raymond more than he wanted to live himself, and saw the gun turning down. Raymond prepared to brace his feet and throw himself back against the cop's legs, but he didn't have the leverage yet, he was just a limp sack of organs falling to the floor. He heard the first shot.

Stennett was the first to fire, but Martinez was right behind him. By drawing attention to himself Martinez had given his old partner time to get his hand on his gun. The young officer on the floor by the bathroom didn't fire at all. He had his gun out and thought he was pulling its trigger, but in reality he was just screaming.

Stennett would have stopped after his first shot if he'd been thinking, but he wasn't, and he wasn't aiming. He was no marksman, he couldn't shoot to wound. He couldn't shoot at all without thinking in some way his own life was in danger. He had no idea where Kreutzer's gun was pointing. Stennett fired in a frenzy of terrified self-preservation. He pulled the trigger of the empty gun twice more after Kreutzer had been thrown back against the couch and was falling sideways over its arm.

Raymond was the fastest person in the room. He scrambled on hands and feet toward his desk as if he knew he would be the next target. No one paid any attention to him. No one saw him open the bottom drawer of the desk.

Stennett was the only one to approach the body. Kreutzer's legs were stretched out, not even twitching, but Stennett went cautiously, the empty pistol still hanging at the end of his arm like a part of his hand. His old partner said, 'Shit,' and kept saying it as he went out to the secretary's desk and the phone.

Stennett relaxed a little when he saw Kreutzer's gun on the floor far out of reach. Another step and he could see Darryl was no threat to anyone anyway. Blood had stopped bubbling out of the half dozen visible wounds in his chest and stomach. More blood was drying on his chin. Darryl's face was frozen in a wince. His left wrist was bent at a terrible angle. That looked like the most painful wound of all. Stennett's stomach rose into his throat, as it always did when he viewed a freshly dead body. Darryl was so newly dead he still looked like a human being. Even with those wounds the spell could snap and that bloody chest begin rising and falling again. They could repair the damage, undo what had happened. The moment was so recent it seemed possible to take it back. It was so stupid for him to lie there and stay dead.

There was a flash. Stennett jerked around, startled, lifting the useless pistol, turning straight into a second flash. Raymond lowered the camera.

'Those'll be good,' he said.

'I told you how I feel about pictures,' Stennett said. 'I work undercover. I'm gonna go on working undercover.'

'Not after these hit the papers,' Raymond told him, indicating the camera. 'I'd be real surprised if both papers don't run shots like these.'

Stennett stepped closer. 'Those aren't going anywhere.'

'Come and take it from me,' Raymond said, no longer making a pretense of joviality. 'Come on.' When Stennett made no further move the lawyer said, 'I'm going to burn you out of the east side, man.'

'Why? I didn't do it. You know I didn't do it.'

'Just dumb luck you didn't. Kreutzer did it using your methods and going after your targets. It wasn't just coincidence the evidence against him pointed to you too. He was your damn protégé. You were his idol. You might even've given him the idea. Like maybe when he told you Frazier had lied to him you bragged about what you'd done to guys who'd lied to you? I was right about that, wasn't I? And Darryl decided he'd try the same thing. He wanted to be just like you. He as good as told me so. This time he was a little bit off about how much force to use. Maybe next time he would've been a little bit off about which black man to beat up. You're the wrong hero for guys like him. I want you out.'

'Of the east side. You don't care if I go practice my scummy methods somewhere else.'

'I'm not a hero,' Raymond said. 'I'm not trying to clean up the world. Let the north side worry about itself. I'd like to see you try to pull your shit on the north side. You'd have so many white parents screaming for your ass ... But that's their worry. I've just got my own little piece of the world to take care of.'

'That you don't even live in,' Stennett said hotly.

'That I don't even live in, that's right, but I got people there.'

'Yeah? You think about your people. Your father did my job, man, the east side 'be *littered* with bodies. He wants these people out worse than I do. You ask *him* if he wants me to stay on the job. You go call him –'

Raymond cut him off. 'I know how much they hate the pushers, you don't have to tell me. If my father and men like him come out of their stores one day with clubs and guns and drive that trash right into the river I'll cheer them on. And I'll be there to bail my father out of jail when he gets arrested and I'll defend him and I'll get him acquitted. But he's a citizen and you're a cop. Cops can't resort to that. There's too much power behind you.'

'Power,' Stennett snorted.

They'd both grown quieter. 'I know you've got a hard job,' Raymond said. 'It's an impossible job. And the law makes it harder. Laws mean you make fewer arrests because you need to make it legal, and sometimes a guilty man goes free. But your way sometimes an innocent man is going to get beat up or killed by somebody wearing a badge and that's worse. If it's too tough for you to do your job without breaking the law then go turn in your badge and your gun and get a black mask and a cape.'

Stennett listened to the end, but then shook his head, doggedly. There weren't enough words in the world to change him. 'You're not taking me out,' he said. 'You don't have the right. You left, a long time ago. You're not part of it anymore. I am. The east side's my territory. I care about it as much as your old man. I won't let it go. You can't make a decision like that for everybody there.'

Mike Stennett wasn't a debater. Conversation was wearing him out, bringing the whole long day down on him. He spoke in a low voice, but Raymond, watching his face closely, saw his eyes glistening. Stennett pointed at the camera. 'You're not doin' nothing with that before we talk some more.'

'Talk where, Mike? Here? Alley? Some dark parking lot? You pick your spot. Come on, take a shot now, when I'm expecting it.'

Stennett leaned close as if he would. 'You didn't have to send me to jail, you son of a bitch. He would've come to me.' Indicating the body on the floor. 'I woulda brought him here, like we said.'

'Would you, Mike? If you'd been a free man, free to make your own plans? Well, I just wanted to lend some urgency to the proceedings. To make you *and* Darryl think about it harder.'

Stennett still looked like he might do something, for several seconds. Then he seemed to call it quits, and returned to the subject of the camera. 'We'll talk,' he repeated wearily.

Raymond's tone lightened. 'We'll talk right now, as a matter of fact. I'm still your lawyer, remember? And we have to be back in court in the morning.'

Stennett looked at him aghast.

CHAPTER 15

'He's right about one thing. I *don't* have the right.'

Denise was sitting at the dining table in her robe, looking a little bleary-eyed in spite of the half a cup of coffee, ready to leave. She'd found him like that half an hour earlier, sitting on the couch, staring, wearing an expression as if someone were sitting beside him telling him something he didn't want to hear. He had started talking as soon as she'd walked in, recounting again his threat to expose Stennett and Stennett's response.

Petey was asleep. It was barely six o'clock in the morning.

'Of course you do,' Denise said. 'You're not going to let that white cop tell you you don't have the right to protect what's –'

'White's got nothing to do with it,' Raymond said. His voice was tinged with weariness but not with uncertainty. He'd been going over it all, over and over, for hours. He hadn't let his client see it the night before, but Mike Stennett had gotten to him, deeply, with that one sentence. 'I *don't* have the right. The east side's more his than it is mine. People *want* him there. I'm the one who's got no business there. Who died and left me king of east side? All I ever wanted from that place was out. Now I'm going to make the decisions for everybody there? It's Stennett who's got the stake there. He's stuck it out all these years. Just like Pop. You should've seen him when I told him I was going to drive him out. He looked like he wanted to cry at the thought of it. It'd be like exile for him. That's how I turned him last night, you know.

Stennett'd never have turned in another cop like he did if he hadn't seen that *not* doing it would cost him the one thing he loves the most. Being a cop. Fighting crime.'

He said the last sentence ironically, but Raymond was thinking about those witnesses he'd called in defense, those solid east side businessmen who approved of the work Mike Stennett did. If he'd convinced no one else, Raymond had convinced himself of those witnesses' sincerity, and of their correctness.

'*I'm* the one who doesn't belong,' he concluded. 'Nobody wants me there, taking up for criminals.'

Denise had come awake. 'You *do* belong,' she said. She sounded so intense her voice lifted Raymond's head. 'You swing too far, Raymond. When did you go from thinking he was the devil to thinking he's some kind of hero?'

'He –'

'Maybe he is, sometimes, to some people. But you know very damn well what he is other times. That man drops over the edge way too easy. He acts like he doesn't even know he's dealing with human beings. Maybe you shouldn't take him out completely, but he needs somebody keeping a rein on him, somebody who cares as much as he does.'

Raymond nodded as if he understood. 'Someone like Lawrence Preston. He used to be my hero, you know. I wanted to *be* Mr Preston.'

Denise sighed. Her husband had just sidestepped. He did that so well she still didn't know, after their years together, if he did it deliberately or not.

'Honey,' she said, 'Mr Preston has the best heart of anybody who ever lived. But all that old man's ever known was fight, fight, fight. My side, my side, my side. It was easier for him than it is for you.'

Raymond gave her a stern look, and opened his

mouth, to correct her, she knew. Denise cut him off. 'I
know, he had it lots tougher some ways. But it was
easier for him to decide the right thing to do. He never
fretted over a case like you have over this one. He
could never look out of the other man's eyes the way
you've been doing.'

Raymond was unconvinced. Denise had one more
thing to say. 'I'm proud of you, honey.'

He tried to act as if he hadn't heard that. But he felt
easier than he had in days. Even if everyone else in the
world would scorn him for what he'd done or was
about to do, he still had Denise on his side.

He took the roll of undeveloped film out of his jacket
pocket. 'But what do I do with this?' he asked.

Denise didn't answer, but he was sure she knew.

Testimony may be heard in a trial any time *before* the
arguments to the jury are concluded. Once a verdict is
reached, certainly, the evidentiary portion of trial may
not be reopened. That's what the rules provide. And
they were bound by the rules. They were creatures of
rules. When they chose to invoke them.

When Raymond presented Judge Byrnes, who had
been forewarned of the nature of the new evidence,
with a defense motion to reopen the testimony, and
the prosecution joined the motion rather than opposing
it, the judge ruled, 'In the absence of objection, I
grant the motion.'

The jurors seemed to find nothing odd in their guilty
verdict being stricken and witnesses taking the stand
again. They did not appear offended. They also seemed
unsurprised to see Raymond taking the witness stand.
After defense counsel, the defendant, and Bernardo
Martinez testified concerning the events of the night
before, the jury retired. Mike Stennett, who had been

sitting impatiently through the proceedings, turned immediately to his lawyer, as if their conversation had barely been interrupted.

'You may be right,' he said, causing Raymond to look at him as if an imposter had taken his client's place.

'About what?' he asked skeptically.

'About me,' Stennett said quietly. They were walking away from everyone else in the room, to a quiet corner behind the bailiff's desk. 'I thought all night about what you said,' Stennett continued. 'You know, it wasn't anything I hadn't thought before, but after last night –

'I kept seeing that kid on the floor. Darryl. You know what it's like to look at a dead guy and think it could've been you?' Raymond didn't interrupt. 'Darryl wasn't me, Darryl was a little know-nothing bigot. But maybe you're right I helped put him there. You understand why I work alone? Because I can live with the way I work. I can sort out the good guys from the bad guys and the half-and-half guys. But somebody like Darryl doesn't make those distinctions. I didn't want him following in my footsteps. I didn't want a protégé.' The word Raymond had used the night before.

'So maybe you're right about me. Maybe I'm – best out.'

Raymond found this contrition hard to believe. He was relieved when Stennett hurriedly added, 'But before you make up your mind I want you to hear somebody else.'

'Who?'

'I'll get him.'

Stennett hurried away, through the gate in the railing and out into the spectator seats. If Raymond had been skeptical about his client's change in attitude, he found completely unbelievable the man Stennett was now pulling forward as a witness on his behalf.

'Ask him,' Stennett said, depositing the unwilling witness in front of Raymond.

'I'm sorry, Mr Burkwright,' Raymond said. 'He shouldn't have dragged you over here. We've got no power over you.'

'I come on my own hook,' Haley Burkwright said sullenly. 'He said you got something I can clear up. I'm not saying I've said anything wrong already. But I want you to know I got no grudge against anybody.'

'Good,' Raymond said. 'You're not under oath now. The trial's over. Really over, this time, I think. You don't have to answer anything.'

'Ask him about the "beating",' Stennett said impatiently.

Raymond turned to his client. 'I didn't cross-examine him about it during trial because –'

'I know why you didn't. But ask him now.'

Raymond said quietly, 'Mr Burkwright, it seems clear now that you never saw Gordon Frazier in the parking lot of the church. It was somebody else with Mr Stennett here. You never even got a good look at the face of the other man, did you?'

'I know it was *him*,' Burkwright said firmly, pointing at Stennett, which answered the question.

'And you saw him hit someone,' Raymond said. During trial he hadn't cross-examined Burkwright about the beating he'd witnessed because by that time Raymond had known it was irrelevant. It didn't much matter to the defense what Haley Burkwright saw Mike Stennett doing to someone in the parking lot of the church, because it wasn't Gordon Frazier being beaten. It wasn't the murder victim; it wasn't the night of the murder. Raymond had known, as the prosecutors hadn't, that what Stennett had been doing in that parking lot didn't matter to the court case.

But it mattered now.

'You saw a black man on the ground, pleading, and you heard this man, this police officer, threatening him. Is that about right?'

'Threatening don't half describe it,' Haley Burkwright insisted. 'He said he's gonna kill him.'

'Good. And what did he do? What did Officer Stennett do?' This was the question Raymond hadn't bothered to ask during trial. Haley Burkwright had testified he'd seen Stennett beating someone to death. But how much of that was conclusory, based on his mistaken belief that the man he'd seen Stennett hitting *had* ended up dead? They'd had medical testimony about the extent of the injuries to Gordon Frazier, but that's not who Stennett had been seen hitting in the church parking lot.

Now Burkwright grew more hesitant. 'Well, I told you about that one punch. Lifted the boy right off his feet. And I think he must have already hit him before I was looking.'

'But what you saw was one punch?'

'Well – I think he hit him again after I come down into the yard.' The witness looked to Stennett, uncertainly, for confirmation. Stennett just looked back at him, arms folded.

'Did Officer Stennett kick the man when he was down on the ground?'

Haley Burkwright scratched his cheek as he looked off into space. 'No,' he finally concluded.

'Stomp on his back or anything like that?'

'No, I never saw him use his feet. But when he turned and give me that look . . .' He returned to familiar ground, with no more uncertainty. Raymond let him talk himself out.

'Thank you,' he finally said. 'Thank you for talking to us.'

Burkwright looked mollified. He actually smiled at Raymond – but not at his client – before withdrawing.

'See?' Stennett said immediately. 'One punch. That's all he saw. That's all it was.'

'He saw a man down on the ground.'

'Well, it was one *good* punch,' Stennett said. 'But it wasn't any fatal beating. Not even close. You heard him say during trial the guy jumped up and took off running as soon as I turned my head. You try running that fast if somebody's just half beat you to death.

'Look.' Stennett stepped in closer, as if to exclude the rest of the world, as if Raymond had become his only judge that mattered. 'I lost my temper that night, not for the first time, as you very well know. It was a mistake. I know that, too. But I didn't come close to killing anybody. I never have. I'm not Darryl.'

'Darryl's wasn't deliberate either,' Raymond said. 'As long as you keep "losing your temper", nobody's safe.'

'I told you it was a mistake,' Stennett insisted. 'You know how I operate, it's fine line after fine line. Sometimes I slip up. But I do more good than harm. Lots more. If not for me –'

'This is your apology?' Raymond asked. 'This is your act of repentance?'

Stennett stepped back. His voice lost its edge. 'You do what you want,' he said. 'I'll go along with it.'

He walked away. *This* was his act of repentance, Raymond knew: leaving the decision in Raymond's hands. But Stennett's meek acceptance didn't ring true. *He thinks I'm going to set him loose*, Raymond thought. *What'll he do if I don't?*

★

The jury was out for a much shorter time than they had been the day before. But it still began to seem long to Mike Stennett, after his talk with Raymond. 'What's taking them so long?' he complained. 'There's only one way to go this time.'

'I wouldn't be so anxious for them to come back,' Raymond said. 'There's no predicting juries. Maybe they feel attached to their guilty verdict. Maybe they're getting ready to come in with another one.'

Stennett didn't look startled. The same thought was obviously occupying his mind. He glanced across the room at the larger bailiff. 'Listen,' he said. 'This time –'

Raymond laughed.

When the jury did return, Judge Byrnes was more informal about receiving the new verdict. 'Read it,' she said, and the foreman laboriously unfolded his short sheet of paper and again read the whole sentence, only slightly amended from the day before. Aware of the contrast, the foreman emphasized the new word: '. . . find the defendant *not* guilty . . .'

There was no eruption in the courtroom. It was a quiet, still moment. For everyone, that is, except the defendant and his attorney. 'Come on,' Raymond said, and they moved, faster than anyone else in the room. Past the jury box, past the bench, from which the judge glared at them. *You haven't been dismissed yet*, she would have said, if she hadn't been occupied with thanking the jury for their service and releasing them. Raymond led Stennett through the door at the front of the courtroom that gave into the court offices, and through those into the courthouse hallway.

'Now hurry,' he said.

Two or three reporters, along with photographers, had guessed what they were up to, after Stennett's camera-shy performance the first day of trial, and emerged from the courtroom forty feet behind Raymond and Stennett. 'Detective Stennett,' one of them called, but Stennett didn't turn his head. A smile was on his face. The way Raymond was almost running down the corridor beside him, away from the photographers, must have meant the lawyer had made up his mind, the right way.

They reached the stairwell and Raymond tugged him up rather than down. Up two flights to the quiet fourth floor, where they paused until they were sure any pursuit had headed down to the street. Then Raymond and his client walked, looking for a quiet corner. As they walked, Raymond displayed the small roll of film that held Stennett's face; that held, in a small way, his career as an undercover cop.

'I've decided to let you have this,' Raymond said. Stennett gratefully reached for it, but Raymond's face and grip told him there was more. '. . . eventually,' Raymond continued. 'If you earn it.'

'Earn it?'

'I'm taking you at your word. You love the east side so much, I want to see you do more than bust heads there.'

Stennett looked at him suspiciously. 'You're sentencing me to community service? Man, I already do more for that place than any –'

'This is not a discussion. This is my proposal, and you can take it or leave it. If you leave it I carry this down the hall to the press room and drop it off for this afternoon's editions.'

'Let's hear your proposal,' Stennett said.

'I want you to become sort of a Big Brother.'

'What?'

'You tugged at my heartstrings, Stennett, with your

tale of the two orphans. But what've you done for them besides try to find their mother's killer?'

'Done for them? What do you want –'

'I'm sorry, are we discussing? Good. I have your first client. She's a little girl whose mother was living with Gordon Frazier when he died. She –'

'Debby Pease?'

Raymond looked at his client with surprise, almost with admiration. 'You know about her?'

'What kind of cruddy investigator d'you think I am? I found Kathy Pease, and her kid. Cops assigned to the case didn't, D. A.'s investigators didn't, but I did –'

'So did I. So you know about Debby's problem. That's what I trade you for the film. You take care of the orphan you left behind.'

'You know damn well I didn't –'

'Your protégé, then. You pay Darryl's dues.'

Stennett was looking at him, chewing his lip, obviously mulling over both whether he could trust Raymond and what he could do about it if he didn't. The roll of film was within lunging distance. Stennett thought about that, thought better of it.

'Listen, just give it up,' he tried instead. 'You don't have the right to make me do some silly –'

Raymond shook his head. 'That's not gonna play with me anymore, Stennett. If I don't have the right, that's your bad luck, 'cause I'm doing it anyway. This is your only out.'

'What makes you think either of them'll let me near 'em? What do I tell 'em, "My lawyer assigned me to you"?'

'Your charm?' Raymond said. 'Your winning ways? I didn't say I cared if you could do it or not. If you can't handle it –'

'Bastard,' Stennett said. He looked again at the roll of film as Raymond put it in his pocket, then abruptly wheeled and hurried away.

It was some time later when Raymond made his way to Tyler Hammond's office. He was unsurprised to find Becky there as well.

'I think we can consider this a mutual victory,' Raymond said.

Becky nodded toward Tyler. 'That's what he's telling me,' she said, unconvinced.

Raymond smiled at her. 'You hate to lose, don't you, Becky? You're on the right side, then.'

'And how do you feel about winning? About putting Mike Stennett back on the street?'

Raymond didn't feel like talking about his experiment in private justice. He didn't even know yet if Stennett would take him up on it. 'I can live with it,' he said.

'You know the saving grace of this whole business for me?' he added. 'Finding out there're cops like Bernardo Martinez, who disapprove of cops like Stennett, who won't work with them. And that cops like Martinez get promoted.' After a moment's study of that thought, Raymond pronounced what he thought was the benediction. 'Well, children, we went about it in a weird way –'

'Yes,' Tyler said, 'like coming to us for help with the sting and having your client sent to jail. That shocked him, didn't it? That wasn't part of the scheme as far as Stennett was concerned, was it? Neither, I think, was him punching you. How long would you have left him in jail? That was a poor risk, I thought, hoping a murderer would have such a guilty conscience he wouldn't let Stennett serve time for something he didn't do.'

'Putting Mike in jail wasn't just to flush Darryl out. I thought it'd help, but it was for Stennett's instruction, too. I think he already knew who the murderer was, or had a real good idea. He had better clues than I did. He knew Darryl Kreutzer had almost arrested Frazier a few days before his death, and got mad when he heard Frazier'd lied to him to talk his way out of it. Stennett probably remembered who he'd given that gun to, too. I wanted to give him a taste of what it would cost him to cover it up.'

Becky was giving him that look again, as if her brief feeling of understanding him had evaporated. Tyler cleared his throat. 'Well, actually . . .' he began. 'I talked to the jurors afterwards. There wouldn't have been much point in our conducting a punishment phase anyway. They had already decided what to give him.'

'No, that's not possible,' Raymond said, sounding serious. 'The judge's instructions told them not to consider punishment.' Becky gave him the look his joke deserved. The jury had honored that instruction as much as juries ever pay attention to judges' instructions. Raymond grinned. 'Twenty?' he asked.

Tyler shook his head. 'Probation.'

'What?' Raymond cried angrily.

Tyler looked embarrassed, as if he'd been in on it. 'That's how they reached a verdict. They weren't sure he'd really done this one, but they didn't think he should be a police officer anymore. So they decided to convict him but let him off lightly.'

For a moment Raymond found no words to express his disgust. But he did make a prediction that would never be tested. 'There's people would've burned this city down over a verdict like that. Like me, for example.'

'You thought he was guilty, didn't you?' Becky asked.

'Doesn't matter what I thought. Now I know.'

'Yes. Thanks to the jury convicting him, giving you that hammer to hold over his head, and to draw Kreutzer out. But what if you'd won the trial to begin with? What if they'd acquitted him? What would you have done then?'

Raymond hadn't been able to answer that for himself. He didn't try to answer it for her. 'That's a very good question. Better than any question you asked during trial. But I trusted the jury to do what juries do best.'

'Get it wrong,' Becky guessed.

Raymond looked at her reprovingly. 'Convict, I meant. Rebecca, you are so cynical.'

When he came out of Tyler's office the first thing he saw was a man sitting beside the secretary's desk, chatting with the secretary, holding his hat in his lap. 'Are you turning detective?' Raymond asked, surprised. 'How'd you find me here?'

His father was glad of the chance to give him a knowing look. 'Son, there are people in this building who know everything that goes on in this old courthouse. You just have to find the right one to ask.' He was saying it as much to the smiling secretary as to Raymond.

'Come on, Pop.'

They were down on the first floor, heading for the outside doors, before his father got around to saying, 'Raymond, you don't need me to tell you what a great thing you did. You were every bit as good as I expected. I'm proud of you.'

'Thanks, Pop.' He smiled but had to make a little

joke. 'Lucky thing you weren't on the jury. I needed them to find him guilty yesterday.'

'Well, I damned well would have found him guilty too, after what I heard of the State's case.'

'What?' They were on the stairs outside the courthouse, heading down to the sidewalk. Raymond stopped and stared.

'Certainly. I approve of what he does, but I never said he should get away with murder.'

'I thought you did.'

Enunciating distinctly, his father said, 'I was speaking figuratively.'

Raymond laughed. A little huffily, his stern old man said, 'I'm entitled to my opinions.'

Raymond continued to laugh. 'That's right, Pop. I don't think anybody else'd have 'em.'

Maybe to cut off his son's laughter, maybe just making conversation, Mr Boudro asked, 'What did Denise say?' assuming, correctly, that Raymond had called her.

'Said she was proud of me,' Raymond said quietly, almost shyly. Raymond had asked her another question, to confirm her approval of the offer he'd made Mike Stennett. 'There wasn't just one right thing to do, was there?' he'd asked.

Denise's laugh had come warm and liquid over the phone line. 'Honey, I told you that. There's at least two.' Set Stennett loose, but not unfettered. The cop had to have an opponent as intense as he, keeping him in check with equal passion.

His old man was nodding. But his expression was a tiny bit troubled. 'Denise is proud of you and so am I. But it certainly was strange, wasn't it? You know, Raymond, some people – from both sides – won't approve of the way you went about it.'

Raymond didn't break stride. He was heading toward his car. The workday was over. He thought he'd go by the school where Denise worked before picking up Petey.

'I'll just try real hard to live with that,' he said.

SIGNET

Published or forthcoming

TRIAL

Clifford Irving

They called it suppression of evidence and disbarred him from the 299th District Court for two long years.

Criminal Defence lawyer Warren Blackburn came back from the wilderness to pick up the crumbs – and found two cases just like the one that brought him down.

But this time he was ready to back his judgement and fight. Fight for justice and a fair trial against a legal system that would do anything as long as it got a deal . . .

'Riveting legal edge-of-the seater . . . Has Texas and American Justice systems by the tail' – *Daily Telegraph*

Published or forthcoming

FADE THE HEAT

Jay Brandon

Mark Blackwell is District Attorney of San Antonio, city of favours and pay-offs. His success has cost him his marriage and family life. Now his son stands accused of rape.

During the trial that follows Mark is torn apart, caught in the judicial wheel that he has set in motion. As the pressure builds, the media and his rivals move in for the kill. Suddenly he has everything to lose and nothing to gain . . .

'A clever plot, a gripping novel' – Tony Hillerman, author of *Talking God*

'Tension radiates from every page . . . guilty of being an enthralling read' – *Today*

Published or forthcoming

THE RATING GAME

Dave Cash

Behind the glass-fronted walls of CRFM's 24-hours-a-day nerve centre in the heart of London, three people fight for control of their lives as the tycoon powerbrokers of international finance move in for the kill . . .

Monica Hammond, the radio station's beautiful and ruthless Managing Director – nothing was allowed to stand in her way . . . until one man discovered her fatal weakness.

Nigel Beresford-Clarke – CRFM's greatest asset – hopelessly betrayed by his love for a schoolgirl . . .

And **Maggie Lomax**, uncompromising and tough as nails – then her outspoken broadcasts pushed the wrong people too far . . .

They're ready to play . . . *The Rating Game*

SIGNET

Published or forthcoming

HAVING IT ALL

Maeve Haran

Having it All. Power. Money. Success. *And* a happy family. Liz really believed she could have it all. So when she's offered one of the most important jobs in television, she jumps at it.

But Liz discovers that there's a price to be paid for her success and that the whole glittering image is just an illusion. And one day she's faced with the choice she thought she'd never have to make.

Liz decides she *will* have it all – but on her own terms.

'Will touch cords, tug heartstrings. Every woman's been here' – Penny Vincenzi, author of *Old Sins*

'Realistic, compassionate, but still as pacey as they come' – *Cosmopolitan*

Published or forthcoming

38 NORTH YANKEE

Ed Ruggero

When an unarmed convoy of American troops on a training exercise is ambushed by North Koreans near Hongch'on, the fragile peace that has existed since 1953 is shattered, and once again the US Army is in the front line of a war on foreign territory.

38 North Yankee is the blistering story of the men and machines on both sides as the powder-keg of Korea explodes into a bloody and ruthless struggle for military supremacy.

Published or forthcoming

Blood Knot

Sam Llewellyn

Bill Tyrrell has locked the door on his crusading past. As a reporter, he's seen conflict and pain close up – and not once have his words ever saved a life. Now he's back in England, living on the antique cutter *Vixen*, the only legacy from his long-vanished father. But the journalist in him can't be buried. Not when a Russian sea cadet gets wrapped round the *Vixen's* propeller under the eyes of a Cabinet Minister – and Tyrrell becomes the scapegoat . . .

It is the first in a series of harrowing accidents. And suddenly the past begins to open up all over again, as Tyrrell's battle-hardened reporting reflexes lure him into a dark maze of political cover-ups and violent death . . .

'The best seabourne thriller in many a tide'
– *Daily Mail*

SIGNET

Published or forthcoming

BASIC INSTINCT

Richard Osborne

A brutal murder.

A brilliant killer.

A cop who can't resist the danger.

When San Francisco detective Nick Curran begins investigating the mysterious and vicious murder of a rock star, he finds himself in a shadowy world where deceit and seduction often go hand in hand. Nick can't stay away from his number one suspect – stunning and uninhibited Catherine Tramell – a novelist whose shocking fiction mirrors the murder down to the smallest, bloodiest detail.

Entangled in love and murder, Nick is headed for trouble, with only his basic instinct for survival to keep him from making a fatal mistake . . .

Ira Levin
author of *Rosemary's Baby*

Thirteen hundred Madison Avenue, an elegant 'sliver' building, soars high and narrow over Manhattan's smart Upper East Side. Kay Norris, a successful single woman, moves on to the twentieth floor of the building, high on hopes of a fresh start and the glorious Indian summer outside. But she doesn't know that someone is listening to her. Someone is *watching* her.

'Levin really knows how to touch the nerve ends' – *Evening Standard*

'*Sliver* is the ultimate *fin de siècle* horror novel, a fiendish goodbye-wave to trendy urban living … Ira Levin has created the apartment dweller's worst nightmare' – Stephen King

SIGNET

Published or forthcoming

MADONNA
UNAUTHORIZED

Christopher Andersen

'Power is a great aphrodisiac, and I'm a very powerful person . . . ' are the words of the highest-paid woman in show business.

The words of Madonna. Self-made icon. The most famous woman in the world. But how did she do it? And what *really* happened along the way?

MADONNA: UNAUTHORIZED
looks beyond the carefully constructed public image of a star who has clocked up more hit singles than the Beatles.

More shocking than anything she has so far dared to reveal . . .

MADONNA: UNAUTHORIZED
covers it all, from abortion to AIDS, from marriage and Marilyn to men she forgot, from women and Warren to ruling the world . . .

'Compulsive . . . the controversies, the triumphs, the lovers . . . diligently chronicled'
– *Observer*

SIGNET

HONEST ILLUSIONS

Nora Roberts

Young Luke Callahan was wild, spirited, a thief – and a runaway scarred by years of abuse. Drawn to the magician's tent at a carnival fairground, destiny and hope fuse when he crosses the path of master conjurer Max Nouvelle. Taking Luke into his home Max reveals to him a new world of wondrous enchantment: magic.

As Luke's artistry and ambition grow over the years, so does his smouldering passion for Roxanne, Maximillian's beautiful, talented daughter. Revelling in their adventures on and of stage, the trio use their magicians' skills to relieve the rich of their jewels and works of art – a lure as exquisite as that of the honest illusion . . .

'Move over Sidney Sheldon, the world has a new master of romantic suspense, and her name is Nora Roberts. *Honest Illusions* is an explosive novel of obsession, passion and intrigue that pulses with excitement from beginning to end' – Rex Reed